INTERSECTIONS

A NOVEL

POORNIMA MANCO

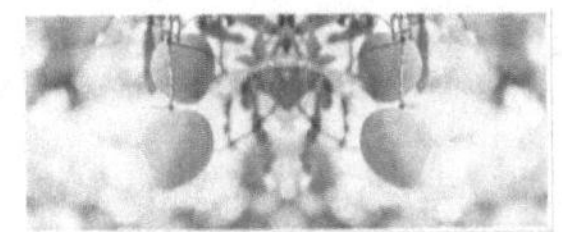

How shall a man escape from that which is written; How shall
he flee from his destiny?

— FIRDAUSI

PROLOGUE

The roads are slick with moisture, an unseasonal rain shower having stopped only moments ago. Light bounces off the puddles accumulated in the potholes that pockmark Delhi's streets like craters on the moon's surface. At 1 a.m., there isn't a soul to be seen on the deserted roads. Even the street dogs have retreated from their nightly patrol. A lonely watchman yawns as he checks his digital Casio watch, a Diwali gift from the master of the household. He rubs his eyes and peers into the distance, wondering if he imagined the sudden screech of tyres.

A car rounds the corner, careening from side to side erratically. The watchman jumps up from his post, his reflexes kicking in immediately. The car seems to head directly towards the house, towards him, but suddenly veers to the left. Then, just as quickly, it rights its course, heading off towards the main road.

The watchman shudders, wide awake now. Drunk drivers, he thinks to himself, chanting a little prayer. He hopes the driver gets home safely, more concerned for the safety of the itinerant workers and street hawkers who sleep on the roadsides than for the idiot driving the car. Even as the thought crosses his mind, he hears a loud crash, an ominous scrape of metal, and then complete silence.

He runs towards the noise, praying it isn't what he thinks it is.

Fearful of getting involved with the police, of having to bear witness, he fights the impulse to pretend he heard nothing, saw nothing. Instead, as he turns the corner, he quickens his step, his mouth falling open at the sight of the mangled metal that has hit the banyan tree at a catastrophic speed. No one could have survived this impact, he thinks to himself. But the low moan he hears confirms that someone has. He shines his torch into the car, only to see a jumble of limbs, blood, so much blood, and a pair of lifeless eyes staring right back at him.

The torch wavers, nearly falling out of his hand. He reaches for his whistle, hoping to alert the chowkidars nearby to the calamity, but just as he does, a hand plants itself against the window, reaching up, streaking blood all over the glass. A face stares out at him, the gash on her cheek loud and gaping, oozing thick red blood as she mouths, "Please... help..."

PART I

Pari

CHAPTER 1

When I was a little girl, all I ever wanted was to be pretty. Later in life, someone said to me that only shallow people wanted shallow things. Was wanting to be pretty shallow? Perhaps it was. But at the age of eight, I could not think of anything beyond how nice it would be to have perfect white teeth, a fair face, and a cute smile. I wanted so much to live up to my name. Pari meant fairy—delicate and beautiful. I was neither.

Amma had once told me that I was named Pari because when I was born, my paternal grandmother had said that I looked exactly like a fairy. Amma had said that she'd thought I looked like a scrunched-up little monkey, but as I was the first granddaughter in the household, everyone had agreed that Pari it would be. It was an unusual name for a South Indian girl, but my great-grandmother was actually from Peshawar, and we had some odd names in the family, like my uncle, Angar. People always wondered why some of us had been given such unusual names in a traditional family like ours. Amma had said it was because the women in Appa's family were eccentric. I didn't know what that meant, but I hoped I hadn't inherited it.

I didn't know what Indian fairies looked like, but the pretty ones

I'd seen in the library books looked nothing like me. They were blonde with gauze-like butterfly wings and large blue eyes. I may not have looked like them, but that didn't stop me from borrowing the books, or from praying every night before I went to bed that I'd wake up the next morning blonde, blue-eyed and fair.

I pored over those stories, dog-earing the books; hoping and praying that my dreams would come true somehow. That once I had transformed, I would no longer be the gawky, awkward girl with no friends. Instead, all the girls at school would vie to sit with me and share their lunch boxes. That they wouldn't make fun of my sticky-out teeth, or the constant colds that plagued me. I would be one of them, yet stand apart by being more dazzling than anyone else. I prayed so hard every night, and was disappointed every morning when I looked into the mirror to see the same face staring back at me.

No-one understood my obsession with those fairy books, but I'd once overheard Amma telling Appa that as long as it kept me out of trouble, she didn't mind. I wondered if I could get Srinivas interested in the books too?

"What are you up to, *ghodi*?" Srinivas pulled my pigtail as he walked past. I showed him my book, hoping he'd sit with me for a bit, but he was already heading out to play cricket with the boys of our locality. Five years older, he was not interested in playing with me anymore. In fact, he was hardly ever home these days.

"It's that Chopra boy! I'm telling you, Rajan, that boy is a terrible influence... The other day I heard he was smoking behind the servants' quarters, borrowing *beedis* from the Nepalis..." I'd overheard Amma complaining to Appa about Sri's absences.

Amma's constant worrying didn't stop me from loving my brother just as he was, even if he called me a horse and neighed every time he wanted to irritate me or make me cry. I suppose I did look more like a horse than a fairy. It didn't help that I had inherited Appa's long, thin face and protruding teeth, but I was only eight, and at school Margaret Ma'am, our Principal, had a framed picture of an embroidered quote that said, "More things are wrought by prayer than the world dreams of".

Amma and Appa were deeply religious, too. We had a small temple room in our ground-floor flat. Every morning and evening, Appa would light incense sticks and pray for his ancestors and for us, smearing sandalwood paste on his forehead as a mark of his faith. He always wore his sacred thread under his shirt, and never ever touched meat or alcohol. Srinivas' rebellious behaviour troubled him far more than he let on.

Our family was a strange mix of old and new, traditional and modern, Muslim and Hindu. Just like our country, which had so many faiths, languages, dialects, foods, customs, behaviours, and clothing, that travelling to a new state within India often felt like travelling to a foreign land.

Srinivas and I were Tamilians with a dash of Peshawari. The latter part did not show in me; not in my build nor in my looks. Srinivas, on the other hand, did not have the typical lanky build of a South-Indian. He was lean but muscular, with sharp features and large almond-shaped eyes. The only features we had in common were our long, thin fingers, and the way we sneezed—multiple little sneezes in rapid succession. Tiny, kitten sneezes that Amma said was charming in a girl but ridiculous in a boy.

At eight, I didn't think we were extraordinary as a family. Both Sri and I identified as Delhiites. We had been born and raised in New Delhi, and even though Amma and Appa spoke heavily accented Hindi, we were as comfortable speaking Tamil as we were Hindi or English.

Now, as Amma railed against the Chopra boy in Tamil, I set aside my fairytale book and went to stare outside the window, beyond the playing field, to see if I could spot Sri anywhere. I hoped he wasn't smoking *beedis,* as Amma suspected. Not only was it against our values, but if he annoyed the Gods, they wouldn't grant me any wishes, would they? I was, after all, related to him.

But, if someone had asked me what I wanted more—to be pretty, or for Srinivas to be on the right path in life, I would have chosen his well-being every single time.

CHAPTER 2

There was blood all over her shirt when I saw her outside the girl's bathroom during recess. She was holding on to her mouth as the blood trickled out from between her fingers.

"You're bleeding," I pointed to her face.

She nodded her head, then took her hand off her mouth to show me the tooth that was still dangling in there.

"I pried pu poolll orff…"

She had tried to pull her loose tooth out. Silly girl. Amma's warnings flashed through my mind, even as I touched my own wobbly tooth with my tongue.

"Come on, let's go to Mrs Seth." I led the way towards our Vice Principal's office. New girl didn't know the layout of the school yet.

She caught up with me, still holding her mouth, not bothered by the stares we were getting from the other students. I noticed a few drops of blood had splattered on her brand new white shoes.

"Oh, your Amma won't be happy with that," I jerked my head towards her feet.

She shrugged, then her eyes crinkled as she smiled from behind her hand. I smiled back. I liked her already.

Mrs Seth was kind, a lot kinder than her husband who thrashed the naughty boys in our school daily. She always looked a bit afraid of

him too, but with his booming voice and his angry face, who wouldn't
be?

"Oh, what's happened here? Come here, let me see…"

Then, even as we were both distracted by a group of senior boys
yelling as they scored a goal on the football pitch, she took a clean
cloth and yanked the tooth out, wrapping it in a handkerchief and
laying to the side. Then she got the new girl to gargle and finally put a
spoon of sugar in her mouth with a drop of *Amritdhara*. The entire
room reeked of camphor and mint, but it was a smell I was used to, as
it was the go-to in my home as well. New girl wrinkled her nose as
she was made to swallow the sugar decoction, but the bleeding
stopped instantly and I could tell she was surprised by this.

"You should be okay now, but ice it when you get home, and next
time, let the tooth fall out naturally."

New girl nodded, then held her hand out.

"May I have it back, please?"

Her speech was much clearer now, but both Mrs Seth and I were
perplexed by her request. What did she want her old tooth for?

"The tooth fairy won't leave me a rupee if I don't put the tooth
under my pillow," she said slowly and deliberately, as though we were
children who needed something simple explained to them.

My ears perked up immediately. I'd never heard of the tooth fairy.
Why didn't I get any rupee coins when I lost my teeth? Mine just went
in the bin!

New girl told me all about tooth fairies on the way back to class.
About one called Angelina, who visited her home regularly, the little
fairy house she'd built for her, and the notes this fairy left in her
pretty handwriting. I was enthralled. I wanted a fairy house, and my
own fairy.

"M… my name is Pari, which means fairy too," I stuttered out,
cheeks reddening.

"Oh, how pretty! You could be the basketball fairy. You're so tall,"
she grinned up at me, her gums still raw, a drop of blood clotting next
to her front tooth. "My name is Samira, but it's not as pretty as yours."

"I like it."

We smiled at each other, and then we became friends.

Truthfully, the first day Samira had arrived in school, nearly everyone had wanted to be her friend. With her auburn hair, fair skin and dimpled smile, she had looked so much like the fairies in my books that a pang of longing had gone through me as Margaret Ma'am had introduced her to the class. She'd been seated next to Alka, three rows ahead of me, and from the way Alka had taken her under her wing, I'd resigned myself to losing another potential friend.

When the tooth incident happened, I thought little of it, doing what I would have done for anyone else, anyway. I figured that someone as pretty and popular as her was hardly likely to want to be friends with me.

Yet, day after day, Samira sought me out in school. From changing seats to sit next to me in class, to sharing her exotic peanut butter sandwiches with me (I had never tasted peanut butter in my life!), Samira was single-minded in her determination to make me her friend. I was alarmed initially before realising that somehow, in some completely random and irrational way, my prayers had come true. The magic had happened.

I never turned into the fairy that I had wanted to be, but life had given me the next best thing. I became friends with a fairy. A beautiful, kind-hearted, bright, funny, and talented fairy.

CHAPTER 3

"Where did you pick up this porcelain doll from?" Amma asked me the first time I brought Samira home after school. All month, all they had heard was "Samira this" and "Samira that". Srinivas had begun yawning loudly every time I mentioned her name. Even Appa had finally told me to "calm it down". I was annoyed that nobody could see how important this was. This was my first real friend, someone everyone wanted to be friends with, but she had chosen *me*!

So when I had asked Samira if she wanted to come home after school one day, I was surprised that she didn't agree immediately.

"I have to ask Mama."

She had blinked and looked away, and I'd wondered if her Amma was strict and didn't allow her to go anywhere. In the end, after multiple reminders, she had finally agreed to come. I'd whooped and hugged her, ignoring all the jealous looks the other girls had thrown us.

From the first week that Samira had walked into school, everyone had competed to be near her. She fitted into school quickly, with nearly all the teachers choosing her to read in class, or selecting her for inter-house competitions. She was sporty and intelligent, she could draw, she could act, she could dance. I had never met anyone like her before, and I knew that I was lucky she had picked me.

"I am not a doll, I am Wonder Woman." Samira declared to Amma, her chin jutting out.

"And what is a Wonder Woman?" my Amma asked, hiding her smile in her words.

Before long, she had pulled the comic books out of her schoolbag and was showing Amma exactly what Wonder Woman was. I watched how quickly Amma fell under her spell, and just for a moment my heart felt as if someone had squeezed it, but then Samira looked up at me, smiled and said, "Pari, I've got you a copy of the latest one" and the moment passed.

Our first playdate involved Samira exploring the whole house, fascinated by all the steel utensils in Amma's kitchen.

"Everything is so clean," she whispered to me, before skipping to the next room. I wondered what kind of house she lived in. Then I tried seeing the house from her eyes. We weren't a rich family, but we were well-off thanks to Appa's high-level government job, because of which we had this three bedroom flat. Amma was very particular about cleanliness. After the maid had swept and swabbed the house daily, Amma would still get down on her knees to clean the odd spot of dirt that may have been missed. As for the kitchen, that was Amma's pride and joy. Not only was she a wonderful cook, but she made sure that the kitchen and the utensils were spotless at all times. I wondered once again what sort of house Samira lived in, but was too shy to ask.

"Is that your guitar?" She stroked the strings absently.

"No, my brother's."

"Srinivas?"

"Yes."

"Where is he?"

"Probably playing cricket."

"Does he not come home straight after school?"

"Not always. He plays for the school team and stays back to practice. Do you want to see my room now?"

"Yes, okay. Do you have any toys we can play with?"

"I have a Barbie."

"Eugh, I *hate* Barbies. I like cuddly toys."

"Well, I don't have any of those."

"Then we can make some."

So we took the pillows off the bed and twisted them in the centre, pretending they were our dolls and proceeded to create a story around a mummy doll and a daddy doll who had naughty children that needed spanking.

When Amma came in with snacks later, I could tell she was horrified at the state of the room. But then Samira gave her one of her dimpled smiles and all was forgiven.

How Samira persuaded her mother to let her come to ours so frequently after that first visit was always a mystery to me. From a hesitant start, she began coming over nearly every day. Amma loved cooking for her, and Samira loved all the attention she got from us. Except for Sri, all of us, even Appa, enjoyed her company. She was like a little ray of sunshine, Appa said once after she had left. A ray of sunshine that danced into our lives and lit up everything.

From the way she exclaimed over each *sari* that Amma wore, to how patiently she listened to Appa's long and winding lectures on what being a brahmin meant (being true in thought, word and deed), politely ignored all of Sri's frowns and jibes, and agreed eventually to playing with my Barbies, she endeared herself to all of us.

"She doesn't talk about her Amma and Appa much, does she?" Amma said after Samira's driver had picked her up one evening.

"No," I replied, thoughtfully.

"Now, that is strange, Pari. Poor child. I wonder what the problem is," Amma said, before wandering back to the kitchen.

I didn't think there was a problem or Samira would have told me. We shared everything: secrets, hopes, dreams, and prayers. We were best friends, and nothing and nobody could come between us.

CHAPTER 4

"She's like a pale ghost that lives in our house," Srinivas threw a shelled peanut at me. I ducked, but it still hit my ear.

"That's not nice!" I pouted at him.

"Who says I have to be nice? And why is she always here? Doesn't she have a home to go to?"

"Of course she has a home, but I like having her here, and Amma doesn't mind. You're always out with your friends. Why can't I have her over?"

"I don't care. Have her here. I just don't want to keep tripping over her. And keep her out of my room."

"How...?"

"I found her hairband."

"Oh."

It was true that Samira loved to go into Srinivas' room and examine his books and posters, fiddle with his guitar and sigh about how much she wanted a big brother. I'd told her it wasn't all that special because big brothers were bullies who pulled your hair and called you names, but she wasn't convinced. I suppose she knew I wasn't being totally honest. I loved Srinivas more than the world.

"She's an only child, Sri! She's lonely."

"Whatever. You asked what I thought of her, and I've told you."

He threw another peanut at me, but I dodged this one successfully. I went and sat with him on the windowsill.

"Are you still friends with Rakesh?"

Rakesh Chopra was the boy who had been caught smoking *beedis* near the servant quarters, but that wasn't the reason he'd been suspended from school. Nobody would tell me why.

Srinivas shelled another peanut and handed it to me.

"Yes, I am."

"Even after Appa and Amma forbade it?"

He shrugged and popped a peanut into his mouth.

I didn't understand it. Rakesh was nowhere near as smart or as handsome as my brother, yet he had a strange hold on him. Amma complained constantly about it, and now, even Appa had decided that Srinivas needed to cut off from this boy. Why wouldn't Sri listen?

I knew they still met up after school. I'd seen Rakesh waiting at the bus stop.

"Sri, what happened?"

"What do you mean?"

"Why was Rakesh suspended from school?"

"Oh, that. Nothing that you should be worrying about."

"But I am. Please tell me."

"He was caught smoking."

"More *beedis*?"

"No, something stronger."

"Cigarettes?!" I gasped, shocked that a thirteen-year-old boy could have access to them.

"Ha!" Srinivas ruffled my hair. "Stronger than that, but you don't worry your head about it, *ghodi*."

Then he sauntered away, leaving me wondering what could be stronger than cigarettes.

As Amma oiled, combed and plaited my hair that evening, I asked, "Amma, was Sri always a naughty boy?"

She paused mid-combing. I tried to turn to see if I'd annoyed her, but she yanked my hair gently into place before answering, "You know Pari, when Srinivas was younger, he was so intelligent that the teachers were worried that the course work bored him. He would race through everything and then either make mischief or fall asleep in the classroom."

"Then?"

"Your Margaret Ma'am asked if we wanted to move him up a grade."

"Did you?"

"We were thinking about it, and then that infernal Chopra boy became friends with him..."

"The one who smokes *beedis*."

Amma tied the hairband at the end of my plait, then turned me around to face her.

"What do you know about it?" She looked so fierce that I trembled.

"O... only what I heard you tell Appa."

"Has Sri said anything to you?"

"No, Amma."

I'd thought of asking her what was stronger than cigarettes, but didn't want to right now. What if Sri got into more trouble?

"Anyway," she sighed, getting up, "ever since that boy entered his life, Srinivas lost all interest in studies. Such an intelligent boy, wasting his life in this way."

She adjusted her pleats, then looked at me, her gaze boring into me.

"Don't you ever do that!"

"No, Amma." I said, quietly, submissively.

At school, Sri was popular because he was good at cricket. He was a good fielder, but an even better bowler. At thirteen, he was already a part of the school team, and was away often, playing matches against other schools. Everyone knew R. Srinivas. Nobody knew R. Pari. We didn't even look alike, or I might have basked in some of his reflected glory. Hardly anyone put two and two together to work out that we were siblings. I never spoke of it, and Sri didn't, either. Sometimes, he would wink at me or pull my pigtail, but mostly, he was in a completely different secondary school building, or away playing matches. We rarely crossed paths, and although I hero-worshipped my brother at school, I was too awestruck to speak to him.

Rakesh, on the other hand, was like his shadow. He was always hanging around Sri. From the moment they met at the bus stop in the morning to the time they parted ways in the evening. I supposed Rakesh was to Sri what Samira was to me. A best friend he could confide in, someone who understood him. But where Samira was our ray of sunshine, Rakesh was like a dark storm cloud that followed Sri around. It wasn't just Amma and Appa's distaste for him that had rubbed off on me. I genuinely did not like him, either. He reminded me of a snake, slithery and dangerous. I wished Sri would stop being friends with him.

CHAPTER 5

Everyone knew now that Samira and I were inseparable. Best friends for life. We sat together at assembly, shared our lunches with each other, chatted non-stop, took part in the same activities, and could be found within a foot of each other. My dream had come true in a way. Being friends with Samira brought me all the attention I'd ever wanted. Suddenly, I became popular. Girls wanted to talk to me, boys didn't push me around as much, and even the teachers started noticing me.

Sometimes I looked at Samira and wondered how one person could have everything. Amma had always taught me to be grateful that we were well-off, healthy and had a roof over our heads. She showed me the beggar children who would come up to our taxi at the traffic lights while we rolled up our windows. They would beg us for money, their hands moving from their mouths to their stomachs, their hair matted and dirty, the rags on their thin bodies clinging to their sweaty skin.

"Look, Pari, look at how these poor children live. They have no homes, they sleep under the bridge at night, they barely have enough to eat or wear. See how lucky you are?"

"Why don't we give them some money, Amma?"

"No, no. You give one, and suddenly they will all swarm to the car. How many can we give to?"

"But Amma, even if we give to one..."

"Shhh," she'd look annoyed and ask the driver to move on as soon as the light turned.

Yes, I was lucky; I knew that. I was surrounded by similarly lucky children who had parents, homes, clothes, enough food, and were being sent to a good school. But Samira was different. Even amongst us, she was special, blessed with a different kind of luck. Years ago, I'd read a story about a man who turned everything he touched into gold. Samira was like that.

She was always in the top five in the class rankings. She spoke so beautifully that she would be chosen to recite a passage every morning in assembly, her sweet voice and anglicised accent making even the most boring extract sound fascinating. When she danced, her movements were lithe and graceful. Margaret Ma'am had once called her a 'cherub', and when I had looked up the meaning in the dictionary at home, it said: a beautiful or innocent-looking child.

Yet, Samira wasn't a goody two-shoes. She had a sense of mischief, and could have a group of girls giggling helplessly over the way she mimicked our teachers. Her jokes were naughty, and she told them with such a straight face that it took a moment or two for them to sink in, before we were in splits of laughter again. She could poke fun at herself too and never took her popularity for granted.

Then there was another side to her that would surface unexpectedly. A vicious side. She couldn't bear fake people and would cut a girl off if she were fawning over her.

"Don't butter me!" she'd snap, delighted to use the Indian phrase she had stumbled upon, adding her own twist to it. "I'm not a toast!"

Not everyone was kind to her, either. The girls she had rejected or overlooked, and the boys she had ignored, said unkind things about her behind her back. Sometimes those things got back to me, but I loved her so much I never told her anything that could hurt her. Not that she would have cared about what anyone thought or said.

In her indifference to other people's opinions, she reminded me of Sri. I, who had always cared so much about acceptance from others, envied this quality. I wanted to have the same aloofness but somehow couldn't.

"What are you thinking of, Pari?"

"Hmmm... that new movie, 'Superman'. Everyone keeps saying how good it is. I've asked Appa to book us tickets for Saturday. Have you seen it yet?"

"No, not yet."

She looked sad for a minute, then dipped her head and carried on colouring the sketch she'd drawn at the back of her rough book.

"Do you want to come with us?"

Her head snapped up, eyes shining.

"Could I?"

"I'll ask Appa to book five tickets." I patted her hand, curious why she never went to the movies with her own family.

"Thank you," she beamed at me, and just for a moment, I thought of letting it go. But curiosity overcame me.

"Do your Amma and Appa not take you to the movies?"

She looked startled. This was the first time I had asked her a direct question about her parents. Then she shifted her gaze before looking down at her book again.

When she spoke, her voice was hushed.

"My Papa is away at work, and my Mama..."

She paused, then looked at me with a big smile on her face.

"I like going with you and Uncle, Aunty and Srinivas. It's like one big, happy family, isn't it?"

My family, I wanted to say, suddenly annoyed, but I bit back my words. Samira was my best friend, and if sharing my family was the price I paid for being friends with her, then it was a small price to pay.

CHAPTER 6

"Ten out of ten!" Margaret Ma'am smiled at me as she handed the maths test back. "Well done, as always, Pari."

I smiled back shyly. Margaret Ma'am was our principal and also our maths teacher. She was the only one who had ever paid me any attention in the days before Samira had joined school. I knew it was because I was good at her subject, but somewhere inside I also believed that she liked me for me.

I walked back to my seat, unable to suppress my grin.

"How much did you get?" Samira asked, leaning in. Her hair had come loose from one plait, and a bit of jam was stuck to one side of her mouth.

"Full marks."

"Show me!"

I showed her. She stiffened and turned away.

"How much did you get?"

"Eight out of ten."

"Which ones did you get wrong?"

"Doesn't matter. They were silly mistakes, anyway. Margaret Ma'am said I'd ace the next one."

"I'm sure you will," I said, smiling at her. But I decided not to tell her about the jam.

In the six months that we had been friends, a few things had started annoying me about Samira. One, that she was never on time. Always full of excuses, she delayed me too, and we had got punished a few times because of her. Two, she was competitive about everything! Yes, she was good at most things, but she couldn't bear it if I got more marks than her in anything. I worked hard, much harder than her, and I deserved my grades. Three, she had never invited me to her house. Even Amma had commented on that. Was I not good enough to meet her parents?

She had become a part of our family. She knew everything about us, even our troubles with Sri, but I knew so little about her family. I thought we had no secrets between us, but now I believed that Samira did keep many secrets.

And why did she need to be in the limelight all the time? Why did it bother her if some of it came my way, too?

Srinivas had warned me about her.

"That girl wants all the attention, all the time, Pari. You be careful of her."

"But she's my best friend, Sri!"

"Girls like that are no one's best friend. They care only about themselves. You watch. The day you overtake her, her true colours will show."

"You're just saying that because she spilled tea on your rug."

"No, I'm saying that because I know people like her. Selfish and spoiled."

"Girls like her?"

"Maybe."

"Do you have a girlfriend, Sri?"

"Don't change the topic, *ghodi*!"

Now I wondered if that was true. Had Samira only made friends with me because I was no threat to her? She was pretty; I was not. She was popular; I was not. She was talented; I was not. The only thing we were well-matched in was studies. Was that why she couldn't take it if I beat her there?

"Pari," she said suddenly, looking up. "I'm sorry."

"What for?" I wondered if she'd read my mind.

"For being angry that you got more marks than me."

"It's okay."

"No, it's not okay. If you teach me how you did those sums, I'll practise your spellings with you."

That's when I decided to tell her she had jam on her face.

Amma said that sometimes, if we were in someone's company for too long, we became tired of each other. Where once we had only seen the good qualities in that person, we started focusing on only the bad ones. She said that in a marriage, once the 'honeymoon period' was over, couples fought a lot because suddenly they only saw the other person's faults.

"But I am not married to Samira, Amma!" I protested.

"I am not saying you are, but you have barely taken a break from each other. Even Appa and I argue when we spend too much time together. So do you and Srinivas. All I'm saying is that maybe for a short while, curtail her visits here. A bit of space will do you both good."

"What if she stops being friends with me, Amma?"

"I think she needs your friendship far more than you need hers, Pari."

"That's not true, Amma! You don't understand. No one wanted to be friends with me before Samira joined the school. Now, everyone knows me and talks to me."

"You cannot depend on someone else like a crutch for the rest of your life, Pari. You need to learn to make your own way." Amma patted my head. "Trust me, child, if your friendship is true, it will survive everything."

So, I took Amma's advice and cooled things off for a while with

Samira. At school, I still sat with her, ate with her, and played with her. But when she wanted to come over, I made excuses. I could see she was hurt, but something made me want to test Amma's words.

Would our friendship survive if I didn't give in to all of Samira's demands?

CHAPTER 7

"Pari, what is this nonsense? Why am I being dragged from one shop to another?" Amma was annoyed, and when she frowned, a line appeared between her eyebrows.

"Sorry, Amma. I just want to find the right present for Samira."

"It's as if she's going to meet the Queen of England," Amma grumbled, but I ignored her. Samira had finally invited me home for her birthday and I was excited beyond belief. Nothing would ruin it for me. Not Amma's grumbling or Srinivas' teasing.

After a month of not coming to our home after school, Samira had come over to me during recess and asked, "Would you like to come to my birthday party next Sunday?"

"Is anyone else invited?"

"Only you from my school friends. Rest is all family."

"I'd love to come over!"

As Amma had said, our friendship had survived the month, and the invitation had only proven that we were indeed best friends.

It was at the fifth shop that I finally spotted what I'd been looking for.

"There, there it is!" I pointed at the shelf, jumping up and down.

The shopkeeper pulled the box off the shelf and handed it to Amma.

"Four hundred rupees!" Amma gasped.

"Please, Amma!"

"What is so special about this doll?"

"She cries, and when you give her water in the bottle, she does *susu*."

"A doll that does *mutram*! I have to pay so much money for this?"

"Please, Amma! I promise not to ask for anything else this year. Plllleeeeaaaassseeee!"

"Hmm," Amma looked at the doll and then at me, one eyebrow raised. "Well, I will make sure you remember that when you ask for a new pencil box."

"I promise, Amma!"

So the *mutram* doll, as Amma named it, was bought and wrapped with an enormous bow to present to Samira on her birthday.

On Sunday, Appa drove me to Samira's house, which was in Gulmohar Park. It took us a while to find her place, as Appa had never really driven to this area before. The houses were large with enormous gardens and grand gates, and had Gurkhas sitting outside in their little cabins. Even Appa looked impressed. Our modest Saket colony did not compare to this rich residential area where every house reflected the wealth and status of its inhabitant.

"What does Samira's father do again?"

"I don't really know, Appa."

"Find out, will you?"

"Okay."

Appa had never displayed the slightest curiosity about my friends' families before, so I took it as a good sign.

Ultimately, we found her house through a combination of good luck, bad directions from a roadside hawker, and my observational skills.

"Look Appa, balloons!"

The floating multi-coloured balloons tied to the wrought-iron gate signalled a birthday party, and I was pretty sure that was Samira's house.

"I'll pick you up at 7 p.m. Be ready." Appa dropped a kiss on my forehead before driving off.

The Gurkha saluted, then opened the gate to let me in. Several young children were running around on the lawn, and I could hear loud music and the sound of laughter from inside the large house. Samira hadn't told me it was going to be this big of a party. My fingers shook as I rang the doorbell. When no one responded, I stepped in, hoping I hadn't made a mistake in identifying her home. A large lady wearing a cobalt-blue kaftan with matching eyeshadow looked down at me and smiled.

"Hello! Are you Samira's friend?"

I gulped and nodded.

"Sam!" she yelled so loudly I nearly dropped the box I was carrying.

Suddenly, Samira appeared. She was wearing a pale blue lace dress with a satin ribbon at her waist and one in her hair.

"Pari!" she squealed, "You made it!"

I grinned and handed her the present, my nervousness evaporating instantly.

"Come on!" She threw my present to one side and grabbed my hand. "I want you to meet all my family."

Samira was an only child, but her extended family was large. Very large. There were *chachas, mamas, buas, tais* and all their children. She took me through them like a whirlwind, introducing me as her "best friend", and a warm glow settled somewhere within my chest.

Then we came up to a tall, slim lady who held a cigarette and a glass in one hand while she repeatedly poked a fat man in his chest with the finger of the other as she talked.

"Mama," Samira seemed hesitant for the first time as she addressed the lady.

"What, precious?"

The lady turned, and I bit back my gasp. I had never seen anyone as beautiful as her in my entire life. From eyebrows that arched over honey-coloured eyes to auburn hair that tumbled in waves over her back; from her dimpled smile so like Samira, to her pure, fair, white skin—she looked like she'd stepped off a movie set. Wearing a low-cut yellow blouse with green bell-bottoms, she didn't look like any kind of mother I had ever seen before.

"This is Pari." Samira introduced me, her eyes not moving from her mother's face.

"Well, well, well. We finally get to meet the basketball fairy!" She bent down and placed a kiss on my cheek, her perfume so strong that I felt I would pass out from the scent. "So, you're the girl whose house our Sam goes to all the time?"

"Y... yes."

"Tell me, darling," her eyes focussed on me intently. "What's so special about *you*?"

Samira

CHAPTER 8

I wish I had a different mother. Someone who loved me more than she loved herself. Someone who wore *saris*, cooked delicious meals, and kept the house clean. Someone who was normal.

Mama had behaved badly with Pari and this was when she was in one of her 'good phases'. I watched Pari's face whiten as she absorbed the nastiness behind Mama's question, but before she could formulate an answer, I dragged her away to meet Papa.

"This is my Papa," I said, holding his hand. He looked so handsome today in his black polo-neck and brown check jacket. When Papa was home, I felt like everything would be fine. He had promised to be home for my birthday and here he was!

"Hello," he smiled at Pari. "You're the lovely girl we keep hearing about. Thank you for making our Sam so comfortable at school. She was very nervous before joining."

I could see Pari relax now after the strange encounter with Mama. She smiled that buck-toothed smile of hers and I felt glad that I had called her over when Papa was home. It would never have worked otherwise.

For the past month, I'd felt Pari pulling away from me. She never told me why she had stopped inviting me back to her house, and it hurt to think that I wasn't welcome. Had I said or done something to put them off? Had I not been a proper friend to Pari?

I knew good manners meant that after months of going to Pari's house and enjoying her family's hospitality, I should have invited her over in return. But with Papa away, and Mama the way she was, how could I? Fortunately, Papa was back, and I felt safe enough to call her home finally.

Now here she was, my best friend, in a canary yellow frock with red buttons that clashed horribly, looking around the house in awe. I suppose the house was quite grand compared to her flat, but it was a cold and heartless place to live in. I would have traded places with Pari in an instant if she'd asked. There was so much love and laughter in her home, and so little in mine.

With all my cousins gathering around me, we decided to go upstairs to my bedroom while the adults mingled downstairs.

"You have such a big house, Samira. How many of you live here?" Pari looked at my room, which would have fit half their house in it.

"It's just the three of us, Pari, and then the maids, and the driver who lives in the garage room."

"And it's clean today," my cousin from Kanpur interjected. "Aunty must have been on their case because we were coming."

"Who?" Pari looked confused.

"Ignore her. Come on, I want to show you my cuddly toys."

The rest of the cousins had followed me upstairs and now settled around the television. Someone put 'Carry On up the Khyber' in the new Video Cassette Recorder that Papa had bought on his trip abroad. I could see Pari's eyes widen as the movie started playing. One of the older cousins must have taken it out of Papa's collection, not bothered that there were young children in the audience. Typical.

"Come on..." I wanted to take her away from there, away from the regular chaos of my life, towards the part of my life that gave me comfort.

I opened the door of my dressing room, pulling her inside.

"These are my babies." I pointed to my cuddly toy collection.

She looked at the hundreds of teddies, doggies, cats, pandas, llamas and other assorted animals in astonishment.

"Do they have names?"

"Each and every one of them." I smiled proudly.

Soon, we took some of them down and made a circle with them. I brought my porcelain tea-set out of the cupboard and we had a tea party, pretending that I was Alice and Pari was the Mad Hatter.

A good hour passed with us giggling and chatting until Divya yanked the door open.

"There you are! Aunty's been calling out for you to cut your cake. Hurry up! We want to finish the movie..."

Outside, my carpet was littered with their trash. Chips, spilt Coca-Cola, half a sandwich and a beer bottle that had been kicked under the sofa.

"You need to clean this up before you leave," I hissed at Divya, but she just shrugged and walked away.

I could see Pari taking it all in, and I wondered what she thought of me now.

Downstairs, a large pineapple cake with nine candles sat in the middle of the table. Streamers and balloons hung from the chandelier above. There were kebabs and samosas, and I knew that Mama had ordered *biryani* from Karim's for later. I had begged for a vegetarian dish for Pari, but I don't know if she had listened.

"There's our birthday girl!" Aunty Julie boomed, her blue eyeshadow having creased into a mess above her eyes. Everyone had gathered around the table, and one of the uncles had pulled out a large Leica camera to take pictures. He started clicking as soon as I came down the stairs.

I held Pari's hand securely as I made my way into the centre of the crowd. I could feel her fear at being surrounded by so many strangers, and gave her hand a quick squeeze. She squeezed back. Our secret code for "I'm here for you." Maybe she had picked up on my nervousness, too.

My eyes searched for Papa as the candles were lit.

"Blow them all out at once and make a wish!" Aunty Julie commanded. I closed my eyes and blew them out, my cheeks puffing out like a blowfish.

"What did you wish for?" Divya asked me, her eyes narrow with envy. I just shook my head and smiled before turning away from her.

My whispered wish remained in my heart.

"Please God, let Papa and Pari stay in my life."

CHAPTER 9

If Pari thought any differently of me after my party, she never showed it. She was still the kind and sweet person she had always been, and I loved her even more for it.

"What's this?" she asked, opening the little bag I had just handed her.

"It's my return gift, and a thank-you card."

"Oh." She looked a bit startled by this.

"Thank you for my doll. I loved her." I smiled. It was true. The doll was now my favourite toy, even more than all my cuddly animals.

"What have you named her?" she asked, cocking her head to one side.

"Hmmm..." I teased, putting a finger under my chin and looking up at the sky, "I don't know... I haven't thought about it..."

Then, as her face fell, I pulled her into a hug and said, "Why, Pari, of course!"

Just then, a group of girls passed us, sniggering. Mala and gang. Ever since I'd turned down their offer to join their little club, they had made it their mission to make snide remarks or be mean to me. To make matters worse, when they saw that it didn't bother me, they had started picking on Pari.

"Hey ugly, don't hug her too hard, you may rub off on her!"

Pari's hurt silence made me react more harshly than I should have.

"Rather her than you dumbos!"

They sniffed and turned away.

"Why are they being horrible?" Pari whispered. "You've always been so popular. I don't understand it."

"Just ignore them, Pari."

Truth was that very few people liked me for who I really was. Either they wanted to be friends because I was pretty or because I was rich. No one really cared about what I was like on the inside, except for Pari. With her, I could be myself, even the part that wasn't always nice.

Margaret Ma'am walked past just as a ball of paper came flying and hit Pari on the head.

"What's this?" Ma'am picked up and unrolled the ball that had a crude drawing of two stick figures, and someone had put a love heart around them. She looked around for the culprits but seeing no one around, she tucked the paper into her skirt pocket.

"Are you okay, Pari?" she asked, her face grim.

"Yes, Ma'am."

"Do you know who did this and why?"

"No, Ma'am."

"And you, Samira?"

"No, Ma'am."

"Very well. I'll put Mr Seth on the case. When he finds out, whoever did this will be *very* sorry indeed!"

Her voice had risen at the end of the sentence, and she stared into the distance, her hands clenched by her sides.

"You two, get back to class now. If there's any more trouble like this, come straight to me."

I wasn't a tattle-tale, and was more than capable of handling things on my own, but I worried for Pari. Although only six months younger, sometimes I felt like she was years younger than me. She had shown me the fairy books she was still obsessed with, and I remembered having outgrown them when I was five. I knew she thought she wasn't pretty, but if only she could understand that being pretty meant nothing. If there was nothing good on the inside, what did the outside matter?

Pari was innocent and sweet. She wouldn't harm a fly. Mala and the gang knew that, too. So, they bullied her when I wasn't around, and enjoyed watching her cry. They picked on her because they couldn't pick on me.

One word to Srinivas, and I knew he would sort them out. But he had never warmed to me like the rest of the family had, and I was afraid to approach him. So, I had my own little plan. Something that would ensure they would leave us alone forever.

At recess on Tuesday, I turned to Pari.

"I have to go see Mrs Seth. I have a tummy ache."

Pari immediately put her sandwich down.

"I'll come with you."

"No, no. You eat your lunch. I'll be back soon. I just need a bit of that smelly medicine."

Reluctantly, she picked up her sandwich again. I made sure I called out as I passed Mala and gang, "Wait here for me, Pari. Don't go anywhere."

I saw her nod as I turned and headed towards Mrs Seth's office, knowing it wouldn't be long before Mala started with her taunts.

As soon as I had turned the corner, I switched directions and went in search of Mr Seth.

It was all very well telling a teacher something, but showing them was what really counted.

Mala was taking special pleasure in grinding Pari's sandwich into the grass when Mr Seth came up behind her and boomed, "What do you think you are doing?"

Her friends scattered like cockroaches in daylight, and Mala stood trembling under his furious glare.

They never bothered us again.

CHAPTER 10

"Mama, wake up!" I stood over the lump on the bed. It was 7 a.m. and Papa had already left for his jog, which was why I needed Mama to wake up. She didn't stir.

"Mama!!" I shook her now, worried.

The lump groaned and turned over, throwing the covers off. Her face looked muddy from last night's makeup. I'd heard the maids complaining about "Madam's dirty pillow cases". Mama never washed her face before going to bed. Her *kajal* had smudged under her eyes, and she looked a bit like my panda. I suppressed a giggle, keeping my face serious as I looked down at her.

"What?" she snapped at me, her eyes open just a slit.

"I need money."

"Don't we all..." She closed her eyes again.

"Mama..." I shook her again. "It's for the picnic. Today is the last day to hand it in."

"Ask your Papa."

"He's not here."

Her eyes snapped open.

"Where is he?"

"He's gone for his jog."

She closed her eyes and sighed.

"Take it out of my drawer. There's a green pouch in there. Now, leave me alone."

I opened the drawer silently, found the pouch and took Rs 200 out. Then, for good measure, I took another Rs 100. I'd buy some pastries for Pari and myself. Mama hadn't even asked how much I needed. She wouldn't care.

"Shut the door behind you," she called out, her voice muffled under the covers. I knew she'd sleep till noon at least.

On my way to the bus stop, I ran into Papa.

"Sam, you're up early!" He grinned and ruffled my hair.

"Not really, Papa. This is my normal school time." I smiled back at him, while smoothening my hair back.

"Shall I walk you to the bus stop?"

I nodded happily. I didn't care that he was all sweaty and smelly, just that he was here, and that he would spend the next few minutes walking with me.

"We are going to Surajkund for a picnic next Friday," I informed him, swinging my satchel with one hand and holding on to his hand with the other.

"Well, that's a very pretty place. Isn't there a lake there?"

"I don't know Papa, I've never been."

"I think I went as a boy once..." He got a faraway look in his eyes.

I yanked at his hand to bring him back to me again.

"You're not going away again soon, Papa?"

"I've just come back!" he laughed down at me. "You want me to leave already?"

"NO!" I said too strongly, perhaps because he looked shocked. "I mean, I don't want you to go at all," I added, softly this time.

"Sam, it's my work, you know..." He looked sad, then switched expressions swiftly and smiled down at me.

"What do you do Papa?" I didn't really care because I hated the job that took him away from me so often, but Pari had asked, so I asked.

"I, uhhh, work with foreign investors. I supply them with Indian goods to sell in foreign markets."

"Is that why you travel so much?"

He squeezed my hand and nodded towards the road.

"Is that your bus?"

It was.

On the bus, I stood on the second step at the front door. That was my place, and the other students always made way for me. I loved feeling the chill of the morning air, watching as we drove past the roadside hawkers setting up their *redis*, the shopkeepers opening the shutters; the cyclists pedalling furiously to get to work. School started at 8:30 a.m. and finished at 1:30 p.m. before the day got too hot to study or to teach.

When we had lived in England, I remembered days and days of grey and overcast skies. Of shivering on my way to pre-school, bundled up in my black parka, gloves and a hat. This constant sunshine still felt like a miracle. Even the winter days were bright and sunny.

Mama complained about the heat constantly, moving from air-conditioned house to air-conditioned car to an air-conditioned club. She couldn't understand why I loved playing outside in the sun.

"You'll ruin your complexion!" she would huff at me before wandering back into her room and shutting the door.

Now that Papa was home, I knew I'd find him sitting out in the garden when I came home from school. He enjoyed the sun just as much as I did.

Pari had started inviting me over to her house again, and I was glad but also kept declining, as now I wanted to go home and spend time with my father.

"He works with foreign investors and travels a lot for his work," I explained to her as we walked to class together. "When he's home, I like being home, too."

"And when he's not?"

"Then I can start coming over again. I mean, I will still come over, but not as much as before. If he has gone to his office, then I'll come over on that day."

"Does your Amma," Pari paused, "your Mama mind that you spend so much time at ours?"

"Of course not! She's happy I have a friend like you." I side-hugged Pari, not meeting her eyes.

Did Mama mind? I didn't think she cared enough to mind.

CHAPTER 11

It was getting dark earlier than usual, as winter was approaching. Pari and I were walking back from the market, chatting and giggling, when an old man with a bicycle stopped us. He was wearing a *dhoti*, and had a cloth tied around his head. A small bundle was clipped on the rear seat of the cycle that he dragged along with him.

"D...?" he asked as both of us halted a few feet away from him. He looked at me directly as he said this. Pari held my hand, pulling at it, but I moved closer to him.

"What?" I asked.

"*Dhobi?*"

I knew there was a press-wallah round the corner from Pari's house. Every evening he delivered freshly ironed clothes: Uncle's shirts, Aunty's *saris*, blouses and petticoats, Pari's and Srinivas' uniforms. I thought maybe the man was looking for him.

"There is a press-wallah there..." I pointed to the left.

The man grinned toothlessly and called me closer. I sensed Pari's hesitation, so didn't go any closer. But he brought his cycle forward and I could smell the sweetness of *paan* on his breath, his unwashed smell along with something dirty and desperate as he leaned towards me and asked, "*Dogi?*"

I backed away hurriedly, my heart thudding as Pari dragged me home. Neither of us knew what he wanted, but we were scared, and as soon as we got home, Pari burst into tears.

Aunty ushered us inside, asking what was wrong, but we couldn't stop trembling. Then Uncle, who had just come home from work, asked Aunty to make us strong, hot cups of tea with lots of sugar in them. As we sipped on the tea, the trembling settled a bit. Srinivas walked in just as we were telling Uncle and Aunty what had happened.

"... then he asked Samira '*dogi?*' And we didn't know what he wanted, but he seemed so wicked, and we ran from there..."

Uncle and Aunty exchanged looks. Srinivas' face turned red.

"Who said this? Where did this happen?"

Pari repeated the entire story to him again. I was still confused about what the man had wanted. I had no money. What did he want me to give him?

Srinivas looked at my face. Then he spoke to me for the first time in all the time I had been coming over to Pari's house.

"Don't you worry, Samira. That man will never bother you again."

"Sri..." Aunty grabbed his hand. "What are you going to do?"

"Don't worry, Amma."

Uncle looked at Srinivas.

"Don't do anything stupid. The man could be from anywhere. He could have been passing through. The girls just need to be more careful from now on, maybe come home before sunset and not talk to strangers."

Srinivas just stood up, cracked his knuckles, and walked out of the house again.

Aunty gathered up our tea cups and said softly to Uncle.

"Let's drop Samira home now."

I didn't want to tell Papa what had happened, but something about the entire incident made me feel dirty. Why had that man looked at me as if he wanted to eat me up? What was it about me?

I stood in front of the mirror and examined myself. I wasn't as tall as Pari, but in the last few months, I had grown a few inches. My hair was always tied back in a ponytail and sometimes I wished my skin was a little darker so that I'd fit in with the girls around me. Was it my colour, or the way I'd laughed? Was it something I had said?

Uncle's words rang in my ears.

The man could be from anywhere. He could have been going anywhere. He could be outside our house right now, asking to see me, wanting something from me. I quickly drew the curtains at my bedroom window, suppressing my shudder.

After showering, I put my dirty clothes in the laundry basket, then walked towards Mama-Papa's room. Just as I was about to knock, the door opened and Mama stood there in a long black dress, her hair piled into a topknot. Papa was adjusting the cuffs on his shirt, and he spotted me in the mirror.

"Sam, sweetie, come in! Are you okay?"

Mama looked at me blankly before calling out, "Maryam, bring two whiskies up to our room."

"Are you going out, Papa?" I asked, careful not to show any emotion.

"Yes," he sighed over-dramatically, "your Mama is dragging me to some party with her."

"Dragging you? Really, Raj!" Mama settled herself elegantly on the settee as Maryam walked in with their drinks. "It's high time you showed your face, or your wife will get snapped up by another suitor."

Papa cast a quick glance my way before saying, "Not in front of the child, Nina."

"Oh," Mama said, looking at me, "I'd forgotten she was there."

"How was your afternoon at Pari's?" Papa asked quickly.

"It was okay," my teeth chattered a bit. "There was a man..."

"Yes?" Papa took a sip of his drink.

"I... he..." I tried explaining, but ran out of words.

"Madam," Maryam, the maid, interrupted, "the driver is back from the petrol station. He's asking if you're ready to go?"

Mama glugged her drink and stood up.

"Come on, Raj, chop-chop! *Allons-y!*"

Papa planted a swift kiss on my forehead, and then they left.

I sat on the edge of their bed, suffocating under the lingering fumes of his cologne and her perfume.

CHAPTER 12

I didn't think we were outsiders, but Pari and I were so close that we didn't really bother to make an effort with the other girls, which wasn't really a good thing because if one of us wasn't around, the other one had no one to talk to or play with. Pari had once told me that she spent an entire week, the week that I didn't go to school because I was sick, without speaking to another person in the class. I felt bad and decided we needed to have more friends.

On the bus to Surajkund, I asked if we could sit at the back with Preeti Joshi and her friends. Luckily, she was not horrible, like Mala and the gang had been to us. Preeti was just sunshine and giggles, and was terribly impressed that I had spoken to her.

"Would you like a *pakora*?" she offered from her tiffin box and I accepted, even though I didn't care for *pakoras*. Pari took it off me as soon as Preeti's attention was diverted.

Preeti, Sakshi and Laila were nice enough girls, and we talked about *Amar Chitra Katha* comics which I rarely read, Amitabh Bachchan movies that I wasn't allowed to watch, and the many festivals and fasts their mothers participated in. It was like landing on a different planet.

"What do *you* watch then, Samira?"

"Umm... mostly English films."

I didn't want to come across as snobbish because I wanted to be like them, but as Pari reminded me later,

"It's because you are not like them that they want to get to know you. They aren't interested in me, are they?"

It was true that even though I was only doing this for Pari's benefit, they barely spoke to her, choosing instead to share their food, their comics and their life stories with me. I wished they'd try with Pari. Then they would find how funny and silly and kind she could be, too.

"This is an artificial lake," Mrs Nagpal droned to us.

"Just like her hair," one boy whispered loudly to another, loud enough that Mrs Nagpal heard and her neck turned red, but she carried on. "It was constructed by King Surajpal of the Tomar dynasty..."

"Why do you watch only English movies?" Pari asked me, while the other girls gathered together on the embankment facing the lake.

"Dunno. It's all Mama ever buys. She is English, you know."

"Is she?" Pari's eyes widened.

"Yes, I have an English grandmother who lives in Coventry. I was born there."

"Is that in London?"

I laughed then.

"No, silly, it's nowhere near London."

"My great grandmother was from Peshawar."

"Where's that?"

"It's in Pakistan now, but used to be a part of India."

"Is that Aunty's grandmother or Uncle's?"

"Appa's. But she married a Tamilian man, and now we are mostly South Indian."

"So, you are a mongrel, just like me." I liked her even better now.

"Why do you say that?" Pari looked hurt.

"I'm not saying you're a dog! It's just what Mama calls me sometimes..."

Just then, Mrs Nagpal looked over at us and said, "Do you know what Surajkund stands for, girls?"

"It means Lake of the Sun, Ma'am." I answered, glibly. Mrs Nagpal looked impressed. I didn't tell anyone that I had borrowed a book about Surajkund from the library. Looking at the old black and white pictures in it, I'd tried imagining Papa as a young boy, visiting Surajkund. Had he gone with his family? The same *chachas* who seemed so old now? Had *dada-dadi* still been alive then?

Pari said something to me, and I looked at her.

"How do you know all these things, Samira?"

I shrugged.

"I read it somewhere."

If Pari loved numbers, then I loved books just as much. Books had been my constant companions throughout life. I could thank Granny Elizabeth for my love of reading. She was the one who had introduced me to Enid Blyton when I was younger, and every year, without fail, on my birthday she would send me money with a card that said, "Buy more books!"

Often, when Papa was away, and I felt sad, I would put all my cuddly toys on the bed, put on the bedside lamp, and re-read all my favourite books well into the night. Mama rarely bothered to check on me, and the maids didn't care what time I went to bed.

Mama and Papa read nothing except magazines and newspapers. Vogue, Marie Claire, Time, Newsweek, and three daily papers cluttered the study on the ground floor. I was allowed to keep my books in the small fifth bedroom that also housed Mama's fur coats in their garment bags, pockets stuffed with mothballs. The smell of old books and mothballs became my favourite smell in the world.

I read anything I could get my hands on, even the magazines and occasional newspaper articles. When I ran out of things to read, I would borrow books from the library, chewing through those as well.

It was from books that I finally understood what that man had been after. It made me feel sick all over again.

CHAPTER 13

I'd been begging for Pari to come and stay overnight for months when one day, suddenly, Mama just agreed.

Excited, I phoned Pari straight away. Srinivas answered.

"Hello?"

"Oh... ahhh... it's Samira."

"Yes?"

He sounded annoyed, like he couldn't wait to hang up on me.

"Is Pari there?"

"No, she's out with Amma."

"Can you tell her I called, please?"

"Yeah, okay." Then I heard a click and the dial tone came back on. I didn't think he would tell Pari I had called, but she called me back within two hours.

"Sri told me you had called?" She sounded breathless on the phone, as if she'd been running.

"Where have you been?"

"We went shopping. For food stuff." She yawned. "Then we ate so many *parathas* at this restaurant. I just want to sleep now."

Sunday was for resting. That's what Mama had done all day. Papa had left on some mysterious errand in the morning, and I had watched a cartoon film before getting my homework done. Pari's day sounded more fun.

"Guess what?"

"What?"

"Mama said it was okay for you to spend the night here."

"Really?" She sounded excited, but then said, "I'm not sure Appa will allow it."

"I'll speak to him." I was confident I could change his mind. Very few people said no to me.

"Let me ask Amma first. She might be able to persuade him."

"Pari, I'm going to get Cassata ice cream and we can watch 'The Sound of Music' together. It'll be so much fun! Next Friday, okay?"

"Okay, I'll try."

On Friday, as we walked towards my bus after school, Srinivas came up behind Pari and grabbed her in a headlock.

"Where are you going, *ghodi*? Our bus is that way."

I watched her struggle to speak, trying to break free, and I spoke up for her.

"She's coming over to my house for a sleepover."

"A *sleepovah*?" he mimicked my slightly Anglicised accent. "What do you mean, m'lady?"

Pari finally escaped the headlock, her face flushed, eyes flashing.

"Amma and Appa have allowed it, unlike your stupid secret meetings with Rakesh!"

"Ohhh." Srinivas stepped back and looked at Pari, his face expressionless. "Right. Go have fun then with the fifty billion stuffed toys, thousand and one books, and Zeenat Aman."

Then he put his hands in his pockets and walked away, whistling something tunelessly.

"What did he mean?" I looked at Pari, who smiled weakly.

"Nothing." She straightened her collar, then bent her elbow towards me, inviting me to walk arm-in-arm with her. "He's just angry

because Appa found out that Rakesh and he had beaten up... oh..."
She bit her lip and stopped.

"Beaten up who? What happened?"

"You know that man? The one who bothered us?"

"The *dhobi* man?"

"Yes. They found him and beat him up."

"What? How?"

"I don't know. But he's in trouble with Appa and not allowed to stay after school for cricket practice."

I linked arms with her, and we walked over to where my bus was parked. She never did tell me who Zeenat Aman was. I found out much later that she was a glamorous Indian actress who looked like my Mama.

We walked in on my parents having a fight. Mama had just taken a cushion and thrown it at Papa.

"You bastard! You promised..."

Her face was streaked with tears, her hair a mess, the blouse falling open to show her lacy red bra.

Pari and I stood frozen at the door. No one noticed us.

Papa picked up the cushion.

"Nina, calm down. It's only a few months. I'll be back before you know it."

"Liar!" Mama screamed, picking up a vase this time. "You know what you are? You are the Fall Guy! Every single time." She bit out the words. Then her gaze fell upon us and she wiped the back of her hand across her face.

"Girls," she muttered tonelessly.

Papa spun around, then ran his fingers through his hair, patting it down, before putting on a smile.

"Why, hello! Are you back from school already?"

"Where are you going, Papa?"

I didn't care that Pari was there; I didn't care that she had seen my parents fight. All I cared about was what I'd heard.

"Ah, Sam, it's work." He looked embarrassed, and Mama snorted from behind him, not bothering to hide the whisky in her glass.

"How many months this time?"

"Oh, darling. I don't know. Six, maybe eight."

"No, Papa!" I ran over to him, clasping him around his waist. "Please don't go! Please don't leave me again..."

I started crying noisily, snot coming out of my nose, tears running down my face and wetting his T-shirt as Papa tried to remove my arms from around him.

"Shhh Sam. Stop. What is your friend going to think?"

I'd forgotten all about Pari. I could only think of what lay ahead—of days and days of no Papa, and just *her*.

"Papa please! I promise I'll be good. I'll get the best grades in class. I won't lie, I won't steal. Please stay!"

But, of course, he didn't.

CHAPTER 14

"Now, this girl will be good on television." Aunty was brushing my hair as she said this. Pari nodded.

"Maybe you could read the news, like Gayatri Acharya?"

I shut my eyes and felt the soothing rhythm of the brush stroking my scalp and running through my hair. It had been a few months since Papa had left, and I didn't know what Pari had told her parents, but they had very nearly adopted me. Mama didn't care. As long as I made it home by 6 p.m. daily.

Today we were discussing careers. Pari wanted to be a dentist, but I figured that was only because she wanted to fix her own teeth. I didn't know what I wanted to be, but Aunty had said I would look good on television. I couldn't imagine sitting behind a desk and reading out boring headlines.

"No, you'd be really good at it. You speak so well, Samira." Pari added.

Srinivas walked through the room.

"Maybe she could be a taxidermist?"

"Sri!" Aunty's voice held a warning in it, and he just grabbed a handful of peanuts, winked at Pari and walked out again.

"What's a taxi...?" Pari asked, and I looked at Aunty's face in the mirror.

"Nothing. Sri is just being a stupid boy. There, all done." She patted my head, and I looked at myself in the mirror. No one had ever done my hair in a French plait. I tried blinking my tears away but caught Aunty's eye, and saw her gulp and blink her eyes too.

"Now, we look like sisters!" Pari grinned, her front teeth looking even larger than usual.

Uncle rang the doorbell just then, and as Aunty took his coat from him and asked him about his day, I wondered why my Mama and Papa were not like this.

As if she'd read my mind, Pari asked, "How is your Mama now?"

On the night of the sleepover, after Papa had left, Mama had finished the entire bottle of whisky and sat Pari and me down in front of her. She had cried and slurred and spoken about lost years. Then she had slumped back in her chair and watched the fan rotate above her. Pari and I had slipped away to my room where I'd sobbed into my pillow all night while Pari had held me tight.

"She's..." I nearly said okay, but changed my mind. Pari deserved the truth. "She's just her."

Pari squeezed my hand and led me out into the garden to play.

In the summer holidays, Pari left for Madras to visit her family there. We hugged each other and promised to write every day. Mama had been speaking of going to Coventry, but in the end we didn't. I stayed home, read my books, played with my toys and watched the same old movies on repeat. She woke at noon every day, spoke to the maids about dinner, got Raju the driver to take her to the club, and came home at midnight. She barely spoke to me, and we never spoke of Papa.

I wrote to Pari daily; long and rambling letters of what we would do when we met, where we'd go, and what we'd eat. She wrote back, telling me about Aunty's mother, who wore nose rings in both nostrils and said *"ayyo"* in every sentence. I told her I'd added another cuddly toy to my collection, after Mama had allowed the maid to take me to the toy store in Greater Kailash Market. She told me about all the temples they had visited in a place called Mahabalipuram. I told her about all the books I'd borrowed from the library. She told me about her grandmother's parrot, who sat on her shoulder and drank tea out of her cup.

I missed her.

When school re-opened in July, I was ready and dressed, with a French plait that I had practised all summer long. The bus journey seemed to take forever, and when a few girls turned and smiled at me, I smiled back but chose not to speak to them. They were not Pari.

I stood on the second step at the front door, and as soon as the bus halted, I jumped out and ran towards my classroom. Pari was standing with her back to me. She was talking to a plump girl who wore glasses. As soon as I reached out to tap her shoulder, she swung around grinning.

"Samira!" she squealed.

"Pari!" I squealed back.

We hugged for a long time.

Then she turned to the plump girl, who looked at us both blankly.

"This is Roma. She's just joined the school. Her Maa is our neighbour, so Amma told me to take good care of her."

I noticed how Roma moved closer to Pari as she said this and felt a sudden stab of jealousy. Who was this girl? And why was she so close to my Pari?

Roma

CHAPTER 15

I was not a Delhiite. I could pretend to be one on the outside, but I knew I would never feel like one in my heart.

I had not wanted to leave Calcutta, even though I knew Baba's job was a transferrable one. Calcutta was home. It was where I'd been born; it was where Maa and Baba's families lived, and as the youngest children of both families, Ria and I had been spoiled by everyone. For some years, before coming to Cal, we'd lived in Hyderabad. I had few memories of the place except for a painful wasp sting I'd suffered at school. When I was six and Ria was only two, we had moved to Calcutta after Baba got his first promotion. Maa was excited to be going back, and even Baba seemed pleased.

Four years later, when Baba announced that he had gotten another promotion, I saw Maa's face fall.

"Ripa, I cannot turn down this opportunity! I will be close to the nerve centre of power in Delhi; it could lead to even better prospects."

I didn't understand a word of what Baba was saying as I watched them from the opening in the door, but I observed Maa trying to smile for his sake and realised that I would have to do the same. Ria had no problem expressing her emotions as she threw herself down on the floor and had a tantrum when given the news. It took many *rasogollas* before she was pacified.

"Bubu," she asked me later at night when we lay in bed together, "We don't speak any Hindi. How will we manage in Delhi?"

"I don't know, Ria. Go to sleep now."

Baba sat us down a week later and told us that he had been in touch with an old colleague of his, a man named Rajan, who had a daughter my age. He had decided to move to the same neighbourhood as him so that we would know someone before starting out in a new city.

"You remember, Ripa? We met them at Alok's wedding?"

Maa shook her head.

"They only had a son then. A very naughty boy who pulled all the sweets off the table..."

"Oh yes, I remember now. His mother, what was her name?"

"Hema."

"Yes, Hema, she was so upset, she took him outside the *pandal* and thrashed his bottom."

They smiled at each other, remembering a moment when neither Ria nor I had existed.

"This girl..."

They both looked at me.

"Does she speak *Bangla*?"

Baba laughed, then pulled me onto his lap.

"Roma, she speaks English. Don't worry, I'm admitting you to the same school as her. It's an excellent school, one of the best in Delhi, and it's English medium, just like the one you go to now. You will have no problem conversing with anyone."

"But Onir, how will the girls do Hindi lessons? They don't know a word."

"We'll get a tutor. I'm telling you girls, before you know it, you will be *pukka* Delhiites!"

. . .

I didn't want to be a Delhiite. Calcutta was home. It was where all our family lived, and I enjoyed being one of the youngest, always indulged, always treated like a princess. How would it be in a strange city where I couldn't run to one of my aunts or uncles if I got into trouble with Maa or Baba? Who would protect me there?

After her initial tantrum, Ria accepted that we were moving and tried to get me to be happy about it too.

"Bubu, it will be fun! We'll get to meet new people and make new friends, no?"

I frowned at her enthusiasm. Ria had always been irritating in how she turned everything negative into something positive.

"Well, I don't want to go!" I finally said it aloud, even though in front of Baba I had pretended to be excited about the move.

I lay on the bed, my arms crossed, a frown on my face. Angry at Baba for taking us away from our home, angry that Maa always gave in to him. When I got married, I would make sure that my husband listened to me and not the other way round.

Maa came into the bedroom just then and saw my expression.

"What is the matter, Roma? Did something happen in school?"

I sat up.

"Why do we have to go, Maa? Why can't Baba stay here?"

"Roma, it is for our benefit only. Baba's promotion means he is doing well at work, and will get a better salary, too. Then we can all have nice new things."

"Can I get a Walkman?"

"A what?"

"It's a personal stereo that I can listen to my tapes on."

"Ohh, I don't know. I will have to ask Baba."

Later, Ria said to me, "Isn't that Walkman thing really expensive, Bubu?"

I shrugged. It was the least Baba could do for me.

CHAPTER 16

I found out later that most Bengalis moved to Chittaranjan Park, or C.R. Park as it was commonly referred to. Baba deliberately avoided it, as he wanted us to live among other Indians and not just Bengalis.

When Mr Rajan called us over for dinner, they had all just returned from their summer holiday in Madras, and looked very tired. We were equally tired, having shifted from Cal to Delhi just the week before.

Still, Hema Aunty cooked us a lavish meal of rice, *sambhar*, aubergines, potatoes and curd. They didn't eat fish as they were Brahmin vegetarians, Maa had told us earlier, warning Ria not to be a fusspot. I watched Ria play with the rice on the plate, clearly not liking these new flavours. But I enjoyed every morsel and even asked for seconds.

Pari (such an odd name for a girl) asked me what subjects I liked, and I said *Bangla* because I couldn't think of anything else. She looked perplexed, as if she couldn't make me out. Her brother, who sat at the table in complete silence, wolfing his food down, suddenly looked at her and said, "That's Bengali, *ghodi*, a completely different language from Tamil, okay?"

"I *knew* that!" she glowered at him, wrinkling her nose. Her teeth stuck out quite a bit. She was really quite ugly.

Later, as Ria lay on her stomach, flipping through a comic, I tried making conversation with Pari and her brother, Srinivas.

"How long have you lived here?"

"All our lives. Appa has been stationed here since Sri was born."

"We love Delhi." Srinivas looked at me, as if sensing that I did not.

"And your school?"

"What about it?" He chewed on his nail, spitting it out near where Ria was lying. I glared at him.

"Do you love your school, too?"

"Yeah, whatever. It's school." He shrugged and got up.

"Sri! Amma said you had to stay."

"Well, I'm not going to." He grinned. "When you two walk into school, it'll be like Laurel and Hardy."

Pari frowned as he left, and I looked down at my hands.

We didn't stay long after that. We were still tired from the move, and they from their vacation. At home, Maa said to Baba, "I'm not sure that Hema and I will be friends. She's too..."

Baba gave her a warning glance and told us to get changed for bed.

Ria and I lay together in the darkness, as I tried to listen to the whispered conversation in the living room.

"Bubu?" Ria said.

"What?"

"What's *ghodi*?"

"Hmmm?"

"That boy called his sister that."

"Oh, I think it means horse. *Ghōrā.*"

She giggled in the dark.

"She does look like a horse!"

"Shut up Ria, I'm tired."

. . .

Delhi was noisy, dusty, aggressive, and confusing. After arriving at New Delhi Railway Station, Baba had ordered a taxi and brought us to this new apartment in a place called Saket. Then he had stood for ten minutes arguing with the taxi driver about the fare and the extra he wanted to charge for taking our suitcases up to the first floor.

"This would never happen in Cal," Maa had stated in dismay.

The apartment had two bedrooms and Maa and Baba had given Ria and me the larger one, but it was the one that overlooked the street. Their bedroom had a nice view of the garden. I had wanted the garden view, but Maa told me not to be fussy.

With our furniture arriving by lorry a week later, that first week we had slept on the bamboo mats Maa had brought along from Calcutta. On our very first night, there had been a power cut for several hours, and without a fan, we had sweated till our night clothes were wringing wet. Mosquitoes had bitten us all over our arms and legs and we had barely gotten any sleep.

"I hate Delhi!" I had declared to Ria in the dark and gotten a sob in response.

A few days later, Baba took us to the school we were to attend. Kinara Public School had massive gates that opened into a large car park that led to a walkway flanked by trees on either side. From between the trees, I made out two large buildings.

"Why are there two schools here?"

"One is the senior school building that you will go to, and one is the junior school that Ria will attend."

Ria tugged at Baba's hand.

"Why can't I go to the same school as Bubu? In Cal we did."

"You are still in the same school, Ria, just in different buildings. Look at that big field between the schools. I'm sure you'll run into each other there."

"Why are we here, Baba? There are no other children here right now?"

"Like I said this morning, Roma, you are going to meet the Principal of the school—Miss Margaret D'Souza. She wants to welcome you."

Miss Margaret D'Souza was a tall, plain-looking woman with curly hair and glasses. She wore a *sari* but walked like a man in it. She held out her hand to me when Baba introduced us and I just stared at it till Baba asked me to shake it. I had never shaken hands with anyone before and thought it was a strange custom. When it was Ria's turn, she pumped her hand up and down, grinning cheerfully.

"These are my girls, Miss D'Souza. It has been quite an upheaval for them, so I hope you will take care of them."

"That's what I am here for, Mr Bannerjee. We pride ourselves on our pastoral care. Don't worry, I'll make sure the girls settle in well."

She smiled kindly at us, but I stayed stony-faced.

"You said that they've met the Rajan children already?"

"Yes, Mr Rajan is a colleague, and he invited us over for dinner a few days ago. I think the children got along pretty well." Baba smiled at us and I kept my expression deliberately blank.

"Well, how about if I place Roma in the same class as Pari? That way, she will at least have a familiar face on her first day in school. As for this one," she turned to Ria with a twinkle in her eye, "I don't anticipate her having any problems fitting in."

CHAPTER 17

We met with the Rajan family just one other time before school started because Maa wanted to make sure she had gotten everything we needed for school with Hema Aunty. They sat and went through the list together while Pari took us out into their garden. We had a first-floor apartment, so we had no garden, but we did have a balcony which Ria pointed out to Pari as it overlooked the Rajans' garden. I wondered why Baba hadn't procured a ground-floor apartment for us too. Maybe Pari's father had a better position than Baba did. Curious to see how they had decorated their house, I tried peeking into the rooms I hadn't seen on my first visit here, but the curtains were all drawn.

Maa and Hema Aunty were still chatting, so Pari had to entertain us. Fortunately, her awful brother was nowhere to be seen, much to my relief.

There was a skipping rope lying on one side near a double swing in the garden, and Pari asked me if I could skip. I shook my head, but Ria jumped up, asking if she could. They skipped together, and I watched them, my head hurting slightly. I took my specs off and cleaned them with the hem of my skirt.

Watching them skip and laugh together, I wondered how Ria always managed to make friends so easily. Even in Cal, I had just one friend—Gracy. When I had told her I was leaving for Delhi, she had made a big 'O' with her mouth and said nothing.

Gracy and I had ended up being friends because no one else wanted to be friends with us. Gracy, because she always smelled funny, like she didn't take baths, and me, because I mostly didn't like people and couldn't be bothered to be nice to them. In the new school, Maa had told me to make more of an effort.

"It's a new beginning for you, Roma. You can have lots of friends, but you have to try. Remember, it's about give and take. You cannot expect everybody to do what you want, okay?"

I had nodded absently. It was true that I had bossed Gracy around, but that was only because she could never make up her mind about anything. What would she do without me?

"Bubu, don't look so grumpy! Come and join us," Ria called out to me mid-skipping.

I shook my head again. I didn't want to skip. I hated all forms of physical exercise. Baba teased me about my weight all the time, but I didn't let it upset me. Sometimes, when no one was watching, I would go into the kitchen and raid the snacks.

I wish I'd brought my Walkman with me, but Maa still hadn't unpacked it from all the boxes piled up in the corner of our bedroom. Music was my escape, and right now, life seemed unbearable. This new city, new language, new neighbours, new school—everything was overwhelming.

Hema Aunty came out just then with a plate of some round, hard things, which were actually quite tasty.

"This is *murukku*. We brought it from Madras." She gave us glasses of Gold Spot, too. "Your Maa and I will be another half an hour, so keep yourselves busy till then."

Pari and Ria came and sat down next to me, reaching for the snacks and crunching on the *murukku* with big swallows of their drinks.

"School is good," Pari said to me.

"Hmmm?"

"You asked Sri the other day if he loved school. I don't think I *love* school, but it's good. The teachers are nice, mostly. Margaret Ma'am is the nicest."

"We met her last week," Ria piped up, putting her piece of *murukku* to one side. So fussy, always. I grabbed it and bit into the crispy deliciousness.

"Really?" Pari asked. "Where?"

"At school. Baba took us to meet her. She is very nice, and she shook hands with us..."

Ria kept babbling, and I looked around the garden, only half-interested in their conversation until I heard my name.

"You are going to be in the same class as me?" Pari was looking at me now.

I nodded. What did it matter? It wasn't like I wanted to be friends with this horsey girl, but if it meant that I had a safety net in a new environment, I needed to make an effort with her. Like Maa had said.

"Are your classmates nice?" I asked, feigning a polite interest.

"Yes, most of them are. The boys are, you know, messy and smelly, especially after football. They might tease you a little in the begin-ning, but if you ignore them, they'll leave you alone. If they don't, we can always go to Mr Seth. They are frightened of him." She took another bite of her snack. "The girls are okay, although a few of them are mean, but that's only because they're jealous that I'm friends with Samira."

"Who is Samira?"

"My best friend in the whole wide world!" she beamed at me, and I noticed a bit of the *murukku* stuck in her teeth. I looked away.

"She is so nice and kind *and* smart. Sometimes she is careless, and she's always a bit late, but she's the best."

I didn't really care. I missed Cal. I didn't want to be here. I didn't want to go to this new school and meet these smelly boys and mean girls. I didn't care about Pari or her "best friend in the whole wide world". I just wanted to be left alone!

Pari reached forward and patted my knee.

"You'll like her. She's very kind."

CHAPTER 18

I didn't like her. She didn't like me either. I could tell straight away. She narrowed her eyes the first time she saw me—when Pari had introduced me to her, after all their squealing. Maybe she felt I was trying to take her friend away from her. I wasn't. I just didn't know anyone else. So I stuck close to the both of them and put up with all her sighs and frowns.

This school was different from the one I had gone to in Cal. There were boys here, just as Pari had said. It was called a co-ed, Baba had told me. Aside from my cousins, I had never spoken to boys before. They were a strange and alien species, and really quite smelly too.

The class teacher, a bird-like woman by the name of Mrs Nagpal, made me sit next to a boy. I sat stiffly, barely acknowledging his presence, turning to look at Pari, who was only two desks away. She smiled reassuringly at me, and I turned back to face the blackboard.

Mrs Nagpal scratched her hair, which did not look real. Then she started calling out names to take attendance.

"Roma Bannerjee?"

"Present," I answered, like all the other students.

"New, hey?"

I looked at her as she stared at me through her half-moon specs. The boy sitting next to me said, "Stand up. She's talking to you."

So I stood up.

"Where you come from?"

"Cal... Calcutta."

"Oh, Bengali?"

I nodded.

"Good, good. Very smart peoples, the Bengalis."

It was my turn to stare at her. I wasn't very smart; I was average. The only thing I was good at was singing, but that wasn't exceptional either, as everyone in my family sang well. *Rabindra Sangeet* was a religion in our household.

"I will put you in the Blue House."

I'm not sure where I found the courage to ask her, but it came out in a rush.

"Please, Ma'am, can you put me in Pari's house? She's my friend!"

She stared at me, then looked around for Pari.

"Pari Rajan?"

"Yes, Ma'am?" I heard Pari answer, but I didn't turn around, focussing instead on a black spot on the wall somewhere over Mrs Nagpal's right shoulder.

"Which house are you in?"

"Yellow House, Ma'am."

"Okay," she said with a sigh, "I'll put you in Yellow."

Later, Pari said to me, "Blue House is the top house. You could have been with Samira. Why did you choose Yellow?"

"I wanted to be with you," I answered quietly, not looking at Samira directly.

My first few days in the new school had shown me how important it was to have someone on my side, a friend who could help me find my way. Pari had shown me around the school grounds, had told me which snacks were the best in the cafeteria, explained that if I needed to use the toilet, it was best to go in the third period before it got too stinky. She'd shown me the water fountain where the water came out the coolest, and had taken me to the Arts and Crafts Room, the

Drama Club and the Music Room. As I had walked with her, I'd heard the sniggers.

"Hey Pari, who's the fatso?" a boy had called out on my second day in school.

She had turned on him and given him such a dirty look that he had slinked away.

From that day onwards, I had edged even closer to Pari, knowing that she wouldn't abandon me, even if it meant putting up with Samira.

At home, Maa encouraged our friendship.

"Sometimes Roma, one has to make friends with unexpected people. Now look, I have made the effort with Hema. You do the same with Pari. It will be good for you. She is a nice girl and very intelligent too. She will help you with your homework."

"But Maa, she already has a best friend. That Samira girl."

"So? You cannot have only one friend in your whole life. It is good to have lots of friends."

I thought of Gracy then, and how she had never once written to me after I had left Calcutta. Then again, I hadn't bothered with her either. Both of us had known that we were only friends with each other because there was no one else, and now there was no need to pretend. Maybe Maa was right. It was time to make a fresh start and make more friends. Ria had already come home with stories about all the girls she had befriended. Why couldn't I do the same? Even if it meant tagging along with Pari and that awful Samira, I'd make sure that I became a part of a friendship group as well. Come what may!

CHAPTER 19

"Gosh Pari, she's like a leech! Always hanging around us. Can't you get rid of her?"

Eavesdroppers never hear good of themselves, Baba had told me once when he stumbled upon me spying on the adults. But I couldn't help it. Over the years, I had come across such juicy tidbits of gossip and information which I had stored away to go over later. Now, however, what I was hearing wasn't pleasant, even if it wasn't entirely unexpected.

I had been looking for Pari after class had ended because I needed her to show me where the uniform shop was. After hunting for her for ten minutes during our recess, one of the girls told me where Pari and Samira liked to hangout. Near the rundown old school office. She'd pointed me in the direction. I could have asked her where the uniform shop was, but some strange instinct made me go looking for them.

Sure enough, they were sitting on the steps, talking to each other. I hid behind the wall, waiting to hear what Pari would say.

"Samira, she's not that bad. She's just a little shy. Once she makes other friends, she won't hang around us as much. Anyway, didn't you say we needed to expand our friends' circle?"

"Yes, but I meant some of the other girls. This fat, grumpy one is not what I had in mind!"

"Sam, that's not nice! People have always said unkind things about my teeth, but it never bothered you. Why does her being a little plump annoy you so much?"

"It's not just that. She's just weird. Always staring, hardly speaking. And she just creeps up on us, like a ghost!"

Pari started giggling.

"What's so funny?"

"You know, Sri used to call you a pale ghost when you started coming over to our place..."

"What?! You never told me this! That's horrible..."

I slinked away from there, not wanting to hear anymore. Maybe it was time to make other friends, but Samira needed to be taught a lesson. Miss High-and-Mighty thought she could get away with saying whatever she wanted about people! She would learn that not everyone thought she was as amazing as she pretended to be.

Right from the start, Samira had irritated me. I knew she didn't like the fact that I was friendly with Pari, and only put up with me because Pari said she had to. But even if Pari had not been there, I would have still disliked Samira. She was just too cocky, too sure of herself. Yes, she was pretty, but I'd seen prettier fisherwomen. And so what if she spoke with an English accent? What was so special about that? Why did everyone give her so much importance, as if she was something special? She was just a normal girl, like Ria or me.

Yet, something about her fascinated me, too. It was the ease with which she attracted people to herself. Teachers, students, boys, girls, everyone was under her spell. She didn't even have to try. It was as if her very existence was a marvel.

One evening, when Rajan Uncle and Baba were having tea together, I interrupted them to ask, "Why do some people have all the luck?"

"Well," Baba paused to think about it, "that may be because they were born under a lucky star. What do you think, Rajan?"

"Oh, I agree. Those ruled by Jupiter have a tremendous amount of luck in their lives." Rajan Uncle was a big believer in astrology.

"Was it someone specific you were thinking of, Roma?"

"No. Just a general question."

"Don't forget Roma, you can also make your own luck. Hard work and determination are better predictors of success than luck on its own."

Before Baba started another one of his lectures, I left them to talk about planetary conjunctions in horoscopes, and stood on the balcony staring down at Pari's garden. I knew Samira was over at hers, which was why Pari hadn't invited me that evening. Normally, it would not have bothered me, but I felt angry at being left out. Everyone around me had friends. Even Maa had met some new neighbourhood ladies whom she got along with. Why did I have to suffer in silence?

Samira might have been the luckiest person I had ever met, but I wouldn't let her muscle me out of the group. I decided right then that I wasn't interested in making other friends. I would stay friends with Pari and put up with Samira. Who knew? In time, maybe I'd find a way to cut her out.

CHAPTER 20

Baba was perhaps the only one out of all of us who settled into living in Delhi comfortably. The rest of us struggled—Maa with finding good places to shop for fish, Ria with Hindi, and I, with everything.

I didn't like the school; I didn't like the boys. I couldn't understand the language even though the tutor tried hard to teach us, and most of all, I hated having to hang around girls who didn't want me around them.

"Maa, I want to go back to Cal," I moaned while shelling peas.

She looked at me and nodded. She had been having a difficult week as well, after having spoken to her sister on the phone.

"Me too," she said now, her face sad.

Then Ria looked up from her homework and started sobbing. We huddled together and cried for a bit. Then Maa wiped her eyes with her *sari*, and said, "Now, you know we can't go back yet. Baba has promised we will visit next year. We have to learn to fit in here, and it will be hard in the beginning, as anything new is." She gave me a shaky smile, and I could tell how much she was missing her home and family.

"Maa, why can't Baba stay here and work, and we go back to Calcutta?"

"Eesh! What a thing to say. A wife's place is by her husband's side, and we all have to stay here with Baba and support him."

Just then, the doorbell rang and Maa went to answer it. Ria set her notebook to one side and sat up.

"Bubu, that fair girl isn't nice to you, is she?"

I knew she was referring to Samira, but pretended I didn't understand.

"Who?"

"The pretty one who is always with Pari. I saw the way she looked at you today."

"Hmm. I don't care."

"Why don't you make other friends?"

"I will, but not right now. Want to come to Pari's house?"

"I have homework."

"You study then. I'm going to play with her."

"What if that girl is there?"

"Let her be."

Samira wasn't there, and Hema Aunty let me in with a smile.

"Pari, look who's here."

Pari came out, holding a *bhutta pora* in her hand, and immediately my mouth started to water.

"You want one?"

I nodded.

Soon, we were sitting on the double swing in her garden, eating our corn, swinging gently backwards and forwards.

"Pari?" I asked.

"Yes?"

"Will you help me with my Maths homework? I am not very good with numbers."

Pari nodded, her hair oiled and slicked back into a plait, the small bindi she wore on her forehead slightly askew.

"My Appa is very good with numbers. Sri is as well. If I can't teach you something, they will."

I nodded back at her, suppressing a shudder at being taught anything by that brother of hers.

"I brought something. You want to see?" I asked.

I pulled the Walkman out of my bag and laid it between us on the swing.

"What is it?" She touched it lightly.

"A Walkman."

"Walkman," she repeated, looking mystified. "What does it do?"

"Here, listen."

I plugged in the headset, hit play, and handed the headphones over to her, motioning for her to put it over her ears. I watched her wonder-struck expression with pride. Olivia Newton-John's 'Magic' was playing, and only Pari could hear it. It was her own personal music player.

"This is amazing!" she breathed.

"I know! I also have Michael Jackson, if you want to come over tomorrow to listen."

Her face lit up, then fell.

"Oh, Samira is coming over tomorrow."

"Bring her too. We can all play at mine."

"Really? You don't mind."

"No, not at all." I shrugged nonchalantly.

The next day, she turned up along with Samira. It was obvious that Samira had come against her will, as she glared at me when I opened the door. But I knew just how to sweeten her up.

"Maa, my friends are here!"

I let them in.

"Come, come girls. Here, look, I have some *sandesh* for you."

Maa handed out the sweets, and I could tell from Samira's expression that she had never seen anything like it before.

"It is our sweet," Maa answered, smiling at her, "you must try. You will like it very much."

She took a hesitant bite, and from the smile on her face, I knew that her sweet tooth had won out. Samira being Samira thanked Maa profusely for the "delicious sweets" and I knew that it was only a matter of time before Samira accepted me into the fold.

Later, Maa said to me, "That child is delightful. So well-mannered and sweet. I'm really glad you are making friends with the right sort of girls now, Roma. I never liked that Gracy."

What Maa didn't know was that I had not changed my mind about Samira. I still disliked her intensely, but if fitting in meant making friends with the enemy, I would do it. Maybe her lucky star would shine some of its light down on me, too.

CHAPTER 21

Maa got used to having the girls over. Even Hema Aunty commented that it was nice for her to get a break now that they came over to us. We became a reluctant gang of three, most of the reluctance coming from Samira. She wasn't impressed with my Walkman, the Russian novels that Baba read, or Maa's *macher jhol*. The only thing that impressed her was the *sandesh*. And our singing.

One time, quite by accident, I joined in Maa's humming, and before we knew it, we were singing an old Bangla song together. Both Pari and Samira stopped in their tracks and watched us, open-mouthed. Ria joined in, eager to get some attention too, and the three of us sang unselfconsciously, our voices in perfect harmony. When we stopped, Pari remained open-mouthed, but Samira looked at Maa and said, "Wow!" She didn't look at me, but I knew she had been impressed. I'd seen her expression.

From then on, I'd hum something every time I was with them, and Pari, without fail, would ask me to sing it. I could tell it irritated Samira, but she never said anything, and I knew it was because she had no talent in music. She was good at studies, sports and dance, but she could not carry a tune.

Mrs Nagpal cornered me outside the classroom on a Tuesday morning.

"Roma."

"Yes, Ma'am?"

"You are singer?"

"No Ma'am."

"No, no, you are not to lie to me. I hear you sing from open window."

I looked at my shoes.

"I want you to join music group." It was not a request, it was an order.

Later that afternoon, I signed up. From then on, I discovered that my talent, so commonplace in Cal, was considered something extraordinary here.

"She sings like a young Gita Dutt."

"Oh no! More like Lata Mangeshkar."

I could play the *harmonium* too, and soon, alongside singing, I would substitute for the music teacher in leading the assemblies in her absence. Never in the school's history had a twelve-year-old led the assembly, and I began gathering a fan following of my own.

I could have stepped away from Pari and Samira then. I nearly did, several times. But some strange affinity had brought us together, and it kept me tied to them for the rest of the school year.

In February 1983, when we were sitting our end-of-term exams, a tall handsome man walked past our classroom with a short skinny girl in an ill-fitting uniform. He peeked into the classroom and waved at someone. I turned to see Samira waving back, her cheeks flushed, a big smile on her face. I wondered who he was and why Samira looked so happy.

After the exam, we chatted about the questions. Pari and Samira seemed confident that they had done well. I hadn't, but Maa and Baba never had high expectations from me when it came to studies, even though they often exhorted me, *"Kaṣṭa nā karalē kēṣṭa mēlē nā!"* No pain, no gain.

They still hadn't worked out that I hated studies and found exams painful. Ria had the brains in the family. All I wanted to do was to pass my examinations to get into the next grade, and I just about managed to do this.

Pari and Samira kept asking me how I had answered question 4 in the Maths paper, so to deflect their attention I asked Samira, "Who was that man who waved at you? And the girl with him?"

"That was my Papa!" she said proudly. "And the girl is just the driver's daughter."

"What's she doing here?" Pari asked, curious now.

"Well, Raju, our old driver quit. So now we have Umesh, and he has two children. One is that girl and the other one is a baby boy. Papa has enrolled her here. He said she deserves a good education, just like me."

"A driver's daughter?" I gasped.

"Why not?" Samira looked me in the eye.

"But how will she manage? Does she speak or write English?"

"She'll learn. She's smart. If you can learn Hindi, why can't she learn English?"

"Which class will she be in?" Pari asked, leaning forward.

"That I don't know. I suppose Margaret Ma'am will decide, depending on how she performs in the interview. But Papa wants me to keep an eye on her. And I will." She stuck her chin out in a determined manner.

We digested this news silently.

"What if Margaret Ma'am places her in our class?" Pari asked.

"I don't think that'll happen. She's not *that* smart." Samira grinned at Pari.

But what if it did? Would this driver's daughter become a part of our group too?

Madhu

CHAPTER 22

I did not belong here. I was an outsider.

When Pitaji took a new job as Sehgal Sahib's driver, he was more than happy to leave us behind in our little village near Patna in Bihar. Mataji insisted on going with him. The last time he had left us in this manner, she told me, he'd taken up with that whore, Mallika. 'Queen of his heart', he'd called her until she'd stolen his money and run away with another lover. This time, Mataji insisted, she would stay with him and watch his every move.

"And Lallan?" I'd pointed to the baby suckling at her breast.

"It's a boy, and he's proud I've finally given him a son, after ten years of waiting. He won't object."

Pitaji didn't dare object; he was too scared to. So, we moved to Delhi in the cold month of January. My nose ran constantly, my hands felt frozen and my hair was all matted from the journey. Mataji and Pitaji were tired and dusty too when we arrived late in the evening to see the one room home that would house the four of us. At least it was a pukka building, unlike the mud hut we'd lived in before.

"Look, the Sahib has even given us a heater!" Pitaji pointed to a small metal box with wire grills. Soon we were huddled around it, with Mataji feeding Lallan again.

"How did you get this job?" she asked Pitaji.

"We have the same boss," he said, warming his hands in front of the orange glow of the wires.

Mataji started laughing.

"You and the Sahib have the same boss?" she mocked. "Then how is it that you get this small room, and the Sahib lives in a *mahal*?"

"Shhh!" Pitaji frowned. "They can hear us if we speak too loud. We have the same boss, but we don't have the same job! Sahib has more responsibilities... and more to lose."

"So, when do we get to meet this very important Sahib of yours?"

"Tomorrow. He wants all of us to go to the house."

"Then let us eat and sleep. We want to be well rested to make a good impression on him," Mataji said, while unwrapping the last four *rotis* and *achaar* from the cloth *potli* she had carried all the way from Bihar. "I hope you'll make enough money soon for us to buy vegetables again."

The complaint in her voice was clear enough. Pitaji had wasted all our savings on the whore. We had been surviving on plain *rotis*, onions, *achaar*, *dahi* and rice for the past few months. I was short for my age and Mataji was just skin and bones, sometimes unable to produce enough milk for Lallan.

"I will be paid well," Pitaji replied sullenly.

"And you will hand the money over to me," Mataji responded, her voice steely as she handed a dry *roti* to me. I chewed on my food slowly, watching Lallan suckle at her breast with his eyes closed and moving in some baby dream.

At home, in our village, I had been considered a very bright girl. The first few years in school, the headmaster had pointed to me and said, "This girl will go places. Her brain is very big."

All the other students had looked at the size of my head, confused because it looked the same size as theirs—where was this big brain hiding then? I had hoped then that going places meant that I could go from the village to the city of Patna, and get to study in a proper school. But when Mataji had fallen pregnant with Lallan, she had pulled me out of school, saying she needed help at home. I was ten years old, and more than capable of cooking and cleaning. Going to school was a waste of time, she had insisted, ignoring my tears and pleas.

Pitaji had wanted me to study, but he was already in a lot of trouble because of his affair with Mallika, so he had kept quiet. But one day when Mataji had fallen asleep while feeding Lallan, he had taken me to one side.

"Madhu, I'm taking up a job in the city."

"In Patna?"

"No, in Delhi." He had looked behind him, just in case Mataji had woken up and overheard. "Once I have earned enough, I will send money home and make sure you start going to school again."

"Mataji will not let me."

"She will. Just let her calm down, then she will listen to me."

"But I have already lost one year."

"So what? You will make it up. Your headmaster said that you were the brightest child he had ever met. Are you telling me you can't make up for one year's work?"

He had pinched my cheek and winked at me, and I had felt my heart expand at the thought of returning to school.

What neither of us had realised back then was that Mataji would be stubborn and insist on going to Delhi with Pitaji. What would happen to my schooling now?

CHAPTER 23

I had only seen such big houses in Hindi movies. I saw Mataji look up in silence at the large, glittering light, which I later found out was called a 'chandelier'. She had Lallan tied on her back, and had covered her head with her sari *pallu*. Pitaji wore a white shirt with a *haldi* stain he had tried washing off unsuccessfully. I was dressed in an old frock with a big, old, moth-eaten brown sweater that had once belonged to Pitaji, and I had rubber *chappals* on my feet. Mataji had tried combing the tangles out of my hair, and had torn off a bit of her *dupatta*, telling me to use that to wipe my nose rather than the sleeve of the sweater.

We stood together in this grand living room at 8 a.m. waiting for the Sahib to arrive. The maid who had let us in wordlessly had given Mataji a vicious look and said, "Don't touch anything!" Then she had left us standing there, feeling lost and uncomfortable.

Pitaji shuffled his feet and cleared his throat.

Mataji asked, "Do you think he's forgotten?"

Just then, a young girl walked into the room, an apple in her hand. She saw us standing there and stopped.

"Who are you?" Her voice was low and smooth but haughty; her Hindi smoother than the rustic Hindi I was used to.

"I am new driver, Missie*ji*."

"Oh. I am not Missie*ji*. My name is Samira."

"Yes, Samira*ji*."

Pitaji grovelling before a girl of my age was unpleasant to watch. Her gaze flicked over us and settled on me.

"What's your name?" she asked.

"Madhu."

"Madhu," she tasted my name. "That means honey. *Shahad*. Did you know that?"

I shook my head. I didn't know names had meanings. No one had ever told me that before.

"How old are you?"

"Eleven…" Then I corrected myself. "Twelve."

"Missie*ji*, Madhu can help in the house if you like. Small jobs. She can buy milk or *subzi*. She can sweep or brush your hair. She is very good with her hands." Mataji said it all in a gush of words.

Samira*ji* looked at her in surprise.

"I don't need a maid! We have two already. Anyway, you'll have to ask Mama all this."

"Ask Mama what?" A tall man walked in, wearing shorts and sweating heavily. He spotted us at the same time as he spoke to Samira*ji*.

"Umesh! Sorry, I'd forgotten you were coming today. I'd gone out for a jog."

Samira*ji* poked a finger in his stomach.

"Papa, I have to go. I'll miss the bus otherwise. Kiss!"

He leaned down, smiling, and she kissed him on his cheek and skipped out of the house.

Then he turned and looked at me.

"How old are you, little one?"

"Twelve," I answered shyly, looking at the marble tiles on the floor that had little kites drawn on them.

"Do you go to school?"

I shook my head, keeping my eyes on the floor.

Mataji started up once again. "Sahib*ji*, Madhu is very good around the house. She can cook and clean, or if you want, she can take care of Missie*ji*. We are very grateful that you are housing us. You won't regret it. My baby is small right now, so I cannot do too much, but Madhu will help. She is very smart, a quick learner. Any jobs you'd like her to do..."

Sahib*ji* held up his hand as if to stop the flood of words. He looked at Pitaji then.

"Umesh, you didn't tell me you were bringing your family with you? Are those living quarters sufficient for all of you?"

Before Pitaji could answer, Mataji jumped in again.

"Please, Sahib*ji*, we are poor people. We have lived in mud huts all our lives. To us, that room is like a palace." She folded her hands and tried to touch his feet, but nearly lost her balance as Lallan weighed her down.

Sahib*ji* righted her, then addressed Pitaji again.

"I have no objections to having your family here, but I insist that this child gets an education."

Pitaji threw a quick glance in my direction.

"I will look for a government school right away, Sahib*ji*."

"Why? She can go to the same school as my daughter. I'll make arrangements for her to be seen there."

Both Mataji and Pitaji were stunned into silence. This was a completely unexpected development, and they didn't know quite what to make of it. I didn't, either. A part of me was thrilled that I could return to education thanks to Sahib*ji*'s kindness, but another part was afraid of going to an unfamiliar school where I would stand out, and not in a nice way.

I had seen how Sahib*ji*'s daughter had looked at me this morning. As if I was an insect that had crawled out from beneath a rock. How would I cope if everyone treated me that way?

CHAPTER 24

Sahib*ji* insisted that Pitaji took the day off to settle us in. He handed him an advance on his salary, telling him to buy all the necessities we needed. As soon as we were home, Mataji snatched it out of Pitaji's hands. She put Lallan down, then turned to face us, her hands on her hips.

"What is all this nonsense, Lallan's father?"

"What nonsense?"

"About Madhu going for an interview at this big school! Can't you see I need her here?"

"To do what? You can make two meals a day and wash a few clothes, can't you? This is an opportunity for our daughter to be educated, and that too, in a proper school. Why are you being so difficult?"

"Opportunity? What will she do with all that studying? We have to marry her off in a few years. Who in our *biradari* will marry an educated girl?"

"It's an English medium school. This will be good for her."

"She cannot speak English..."

"She will learn..."

"And wash somebody's dirty dishes after learning a few words in English? Don't give her ideas!"

On and on they went, arguing about it. I turned my back on them and closed my eyes, lying on the thin mattress on the floor. I was warm and fed, and that meant something. Besides, there was no point in interfering. Mataji would have her say, no matter what Pitaji or I thought or wanted. But Sahib had been very firm, and I couldn't imagine that Mataji would refuse him. After all, our livelihood depended on him.

What kind of man was he that my education mattered to him? I was a nobody, yet he had looked at me with such kindness. Not all city people were bad, as they often claimed in the village. Sahib*ji* was a good man, and now I was glad that Mataji had insisted on coming to Delhi.

Two days later, I was presented to the Memsahib of the house. She had large honey-coloured eyes, reddish brown hair and skin as white as the marble I'd stood on a few days ago. Now, I stood in front of her in the same brown sweater, the only one I owned, and Sahib said to her, "Well?"

She looked at me up and down and then leaned back in her chair.

"Honestly Raj, what do you expect me to do with this?"

"Nina, work your magic. Do something altruistic for a change."

"Why all the *charrideee*, Raj? Guilty conscience bothering you?"

I wasn't sure what they were talking about, but I knew that it wasn't about me anymore. They spoke rapidly, mixing English words with Hindi. I later found out that most educated people in Delhi spoke this way. It was called Hinglish.

"I'm just trying to do something nice for someone, Nina. There was a time you would have jumped upon the chance..."

"Yes," the beautiful woman sighed, "but that was before I found out what you were really up to."

"This lifestyle of yours," he said, but she put her hand up as if to push his words away.

"Whatever." She looked at me again. "I'll do it for the kid. Maybe this is her only chance in life. What have I got to lose, anyway?"

He dropped a quick kiss on her forehead, and she flinched away from him.

"Attagirl! I'll be out all day, but see if Sam's old stuff fits her. Also, try her English out. Her father said she's smart. Find out if she is."

"How on earth are you going to convince the school to admit her?"

"They have an SC/ST quota, and a little nudge in that direction should help."

"SC/ST... What?"

With a quick glance at me, he lowered his voice and said, "Scheduled Caste/Scheduled Tribe."

"She's one of those?" Her eyes flicked over to me again.

"Does it bother you?"

"Not in the slightest." One shoulder on her sweater fell as she shrugged, revealing a dark mole on her creamy white skin. "Operation ragpicker will begin straight away!"

After Sahib*ji* had left, she called me over to her and told me to turn around.

"Goodness, child, you're so thin! You need some feeding. Maryam!" She went from speaking softly to letting out such a huge bellow that I jumped.

She grinned at me then. "It's okay. My bark is much worse than my bite."

I didn't know what that meant either, but I smiled back at her shyly.

She put a finger under my chin and said, "Why, you're really quite a pretty little thing when you smile."

I felt warm all over, as if the sun had directed all its beams towards me.

Maryam, the maid, arrived at the door and gave me a suspicious look.

"Madam*ji*?"

"Pull out some of Sam's old clothes from the trunk. Let's see what fits this one here." Maryam nodded her head and turned to go. "Oh, and get her to take a hot bath. She needs it."

CHAPTER 25

Memsahib didn't like me calling her Memsahib. She wanted me to call her Nina. But Mataji and Pitaji were horrified at the thought. Call her 'Aunty', they said.

"Do NOT call me Aunty!" she said, glowering down at me.

Ultimately, we settled on Nina*ji,* which was respectful enough for my parents, and informal enough for Memsahib.

Susannah, the nicer of the two maids, was the one who pulled out all of Samira*ji*'s old clothes and made me try them on. Most of them hung off me. I was too little and too thin for them.

"Goodness, child, you're like a scarecrow!" Nina*ji* cried upon seeing me try a dress that was two sizes too big. "We'll have to get Tailor Master in to get them all altered."

Nina*ji* had already spoken to Mataji about daily baths. She said I could use the maid's bathroom with the geyser, so that I could have hot water to bathe in. Then, getting me to put on the only dress that fit, with a small woollen jacket, thick socks and Samira*ji*'s old sandals, she called for the driver.

Pitaji answered the door in his uniform, driver's cap in hand.

"Memsahib*ji*?"

"Oof, stop calling me that. I need you to take us to Vikram Hotel in Lajpat Nagar."

"Yes, Madam*ji*."

Nina*ji* rolled her eyes and got into the car, indicating to me to get in beside her. Pitaji kept stealing glances at me in the rearview mirror, but would not look at me directly.

"So, Madhu." Nina*ji* had put on huge sunglasses that made her look like a bug. "Can you understand *any* English?"

I nodded, too shy to say anything. In my school in Bihar, where the standard of education hadn't been good, I had still done well in all my subjects. I could read English slowly but speaking it was a different matter.

"When we get home, I'm going to pull out some of Sam's old books and test you. But first, let's get all that awful hair cut off!"

Pitaji parked the car and opened the door for Nina*ji*. Then he did the same for me, but from under his driver's cap, he gave me a wink. I kept a straight face, knowing Nina*ji* would not approve if I gave in to my giggles.

She glided through the lobby of the hotel, waving to some of the staff, and I galloped behind her, trying to keep up with her long stride. I saw how everyone stared at her and felt enormously proud to be in her company. She wore blue jeans with a brown top that had turquoise gems sewn into the collar, and lots of fringe bits hanging off the sleeves. Her hair was pulled into a topknot because she had declared it was "too dirty to leave down, and Asif would sort it out for her, anyway."

Nothing about her was dirty, though. She looked like she had stepped out of one of the paintings that were all over the house. Beautiful, fair women with tiny waists and enormous chests who never smiled.

Mataji had asked Pitaji after meeting her, "What kind of woman is that?"

Pitaji had said, "She's a *gori* from England. That's why she wears those funny clothes and sleeps till the afternoon. She is not adjusted to India."

"And you want our daughter to be handled by her?"

"Look at how she lives, what she looks like. If Madhu gets to be even ten percent of that, I will consider her life made!"

Mataji had narrowed her eyes but kept quiet. For now, her bread was being buttered quite nicely, and she was happy to go along with the whims and fancies of her employers. But she didn't like it. Not one bit.

"What is this Nina?" Asif said, running his hands through my hair, his fingers getting caught in the tangles.

"Don't ask! Another project Raj has lumbered me with."

"That husband of yours!" He winked at her. "How is the gorgeous man?"

"Alive," she said, her voice flat. "Anyway, just cut it all off. Give her a Mia Farrow."

"She's certainly got the bone structure for it. But where have you picked this urchin up from?"

"She's the driver's daughter."

"Hmmm. Why don't you get your hair washed while I tackle this mess?"

He seated me in a chair that rotated, and I nearly fell off from the shock of it. Then he asked for some cushions and got me to climb on top of them.

"You're twelve?" he asked in a funny tone. "You look about five. Now, sit up straight."

He took a large pair of scissors and snipped off all the tangled ends. I looked at my hair in the mirror and felt like crying. There had been a madwoman in our village who had taken the sickle and cut off all her hair. I looked like her right now.

"Don't worry! Go with Sultan and get your hair washed. When I'm finished with you, you won't even recognise yourself."

Propped up on another chair, I leaned back over the basin as Sultan ran warm water over my hair and massaged my scalp with something that smelled lovely. Shampoo, Nina*ji* told me later. It was the best feeling in the world, the feel of his fingers on my scalp, the fragrance, this unusual experience.

I could see why Pitaji had wanted me to study well and study further. If this was the life on offer, then I was more than willing to put in the work.

CHAPTER 26

When Samira*ji* saw me the next day, she wouldn't stop laughing.

"You look like a boy!" Then she stared, came forward and touched the blouse I had on. "Mama!"

Nina*ji* walked into the room, holding a glass in one hand and a cigarette in the other.

"Oh hush, Sam. What's all the racket about?"

"She's wearing my top!"

"So? I gave it to her. It doesn't fit you, anyway."

"But it was my favourite top! And I was going to put Albert in it."

"Now, who the hell is Albert?"

"My Dalmatian."

"Sam, you're being ridiculous! And you need to grow out of those cuddly toys. You're twelve! I'm going to tell Maryam to get rid of them."

Samira*ji*'s face turned white.

"No, Mama, please don't do that. I don't mind. You can give the girl anything. I don't care."

"Very well. Be off with you then." She waved her fingers towards the door, and Samira*ji* left silently.

"Come here, Madhu. Sit next to me. You don't say much, do you?

Right, let's start with this storybook. It's for five-year-olds, but I want to see how well you read..."

I think Nina*ji* liked me because I was like her own personal doll. She dressed me up, changed my hair, told me how to walk, how to talk, how to sit and I never complained. It was obvious I adored her. I had never met anyone like her before. All the women I had seen were beaten down by life, poverty, and by the men in their lives. And here was a woman so vibrant, so stunning, even life seemed to bow to her.

The maids learned to treat me with respect. The one time Maryam had switched off the geyser so that I couldn't get hot water, Nina*ji* exploded.

"Maryam, I will cut a day's wages from your salary! How dare you! Madhu, you use my bathroom henceforth."

The maids gasped at the audacity of the driver's daughter using the Memsahib's bathroom. Even I was taken aback at how much attention she gave me. It was strange that she was so distant with her own daughter and yet so close and comfortable with me.

"You have won the lottery!" Pitaji smirked at me as we ate our *chapattis* with *tinde ki sabzi* and *arhar daal*. We had even had chicken curry a few days ago. Mataji had put on weight. Her cheeks looked fuller, and she didn't worry about producing enough milk for Lallan now. But she was not pleased with the situation and made sure we heard about it.

"Why is that woman so focussed on our daughter when she has one of her own? That child is always in her own room or out of the house, and our child is always with the memsahib. Something is not right!"

"Sushila, *tujhe aam khaane hain ki guthliyaan ginnee hain?*"

Pitaji was not one to look at life as a half-empty tumbler. For him, his glass was overflowing, and he didn't see any need to question it.

"Tell me," she asked, looking at my face, "has she ever done anything to you?"

Confused, I stared back at her.

"What?"

"Has she touched you in a funny way?"

"Sushila!" Pitaji's voice had taken on an edge.

"No," I shook my head. "Nina*ji* is very nice to me. She wants me to do well, to study and improve myself." My tone had the tiniest bit of blame in it, and Mataji was quick to pounce on it.

"Ohh, so she is better than your mother, who only wants you to cook and clean?"

I stayed silent.

Mataji stood up, muttering.

"Well, if something happens, don't come running to me. Mark my words, there is some funny business going on here, and one day, the two of you will wake up and find out that you've been made fools out of."

Some people always thought the worst of others. Mataji was like that. She thought it was because she was shrewd and could read people, but Pitaji told me it was because she was bitter. She could not bear to see me have a life that was denied to her.

"Did Mataji want to study too?"

"Study? Bah! She wanted an easy life, which I couldn't give her. So now, when she sees you ride in the car with Memsahib, or receive nice gifts, she gets jealous."

"But she is my mother. She should be happy for me."

"Madhu, often, the very people you think will support you are the ones that betray you. Now, listen to me. You keep working hard and do whatever Memsahib tells you to. One day, when you have made something of yourself, your Mataji will have to eat her words."

I hoped he was right. Even though I realised how fortunate I was, it pained me to see it bothering Mataji so much.

That night, as she settled Lallan next to her, I went to the foot of her bed and started massaging her legs.

"Eh, what are you doing, Madhu?" she asked, half-sitting up.

"Taking care of you, Mataji."

She let me massage her legs well into the night, and I hoped that on some level she had forgiven me.

CHAPTER 27

Samiraji didn't like me, and even though I was only twelve, I understood why. It had taken me a while to accept Lallan, and he was my own flesh and blood. I tried to keep out of her way and not flaunt my connection to her at school. I had been put in a junior class because I could not speak English as well as the other students, even though I had surprised the teachers by how quickly I read and understood it.

There was that first day when Sahibji had brought me to school to meet the Principal, when, just for a moment, as we had passed Samiraji's classroom and she had waved to her father, our eyes had locked. There was a strange emotion in hers, a sort of challenge, but I could not decipher it and, overcome by nervousness, I had forgotten what it was.

Margaret Ma'am was a tall lady, with curly hair and kind eyes that twinkled behind wire-rimmed spectacles.

"Mr Sehgal, it's very kind of you to want to do this, but wouldn't the child do better in a government school?"

"I don't see why she cannot be given a place here. Surely, you have a quota to fill." Sahibji's voice was stern, and the lady seemed to deflate in her seat.

"It's not just about quotas, it is also about the child. Children can be merciless, as you know, and Madhu isn't a natural fit for the school. I appreciate your wanting her to have the same opportunities as your daughter, but you might find that she is isolated and picked on because of her background and her inability to speak the language."

"Isn't it your job to ensure that doesn't happen?"

"I cannot be around all the time to monitor what goes on."

As they went back and forth, my mind switched off, focussing on the girls playing basketball outside.

"Madhu?" The Principal had asked me a question that I had missed. I looked at her inquiringly.

"I'm going to ask you a very simple question. If you can answer it, then we will consider giving you a place at the school."

I looked at Sahib*ji*, blinking nervously, and he nodded his head with a little smile.

"What are the names of the planets that rotate around the Sun?"

I was silent for a minute, and then I spoke slowly, "Mercury, Venus, Earth, Mars, Jupiter, Saturn, Uranus, Neptune, Pluto."

Sahib*ji* looked at the Principal and said, "I told you she was smart and a quick study. It's not important where a person comes from, it's where they want to go."

On the bus to and from school, I kept my distance from Samira*ji*. Fitting into school was difficult, just as Margaret Ma'am had predicted, but I kept my head down and worked hard. Soon, even the teachers who didn't care for me accepted the fact that I was trying my best, and the ones who liked me pushed me to excel. I was not going to catch up with Samira*ji* anytime soon, but I wasn't willing to be left behind.

At home, I tried taking on whatever chores I could manage between homework and extra English tuition with Nina*ji*. Mataji hadn't forgiven me entirely, but even she could see that I was trying hard on all fronts. Sometimes I felt like a spinning top that whirled faster and faster, too scared to stop in case I fell over.

Pitaji would often see me drop onto the mattress, exhausted from the day's activities, and say, "Madhu, take a break. You are doing too much."

People often looked at me and saw a small, thin girl who looked like the tiniest gust of wind could knock her over. What they didn't know was that I was a lot stronger and far more determined than I let on.

I did not take my luck for granted. I had known a different life, and there was no way I was going to return to it. Annoying the boss' daughter was a sure-fire way to get into his bad books. So, I stayed out of Samira*ji*'s way at home too.

I would have my lessons with Nina*ji* while she was out at her friend's, and return to my house just before she returned home. On the school bus, I would ride at the back while she stood up front. In school, I would keep my own company, and never once, through word or gesture, did I indicate that I knew her. In this way, I tried my best to stay invisible.

Two months into my attending school, something happened that would change my relationship with Samira*ji* forever.

CHAPTER 28

They always played together, walked to class together and ate lunch together. One was tall and horsey-looking with teeth that jutted out at an alarming angle, the other was shorter but plump, wore glasses, had a slight squint and looked grumpy all the time, and then there was Samira*ji*. At home, I was used to seeing her in her pyjamas, looking like a younger and less pretty version of her mother, and it never really registered with me that she was considered a star at school. There were those that hated her, those that were confused about her friendship with the two plain-looking girls, and those who tried to pretend that she didn't matter. But almost everyone else behaved in a worshipping manner around her, as if she was some kind of royalty that had landed in our midst.

I tried to see it from their point of view, and almost could, but my overriding impression was that of a girl who had been pushed aside by her own mother to make way for me. I felt pity for her, yet a part of me craved the popularity that came to her so effortlessly. She didn't notice it, and if she did, it didn't bother her one way or another. I noticed nearly everything about her and her friends—Pari, the tall one who was like her shadow, and Roma, the fat one who seemed to despise them both, but made no effort to make other friends.

Who was I to judge? I made no effort either. More because I knew my place. Enough people called me 'driver's daughter' to my face, putting me down and making me aware that I would never belong, without my having to grovel for friendship too.

So, I took to hiding out in the library during recess, eating my *paratha* slowly while reading a wide variety of books on different subjects. Devouring all that I could, in the hope that someday I would catch up, if not overtake all those who looked down on me.

It was one of those afternoons when I was tucked away in a hidden corner of the library that I heard some giggling and whispering. I thought I'd heard Samira*ji*'s accented voice, so I inched closer to the shelf, staying hidden.

"It's here, somewhere," Roma muttered.

"But what is so special about it?" Pari asked, trying hard to whisper too, but her voice came out wheezy and thick with cold.

"It talks about sex," Samira*ji* giggled, "That's why Roma is so excited."

"Are you sure? They wouldn't keep books like that in the library!"

"Shut up, the both of you. I'm trying to find it…"

I peeked from where I was hiding, careful not to give myself away. They had their backs to me and were rifling through the books under 'C'. Maybe because they were so focussed on their task, they hadn't noticed something that I saw straight away.

I stepped out from behind the shelf, clearing my throat. They jumped, spinning around to face me.

Samira*ji*'s eyes narrowed.

"Are you spying on us, Madhu?" Her voice was low and menacing.

I shook my head, about to speak, but the fat one, Roma, stepped forward threateningly.

"I've seen you watching us! Why are you always following us around? What did you hear?"

I shook my head again and then pointed to Samira*ji*'s skirt.

"You have a bloodstain on the back. I thought I'd tell you before you walked out of the library like that."

Samira*ji* gasped and craned her neck to look at her skirt.

"No, no, no, no, no! I could've sworn I wasn't due for another week...!"

She looked close to tears. Pari and Roma were staring at her in astonishment. Maybe they hadn't started their period yet. Nor had I, but in a small household like ours, bodily functions had never been kept secret. I had washed enough of Mataji's soiled clothes to know what a period meant.

"We could trade skirts," I offered. "This one is yours, after all."

"You would do that?" Samira*ji* gaped at me. "But mine is stained."

"I will wash as much of it as I can, then wear it back to front with my shirt out. No one notices me. It will be alright."

She nodded, her face flushed. No matter how much she pretended that her status in school didn't matter to her, I realised then that it did. She didn't want to become the butt of all jokes. I already was.

Something shifted that day. Samira*ji* became Samira*di,* an 'elder sister' as she insisted on being addressed as, even though we were only a few months apart in age. I was semi-absorbed into their group, and little by little everyone forgot where I had come from.

Almost everyone. There was one person who would never forget.

PART II

Pari

CHAPTER 29

I finally got my braces at fifteen, and according to Sri, looked like 'Jaws' from James Bond.

"Ignore him," Amma said when he teased me by bringing a rope near my teeth and asking me to chomp on it the first time I came home with the braces on. But how could I ignore what *Paati* had said to Amma when they thought I was out of earshot?

"Get that child's teeth fixed, Hema. She will not find a husband otherwise."

"Amma! There is more to life than finding a husband."

"*Ayyo*, Hema! Only someone who is happily married will say that. What more is there? Everyone needs a companion in life."

"I am happily married, that is true, but if only Appa and you had let me work for a while; find out who I was before I settled down."

"Do you not know who you are? All these stupid western ideas you get from the television! I'm telling you Hema, these western women who wear trousers and have boycut hairs are also looking for the same thing. They also want someone to look after them; take care of them. But they pretend they are what...what is that word?"

"Emancipated?"

"Yes. All unhappy and em... em..."

"Anyway," Amma sighed, "dental work is expensive, and right now, we don't have the money for it."

"Why? Something wrong with Rajan's job?"

"No, nothing wrong there. We are trying to save money to send Srinivas abroad."

"To America?"

"Yes. He is bright, and once he's away from that Chopra boy, we know he will do well."

There was a pause, and I wondered if my teeth had been forgotten about, but *Paati* was not one to give up easily.

"It is okay to focus on the boy's education, but Hema, the girl needs attention too. If you don't have the money, then sell the gold earrings I gave you, get the money and get her teeth fixed. You will thank me later."

"Amma, those were the earrings Appa gave you when you got married!"

"And I gave them to you. What am I—a seventy-year-old widow—to do with them, huh? And you never wear them. Might as well put them to good use."

Amma relented under *Paati*'s iron-will. I wish I had thanked her then, but that would have meant disclosing I'd overheard their conversation. That was our last vacation in Madras, as *Paati* died five months later, and we never took another family vacation to my maternal grandmother's home again.

My teenage years had proven to be a time of huge anxiety for me. Earlier I'd wanted to be pretty, to be liked by the girls. Now, I wanted to be pretty, to be liked by the boys. In our little group, there was no doubt that Samira was by far the most attractive, but lately I had realised that I was the least. Roma was still plump, but over the years, she had also become quite pretty. She had stopped wearing glasses once they had corrected her squint, and she had the sort of hair one saw in shampoo advertisements—long, thick, jet-black and lustrous.

When she smiled, her entire face lit up, and more than one boy had thrown her a second glance. Madhu had a delicacy about her. She was tiny, but perfectly proportioned, graceful, soft-spoken and, while not drop-dead gorgeous like Samira, there was something alluring about her. I, on the other hand, felt like a clumsy, hulking giant next to them. Too tall, too awkward, always aware of my ugly teeth. I knew the boys had cruel nicknames for me. One of them was 'Big Ethel' from the Archie comics.

Paati had hit a nerve when she said that no one would want to marry me. It wasn't like I was looking to get married at fifteen, but if no boy ever spared me a glance save to make fun of me, what hope would there be for me in the future?

One time, when Roma was in her music lesson and Samira in a drama club meeting, I asked Madhu what it was like living in the shadow of such beautiful people.

She looked at me peculiarly and said, "Beautiful how?"

"I mean, look at Aunty and Uncle. They are like movie stars.When they walk into a room, everyone just stops and stares. Then there is Samira, who gets more beautiful with every passing year. How does it feel to live with people like that?"

Madhu thought about it for a while, then answered, "But I don't see them that way. To me, they are just people."

I wish I had her quiet self-assurance. Nothing anyone said to her ever bothered her. It was like she was encased in an invisible armour that no cruel words could penetrate.

CHAPTER 30

"You are coming, aren't you, Pari?"

This was the tenth time Sam had asked me the same question that week.

"Yes," I groaned loudly. "What makes you think I'm not?"

"Well, you didn't come last year..."

"I had jaundice, Sam!" I glared at her. Sometimes her neurosis was too much. "I'm hardly going to miss your 16th, am I?"

She leaned back in her chair, playing with the end of her ponytail, a small smile on her lips.

"Should I call the boys?"

"Which boys?"

"You know, some from our class, some from the classes above?"

Sam had accumulated a legion of admirers that ranged from ages twelve to eighteen. Some of them had written her love letters, others had scrawled hearts around her name on the girls' toilet doors. One had even carved her name on his forearm with a compass.

"I thought it was a family party?"

"So? It's not like Mama's boyfriends don't turn up like clockwork every year!"

I sighed. This was likely a prelude to another rant against her mother. Just as much as Sam idolised her absentee father, she hated Aunty, who had been more of a mother to Madhu than to her.

"Not again, Sam!"

"I know, I know," she put her hands up. "I just wish I had a normal family like yours."

"What's normal? Appa is always working, and Amma doesn't stop obsessing over Sri."

"How is he?"

"Okay, I guess. He's failed another year at college, so now they're thinking of sending him to the US to Amma's brother. They think if he's away from Rakesh's influence, he'll get better."

"Is that Rakesh fellow still hanging around him?"

"Yes, and he's such a good-for-nothing, too. He's dropped out of college and Amma said he's involved in some shady business. I just wish Sri would see him for the blood-sucking louse he is!"

"Hmm. Say, why don't you bring Sri to the party too?"

"You can't be serious! He'll mock everything and everyone. Why do you want him there?"

"Why not? He's cool, and he rides that motorbike, which will just make all the boys so jealous."

"Really Sam, you don't need my brother to make the other boys jealous. They are all falling over each other to get to you, anyway."

Sam looked at me and smiled.

"You wait. Once those braces come off, they'll forget all about me. You'll be beating them off with a stick."

I smiled back. This was why Sam was so dear to me. Despite her vanity, her insecurities, and her goddamn luck with everything, she had such a kind heart. She knew as well as I did that I would never match up to her in looks or style, but that did not stop her from genuinely believing that I had a chance.

"Shhh, Roma's coming. Don't say anything about the party yet, okay? I'm still trying to figure out if I want to invite her."

"Sam!" I looked at her, pained.

Roma walked up to us, her face flushed.

"I hate that P.T. sir!"

"Rao Sir?" I asked. "Why?"

"I was trying to say to him that I wasn't well, and it came out all wrong. I said 'I am not ill' and he laughed in my face. Then he made me do five laps for making excuses!"

Samira started laughing.

"Serves you right! You *are* always making excuses to get out of exercise."

"Shut up, Samira. It's okay for you. You are his favourite, but for people like me, it's hard."

I sympathised with Roma. I wasn't particularly sporty either, and couldn't wait to give up P.T. at the end of the academic year.

"Maybe if you tried a bit harder, you could lose some weight," Samira said, thoughtfully. I could have kicked her. Roma had been trying, unsuccessfully, to lose weight for the past year. We had heard all about the various diets, put up with her staring at our lunches while she ate toast, and celebrated her when she had lost one kilogram just to put it back on the next week.

"Damn, Samira! I'd never have thought of that!" Roma responded, sarcasm dripping off her, "Why don't you try harder at singing, then maybe you won't sound like a *fataa baans*?"

"Enough!" I said, sick to my back teeth of their constant arguments. "I'm going to look for Madhu. When you've both made up, come and get us. Otherwise, leave us in peace!"

I walked away from them, annoyed.

It had been like this for years—the simmering resentment, the constant jibes at each other, the blatant hostility. I could never figure out whether they were fighting over me, or whether they just enjoyed fighting. Yet neither of them was willing to let go. They hung on to the group and to each other, sharpening their tongues with their verbal warfare.

"There you are!" Madhu was sitting in her favourite corner of the library, reading a book while absently munching on a pear. She looked up, surprised to see me there.

"Are you okay, Pari?"

"They're fighting again. I couldn't take it. So, I thought I'd join you."

She shifted to allow me to sit next to her.

"Why don't you just ignore them?" she asked. "Half the time they enjoy having an audience, that's why they do it. Or at least that's why Samira*di* does."

"That's what I don't get. Samira has nothing to prove. Why does she bother responding to Roma?"

"Pari, don't get involved. Let them figure it out."

CHAPTER 31

"I'm just dropping you off *ghodi*, is that clear? I don't want to be hanging around a bunch of teenagers." Sri was combing his long hair into a low ponytail.

"I don't care. It's Sam who wanted you to come." I looked at my reflection in the mirror. The pink lip gloss that I'd put on clashed horribly with the braces, so I wiped it off and applied a lip balm instead.

"How is the ghost-who-walks?" Sri fiddled with the zipper of his jacket as I threw him a glance.

"She's fine. Busy being adored by all." I didn't mean for my comment to sound snarky, but it came out that way.

"Jealous, *ghodi*?"

"Of course not! Sam's like a sister, you know that."

"Then why doesn't she come around as much?"

"Her dad's back. She's spending time with him right now."

"From another one of his 'business trips'?" Sri used his fingers to draw air quotes.

For a while now, we had suspected that all was not what it seemed with Raj Uncle's work. While Sam refused to acknowledge that her father was anything less than perfect, rumours circulated about the real nature of his business, some of them quite unsavoury, too.

"Shut up, Sri! We don't know if the rumours are true..."

"No smoke without fire, baby!"

"Speaking of smoke, can you please not hide your cigarettes in my room? Amma nearly found them the other day, but I spotted them before she did and put them in my jacket pocket!"

"That's where they went!" he grinned at me, looking devilishly handsome. "I thought you'd taken up smoking too!"

"Yuck! Filthy habit. Never ever. I'll give them back to you, if you promise never to put them in my room again."

"Okay, okay. Now hurry up! Gotta get to the Princess's party, don't we?"

Despite his protestations, once Sri had parked his bike in front of her house, he did accompany me inside. It might have been curiosity, but I didn't probe. I liked having Sri with me; it made me feel safe and special. Not only was he unconventionally good looking, but he had an arrogant air about him, and although he was wiry now to the point of being thin, no one messed with him. Just like with Sam, I wanted a bit of his coolness to rub off on me, too.

"Well, well," he remarked caustically, "the Princess does live in a palace. Why's she been slumming it with us all these years?"

"Shhh," I motioned as I spotted Roma in the distance, wondering when Sam had changed her mind and why Roma hadn't mentioned it to me.

"Is that Fatso over there?" Sri elbowed me.

"Honestly, Sri, you have to stop! I won't have any friends at this rate."

"Alright, alright. You go and hang out with your teenage gang. I'm going in search of alcohol. Surely this joint will have some? Where's the alki mother??"

"Sri," I looked at him, "please don't do anything stupid."

For a moment, his shoulders seemed to slump, then he straightened himself up and patted me on my head.

"For you, *ghodi*, I'll be on my best behaviour."

.   .   .

By now, I was familiar with the ins and outs of Samira's family. The many *chachas* and *mamas* that dipped in and out. The merry-go-round of 'uncles'—Nina Aunty's admirers—that always hung around, and now that Samira had her own devotees amongst boys and girls alike, the house was full to overflowing. After pushing my way through the many groups of people, I finally found Samira. She was dressed in a simple white T-shirt and ripped jeans, so unlike the other girls who were wearing bright colours and large plastic earrings, all the rage in Delhi. Even so, she looked stunning.

"Pari!" she called out. "Come on over! Have some punch."

"What's that?" I asked, eyeing the glass suspiciously.

"It's just mixed fruit juice," she laughed at me. "Did Sri bring you?"

She was looking behind me to see if she could spot him.

"Yeah, but I don't know where he got to." I didn't want to tell her that he was probably raiding Uncle's beers right now. "Are you enjoying your party? It looks really busy."

"It's okay," she shrugged, then grabbed my arm and took me to the side. "I had to call Roma. Someone let it slip that I was having a party, and she nearly blew a fuse."

"It was the right thing to do," I nodded sagely.

"Have you seen what she's wearing?"

"I caught a glimpse of her earlier, but no, I didn't notice. Why?"

"Her top is so low cut that her boobs are nearly falling out."

"Oh. I'm surprised Ripa Aunty let her leave the house like that. Maybe Roma didn't realise."

"Please! Roma knows exactly what she's doing, and Ripa Aunty barely has a say these days. She's got all the boys thronging to her like bees to a honeypot!"

This was the first time I had seen Samira display jealousy, and I was taken aback. Insecurity didn't sit well on her.

CHAPTER 32

"Pari, Pari, wait up!" I turned to see the slight figure of Madhu running towards me and stopped just before the canteen for her to catch up.

"Are you okay?" she asked, concern etched all over her face.

I shrugged.

"Look, I know what it looked like, but Nina*ji*... she... I mean, she's a complicated woman..." Her face was earnest as she defended Sam's mother.

"She's *old*, Madhu! And she was trying to kiss my twenty-one-year-old brother!" I was still furious and embarrassed by the whole thing.

"Yes, I know! But she had drunk a little too much, and Srinivas..."

"What about Sri?" I asked coldly, drawing myself up to my full height, looking down at her.

"He didn't exactly help matters," she mumbled, taking my elbow and steering me towards a quiet corner. "I was there. I saw him ask her if she had any whisky, and they were drinking long before you and Sam spotted them."

My eyes filled with tears. Typical Sri. Typical Nina Aunty.

"How is Sam?" Sam hadn't come to school the entire week, hadn't answered any of my calls, and right now, Madhu was the only bridge between us.

"Angry. Very angry. Raj Uncle is trying to calm things down at home."

"Oh, God! Poor Uncle."

Madhu looked uncomfortable.

"He's not exactly blameless, you know. There're things... stuff... that Aunty tells me and I... I just can't take sides anymore..."

"I'm sorry." I looked at her again, wondering how it felt to be a part of that crazy household, and yet keep your sanity. She seemed to read my mind.

"It's okay. I've seen all this before. They will calm down in a few days, and it will go back to being how it was."

"Hmm."

I still wondered, because although Sri had brushed off the entire incident, I'd seen his stricken face as Sam and I had stumbled upon them pawing at each other.

Roma wouldn't stop gloating about the entire episode and I wondered if she was the one who had been spreading the news everywhere.

"Hey Roma!" I caught her outside the Music Room.

"Pari," she smiled at me absently.

"What have you got against me?"

"What?" she stuttered, wrong-footed.

"Have I not been a good friend to you?"

"Y... yes, you have! Of course you have!" Her face reddened as she realised where I was going.

"Then stop talking rubbish about my brother, okay?" I glared at her.

"I... I didn't mean..."

"I know," I said, softly. "But just stop now, okay?"

Her vendetta against Samira could wait. But when it came to my brother, I wouldn't stand for anyone speaking against him.

I looked her in the eye just to make sure she understood. She gulped and nodded.

But rumours have a way of spreading, then mutating. The story took on a life of its own, and before long, everyone was whispering about the 'affair' between Sri and Nina Aunty. Sri's reputation had never been the best, but now Sam's name was being dragged through the mud, too.

When Margaret Ma'am called me into the office, I shuddered to think what she must have heard for me to be called in this way.

"Pari, shut the door behind you, please."

I did, and then stood in front of her desk, eyes downcast.

"Take a seat, Pari. You must be wondering why I called you in?"

I sat down, my cheeks reddening. Then, before I could help it, a tear rolled down my cheek.

"My goodness, child, whatever is the matter?"

"I'm sorry, Ma'am! If I had known what would happen, I would never have taken him there. He just... sometimes... he doesn't understand right from wrong... but he's a good person, really. And it isn't Sam's fault. You should have seen her face... I think she was more shocked than I..."

"Wait, wait—stop, Pari. Here, take a sip of water." She handed me a glass of cool water from the earthen *matka* she kept in her room. The water always tasted fresh, as if it had been drawn from a well. "Now, start from the beginning, and tell me what all this is about."

I stumbled over the story, embarrassed to be relating it, even though it was the more innocent version of whatever she had heard in the first place.

"I see." she steepled her fingers together. "Well Pari, from what you tell me, the people involved were adults and consenting. It is not for me to debate the right or wrong of the situation. As for these rumours you have mentioned, I would ignore them and let them die a natural death. All this will be yesterday's news before you know it."

Puzzled, I looked at her.

"But did you not call me in because of this incident?"

"Oh Heavens, no! I called you in to tell you that I'm submitting your name to the Senior Quiz Team. I think you'll be a tremendous asset to them. So, make sure you prepare well before they grill you."

I let myself out of her office, bemused at the turn of events. For the first time in a long time, I felt that someone had looked at me and really seen me. I wasn't just that 'good-for-nothing's' sister, or that 'gorgeous girl's' friend. I was Pari, smart enough to join the Senior Quiz Team.

I couldn't stop smiling all day long.

CHAPTER 33

Regardless, I didn't tell Appa or Amma about Sri's behaviour at Samira's party, but Sri knew I was mad at him. For over two weeks, I didn't speak to him, ignored all his teasing, and turned my back on him every time he tried to catch my eye.

Finally, Appa asked at the dinner table, "Is everything okay, Pari? Have you and Srinivas had a fight?"

Amma looked between Sri and me, and I already knew whose side she would take.

"No," I muttered, mashing together the rice and curd on my plate with my right hand and scooping it into my mouth.

Sri reached out for a *papadum*, not saying anything either.

Appa set his water glass down and looked at us both.

"It's clear that something has happened, and if neither of you want to talk about it, that's fine. Just remember, we are a very small family. Your Amma's brothers are all settled in the US, and my sister, Malathi, would not leave Kodaikanal even if I was taking my last breath. Angar, my brother, was lost to us soon after he married that Pakistani woman. So, with just the four of us in this household, we need to get along. Arguments and fights are all part of growing up, but learn to make up quickly. Do not let things fester. We cannot have deep divisions in a small family."

It was the most Appa had spoken to us in a long time, and we absorbed his words in silence.

"It was my fault, Appa," Sri spoke up. Then he looked me in the face and said, "I'm sorry, Pari. It won't ever happen again."

I looked back at him, nodded mutely, and brushed the stray tear off my face. Forgiving Sri had never been hard for me.

A month later, when life had fallen back into its usual rhythm, I asked Sri the one thing that had been bothering me all along.

"Why did you do it?"

He looked up from the book he was reading.

"Do what, *ghodi*?"

"You know..." My face flushed.

"Oh, *that!*" he laughed, a short sharp sound. "I don't know. Opportunity, alcohol, an impulse... I couldn't say."

"Do you like her?"

"Who?"

"Nina Aunty."

"Zeenat Aman look-alike? She's pretty, but no, I don't like her in the way you think."

"Sri..."

"Yeah?"

"I worry about you."

"Not you too, *ghodi*! I'll be fine, okay?"

"You say that, but I've seen you with Rakesh, and..."

He set his book down and called me over to him. I sat next to him and put my head on his shoulder.

"Pari, you concentrate on your life. Don't get taken in by what people say about Rakesh. Deep down he's a nice guy, and he gets me." He put his arm around me and said softly, "I know what I'm doing, so stop worrying about me."

"Are you going to the US then? Is that why you've been studying so hard?"

He pulled my hair.

"If I get through the entrance exam, I'll go. I've promised Amma."

I nestled into him.

"I'll miss you, Sri, but I know it will be for the best."

"I'm going to call you over, *ghodi*, as soon as I'm settled there. I'll get you married to some American dude, yeah?"

I mock-punched him in his stomach, happy that we were friends again, happy that he was turning his life around.

"Say, what do you make of what Appa said about his brother?" I asked him.

"That Anger dude?"

"Not Anger—Angar!"

"I don't know any more than you do, Pari. Why do you care? It's not as if we've ever met him."

"Just curious, I guess. Maybe because we both have strange names. I wonder how he got on with a name like that in a South Indian family."

"Clearly not well. That's why he ran off to Dubai and married some Pakistani chick!" Sri guffawed.

"Don't be rude!"

"Rude? I'm just stating facts." He dropped a kiss on my head. "And I like your name, Pari. It's different, it's unusual, and it suits you. Even with those braces."

It was rare to hear such tenderness in his voice, and I nestled closer to him. Whatever the world thought of Sri, I knew he had a heart of gold. I prayed that God would take him out of Rakesh's clutches and allow him to make something of his life. Sri was much, much smarter than me, and he deserved to do well. If he carried on working as hard as he had been, I had no doubt in my mind that he would turn his life around. Then Amma could stop all her worrying, and Appa could retire early.

"Sri?"

"Yes, *ghodi*?"

"Promise me something."

"You know I don't make promises."

"I know. But just this once."

"What is it?"

"Promise me that you won't ever do anything impulsive again, that you'll think before you act."

"Ooh, *ghodi,* you're going all grown up and wise on me now!"

"Well?"

"I can't promise, Pari. But I'll try. I really will."

I closed my eyes and hoped it would be enough.

CHAPTER 34

When the dust had settled, as Margaret Ma'am had predicted, 'the incident' became yesterday's news. Samira and I were too close to let the small matter of my brother and her mother's behaviour come between us. After the initial awkwardness and one brief conversation, we never spoke of it again. Exams were approaching, and we got busy preparing for them. A healthy academic rivalry still existed between us, with one of us inevitably taking the top slot in the class. Yet, we knew that after this year, we would part ways to take up the different subjects we were interested in.

Samira wanted to study Arts, her natural inclination being towards English and history even though she excelled in almost everything. I had been leaning towards maths and economics, and knew that I would end up in a different section from her. Ironically, Roma had chosen to do Arts as well, with music as her elective. I wondered how the two of them would get along without Madhu or I putting out their constant conflagrations.

Madhu was still a class behind us, even though they had advanced her a couple of years already. Supersmart, self-effacing and quiet, I had grown to admire her in the few years I had known her. Whenever I went to Samira's house, I'd see Madhu, but she kept out of our way, sensing that we wanted to spend time with each other.

Occasionally Samira would ask her to hang out with us, and she would without complaint, never asking for any special treatment or extra attention.

Roma, on the other hand, stuck to me like a limpet most days. I had long accepted the fact that I couldn't shake her off as Amma and Ripa Aunty had become fast friends. I didn't actively dislike Roma like Samira did, but something about her unsettled me. She didn't seem happy in her own skin. It wasn't the weight thing., although, in her mind, her figure was her defining feature. I could have told her it wasn't. She sang beautifully, had lovely long hair and a charming smile. She was really very attractive. Yet, I could see that she constantly compared herself to Samira, and kept coming up short. I wanted to tell her that it was a futile exercise, that some people were just genetically lucky, and the rest of us had to make do with whatever our genes had doled out to us. But I refrained, knowing that Roma's competitiveness arose from insecurity. Perhaps if she got to spend time with Samira, she'd see that despite her beauty, intelligence and popularity, Samira's life was far from perfect. As was evinced by the fallout of 'the incident'.

The only time we'd spoken of it, I could tell how furious Samira still was with her mother.

"That woman is like a bitch in heat! She'll attack anything in trousers."

"Samira! That's a wicked thing to say," I'd cried out, appalled. "Sri was to blame as well. There was alcohol involved…"

"There's always alcohol involved!" she'd scoffed. "I'm telling you, Pari, she did it deliberately."

"But why?"

"Because it was my special day! She had to ruin it, and she found the best way to do it. By making out with my best friend's brother. Disgusting!"

"Samira, I can't pretend to understand, but isn't it better to forgive and forget? I've had to, with Sri. Look, it was ugly and unpleasant, but it's not like they're having an affair. It happened once. It was foolish and callous, but let's just move on from it."

Samira had nodded grimly, and we had never spoken about it again. But I didn't mention the rumours that Roma had spread. Things were bad enough between them.

Could Roma not see how hard it was for Samira at home? With Nina Aunty the way she was, and Raj Uncle away more than at home, who did she have to turn to? At least Roma and I had stable home lives. Madhu spoke little of her parents, but I knew her father doted upon her. Samira had told me as much. In so many ways, we were luckier than Samira. Lucky because we had parents who loved us and were invested in us, because we had siblings we could exchange confidences and gripes with; lucky that we had stability. The stability that Samira lacked completely.

Even I had come to realise in the course of the years that no matter how picture-perfect her life looked from the outside, on the inside, it was rotten to the core.

CHAPTER 35

"Amma! Amma?" I stomped into the living room. "I can't find my Madonna tape! Where have you put it?"

It was six in the evening and I had heard Appa come in from work, but hadn't popped out to say hello because I was finishing a particularly tough mock-paper. Now, as I barged into the living room, I saw them both huddled together, whispering, their bodies leaning into each other.

"What? What's happened?" I knew immediately that something had, and my heart sank as I tried to remember where Sri had said he would be. "Is it Sri?"

They looked up at me with similar expressions of bewilderment and grief.

"Amma?" I sat beside her, clutching her hand. "What is it?"

She shook her head and looked at Appa. He looked at me intently before speaking.

"We'll have a new family member join us soon."

My face blanched as I looked at the both of them and then down at Amma's stomach. Surely not?!

Amma caught my look and cracked the tiniest of smiles.

"No, Pari, not that. It's Appa's nephew."

"Who?" I was genuinely perplexed. Malathi Aunty had never married, so who was this nephew?

"My brother's son, Angad. I have to go to Dubai to pick him up."

So many questions jostled for space in my mind, but the uppermost one burst forth.

"How old is he?"

"Sixteen. Just a few months older than you, Pari," Appa supplied.

"Why have we never heard of him? And why is he coming to stay with us? And Amma," I paused for breath, "where *is* my Madonna tape?"

Just then, Srinivas sauntered in, and exactly like I had a few minutes before, picked up on the atmosphere. He came and sat on Amma's right.

"What's going on?"

Amma held his hand and looked at Appa beseechingly.

"You have to tell them, Rajan."

Appa sighed and rubbed his hand over his face before looking into the distance. The tea that Amma had made sat untouched on the little side table, a film of cream forming on its surface.

"I may have mentioned my brother Angar before..." he said.

Sri interjected, "The one who married the Pakistani woman?"

Appa nodded.

"Your great-grandmother and grandmother lived through the partition. They came over as refugees from Peshawar and saw so many deaths and atrocities at that time. Neighbours killing neighbours, friends turning upon each other, fear, hatred, distrust... Over the years, this solidified into a sort of enmity for the nation of Pakistan. In their minds, everything that had happened, everything they had witnessed, was the fault of our Muslim neighbours. Then Angar went to Dubai for work and met this Pakistani girl who he fell in love with, and he wanted to marry her... You can imagine, it did not go down well. There was still so much residual anger and pain that my mother put her foot down and refused." Appa looked so wretched that Amma, in a rare show of physical affection, patted his cheek.

"What happened then?" I asked, fascinated by this bit of family history that had never been spoken of before.

"Angar was just as stubborn as my Amma. At first he tried to reason with her, but when he realised she wouldn't budge, he cut himself off from all of us, settled down with that Muslim woman and never contacted us again."

Sri nodded at Appa to go on.

"We heard occasional snippets of news from friends and acquaintances, but he never reached out, not even after our Amma passed." Appa sighed once again. "I didn't even know he had a son Pari's age."

"Then?"

I could see that Sri was confused. He had walked in after I'd been told we were gaining a new family member.

"Well," Appa continued, "I had a phone call at work today. I'm not sure how the solicitor tracked me down. Maybe Angar had always had my details... not that he ever... anyway..."

Appa seemed lost for words. Amma took over from him.

"Angar and his wife were in an accident. The son, Angad, has no other family that will take him in."

After a moment's shocked silence, Sri asked, "What about his mother's family?"

"Apparently they had severed ties with her, too. So, it's us or nobody for the poor boy." Amma's voice quivered as she said this. "We have to take him in, the poor child. Where will he go otherwise?"

"This boy is going to live with us?" Sri was still trying to absorb this groundbreaking news.

Amma nodded and said, "I know we had nothing to do with Angar and his family. I never even met him. But blood is blood, after all, Sri. How can we abandon him?"

I reached over and hugged Amma, then looked at Appa.

"It's a good thing, no, Appa? We are gaining a brother. It will be a good thing!" I insisted, and somewhere within me, I truly, truly wanted to believe it would be.

Samira

CHAPTER 36

"Bitch!" I muttered under my breath as I slammed the bedroom door behind me. "Bloody bitch!"

I leaned my head against the wall and let the tears flow now that I was out of her sight. In front of her, I never showed any weakness, or she'd sniff it out and go for the kill. Survival necessitated that while Papa was away, I stayed strong, even if on the inside I was a quivering mess.

I picked up the phone to ring Pari, then thought better of it. What if Sri answered? I couldn't bear talking to him after the scene we'd witnessed at my birthday party.

Instead, I decided to listen to the mix tape Arjun had made for me. All love songs, each chosen carefully to display just what I meant to him. I didn't have the heart to tell him that I had five other mix tapes with similar numbers on them. One was from his own best friend.

I put the cassette in and let Whitney Houston's silky voice cover me as I lay on the bed and examined the ceiling. With Papa being away once more, it was the bitch and me, with the occasional lashings of Madhu in the mix. At least when Madhu was around, the bitch's attention was diverted away from me. Her live doll, her ardent fan, her almost-daughter, was so much better than the real thing.

I chewed on my nail. Mothers were supposed to love their children. Why did mine hate me so much? From the barely hidden derision to her outrageous behaviour, everything indicated she abhorred me. But why? Pari had asked me that question once, and now I pondered it again.

It hadn't always been this way. There was a time when she *had* loved me. I remembered the perfumed hugs, the songs she'd sung as she brushed my hair, the cartoon films we had watched together, lying on our stomachs and eating peanuts. A time when she'd hidden rupee coins under my pillow pretending they were from the tooth fairy. Cuddles and kisses when I'd fallen and hurt my knee. Then it had all changed. Abruptly and inexplicably. She had become a remote, brittle and caustic stranger who chose to either ignore me or inflict pain on me.

How could I ask her why, when I could barely vocalise my own thoughts? How could I say, "Mama, why don't you love me anymore?"

Papa had said nothing when I'd told him about Mama's behaviour with Srinivas the very day he returned from his business trip. I'd rather it was me he heard it from than some gossipmonger. He'd looked at me as I'd sobbed hysterically, screamed and shouted, then called me over to him.

"Sam, forget you saw that. Your Mama probably didn't mean it, and she definitely won't have any memory of it."

"Why do you keep forgiving her? Can't you see what she's like?!"

"I see far more than you can imagine." He'd sat me next to him, his hand stroking my hair. "When I married your mother, it was for keeps. I loved her then, and I still love her very much."

"She doesn't love you, Papa!"

"Darling Sam, that's where you're wrong. She loves me too, but her way of showing it differs greatly from what convention dictates. She could have left me a long time ago, but she's hung in there, and that counts for a lot."

.   .   .

I missed Papa. I missed his sense of mischief, his aura of calm, his kindness, his ability to make the most mundane day sparkle with joy. I'd said as much to the bitch today, thinking it was a safe day, that she was in a good mood, hoping that a bit of nostalgia would open her heart towards me.

Instead, her face had twisted as she looked at me from over the rim of her glass, full of some shit alcohol, as usual.

"Oh, you miss him, do you? And what am I? Chopped liver?"

I'd stood up then, not wanting another ugly argument.

"Yes, run away, why don't you? A coward, just like your father..." she'd slurred the last few words, and just as I'd walked away from her, I'd heard Madhu come in.

"Nina*ji*, shhh. Look, the Tailor Master has come with your blouses."

I should have hated Madhu, except that I couldn't. I saw her as a bridge—the only way to reach my mother when I needed to. She soothed and pacified her as none of us could, cajoling her into being softer, kinder even. It was because of Madhu that I escaped the worst of her wrath.

As for Madhu, I knew that her own mother preferred the little brother over her. So, if she was okay with the bitch playing surrogate mother to her, why not? It wasn't as though Mama was transferring her affections from me to her. She didn't have any for me, so what was there to transfer?

I looked at the cobweb that was forming in one corner of the ceiling; a tiny spider making its home, tangles of silken threads waiting to catch an unsuspecting victim. I closed my eyes. Where was Papa now? When would he come home?

CHAPTER 37

"I'm telling you, she's a klepto, Pari!"

"How can you say that?" Pari looked at me, astonished at the accusation I was levelling at Roma in her absence.

"You remember the glittery hairband Papa had brought me from America? I hadn't seen it in a while, and I thought I'd lost it. Then she came in wearing it today. I asked her where she'd got it from, and she said *her* Baba had bought it for her. The exact same thing!"

"Come on, Sam, he might have. I know Uncle travelled abroad a while ago. Maybe she asked him to buy the same thing if she liked it on you?"

"Okay," I leaned forward, "Explain Monica's ring ending up on her finger, or Ashish's pencil that just 'fell into' her bag? Oh, and by the way, any of your stuff gone walkies lately?"

Pari was silent for a moment, before nodding her head.

"I knew it!" I smiled triumphantly.

"But what are we going to do? We can hardly accuse her of being a thief, can we?"

"I say we cut her out of the group. You know I don't like her much anyway, and Madhu won't be bothered if we do."

"Sam..."

"Pari, listen to me," I spread my fingers on the desk, "she'll be in a different section soon..."

"With you..."

"Yes, but not with you. I won't have a problem ignoring her, but you need to finish with her, too."

"Does it have to be this drastic? I mean, let's wait it out. Maybe she'll become friends with other people when you're in a different section."

"Honestly! I can't believe that after all her sneaky and thieving ways, you still want to stay friends with her!" I was livid, and Pari put her hand on mine to calm me down.

"Sam, I know that the two of you have always had this *thing* between you, but try to understand my position in this. What do you think Roma will do if we cut her out? She'll complain to her mother, who will take it to Amma, who will then get angry with me. I'm just trying to avoid all that unpleasantness. Besides, there's already so much going on in my household without me adding more aggravation."

I snatched my hand away and crossed my arms. Then, after a while, I let out a long exhale.

"How is everything? Has Uncle left for Dubai yet?"

"He's leaving on Saturday."

"How long will he be gone?"

"A month, at least, he said. He's had to take time off from work because he will have to settle all their affairs in Dubai before returning."

"With your cousin."

"Yes, with Angad."

"Your family has strange names."

"I know," Pari smiled at me, and with the braces she looked around twelve. I smiled back. Roma's fate would have to wait another day. It was time to cheer my best friend up.

"Come on, let's get some bread *pakoras* from the canteen. My treat!"

. . .

This *thing* with Roma had started almost as soon as I had met her. At first it was because she'd clung to Pari as if she were a life jacket. I had hoped back then that in time she would branch out and make more friends. When she started leading the morning assemblies, singing *bhajans* on the *harmonium*, I'd hoped she'd move away from us and find her own little group of friends. But for one reason or another, she always stuck around.

Resigned, I had even tried making friends with her, but there was nothing about her that appealed to me. She wasn't as smart as Pari, or as kind and patient as Madhu. She was mean-spirited, sly and deceitful. I didn't trust her, and could not get myself to like her.

I'd asked Madhu once how she tolerated her, and she'd said, "Roma is insecure around you, Samira*di*. You bring out the worst in her. She barely speaks to me, as she doesn't think I'm worthy of her attention."

"Worthy? What do you mean?"

"Samira*di*, in her eyes, I've always been a driver's daughter, a scheduled caste person. She may not say it in so many words, but she believes that I am not equal to any of you."

"What nonsense! You are a far better person than she has ever been."

"*Didi*, that's because neither Raj Uncle nor Nina*ji* believe in all this caste stuff, but you do know that Pari's parents are staunch brahmins too? If they knew that I was of a lower caste, do you think they'd let me be friends with her?"

"Madhu, you can't be serious! We are nearly in the 21st century. Are you telling me that all this caste business is still such a big deal?"

"To many people it is. To Roma, it is."

I'd hugged her then, hoping to convey that none of it mattered to me. I didn't think it mattered to Pari either, but then, why had she refrained from telling her parents? As for Roma, it only confirmed my opinion of her. She was a shallow, self-serving, nasty person, and I couldn't wait to get away from her.

CHAPTER 38

On the last day of the mock-exams, Pari called me home. It had been a few months since I'd gone over, and I needed a break from the bitch, so I said yes, but on the condition that Roma wouldn't be there. Pari had agreed with alacrity. Roma had music lessons that day.

Uncle had already left for Dubai, so I guessed that Pari and Aunty could do with the company. Aunty was so pleased to see me that she'd made *dosas,* which she knew I loved.

"Some more *milaga podi,* Samira?" Aunty smiled at me encouragingly, while sliding another *dosa* onto my plate.

I grinned and nodded, remembering the first time I'd dipped my *dosa* in the gunpowder spice and how it had nearly blown my head off. Now, I ate it with relish, even though invariably, sweat beads would break out on my upper lip.

"You have not come for a long time, huh?" Lovely Aunty, who had become plumper as the years went on. Lovely, plump and maternal. All the things my mother wasn't, and I wished she could be.

"I've been preparing for the mocks, Aunty."

"Ah, yes. All you children studying so hard," she nodded her head. "You will do well."

Once again, the image of Mama sprawled on the armchair flashed into my mind. She had never once asked how I was doing or encouraged me in any way. Her only contribution to motherhood had been producing me.

"Amma said we could watch E.T. on the VCR today." Pari grinned at me. We had seen E.T. four times already, but loved it so much that we could watch it on repeat.

After lunch, we sat on the rug while Aunty sat on the sofa behind us, shelling peas and half-watching the movie. At some point, Srinivas strolled in and sat behind us, too. My spine stiffened, but I pretended to be engrossed in the film.

When it finished at 7 p.m. I suddenly realised that Uncle wasn't around to give me a lift home, and Mama would have left for the club, so the driver wouldn't be able to pick me up either.

"I'll take an auto-rickshaw," I insisted to Pari, who looked at Aunty.

"Nonsense! It's not safe. It's already getting dark," Aunty said. "Sri will take you on his motorcycle."

"No, no, it's okay." My cheeks reddened at the thought, but there was no arguing with Pari or Aunty. Srinivas sat on the sofa, jiggling his knee, as if waiting for us to make up our minds.

Acquiescing finally, I perched delicately behind him, tucking my skirt under me and placing one hand on his shoulder. With the other hand, I waved to Pari and Aunty as they waved back.

Without a word, Srinivas started the bike and took off with a roar. As he zipped in and out of traffic, I relaxed and enjoyed the feel of the wind in my hair, semi-watching the buildings, the houses, the shops, the hawkers, and the traffic as we rode past them. There was no conversation; it would have been impossible over the sound of the motorbike, but I liked the feel of his hard muscle under my hand, tightening my grip ever so slightly, wondering what he was thinking about.

We had barely spoken since 'the incident'. The few times I'd run into him at Pari's house, he had either avoided me altogether, or behaved with exaggerated politeness. I didn't know what to make of him, but then again, I never had. Sri had always been an enigma to me. Pari's older brother: remote, attractive, scary, troubled, and troublesome. I often wondered what he thought of me?

In no time at all, we were in front of my house and as he parked, I quickly slid off the back of the bike. It had gotten dark, and the streetlights created little pools of light every thirty metres, but one of them had gone out and not been replaced. We stood in the shadow between the two lights, the slightest of illumination reaching us from the house lights behind us.

"T... Thank you, Sri. For the lift."

He took his helmet off and shook his long hair. Even in the half-darkness, I could feel his eyes piercing into me. I shivered slightly, clasping my arms around my body.

"Samira," his voice was hoarse.

"Yes?"

"I'm sorry."

He didn't need to say anymore. I didn't want to hear him apologise or explain. It would have been too much. I reached forward spontaneously to place my finger on his lips, wanting to stop the flow of his confession, but he pulled me in closer. In the half-light, our lips met. I felt his stubble against my skin, the faint smoky flavour of tobacco on his tongue.

Then, with a hunger that had been growing—for weeks, for months, for years, perhaps even forever—we devoured one another.

CHAPTER 39

Stolen kisses, half-whispered promises, the lightest of touches, secret notes kept in hidden places. Can there be anything more intense and consuming than first love?

Instinctively, we hid it from the world. From Pari, from Aunty, from everyone we knew and trusted. Exposing something so new, so nascent, seemed almost a crime. We didn't want it sullied by people's words, thoughts, or expectations.

Yet, the fire in his eyes, the yearning in every look and passionate touch, seemed to reach into my soul and separate it from my body. I was thrilled and frightened by the intensity of his ardour, by his unspoken wanting, by this feeling of losing myself in our all-consuming desire.

"Sri," I would whisper into his neck as we found old forts and abandoned buildings to hide in.

"Sam," he'd whisper back, as his hands roamed my body, waiting for my inevitable signal to say "stop", "no, not today", even as I arched towards him, wanting more, yet scared to go there; scared that it would be wrong to do it this way. Hidden, cheap, tawdry.

. . .

In the two weeks since our first kiss, we had accelerated through a relationship with eager fervour. We weren't 'boyfriend and girlfriend' to the world yet, it was still too fresh for that, but we acknowledged to each other that this was more than just a passing crush.

"Sri?"

"Hmm?"

"Did you always know?"

"Yes, I think so," he said, his eyes closed, his head on my lap, face towards the sun. "I knew I didn't want to be your big brother, for sure."

I laughed at the memory.

We were hidden in a cool corner of the tomb in Lodi Gardens. I had changed out of my distinctive blue uniform into a white T-shirt and jeans, scared that the denizens of propriety would find us out. Sri was in his usual black jeans and black tee, a uniform of another sort.

"And what if you leave for the US?" I asked, my fingers stroking his brow.

"I won't be gone forever, and we don't even know if I'll get through the entrance exam." His eyes remained closed.

"Of course you will! Pari told me how hard you've been working."

His eyes snapped open. There was a peculiar look in them.

"You do know that Pari only thinks the best of me?"

I nodded. How could she not? Besides, I did as well. Despite everything.

He rolled over onto his stomach.

"Sam, it's not that I don't want to go to the US. It's just that..."

"What?"

"It's someone else's dream. Amma's dream."

"And what's yours?"

"To stay like this, in your arms, forever."

He reached up and pulled me down towards him. Our kiss was quick, circumspect. This was not the time or place.

"Seriously, Sri, what's your dream?"

"We do not know what we want and yet we are responsible for

what we are—that is the fact," he quoted, once more on his back, looking up at the sky.

Jean Paul Sartre.

I looked up at the sky with him.

There was a darkness in Sri that frightened me. A desire to self-annihilate. He'd pass on books on existentialism to me, asking me to read them, to understand the philosophies of Nietzsche, Kafka, Sartre and Beauvoir.

Essentially, he believed that life was meaningless, and that our actions could only take us so far and no further. We were particles of nothingness in an unfathomable universe.

"Then what is the point of our existence, Sri?" I would ask, confused by the messages in the books, only half-understanding them, half-processing them.

"There is none." He would grin at me then, devilishly handsome.

"But there must be! Why would we be here otherwise?"

"Life is chaos and uncertainty, volatility and anarchy. Someday you'll understand, Sam."

"And us?" I would ask, fearful that he would attribute nihilism to our fledgling relationship, too.

"Love is the whole thing. We are only pieces," he would quote Rumi then, bewildering me once again by being a romantic.

He would pull me towards him, chuckling, then crushing my lips under his, and I would forget everything, drowning in the ecstasy of loving him.

For love him I did, with every fibre of my being. With the ache and ravenous craving of an addict. Yet, it had taken me years of not understanding, of not connecting the dots, until the shock of seeing him with my mother had made me realise the depth of my feelings towards him.

I still remained confused. Much as I loved him, there was a part of me that was scared of being consumed whole by the intensity of his ardour. With Sri, there could never be half-measures. He wanted me, all of me—and I held back, unable, unwilling to give him the part of me he desired the most.

"You drive me crazy, Sam! I can't sleep thinking of you. Of all the things I want to do to you," he'd groan, running his fingers through his hair.

I'd feel a delicious shiver of anticipation go through me at his words, then wonder why I didn't succumb. What held me back? Was it fear that once he'd had me, he would tire of me? Or that once he'd had me, there would be no turning back?

CHAPTER 40

"*Samiradi?*" Madhu was at the door, and I quickly hid the note I was writing to Sri. She held a newspaper bag in her hand.

"What is it?"

"I've brought you the pads you asked for." She held out the package to me.

"Just set it down on the side." I sat up and indicated she should come in. "Get me a Fanta from the fridge and get yourself one, too. And there's a packet of chips on top. Bring those as well."

She did as I said, then sat on her usual *mooda*. Years ago, when I had finally overcome my antipathy to her, I'd invited her to sit on my bed. The very next day, these *moodas* had appeared in all the rooms. Was it Maryam who had bought them, or was it Mama who had asked her to? At any rate, Madhu never sat on the bed with me again.

Mama, for all her so-called largesse towards the driver's daughter, was not immune to social or caste hierarchy, even if Madhu thought otherwise. I'd picked up on the tiniest of clues, surprised that she hadn't cottoned on.

Madhu had her own plate and glass, just like the maids. We never ate at the same table and never pretended that we were anything but Memsahib's daughter and Memsahib's pet project at home. At school, it was a different matter.

"Is Kitchloo still bothering you?" I asked her.

She shook her head.

"After you gave me that book *di*, I did well in the Chemistry test. Now he's found a different *murga*."

We grinned at each other. Kitchloo Sir was known for his explosive temper, and while I'd had him wrapped around my little finger within a week, poor Madhu had borne the brunt of his sudden rages for the better part of the year. Personally, I thought it was because he couldn't bear the fact that a driver's daughter could speak better English than him. Kitchloo Sir would always retain traces of his Kashmiri accent, while Madhu's English sounded as good as any newsreader on Doordarshan now.

"How is 9th class, then?" Madhu had done so well in her studies that they had moved her up a year, so she was just a year behind me now.

"Yes, it's okay. You know what they're like, *di*! They keep harping on about the Board exams."

"Yeah, they did that to us, too." I took a swig of my Fanta. "Have you thought of what subjects you'd like to take?"

"I was hoping to do biology. If I could just get better grades in chemistry, then I think they'd accept me into the Science section."

I offered Madhu some chips that she put in her left hand and ate one by one with her right. She was still incredibly skinny, but could eat like a horse. Something Roma was so jealous of.

"I'm really proud of you, Madhu!" I said to her as I munched on my chips. "You're the only one out of the four of us taking Science."

"But *di*, you know I've always wanted to be a doctor."

"Not *always*..." I laughed. She laughed too, in response. There was a time she'd decided she wanted to be an astronaut after reading some book in the library. Until her Mataji had told her to come back down to earth, very firmly.

"How is Lallan?"

"Four years old and very mischievous! You should come and see him."

"Why don't you bring him here?"

The last time I had gone into their home, our converted garage, I'd seen the look on Umesh Driver's face. He still insisted on calling me 'Missie*ji*', and when they all sat at my feet while I sat on their *charpoy* bed, I decided never to visit them again.

"Yes, okay, I will."

"Say, Madhu...?"

"Yes?" She looked at me intently.

"No, nothing." I fumbled with the ties on my top. "See you at school tomorrow."

"Okay *di*." She stood up, dusted off her skirt, smiled at me, and left the room.

I wanted to confide in someone about the complex surge of emotions I was feeling. Up one minute, down the next; a rollercoaster that wouldn't stop, wouldn't let me breathe. I couldn't tell Pari, and I wouldn't tell Roma if she was the last person on earth. But was burdening Madhu with this information fair? What could she possibly advise me?

I walked past Mama's room, then stopped. Pushing the door open quietly, I looked inside. The television was blaring with some nature programme while she sat in front of it, passed out in the armchair. The crystal tumbler lay on its side, a trickle of amber liquid seeping into the carpet. A packet of chips had been opened and barely consumed. A stale, unwashed odour hung in the room, as if it hadn't encountered daylight or fresh air in weeks.

Sighing, I shut the door once again.

CHAPTER 41

On the outside we looked just like any other group of teenage girls—silly and giggly, with our skirts rolled up at the waist, lip gloss applied discreetly enough to miss detection by the teachers, but enough to attract the attention of the boys. We were tall, short, fat, thin, curvy, or underdeveloped, and our personalities were just as mercurial as our teenage temperaments. Underneath the happy tableau, though, there were jealousies that simmered, and the currents that eddied and swirled could have filled reams of teenage sagas.

Perhaps, out of all of us, Madhu was the calmest. Nothing ever ruffled her feathers, and she often played peacemaker between Roma and I. Pari was torn, and I suspected that it wasn't just family loyalty that allowed Roma to stay in our group. In the course of the last few years, a genuine fondness had sprung up between Pari and Roma. They were neighbours, and of late, Pari was spending more and more time in Roma's company. I had been 'unavailable' and otherwise occupied with her brother, but she didn't know that yet. Her response to my inexplicable unavailability was a hurt silence and then a transference of the bulk of her affections to Roma. Still, she hadn't forsaken me completely. We hung out together at school, papering over the cracks with little jokes and anecdotes of the past.

I wanted so much to explain to Pari that I hadn't abandoned her, but how could I, without giving away the reason for my unavailability? Sri had not asked me to keep anything secret, but he had nothing to lose. I was fearful that our relationship would change my dynamics with everyone. From Pari and Uncle-Aunty to Madhu and Roma.

I could just see Roma going to town with the rumours. I hadn't been unaware of the gossip she had initiated after 'the incident', even if Pari thought I didn't know. I could predict how she would treat this information.

"Keeping it in the family, is he? First the mother, then the daughter!"

I could almost hear her sniggers of derision. I could feel the dagger she would stab me in the back with as she feigned innocence and played her *harmonium* as if nothing untoward had occurred.

Who had given her the name 'nightingale'? Why was she compared to this small bird with its powerful and beautiful song? So she could sing. So what? She was no Lata Mangeshkar! She'd sung Eurythmics' 'Sweet Dreams' as if it was an Indian classical song, her voice wavering in a *raga*. Wrecked it completely. I could never listen to it again. She was a serpent, with a forked tongue.

"You're miles away, Sam!" Pari poked me in the ribs, interrupting my poisonous train of thought.

"Huh? Sorry, was just thinking of something."

"They'll be releasing the test centres today. I hope we get the same one." Pari said, a thoughtful look on her face.

"Why wouldn't we?" Roma asked.

"Last year there were two, but in the previous years there had only been one."

As they carried on talking about test centres, I allowed myself to drift into another daydream about Sri. His smokey kisses, his dark, wavy hair, the way his brow creased when he was thinking, his molten brown eyes deep with desire...

"Earth to Samira!" This time it was Roma.

"What?" I snapped, irritably.

"What are you planning to wear to the end-of-year party?"

"A *sari*. Isn't that what all the girls are wearing?"

"Samira*di*, the purple one?" Madhu asked excitedly. She'd seen me sneak it out of Mama's wardrobe when she'd been sleeping.

"Yeah, maybe." I winked at Madhu. She was more excited about the party than I was. I wished Sri could come as my escort. Instead, I'd be fending off silly boys all evening long.

"That will be our last fun outing before the exams," Pari remarked wistfully.

"Then, let's make it count!" Roma replied.

"What do you mean?"

"I'm going to smuggle in some alcohol. Let's get drunk."

Pari gasped. Madhu's mouth fell open, but I just shuddered.

"No way!" I looked at Roma in the face, biting my words out. Madhu and I exchanged a quick glance, and she tilted her head in acknowledgement.

"What? Are you suddenly Miss Goody-Two-Shoes? Don't you want to live a little?" Roma glared at me.

"What kind of alcohol?" Pari sounded intrigued. "I've always wanted to try a drink. Amma and Appa keep nothing but brandy in the house, and we're only given a spoonful when we have a cold."

"Vodka. Baba bought it on his last trip to Poland."

"Won't he miss it?"

"I'll just top it up with water. He doesn't really drink, and he won't notice."

"What if he does?" Madhu asked.

"Baba will forgive me. He always does."

CHAPTER 42

A month until our exams and I had to ask Madhu's Mataji, Sushila, to drape the *sari* for me. It was no good asking Mama, who was once again passed out on the bed, her afternoon drinking having slowly encroached into the mornings.

"Missie*ji*, you will need another safety pin here." Sushila stuck a pin into the *sari pallu,* attaching it safely to my shoulder while I fidgeted uncomfortably. Wearing this an entire evening would be torture, but if all the girls were doing it, I'd be damned if I'd be left out.

I pointed at the perfume and Madhu picked it up and sprayed it on me.

'Poison' was Mama's perfume, and much as I didn't want to smell like the bitch today, I had nothing but 'Charlie', which was much too girly for this grown up look.

I examined myself in the mirror. My hair was tied back in a topknot, and I wore a pair of dangly earrings with crystals that Papa had bought for my last birthday. The purple *sari* had crystals on the border and *pallu* too, and as I twirled, they caught the light.

Madhu smiled at me as she said, "Samira*di*, you look beautiful."

Her Mataji nodded and said, *"Kaala teeka lagao, Missieji."* Then she took a bit of the kohl and put a black dot on my cheek to ward off the evil eye.

I wished Sri was here. I wished he could see me like this.

"Missie*ji*?"

"Yes, Sushila?"

"You look like Nina Memsahib today."

I frowned into the mirror. It was uncanny how similar I looked to the bitch. I didn't want to, and I searched in the mirror for something, anything, that reflected Papa, settling on the shape of my ears.

I wished Papa was here. I wished he could see me like this.

The driver dropped me off at the school gates, and I saw Pari and Roma waiting with a group of girls. Madhu, who was sitting with her father in the front, turned around and said, "*Didi*, have a good time, and don't let Roma bother you."

I nodded at her before allowing her father to open the door and let me out. As I walked towards the group, I noticed that Roma was wearing a purple *sari* too. She had worn hers Gujarati style, *seedha pallu*, probably to hide her big, fat stomach. I put a swing in my hips, knowing that everyone was watching me walk towards them. Roma could try as hard as she wanted. She would never be as sexy as me.

There were lots of speeches. Too many speeches. Some kids were leaving for other schools, and it was a sort of farewell for them. Teachers talked about how wonderful our year had been; some gave us life advice, while others told lame jokes. Kitchloo Sir actually broke down, which elicited quite a few giggles from us. Then, we were led into another hall and the lights were dimmed, music turned on, and we were told to enjoy ourselves.

Pari had had her braces taken off, and as the disco lights hit her face, she looked so lovely that I took her hand to tell her. But the next minute Roma was leading her off somewhere, and Arjun was standing in front of me, asking if I wanted to dance.

I danced, twirling from one partner to another, dizzy with the euphoria of being liked, being wanted. One part of me throbbed with the premonition that something was about to change, and another with the absence of the two men who meant the most to me. My evening of triumph felt hollow without them. In the melee, I tried looking for Pari but didn't see her. Where was she? What was she doing?

Time seemed to pass in a blur. I was dancing one minute, chatting the next, then eating a sandwich someone had brought me. There were always people around me, touching my *sari*, telling me how pretty I looked and asking where I'd got my earrings from. But no Pari. Where was she?

Then suddenly she was there! Grinning at me, displaying her perfectly white, perfectly straight teeth, and I had a sudden pang of nostalgia for my dear buck-toothed friend who had vanished forever.

We danced together, Pari and I, moving to the rhythm of the music, laughing as we got the steps wrong. Then Roma joined us too, awkward and lumbering, and I ignored the irritation, suppressed it, then smiled at her. I wouldn't let anything ruin tonight. She smiled back, looking relaxed and happy for a change. Then I got a whiff of something and knew. I moved closer to Pari and sniffed discreetly.

It was a smell that made my stomach turn, a smell that I had been intimately acquainted with from a very early age. It was the smell of broken promises, betrayal, and anger. A smell of indifference and dissipation. It was the smell of alcohol.

I wanted to say something to Pari, to warn her, but there were too many watchful eyes around us, and Pari looked happy. So happy.

I thought I spotted Sri in the distance, but that was impossible. I peered once again, but he had disappeared. My imagination was playing tricks on me. Then it was Madhu, looking grim, saying something. I turned away, shimmying across to the other side of the room, the lights and the music giving our sports auditorium a soft, incandescent quality.

Someone grabbed my arm, and I shook them off. I was tired of being touched and grabbed by these people. I just wanted to get lost in the music, in this moment. Closing my eyes, I swayed to the song, trying to pin down the emotion I was feeling. Then Madhu was in front of me again, shaking me, saying, "Samira*di*! *Didi*! You have to come with us!"

"W... what?" I shook my head to clear it.

"Nina*ji* has collapsed. We have taken her to the hospital. You need to come with us..."

The world seemed to shrink and expand at the same moment.

Mama!

I thought I'd screamed it, but no one else seemed to have heard. The party carried on around us. I picked up my bag and left quietly.

Roma

CHAPTER 43

Today I saw the most beautiful boy in the world. And I decided right then that someday he would be mine.

He was lounging in the chair with a book in his hands when we walked into Hema Aunty's living room. His brown hair flopped onto his forehead, and he stood up when he saw us come in. My heart beat unevenly when Hema Aunty introduced him as her nephew, Angad.

His skin was like milky coffee, every feature on his face so clearly defined—from his aquiline nose to his sharp jawline; his high cheekbones to the eyebrows that swooped over his deep, long-lashed grey eyes. He was tall and muscular, and so incredibly handsome that my breath caught in my throat.

Later, Pari said to me, "I know! He looks like a model. Just wish he wasn't my cousin."

"What's he like?"

"Quiet. He doesn't say much. But I think it must be hard for him. Losing his parents, moving to a new country, sharing a room with my brother. Oh, and he speaks with an American accent."

"Really?" I said, deeply impressed. "Why, though? I thought he lived in Dubai."

"He went to the American school there."

"Will he be coming to our school now?"

"I think so. Appa's working the details out, but I know he wants to take commerce, so he'll probably end up in my section."

"Lucky you!"

"He's my *cousin*, Roma!" Pari wailed, trailing off as Hema Aunty walked in with the snacks.

"What are you girls talking about?"

"Just the exams, Aunty," I said, hurriedly pulling out the notes I'd brought with me.

When she'd gone, I turned to Pari and asked, "How's Nina Aunty?"

"I haven't heard any more. She was still in the hospital when I called Samira last week."

"What happened to her?"

Pari stayed silent, and I knew it was out of loyalty to Samira, even though they had been drifting apart lately.

"Was it to do with her drinking?"

She looked up at me, startled.

"How did you know?"

I shrugged. It had been a guess, but obviously, a good one.

"She has cirrhosis of the liver," Pari said in an undertone.

"Is that cancer?"

"No, not cancer. But it's not good."

"And Samira's father?"

"He's not back yet. Their driver has been in touch with their boss or something... I'm not sure, it's all very complicated..."

"Is Samira okay?"

"I guess. I mean, she sounded sad and distant the last time I spoke to her, but she could also be busy studying for the exams."

With that, I suddenly remembered the reason we had come over in the first place. While Maa and Aunty chatted in the living room, I spread all my notes out on Pari's bed, going over the underlined portions I had put question marks next to.

A half hour later, I sat back on my haunches, tired from kneeling next to the bed. The sigh that escaped me was long and loud, if completely involuntary.

"Don't worry, Roma," Pari said reassuringly. "You'll do fine. Anyway, you don't need high grades to get into Arts. Besides, they'll keep you in school because of your singing. Not for nothing do they call you the nightingale. Who else will lead our assemblies, hey?"

Just for a moment there, I had a vision of Angad walking into assembly as I was singing. His grey eyes meeting mine, and us falling truly, madly and deeply in love. I sighed contentedly. At least there was that to look forward to.

With the exams just a few weeks away, I would make several excuses to drop in and see Pari.

"How do I do this equation, Pari?"

"I don't understand the concept, Pari. Can you explain it once again?"

I could tell she was perplexed and perhaps even a tiny bit annoyed by my constant visits, but I couldn't help it. Like a moth to a flame, I was drawn to her home, just wanting to catch another glimpse of Angad.

"Where is your cousin today?" I asked Pari the day before the physics exam.

"Sri has taken him out on the motorbike to Connaught Place."

"I see," I chewed on the end of my pen before asking, "Is he settling in well here, in Delhi?"

"I guess. Amma has been spoiling him rotten. It's like she can't do enough for him. Even Sri had to tell her to stop mothering him too much."

"Hmm. What happened to his parents?"

"They were in a bizarre accident. Something called 'Wadi bashing'."

"What's that?"

"Like driving through dried-up riverbeds, only they may not be dry; and if it rains, there could be flash floods. That's how Appa explained it. It was a birthday adventure for some friends of theirs and when they set out, there was no sign of rain. But within minutes, the Wadi filled with water and they couldn't get out. Three couples died. Drowned." Pari said the last bit mournfully, her lower lip trembling.

I nodded and made all the right noises while listening intently. What a way to die! I had never even heard of this 'Wadi bashing'. This snippet of information added to the already glamorous aura surrounding Angad.

CHAPTER 44

Study leave should have been about studying. Instead, when I couldn't go visit, I hung out on our balcony, which overlooked Pari's back garden, looking out for Angad. 'Adonis' I called him, in my mind, dreaming up various scenarios of us together, singing and dancing in the Swiss Alps, like in some Yash Chopra film. Maa caught me staring at the garden more than a few times and wondered if I was having a nervous breakdown.

"Eesh Roma, as long as you don't fail, it is all right. You don't have to look so sad all the time."

I tried putting on a suitably depressed look for Maa, but Ria had me figured out moments after she saw me hiding behind the wall when Angad walked into the garden.

"Bubu, do you have a crush on that boy?"

"What?" I nearly dropped the teacup in my hand.

"You're always out here, mooning over him. He doesn't pay you the slightest attention."

"Shhh Ria!" I hissed at her and went back inside. She would never understand.

• • •

With only a few days before the exams, I suddenly started to get huge butterflies in my stomach. I felt very unprepared, and despite Pari's assurances, I wasn't sure I would pass. So the last few days were spent cramming anything I could fit in. Bits of maths, equations from chemistry and sometimes even body parts from biology, would float into my dreams. That is, when I slept at all.

Baba looked at me one morning at 4 a.m. when I sat at the dining table, yawning and scratching my head.

"Reach high, for stars lie hidden in you," he quoted Tagore to me once again. "Dream deep, for every dream precedes the goal."

I fell asleep with my head on the table, dreaming of Angad.

Perhaps the only fun part of sitting the exams was not having to wear the uniform. I hated that uniform. It made me look even bigger than I was. It was all right for someone like Samira who looked good in anything she wore. Even Pari, with her long skirts and baggy shirts, looked better than me. As for Madhu, she was so slight that it was easy to forget she was there. But I hated the way I looked in the uniform. It emphasised all the body parts I wished to keep hidden: my chunky calves, my thick waist and the large breasts that none of the Sarojini Nagar bras could contain. When I dressed myself, I chose beautiful floaty *salwar* or *churidar kameezes* in rich jewel tones like emerald green, sapphire blue, or amethyst purple. I made sure that the tailor cut the front low enough to just hint at what lay beneath, but not enough to offend anyone's sensibilities. Maa had long agreed that I had a good eye for clothes, and let me pick my own materials and designs. On the occasional foray into Janpath, she would let me buy the export reject shirts and trousers that I wanted, claiming she did not understand 'modern clothes'. The only thing she wouldn't agree to was letting me wear my hair long and loose for the exams.

"It is not a party, Roma. You must respect the rules."

"What rules, Maa? There is no dress code."

But there was no budging her. And so, that was one less camou-flage I could use to keep my little notes hidden. But *dupattas* were useful things too. No one, least of all the invigilators, would ever suspect that under my long floaty sleeves and the sheer chiffon of the scarf, I had the cheat notes to that day's exams.

Only once did I think of what could happen if I got caught, but dismissed that possibility immediately. I was far too clever for that. Besides, it wasn't like I wanted to top the exams. I just wanted to pass. A little sophistry harmed no one, particularly if it was never found out.

There was an edge of desperation to my tactics now. I wanted to stay in the same school as Angad was joining the following year. I couldn't afford to fail. So, with a combination of last-minute mugging of notes, and the little cheat sheets I kept up the sleeves of my *kameezes*, I contrived to pull off a decent score in my Board exams.

CHAPTER 45

On the day of the last exam, I put forward a proposition to Maa. I was willing to sew all the falls on her new *saris*, if she would let me have a party at home.

"What kind of party?" Maa looked bemused. We were not the party sort of people. Most of our socialising happened outdoors, and mostly during Durga Puja.

"A little get-together with a few friends. Hema Aunty and family will be heading to Kodaikanal to introduce Angad to his aunt, so we won't see them most of the summer. And afterwards, we are all going to end up in different sections. So, this may be the last time we can meet as classmates."

"Hmm. Who are you calling?"

"Well, Pari, naturally. Samira and Madhu. Maybe Angad and Srinivas too."

Adding Srinivas to the guest list was a stroke of genius. I figured Maa would see it as me being neighbourly, which is exactly how she saw it.

"Ah, Roma, that is very kind. Pari's cousin looks like a very sad boy. Coming to a party will cheer him up. What shall I cook?"

"Maa," I said, "let's just get some pizza from the market."

"Pizza?"

Maa pronounced it 'peezhaa'. It was an alien, inedible food to her. She had complained about it many times before, saying she could not see why we preferred eating bits of dried bread with cheese and tomato ketchup over her delicious fish curry. Truth was, I didn't want the house reeking of fish when Angad came over. Pizza was modern, a culinary equivalent of the blue Levi's jeans I planned to wear on the day of my party.

"Why all this peezha-sheezha when I can make nice food at home?"

"Because, Maa, we want to stand and chat and eat. That's not possible with rice and curry."

"At least let me get some *rosogollas*..."

"Maa! No! I'm going to buy some pastries from Cakewallah's." My voice was firm and just for a moment, she looked hurt, then she reassembled her features and nodded.

"Okay, *shona*, have it your way."

I smiled triumphantly.

Then I started on Baba.

"Ria," I said the next day at the dinner table, "do you want the Levi's jeans Baba got me from America?"

Ria's ears perked up, but she gave me a suspicious look, knowing how excited I'd been to receive them.

Baba looked up from his plate.

"Why are you giving your jeans to Ria? I brought her a pair too."

"Baba, I have nothing to wear them with..." I sighed and dropped my eyes.

"You have no shirts or tops?" He looked at me, flummoxed.

"Everything is old and faded, and looks so bad with the new jeans."

"Ripa," Baba said to Maa, "how is it our daughter has old and faded clothes? That is no good. You must take her shopping at once. I will give you some money to buy her a nice top."

Ria frowned at me. She was the only one in the household I could not fool. But at least I'd gotten what I wanted.

Now, to send out the invitations.

In my dreams, I imagined opening the door to Angad, him walking into my house, looking deep into my eyes and saying, "I've been waiting all my life for you, Roma."

"You need to stop reading those Mills & Boon books, Bubu!" Ria chided me when she saw me mooning at Angad from the balcony again. "You're getting funny ideas from them."

"What do you know about what ideas I'm getting?"

Ria dragged me into the room and shut the door.

"Bubu, you think Maa and Baba will let you go out with that chap? We are a traditional family. They will want you to have an arranged marriage with a nice Bengali boy. Why are you wasting your time over Pari's cousin?"

There was a ring of truth to Ria's words, and just for a moment, I felt doubt creep into my mind. Was I really living in a fantasy world? Would my dreams never come to pass? Then I set my face and turned to face Ria.

"It's none of your business what I do with my time! You focus on yourself, and stop spying on me."

Ria looked at me, her eyebrows meeting in a frown.

"Fine, Bubu. But don't say later that I didn't warn you."

I took Maa to a boutique in South Extension Market to buy my top. No Janpath stuff would do for Angad. I wanted to look like Madonna for him, a woman of the world.

Maa kept exclaiming over the prices, and I had to hush her more than once when the boutique owner looked over at us with a grim face.

"*Shona*, so expensive!"

"Baba said I could have it."

"Yes, but..."

What neither Maa nor Ria understood was that once I had set my heart on something, no power in Heaven or Earth could deter me.

CHAPTER 46

A week after the exams had ended, I had my party.

I wore my Levi's with a black and white top that had sequins sewn into the sleeves.

Maa was still not impressed with it. "So much money for a top that does not even stay on your shoulders! What good is it?"

I had deliberated between cleavage and shoulder, and chosen to display the latter. I wanted to reel him in slowly, not display all the wares at once.

Now, as I arranged the paper plates and napkins on the table, a couple of sequins fell onto the tablecloth, and I brushed them to the floor hastily before Maa spotted them.

Pari had been enthusiastic about the party, promising she'd bring Angad and Srinivas along. I half-hoped that Srinivas would say no. I'd never much liked him, and suspected that he didn't care for me either. Whenever I went over to Pari's, he'd pass a sarcastic comment or roll his eyes as I tucked into the snacks Aunty provided. Pari had caught him once and kicked him so hard on his shin that he'd stopped rolling his eyes after that. Later, she had told me he was like that with all her friends, even Samira.

As for Samira and Madhu, they had been much harder to pin down. But I needed them here for the ruse to work. After Aunty's hospitalisation, we had barely seen Samira. She sat her exams and left promptly afterwards; the driver waiting for her in the car outside our examination centre. She didn't exchange notes or ask how we'd done either. She kept her distance from us, as if we were diseased and contagious.

I could tell that Pari was miffed at her and hurt by her behaviour. It was like Samira had inexplicably slammed the door in her face. To be honest, I was quite pleased. I'd grown to like Pari and wanted her to be *my* best friend. Especially now that Angad was in the picture.

Persuading Samira to come took a lot of tactical planning. From taking flowers for Aunty, to sending her a card a week later, I made it look like I really cared. Like Samira's pain was my pain; her worries, my worries too. But when I heard nothing in return, I panicked. Maa would never agree to a party if it was just Pari and her brothers. I could just hear her saying, "But you see them all the time. Why all this party-sharty?"

Thinking laterally, I asked Baba to take me over to Samira's on the pretext of dropping another card off. Then I cornered Madhu outside the house while Baba waited in the car.

"How are you?" I asked, concern dripping from my voice. Normally, I didn't even bother talking to her, but now I needed her for my scheme to work.

She looked startled, not expecting to see me outside the house on a Saturday evening.

"I'm okay." She held up a plastic bag. "I'd just gone to buy some eggs from the market."

"How is Aunty? And Samira?" I asked, moving closer to her.

"Yes, they are okay. I mean, better now."

"What happened?"

"Oh, just... Ninaji has a weak heart."

I knew she was lying because her eyes shifted ever so slightly before she spoke.

"That's terrible! I hope she's getting a lot of rest."

"Yes, yes," she nodded, trying to slide past me, but I took another step sideways and blocked her.

"Will you be coming to the party?"

She was silent for a beat, then chewed on her lip.

"I don't think... I mean, it may not be a good time..."

"Nonsense, Madhu! We need to celebrate the end of our exams, and also Aunty's recovery."

"But she isn't..." Then she stopped and shuffled her feet.

"What's the matter?" I asked, dropping my voice to a whisper. Maybe she would spill a few nuggets of information. But Madhu was Madhu, a loyal little lap-dog to Samira.

"No, nothing. I mean... I'll talk to Samiradi about it."

"You must convince her, Madhu! It will be a nice break for her after all the stress."

She shifted the bag from her right hand to her left, and said thoughtfully, "Yes, it would be nice for her to go out somewhere for a change."

A day later, the phone rang with Samira confirming she would come to the party with Madhu for a short while. Success!

CHAPTER 47

Pari was the first to arrive, along with Angad. Thankfully, Srinivas was nowhere to be seen. I ushered them in, blushing slightly as Angad shook my hand and looked me in the face for the first time. I'd already laid out the pizza, potato chips, and pastries on the table.

Maa had looked appalled.

"What is this, Roma?"

"What?"

"The food will go cold like this. And the pastries have cream. They should be kept chilled."

"Shhh, Maa. You don't know these things! This is how we teenagers party."

What she also didn't know was that I had spiked the fruit punch with some vodka. It had worked at the school party and I hoped that it would relax everyone enough for us to get to know each other better.

Angad made a beeline for the punch and poured himself a glass. He took a sip, looked into the glass, then took a larger gulp. I smiled to myself. Pari was saying something, and it took me a second to refocus on her.

"... the pickles from I.N.A Market," she finished, and I didn't have a clue what she'd been talking about. I was about to ask her to repeat herself when the doorbell rang again.

It was Samira and Madhu at the door. I was shocked at Samira's appearance. She had lost so much weight that her clothes were hanging off her. If anything, she looked even thinner than Madhu. They looked like a pair of skeletons, one dressed in black and the other in white. I had to suppress my giggle as I reached forward to pull Samira into a hug.

"Samira, I'm so glad you came! How is Aunty now?"

When she pulled away, she had tears in her eyes. She blinked them away and nodded.

"Thank you for the card and flowers. It was really thoughtful of you."

"Come in, come in. How silly of me to keep you standing here."

They came in, and I noticed Pari's momentary hesitation before she jumped up to give Samira a hug. I introduced Angad to Madhu in the meantime, noting he had refilled his glass already.

Then I saw his gaze fall on Samira, and he seemed to freeze. I could hear the words coming out of my mouth, but I felt as though I was standing a thousand miles away, watching a group of strangers. Samira's wan smile, Pari squeezing her hand, Madhu standing quietly to one side, and Angad, *my* Angad, looking at Samira as though he'd been bewitched.

Maa entered just then to check if we needed anything, and like a jolt of electricity, I felt myself pulled back into my body.

"Hey! Help yourselves to the punch and food," I said with a forced jollity, something hard lodged in my throat.

They did, and then luckily for me, Pari, Madhu, and Samira retreated to one corner, leaving me to chat with Angad.

"Do you like the pizza?"

He shrugged. "Yeah."

"You lived in Dubai, right?"

He looked at me then, his grey eyes piercing.

"I did."

I swallowed.

"Did they have good pizza there?"

I'm not sure what was so funny about what I'd said, but he burst out laughing, and then seemed to relax.

"Yeah, we had good pizza there, too."

Our conversation was random tidbits—school information I tried to impart, girlfriend information I tried to glean, and we meandered happily through several topics. But, every so often, he would look towards her, as if waiting for her to pay attention to him. Thankfully, she never did.

When the doorbell rang again, I was reluctant to answer it; reluctant to break this happy spell. But I got up against my wishes and opened the door. Srinivas stood before me, holding up a bag, his long hair in a ponytail, the expression in his eyes sardonic.

"Pickles for your Maa from my Amma."

I let him in quietly, hoping he'd leave quickly. He set the bag down on the table and whistled at all the food.

"This is quite a spread! Cooked it all yourself, did you, Roma?"

"Of course not..." I blurted before picking up on the sarcasm.

Pari waved to him and went back to her whispered conversation with Samira and Madhu. I saw Samira glance at Srinivas, her face pale, before she dipped her head and listened to what Pari was saying.

I wish I could say that the party was a grand success, but it wasn't. Not really. I didn't accomplish what I'd set out to do, which was getting to know Angad better. Once Sri arrived, they hung out together, and I had to play the perfect hostess by circulating with trays of pizzas and pastries. The mood wasn't as upbeat as I wanted, and the vodka was clearly not enough, as no one spilled any secrets that evening. They didn't want to dance, and the girls stuck to one corner while the boys stood on the balcony and chatted. At times, I felt like pulling my hair out in frustration.

But I wouldn't have called it a complete loss, either.

What I did learn, though, could prove useful in the months to come. There was a definite atmosphere between Samira and Srinivas —a deliberate avoiding of one another, a hyperawareness of the opposite zones they stood in. They barely spoke, but the looks that I intercepted were loaded with what? Anger? Grief? Love?

It would be fun to find out.

CHAPTER 48

A fortnight into the school holidays, I was already bored. Pari and family had left for Kodaikanal, and after the party, I hadn't heard from Samira or Madhu. I couldn't be bothered to reach out to them either. Maa kept asking Baba if we could go to Cal, but he was reluctant, as he had a new boss and wanted to call him home for dinner. Which meant Maa had to cook, and that meant us leaving for Cal was postponed indefinitely.

I had my Tuesday music lessons to look forward to and little else. Ria and I were polar opposites when it came to hobbies or interests. She could play on the street for hours with her friends, come home for a quick bite, and head out again. I, however, enjoyed lolling in bed with my Walkman, music filling those empty hours like nothing else could. She was brown as a berry, her hair short and curly like Maa's. I protected my skin from the sun, not wanting to turn brown and ugly. I washed my hair with *shikakai* and applied a *besan* face pack daily. Ria thought it was enormously funny.

"Bubu, are you trying to look like Kimi Katkar?" she asked me once, when I had the face pack on and was reading Stardust magazine.

I stuck my tongue out at her and went back to reading.

Yes, I admired the beautiful heroines in the magazines, and tried to copy the way they did their hair and makeup. What was wrong with that?

Samira just had to throw on a T-shirt and jeans and would still look like she'd stepped out of a catalogue, but the rest of us had to try harder. I resented the fact that my genes hadn't blessed me with what she had, but was grateful that at least I was better looking than Pari. As for the mousy Madhu, who ever noticed her?

I still couldn't understand why Uncle hadn't admitted her to a government school. People like her could get all the education in the world, but where would it take them? She would still end up marrying a driver or a cook, so what was the point?

Maa called me into the kitchen one day and said, "Roma, I think it's time you started to help me in here."

I took a step back.

"You want me to cook?"

"Yes, why not?"

"Then what will the cook do?"

"Roma, that is not the point. All girls need to know how to cook. You have to take care of your household some day, and how will you manage anything if you don't even know the basics?"

I shuddered at the thought.

"I am going to marry someone rich, and then I won't ever have to set foot in the kitchen."

"Don't be ridiculous! Someday you'll thank me. Now, wash your hands and start peeling those potatoes."

Day after day, Maa harangued me to cook with her, much to Ria's amusement.

"Look at Kimi Katkar getting her hands dirty!"

"You wait till it's your turn!" I'd snap, irritated that she was still allowed to while her time away while I had to slave in the kitchen. But Ria, sensing my irritation, would just laugh and skip away.

Slowly, though, I started enjoying the process. Watching how raw ingredients transformed into an edible, delicious meal satisfied a part of me I didn't know existed. At last, I had another talent besides my singing.

"*Shona*, this is very good!" Baba said, after tasting my *aalu posto*.

"See, Roma, I told you. A way to a man's heart is through his stomach," Maa said.

From that point on, I resolved to become such an excellent cook that no one would be able to resist my food. Especially not Angad.

"Just be careful, Bubu," Ria butted in, "Don't be tasting too much of your own food, or the uniform won't fit next term!"

I could have slapped her.

That summer I decided that to attract Angad to me I would have to become the antithesis of Samira. I would be the wholesome neighbourhood girl who laughed at all his jokes, understood all his pain, and provided a shoulder to cry on. If Samira was unapproachable, I would be accessible; if she was haughty, I would be humble. As long as I could get Pari on my side, it was only a matter of time before Angad saw me as something beyond the girl next door.

People had underestimated me all my life. They saw me as the plump songbird, not particularly intelligent but happy to go along with wherever they wanted to slot me. What they had not encountered was my steely resolve and rigid determination when it came to my own desires.

I desired Angad and I would have him, come what may.

CHAPTER 49

Going into 11th Standard felt like entering some super-exclusive club. Suddenly, we were the seniors. All the junior students looked up to us, and I was immediately put in charge of the Music Room. My results had been so so, but as Pari had predicted, it made no difference to my being accepted into Arts. Samira hadn't done that well, either. It was only Pari who had excelled and been offered science, but she declined, much to her parents' consternation.

Aunty had complained to Maa, "Both my children are so strong-willed, I don't know what to do!"

"But surely, it is better she does a subject she wants, no, Hema?"

"Yes, I know. But with a brain like hers, she could become a doctor or a scientist. Why is she so obsessed with numbers?"

"She wants to be a mathematician?"

"No, an economist. What is that, even?"

Hema Aunty had crumpled her *pallu* in one hand before saying, "At least with Pari, I know that she'll end up doing something worthwhile. But Sri…"

"How are things with him?"

"I don't understand, Ripa. It's like a switch has been turned off. He was doing so well until a few months ago. Now, he can't be bothered.

Rajan and I are so worried about him. And that wretched boy, Rakesh, is hanging around again..."

Just then, Pari rounded in on me, eavesdropping on their conversation from outside the room.

"What are you doing, Roma?"

I bent down quickly and fiddled with my laces.

"I was just tying these, and waiting for you. Should we go out and get some ice cream now?"

Samira and I were in the same section, and just by virtue of having hung out in the same group, we ended up sitting together on the first day. Not that it made any difference, as she was listless and uncommunicative most of the time.

"You okay, Samira?" I asked, suppressing my instinctive irritation with her.

She nodded and bent over her notes as Mrs Mukhopadhyay, the English teacher, droned on about John Donne.

"How's Aunty?"

She scribbled furiously with her hair hanging like a curtain around her face, acting as if she hadn't heard me. Undeterred, I ploughed on.

"Did you have a good summer? We finally made it to Cal, towards the end, which was so nice. I got to meet my *mashi, mesho* and *poribar* after so long." She still didn't respond, so I carried on. "What about all your family? Pari told me how she came to your party once and you had so many people there. All family, no?"

She looked up then, her eyes as hard as flint.

"What else did Pari tell you?"

I swallowed.

"N... nothing else. I just wondered where they are now. I mean, your Baba is away, and your Maa is not well..."

"Roma, I'd really like to focus on the class, so can you keep your questions for another time?"

With that, she shut me down for the day. But not forever.

. . .

I had been waiting to catch a glimpse of Angad all day long, and when I finally spotted him with Pari during recess, I headed straight for her.

"Hi," I smiled shyly at him after greeting Pari. He smiled back, acknowledging me, then bit into the sandwich Aunty had packed for him.

"Where's Samira?" Pari asked me.

I shrugged. I was glad she wasn't around to distract Angad.

"How are you finding commerce?" I asked them both.

"It's okay. There's a new economics teacher, and I really like her," Pari said, still keeping her eyes peeled for Samira.

We chatted together, and I noticed how, after a while, Angad joined in our conversation. "Strike while the iron is hot," Baba had always said, so I invited them over after school to try the *mishti doi* we had brought back from Calcutta.

"What's that?" Angad asked.

"Sweet curds. It's a Bengali specialty. You have to try it," I insisted, and Pari finally agreed, saying that her Amma wouldn't mind them coming over as they were hardly likely to get any homework on the first day of school.

Later that day, as we walked towards the bus stop, I spotted Samira in the distance. She was walking alone, her eyes on the ground. Her misery unloosened something in me. I felt light and happy, as if now I could finally breathe.

I should have invited her to join us. Maa would have wanted me to. Instead, I positioned myself in such a way that neither Pari nor Angad would spot her. I spoke quickly and laughed loudly, making sure that I had all their attention. For far too long, Samira had hogged the limelight. Not anymore. It was finally time to topple her off her throne.

Madhu

CHAPTER 50

I saw and heard everything. I may have been slight, easy to overlook and even easier to forget, but that gave me an immense advantage. In a world where everyone was screaming for attention, I stayed silent. I watched, observed, and learned. Then I filed it all away to analyse at a later date.

For instance, I'd always known that Nina*ji* was an alcoholic. Not just through the whispered conversations between Pitaji and Mataji, but also in the persistent chemical odour of alcohol that she reeked of. At first she had tried covering it with heavy perfumes. Even then, even when I was younger, I'd known something else lingered beneath those exotic fragrances—something malodorous and malignant. Then, she didn't bother anymore, letting her pores exhale her addiction to the world. Now, she lay in bed, wasted and emaciated, her hands shaking, as she doubled up in pain. Her disease and her panacea were one and the same—an amber liquid in a bottled case.

Then there was Raj Uncle—Pitaji's boss, my benefactor, and an all-round good guy. Except that he wasn't. I didn't know what kind of shady business he and my father were involved in, but I did know that while my father was just a foot soldier, Raj Uncle was much higher in the ranks. His 'travel' didn't just comprise going to foreign countries to solicit foreign investors, it comprised languishing in prison for long periods of time too.

Nina*ji* knew. Samira*di* didn't.

Once, long ago, when it had first dawned on me that all was not as it seemed in their household or ours, I had asked Mataji, "How can you support Pitaji when you know he is involved in illegal activities?"

I never forgot what she told me.

"Madhu, when you don't know where your next meal will come from, you will snatch it from another's hand. We do what we have to, to survive."

I envied Samira*di*'s naïveté. She may have only been a few months older than me, but I felt a thousand years wiser than her. In her teenage anger against her mother, she had cast her as the villain, when the villain was much greater and much more lethal than she imagined. The villain was hunger; it was greed, ambition and aspiration. It was everything that fuelled good people and bad. The desire to succeed in an unfair world justified whatever nefarious means were used to get there.

Neither of our fathers were evil, but I knew that they had done evil things, whether directly or indirectly. And sometimes I wondered —would we have to pay the price for their deeds?

In the years that Pitaji had worked for Raj uncle, I had grown accustomed to his absences too. I missed Pitaji just as much as Samira*di* missed her father. My relationship with Mataji was a fractious one. She couldn't understand my thirst for knowledge, for wanting to better myself through education. Her only ambition had been to marry a man who could provide for her and her children, and while she had forgiven Pitaji his straying once, she had never allowed him to forget that she had. Now, she was content to turn a blind eye to all his illegal activities, as long as we were fed and had a roof over our heads.

I wanted so much more.

My desire wasn't for riches. Big houses, fancy cars and foreign travel did nothing for me. I had seen how little all of those things meant if the people inhabiting that life weren't happy in themselves. What I wanted was to make a mark on the world. To do something that would outlive me. Something big, something remarkable, something that allowed me to give back.

Once, when I had ruminated over the possibility of becoming an astronaut, Samira*di* had laughed and asked me which world I lived in. She wasn't being patronising, nor did she think I wasn't capable of it. I knew that her laughter was simply disbelief that I wanted to aim as high as that.

A few harsh words from Mataji had squashed those dreams, but I still nursed another. This one I kept close to my heart, revealing it only to a few people. It ticked every box on my personal checklist.

I wanted to become a doctor. To take my healing skills to remote villages that had no access to medicine, to treat the most marginalised and impoverished. There were so many young girls in places like those with dreams in their eyes and a yearning for a better life. Girls like me. I wanted to help them fulfil their dreams. I wanted to pay forward every bit of goodness and kindness that I had been a recipient of.

And to that end, I worked hard. Harder than anyone else I knew, because to me, my dreams were just the beginning of the life I would attain someday.

CHAPTER 51

"Samiradi, he is here again," I said to her as she spooned soup into Ninaji's mouth. A little of it dribbled from the corner, and she used a white napkin to wipe it off.

Ninaji looked terrible. Her hair was matted and unwashed, dark circles under her eyes, her clavicles painfully pronounced. While she was in the hospital, Samiradi and I had poured every bottle of alcohol down the drain. When she had returned, we had held her as she'd thrashed and screamed, pacified her as she'd shaken violently, and hugged her as she'd sobbed. Alcohol was poison for her system, the doctors had warned. We couldn't allow her to touch a drop.

Now, she was placid and obedient like a little child, content to let us mother her and be her sentinels. But from her vacant expression, it seemed as if she had checked out. The vibrant woman I had first met in this very room had turned into a ghost.

However I had expected Samiradi to react to her mother's collapse, it hadn't been this. I'd expected tears, anger, even withdrawal, but not this touching tenderness. Once the initial shock had worn off, Samiradi had risen to the task of caring for her mother in a way none of us could have anticipated. She had cut herself off from all her friends to devote herself to her mother's rehabilitation. She'd ignored all phone calls and letters, shutting herself in with Nina*ji*, allowing access to just Mataji and me.

But the motorcycled Romeo would not leave Samira*di* alone.

I had known of their short-lived affair from the moment it had started. I had even facilitated her absences by lying about after-school homework clubs and drama practices. That is, when Nina*ji* had been able to give a damn about her daughter's whereabouts.

"Tell him to go away," she said without turning around.

There was a part of me that wished she would let him in, even if I understood why she wouldn't. Yet, another part was glad to see Pari's arrogant older brother brought to his knees.

"She can't see you," I said to him, unable to look at the bleakness in his eyes.

"Why?" he asked, trying to disguise the despair in his voice with a false bravado. He swung between anger and misery. For six months, he'd done little else.

"I don't know. She won't tell me. Now, please go."

Pitaji had had to stop him from forcibly entering the house previously. He had threatened to call the police if Srinivas didn't stop harassing us. I knew it was an empty threat. Pitaji wouldn't want to call attention to himself in any way, but Srinivas didn't know that, and it worked for a while. But here he was again, desperate to see the girl who had promised him the world and then broken his heart.

"Has he gone?" she asked me later, after she had put her mother to bed.

"Yes," I answered.

"Do you think I'm being horrible?" she asked me, weariness lacing her voice.

"I think," I paused for a beat, "I think you're doing what's best for everyone at this point in time."

She sighed and sunk into the armchair, inviting me to sit on the *mooda*. I remained standing.

"I don't know how long we can carry on this way. When will Papa be back?"

"Pitaji said in another month or so."

"Can I not speak to this boss of his?" She had asked me this before and I stayed silent once again. Her shoulders slumped as she accepted defeat.

"I just wish..." she whispered, then stopped. I waited for her to continue. "If only things were different. If only Papa was here, if only Mama was better, if only..."

I wrapped my arms around her as she cried. "If wishes were horses," Margaret Ma'am had once said, "then beggars would ride."

In all the years I had been a part of this household, I had seen their family members fall away one by one. Either they had caught a whiff of Raj Uncle's activities, or Ninaji's blatant alcoholism had driven them away. We hadn't a single phone number to call when she had collapsed, not a single person to turn to. But word had gotten out as it invariably does, and we had braced ourselves for a parade of visitors, a barrage of questions.

None came.

No *chachas* or *mamas* could be bothered to check in on a dying woman and her distraught daughter. It was up to us, as the help, to step in and prop up a family that was on the verge of going to pieces.

CHAPTER 52

At school, I could do little to help her, but I watched as she withdrew from everyone. Pre-exams it had been understandable that Samira*di* had required space, but now she didn't seem to have the energy to invest in anyone other than her mother. I observed Roma usurp Pari's affections and muscle Samira out of the group. I also saw Roma fawning over Pari's cousin, incapable of hiding the violent crush she nursed. But his eyes followed *didi* everywhere, and I knew that Roma could try as hard as she wanted but Angad was already smitten.

A month into the new term, Samira*di* said to me, "Someone's coming home this evening. Can you get my green dress ironed?"

As I took the dress to the *press-wallah*, I wondered if she had decided to let Srinivas back into her life. It seemed unlikely as I had seen no communication between them in the past few months, but if she had, that could be a positive sign. A sign that she was finally emerging from her self-inflicted hibernation, willing to give life and love another chance.

When the doorbell rang that evening, I fully expected to see the motorcycled Romeo at the door. I had been planning an apology all afternoon, hoping he wouldn't hold all the previous months against me. Instead, Angad stood at the door, a large bouquet of red roses in his hand.

We had barely spoken at school. I don't think he'd even registered my existence. I let him in wordlessly. He looked around the living room, taking in the plush sofa, the antique furniture, the gilded mirrors and the fine film of dust that covered it all. No money, no maids. It was just us, and we could just about subsist on Pitaji's wages and the money advanced to us by the boss.

Mataji had harangued Pitaji over it, complaining about having to buy groceries for the main household when that money should have been going towards looking after our family.

Pitaji had looked at Mataji as if he was seeing her for the first time.

"Sushila, these people have been good to us! This is our time to pay them back in a small way. How much do you think Memsahib and Missie*ji* eat, anyway? Stop complaining now and make enough *rajma chawal* for all of us."

Nina*ji* had barely eaten two teaspoons full of food tonight, turning her face away when Samira*di* insisted on feeding her some more.

"I'm leaving the bowl here, Madhu. If she wakes up later, make sure she eats a little more."

I'd nodded, knowing that this bowl of food would go to waste like all the previous ones had. I'd have to dispose of the food covertly in case Mataji caught sight of it and had another fit.

Now, I glanced over at Angad, wondering what was going through his mind as he examined a framed photograph of Samira*di* with her parents. Aged five, her front teeth missing, sitting between Raj Uncle and Nina*ji*, she was grinning unselfconsciously. This was the only photograph in which all of them looked happy and like a normal family.

Samira*di* came down the staircase, ethereally beautiful in her green dress. Where she had been pretty before, the last few months had lent her a different allure. She seemed fragile and fierce, broken yet unbreakable. Angad's desire for this enchanting paradox of a girl was unmistakable.

"I'll be out late, Madhu. Take care of everything," she said, a strange hauteur in her voice.

I didn't understand what was happening, but sensed that there was a seismic shift in the air. She took the roses from him and placed them carefully to the side, then with a forced smile said, "Shall we go? I know this wonderful Chinese restaurant called Chungwa in GK2."

She did come home late. Later than she had in months. Her dress had a slight tear in the back, and when I washed her panties the next day, they were stained with blood. I wondered why she'd given her virginity to this handsome stranger, when her heart belonged to his brother.

And then I thought, maybe that was exactly why.

CHAPTER 53

After something momentous has happened, people will talk of portents—of the signs having been visible if only one had looked, of knowing in their bones that something bad was about to occur. This is exactly what happened after that Tuesday as well.

It was an ordinary day, like all others. It had been exactly a week since Samira*di*'s 'date' with Angad. He hadn't come around again, but I had seen them speaking to each other on different occasions around the school. Samira*di* seemed detached, almost as if he were just another boy who paid her too much attention, not the one that she had given herself to just a few days ago.

There were times when I wished she'd confide in me, but I also felt relieved that I did not have to carry the burden of her thoughts. Carrying the burden of my own was enough.

In the morning as I had packed my bag for school, Mataji had fed Lallan the *khichdi* she had made the previous night. Her eyes were red-rimmed from caring for her sickly son. Pitaji was the only one who had slept through all of Lallan's fretful crying.

"*Suntey ho,* Lallan needs to see a doctor today. His rash isn't subsiding, and I am worried."

"You *toh* worry about the smallest things. He will be fine. Just give him some Disprin."

"Okay, but I am warning you, I will call you at your work if he gets any worse."

Raj Uncle had gotten a land telephone installed in our one-room tenement, just so that he could get a hold of Pitaji when he needed him. It had come to good use after he had left. Mataji didn't hesitate to use it to keep track of her husband, get him to buy groceries on his way home or, on the rare occasion, inform him of an emergency at home. It was the same phone we had used to call the doctor when Nina*ji* had collapsed.

Occasionally, I would receive a call from Pari or a friend from my class. I felt very important answering the phone, speaking into the receiver, marvelling at the fact that our voices were travelling across distance and through time.

At school, I took notes diligently, certain that I would stand first in the class again this term. It had been many years since anyone had called me "driver's daughter". My intelligence, performance and determination had made me a 'topper' in class. Once I had earned the respect of the teachers, the students followed suit.

I still kept my distance from everyone. I had no interest in making friends. School was a place to study, to get ahead. There was plenty of time to make friends once I had attained my goals.

Yet, in a strange sort of way, I did think of Pari, Roma and Samira*di* as my friends. I would meet them at lunchtime, sit with them during school functions, and listen quietly to their silly spats, politely refusing to take sides. Of course, even that had changed in the new term. They no longer hung out together, which left me at a loose end.

I was returning from the toilet when Margaret Ma'am stopped me.

"Madhu, do you know where Pari is?"

"No, Ma'am." Sometimes she forgot that I was a year behind them in school.

"Can you find her for me? Bring her to my office straight away!" There was an urgency in her voice that I hadn't heard before, and as I hurried to Pari's classroom, I wondered what could have triggered that emotion in our normally unflappable Principal.

"Excuse me, Sir," I said, knocking on the door, at the Accountancy teacher who was drawing some kind of chart on the blackboard, "Margaret Ma'am wants to speak to R. Pari."

Pari looked confused as I led her to the Principal's office.

"Am I in trouble, Madhu?"

"I don't know, Pari. I'm just following instructions."

We knocked on Margaret Ma'am's door and waited for her "enter". Inside, she had drawn the curtains, and her office was cool with the air conditioner humming softly in the background.

"Madhu, thank you. You can leave now." She smiled at me and as I turned to leave, she said, "Wait! You are Pari's friend, right?"

I looked at Pari and nodded.

"Then stay. Stay until someone arrives to pick her up."

She handed Pari a glass of water and sat her down on the chair that faced the desk. Then she asked me to sit next to her. I wasn't sure whether it was the air-conditioning or some sixth sense that gave me gooseflesh. Even before Margaret Ma'am had said anything, I reached for Pari's hand and gripped it hard. Pari looked at me, perplexed, but I watched as Margaret Ma'am opened and shut her mouth a few times before clearing her throat.

"Pari," she said, finally, "your father is coming to pick you up."

"Why?" Pari's eyes had grown large and round. "What's happened?"

My grip on her hand tightened.

"There's been... something's happened..." Margaret Ma'am looked close to tears herself.

"W... what?" Pari asked, her voice hoarse with fear.

"Uhh," she looked at the pen she held in her hand, set it down on the desk, then picked it up again. "Your brother, Srinivas..."

"Sri?" Pari whispered. "What's happened to Sri?"

Tears ran down Margaret Ma'am's face as she reached for Pari's other hand.

"I'm afraid that Srinivas is no more."

CHAPTER 54

Life after death. I didn't know what that was like, but I imagined it to be pretty horrible. The rumours that circulated were no better. Some said it was a drug overdose, others said it was suicide.

When Margaret Ma'am announced it during the assembly, she just stated sombrely, "His heart stopped. Sometimes, heart disease goes undetected in young men until it is too late. Tragically, Srinivas is a part of that statistic now."

I searched for Samira*di* in the crowd, zeroing in on how white her face had gone, how she trembled and looked as if she would throw up. Maybe it was she who had stopped his heart, and now she wished she hadn't?

Pari did not come into school for the rest of the month. Eventually, the rumours died down, each person choosing to accept the version of reality that suited them best. I didn't tell Samira*di* of my part in the entire episode, not wanting to add to the guilt she already bore. But I could not stop picturing Pari sinking to the floor, her hands on her ears, shaking, rocking back and forth, trying to block out the cruel words that had upended her world. Nor could I forget Rajan Uncle's face as he had collected her. Shell-shocked, uncomprehending. And then there was Angad.

He'd stood at the doorway as Rajan Uncle and Margaret Ma'am

tried to explain what had happened, his face blank, his eyes shuttered. Was he thinking of his parents' death? He had barely recovered from his own tragedy before landing slap-bang in the middle of another one.

Calling him to the office had been an afterthought, as if everyone had forgotten his existence. No stranger to being sidelined, I had spoken up tentatively, asking if Angad needed to be called to the office too. After all, he was a part of the Rajan household now.

There was no one to hold his hand or break the news gently to him.

Does one become inured to pain through overexposure, or does one feel it even more keenly? Angad's face had given nothing away as he had listened to the news of his cousin brother's untimely death. Just a tiny tic in the corner of his eye had betrayed his impassivity. I'd felt desperately sorry for him, for all of them. How could one survive something like this?

Margaret Ma'am and I had stood together at the door of her office, watching them leave. One stooped figure supporting the weight of a girl who could barely walk, and the ramrod straight back of a young man who had already seen too much grief.

Angad had not been back at school either.

Just after the 5th period, as I rushed to fill my water bottle before the next class, Roma ambushed me near the water cooler.

"Awful, isn't it?" she said, trying but unable to suppress the excitement of a voyeur.

I nodded, desperate to make my escape.

"How's Samira taking it?"

I stopped and looked at her.

"What do you mean?"

"*Arrey*, it's obvious, *yaar*! There was a *chakkar* between them, wasn't there?"

"I don't know what you mean," I responded, stiffly. Now, even more than before, I couldn't stand to be in Roma's company.

"Between Srinivas and Samira!" she pressed on. "I saw the looks between them at the party."

She nudged me into a corner. "Guess what? They found her love notes to him."

I bit my lip, not sure how to respond.

"Now, it's all out in the open and the family can't believe that Samira turned out to be such a snake. Pari is hopping mad!" She could barely contain her glee. "She blames Samira for what's happened, and I agree with her completely."

"Why?"

"What do you mean?"

"Why do you agree with her?"

"Because that's what Samira does, no? She fools around with all the boys, not bothering about how it affects them. She picks them up then drops them, uses her looks and body like a slut. She's just like her mother!"

I drew myself up to my full height, and even then, I was much shorter than Roma.

"So, you don't think Angad is to blame in any way?"

"Angad?" she squeaked, turning pale. "Why?"

"Because the '*chakkar*' was between Samira*di* and him. That thing with Srinivas was over a long time ago. Maybe you should ask Angad all your questions, Roma."

With that, I swept past her, leaving her standing by the water-cooler, open-mouthed.

I felt sorry for dropping Angad in it, but Roma's gloating had pushed me into lashing out. Privately, though, I wondered what all of them were thinking. Did they really blame Samira*di*? Was she to blame? Did she really pick up and drop people the way Roma had implied? This did not align with my opinion of her, but I had witnessed her moving from one brother to another. What did that mean? And what about Angad? Had he felt betrayed by her, too? An unwitting pawn in a game she had played?

CHAPTER 55

When a lorry runs over a pothole filled with dirty water, it splatters the mud on anyone who happens to be nearby.

So it was with all of us. Srinivas' death created ripples of grief, anger, confusion, rumours and denials. When Pari came back to school, I barely recognised the hollow-eyed girl. Angad came back at the same time and seemed unchanged, except for a new wariness that had crept into his every interaction.

Samira*di* had done all the right things. She had sent flowers and cards. She had tried calling to find out when she could visit, but she had been stonewalled at every instance. Even Aunty, who had practically brought her up, wouldn't respond to her messages.

On the day that I had stood outside their house with another letter from Samira*di* to Pari, and Pitaji had waited in the car, Aunty had answered the door, her face heavy with grief.

"Aunty, Samira*di* has sent this…" I'd held out the letter, and she'd taken it silently, then shut the door in my face.

I was a bystander to their anguish, but it did not leave me unaffected. When Samira*di* wept, I cried along with her. When Pari appeared shrunken in her sorrow, I shrunk alongside. The only one who seemed indifferent to all the sadness was Roma. Perhaps that was why Pari and Angad gravitated towards her. In her obdurate determination to march on and away from the central tragedy of their lives, she unwittingly created a safe haven for them. A haven where, even if they could not forget, they could momentarily just be normal teenagers living an unexceptional life.

Raj Uncle returned in November. As always, he turned up out of the blue, looking immaculate in a grey pinstripe suit, as though he had just stepped off a plane.

When Samira*di* caught sight of him, all her steely resolve crumbled and she gave way to great wracking sobs that convulsed her slender frame. Even I breathed a sigh of relief. Maybe now life could return to a semblance of normality.

The new normal was Uncle taking Nina*ji* to a different doctor who prescribed another course of treatment, which involved a complete overhaul of her diet, new medication, and a strict no-alcohol-in-the-house policy. The last bit we had dealt with already.

"Umesh, I cannot thank you enough for taking care of my family in my absence," Raj Uncle thanked Pitaji repeatedly.

"It's nothing, Sahib*ji*. You would have done the same for me."

With Uncle back in the house, two new maids were hired, and soon, the past eight months seemed to retreat into the background like a nightmare that needed forgetting. Even Nina*ji* perked up enough to take a slow walk in the garden every morning and evening, regaining a bit of colour in her cheeks. She'd watch Lallan run around with his toy truck and smile wanly at him, but she was still weak, still sickly, and sometimes the effort of coming downstairs was too much for her.

"Will she get better, Mataji?" I asked one evening as she sat dozing in the garden chair.

"Your Pitaji said that they are waiting for a donor. If she gets one in time, she may recover."

"A liver donor? Do those even exist?"

"How would I know, Madhu?" Mataji said before going back to slicing the aubergines.

Raj Uncle had paid Pitaji back and added a hefty bonus to the sum, which satisfied Mataji immensely. Life had gone back to the pleasant and familiar routine of before, as far as she was concerned.

Yet, for Samira*di*, everything had changed. She no longer took anything for granted. Her anger against her mother had disappeared, her rebellious behaviour retreated completely. I would often see her lost in her thoughts, staring out of the window, her face sad. She never confided in me, but she didn't need to. With Srinivas gone, she had lost her best friend and her proxy family, too. I tried being a friend to her, but knew that I could never take Pari's place in her life or change anything that had happened in the last eight months.

That was the thing about time. It marched on, regardless of the boot prints it had stamped all over your heart.

November slid into December and then January. School was ramping up for another round of mock exams, and Samira*di* and I took to studying together in her room. The *moodas* had been long forgotten, and we often fell asleep in her bed together, books on our chests, the lamp still glowing in the corner. No one minded, least of all the new maids who just accepted me as a part of the family.

To me, Nina*ji*, Raj Uncle and Samira*di* were no different from Mataji, Pitaji and Lallan. We may not have been blood, but they were as dear to me as my own kith and kin.

CHAPTER 56

February was a mercurial month in Delhi, temperature-wise. One day it could be bright and sunny, allowing us to discard our woollen sweaters halfway through the day. But the very next day it would be bitingly cold, the chill penetrating our bones, leading us to huddle around our heaters and drink hot cups of sweetened *chai*. Still, most Delhiites preferred the winter weather to the blazing heat of the summers.

Pitaji had once told me that the reason for the extreme weather was because we were close to the Thar Desert in Rajasthan, which also deposited the finely milled sand-like dust I had to clean off the surfaces twice daily.

Now that Raj Uncle was back, Pitaji was often out late, driving him to and from all the places they conducted their business.

In the morning, I had stumbled upon them talking, and quickly stepped back before they spotted me.

"A new consignment has come in, Umesh. I need to inspect it today."

"Where is it, Sahib*ji*?"

"In a godown near Sharma*ji*'s farmhouse. I have the address."

"What time do you want to leave?"

"Closer to dusk. We are being watched, so it's best to take precautions."

"Will we stay over at Sharma*ji*'s tonight?"

"He has said we should. There are buyers from Geneva who want to see the *Shiva lingam*, and maybe a few other pieces."

"But if we are being watched...?"

"We will take a circuitous route there. It will be easier to lose them in the dark."

"Very well, Sahib*ji*. I'll make sure the car is ready for the journey."

"Take some gunny sacks in the boot as well. We may need to transport a few items to the other godown."

By then, I had already pieced together that their 'business' was the illegal export of antique goods from India to foreign countries. They were smugglers, and while this was their primary racket, I couldn't be sure it was the only one. For the first time, however, I had heard another person's name. Was this Sharma*ji* their boss, or just another accomplice?

When Raj Uncle was 'abroad', Pitaji had often brought work home. The first time, one of the gunny sacks had come loose and a mud-encrusted stone idol had rolled out. It was some kind of goddess with a broken arm and half a face missing.

Mataji had glanced at me before telling Pitaji off in an undertone.

"Why are you bringing these home? Don't you have other places to store them?"

"Only temporarily, Lallan's mother. I will move them tomorrow."

I always wondered how, if the police knew what Raj Uncle was up to, they didn't suspect my father? But then, in some ways, there was still a lot that I didn't understand.

Preoccupied as we were with our exams, neither Samira*di* nor I asked any questions about our fathers' whereabouts that evening. We ate a light dinner and then retired to our respective homes for the night. Nina*ji* had fallen asleep well before us.

At 2 a.m., a car door slammed right in front of the gates. Mataji sat up and I could see her straining to hear what the Gurkha was mumbling. We heard the front door to the house open and shut. Then we waited in the dark, in silence, to hear Pitaji's tread. When he did not appear, Mataji whispered to me, "He must be busy with Sahib*ji*. I'm sure he'll come soon enough."

I wasn't sure whom she was trying to reassure—me or herself. I remained wide awake, nerves on edge. A half hour passed before there was a heavier tread at the doorstep, and a rapid knocking.

Mataji wrapped her shawl around her and opened the door. Raj Uncle walked in quickly, shutting the door behind him. I sat up too, but Lallan lay fast asleep next to me, snoring softly.

In the dim light, I could see that Raj Uncle looked dishevelled. His shirt was stained with mud and there was a wild-eyed look about him. He was holding a small rectangular package that seemed to be Nina*ji*'s *dupatta* wrapped around something. He thrust this into Mataji's hands.

"Sushila, this is all I have right now. I will send you more, I promise. But we have to leave straight away."

"Leave?" Mataji was uncomprehending. "Where is Lallan's father?"

"That's what..." Raj Uncle was sweating profusely in the cold. "I'm not sure if he's... when I left... but I could swear a bullet hit him..."

He wasn't making any sense, but from the way Mataji recoiled, I knew something bad had happened.

"You can stay here, but I strongly advise that you leave too. Go to your village. Hide there for a while. I'll send more money, but now I have to go."

With that, he turned and left.

In a couple of hours, his entire family had fled, leaving behind a widow with just Rs 20,000 to support herself and her two young children.

PART III

Pari

CHAPTER 57

Oh, the lies we tell ourselves! The deceptions we inflict upon our unsuspecting selves, believing that life will give us everything we wish for. Then one day, when all those dreams have turned to ash, we wake up. And we're never the same again.

Sometimes I would think back to the time when my only ambition in life had been to be pretty. I'd wish I could turn back the clock to return to the innocence of those years. If I could redo those wishes, I would only ask for the safety and well-being of my family, instead of wasting it on asking for good looks.

The irony was that I was passably attractive now. My teeth were fixed, and I had settled into my body, but what had that gotten me? How naïve I had been to think that life was smoother for those who looked the part.

"Pari?"

"Hmm?" I looked up at the woman standing in front of me. With brown eyes, an impish smile, and her wavy hair held back with shiny clips, she was the sort of friend one made out of necessity and not choice. But Bela had proven to be a staunch friend nonetheless.

"Want another *chai*?"

I nodded a yes, smiling up at her. Then I checked my watch, gathered up my files, and walked behind her. Bela held the door open behind her, allowing me to catch up. The hallway was empty. It had been painted recently, and there were still signs of 'wet paint' dotted around, which someone had brazenly ignored, pressing their handprint into the paint for all eternity, or at least until the next paint job. I had to smile. How thoughtless young people were; their youth allowed them so much latitude where boring things like consequences did not worry them.

Bela walked briskly towards the canteen, her legs a lot freer in the *churidar* she was wearing. I only wore *saris*. Amma frowned upon anything else as professional wear. *Salwar-kameezes* and *churidar-kameezes* were casual wear in her opinion, and in this instance, I did agree with her.

All the students were in their classes, except an odd child wandering the corridors, ducking as he spotted us. It was a free period for both Bela and me, and a good time to catch up on the week's news.

"Golu threw up again this morning." Golu was Bela's seven-year-old son who seemed to suffer from one ailment after another.

"Did you send him to school?"

"Yes. Amit insisted. He said that Golu is playing up because he hates going to school."

"Still, it might be an idea to take him to the doctor just to rule out something else."

Personally, I thought that Amit, Bela's husband, was probably right. Golu was playing up because Bela caved in every time and allowed him to stay home from school. Either way, it was worth getting a doctor's opinion.

Bela nodded in agreement and paid for the *chai*, which we took to the corner table. She pulled out a *dabba* of *kaju barfi*.

"Mother-in-law made so much of it that I thought I'd bring some into school to get rid of. That woman doesn't understand the meaning of 'diet'!"

I refrained from pointing out that Bela's 'diet' often consisted of *samosas* and *kachoris* gobbled down with her *chai*—deep fried treats that were not slimming fare.

"It could be worse, Bela. At least all your mother-in-law does is try to feed you goodies. Think of poor Mrs Gulati. Her mother-in-law is a witch who is always trying to set her son against his wife!"

"I really believe women like that have been so unhappy in their own married lives, they can't bear to see another woman happy. Even if it is their own sons' wives." She offered me some *barfi* and popped a piece into her mouth too. "You are lucky you have no such *jhanjhat*! Single, footloose and fancy-free."

I swallowed, then responded, "Yes, I guess so."

At thirty-one I was still single, a fact that I had come to terms with a while ago. Bela thought it was modern and liberating. Most others thought I was a sad spinster, always on the lookout for a man.

"How's the new lot?" she asked as she snapped the lid of the *dabba* shut and adjusted the *dupatta* on her shoulder.

"Okay, I suppose. Hormonal teenagers. We were like that once, too."

"Speak for yourself. My parents were so strict, they even monitored my dreams!"

We laughed together, then I picked up my files.

"I need to get a few things sorted before heading to class. Thanks for the *chai*. Next one's on me."

With that, I adjusted the pleats of my *sari* and headed to class XI-C to teach economics.

CHAPTER 58

There were more girls than boys in my class, and in a way, it made things harder. Boys were uncomplicated creatures. They rubbed along fine, fighting and making up without a fuss. Girls were trickier. There were long-held grudges, little cliques that competed for attention, queen bees that expected to be fawned over, and internal politics that were impossible to fathom from the outside. Not that different from my own time in school.

Flashes of memories still ambushed me from time to time. If I glimpsed a girl with dimples, my heart would constrict. If a motorcycle roared past our house, I would rush to the window. There were mornings I would wake up from such a vivid dream of my school days that I couldn't shake off the images for hours afterwards. Yet here I was, all grown up, playing a role I had never envisaged for myself all those years ago.

Today, I stood in front of the class full of new entrants to Year 11, and meditated on just how much had changed in the last fifteen years.

India was more progressive now. We had different television channels that broadcast programmes from around the world. Foreign goods had flooded the market, beauty queens had won international titles, and we were no longer dismissed as an underdeveloped nation with forty percent of our population below the poverty line. We were world players now, and there was a new confidence and awareness that was reflected in the teenagers of the present day. In that, yes, things were quite distinct from my time in school.

I thought back to how different we had been at this age and how small our world had felt. Now, the world had expanded, and the horizons had stretched out. The opportunities these kids had were far more exciting than the ones we had been presented with. Would they use them or waste them?

"Now, we are going to look at a single producer and consumer, and how supply and demand works. This is a part of your microeconomics course…"

I thought back to the time when I had sat with my head bent over my books, absorbing all the information like a sponge, hoping someday to put it into practice. Studying economics had never felt like a chore. It was a language that spoke to me, just as music had spoken to Roma once. Who could have imagined that one day I would end up teaching it?

What was it that George Bernard Shaw had said? "Those who can, do; those who can't, teach." Here I was, proving that to be true. But did Mr Shaw ever consider that sometimes those who wanted to do simply couldn't? Not because they were incapable, but because life hadn't allowed them the opportunity.

"Turn to page 5. Chandan, read the paragraph that begins with Price Theory."

As I taught the class, I could tell how the air shifted from boisterous and chatty to one of quiet concentration. I was a good teacher, and I took solace in that. In no time at all, the students had fallen under the spell of economics, the study of scarcity and choice.

My life, after Sri's death, had been a study of the scarcity of choice. Suddenly, all those paths once open to me had disappeared. I was the sole survivor, the one my parents couldn't let go of. What if they lost me, too? They didn't have the same rights over Angad as they had over me. I was their blood, their baby. Besides, my own guilt kept me rooted; unable to fly and resentful of my circumstances, yet powerless to follow my dreams.

Should I have protested more? Demanded to be let go of. To be allowed to follow my path. But how could I? They had been broken by Sri's loss. How could I possibly betray them, too?

Yet, every so often, a surge of anger would overpower me, a resentment that threatened to spill from my lips. I had never reconciled to the unfairness of my situation.

My phone beeped, and immediately I stopped writing on the blackboard and picked up my bag, motioning to the children to read on their own.

I flipped the phone open to see Amma's message: "Appa's had a fall. Come home soon."

I shut the phone, excused myself from the classroom, and strode towards the Principal's office.

Margaret Ma'am opened the door as soon as I had knocked.

"Pari, all well? You are as white as a sheet!"

"I need to head home, Ma'am. My father's had a fall."

"Go," she said, ushering me out. "I'll take over your class."

I got into the car, my heart thudding, and I turned the key in the ignition. All anger and resentment had fled for now, leaving in its place fear and desperation. Not Appa. We couldn't afford to lose him, too.

CHAPTER 59

The doctor who dealt with us was young and handsome, but I was too distracted to register it until much later. And then I laughed to myself, thinking—how did it matter? I wasn't on a manhunt!

"Has this happened before?" he asked, ticking something off on a chart he held.

"Well," I looked at Amma, who was stroking Appa's hand while he slept, "after the first stroke, he recovered well and even went back to work. But then the second stroke happened at work. He had a fall in the toilet cubicle and wasn't found until much later."

"Which is why the damage has been longer-lasting," the doctor interjected.

"Yes, and recently, he's been doing strange things. It's like he forgets he's sick and tries to get up on his own, or tilts himself out of the wheelchair. I mean, Amma can't be with him all the time, and this time..."

"Hmm, sounds to me like this could be vascular dementia. I'd like to keep him in the hospital to run some tests on him."

Amma spoke up then. "I want to stay with him."

She looked at me, as if waiting for my objections. But I had none to offer. I simply nodded and followed the doctor out.

After filling out all the requisite forms, I went back into the room. Amma had fallen asleep with her head on Appa's arm. I planted a small kiss on her forehead and then smoothed back Appa's hair.

Then I stood there for a moment, watching them. How much they had aged in the last decade! First the shock of losing Sri, and then Appa's strokes, had turned Amma's hair entirely grey. She rarely called anyone over now. Barricading herself against the world was her only defence against pain.

As for Appa, the strokes had reduced my strong and handsome father to a helpless little infant, dependent on us for nearly everything. Once an intelligent man who had read two newspapers every morning before work, he now watched the television with an uncomprehending gaze, drool escaping from the side of his mouth.

These were the people I was angry with? These were the people I resented for wanting me to stay near them? How could I be so selfish?

Once again, I reminded myself to be grateful that I had a chance to take care of my elderly parents. The same parents who had brought us up with such love and care. Would Sri have done the same for Amma and Appa? I didn't know, but I wanted to believe that he would have.

The house felt strangely silent when I returned. We had forgotten to turn the lights on before rushing to the hospital, and I recalled how *Paati* had always said it was unlucky to leave a house totally dark. Slowly, I went about turning all the lights on. In Sri's room, I stopped and stroked his guitar.

Fifteen years had passed since I had lost my brother. A congenital heart disease, they had said, worsened by his drug use. Neither conditions that my parents had been aware of. And then there was the sheaf of letters he had been clutching. Love letters from my best friend to my brother. Something that I hadn't been aware of. How many secrets had he kept from us?

Angad had stood by me as the police had questioned us, each of us shocked into silence by this cataclysm that had rocked our world.

We took it in turns to cry, to rage, to think of ways to turn back time, to do something different that would create a different outcome.

The sound of the phone ringing in the distance snapped me out of my reverie, and I ran to answer it.

"Hello?"

"Pari?"

The line was crackling, indistinct.

"Yes?"

"It's me, Angad."

"Oh, hi Angad." I had forgotten that he rang on the first Thursday of every month.

"Is everything okay? You sound a bit distracted."

"Yes… no… I mean, Appa had a fall today. He's in the hospital now. Amma's with him."

"Oh God! Is he alright?"

"I hope so. The doctor is running some tests. He suspects vascular dementia."

"That doesn't sound good. Listen, do you need me to come?"

He sounded worried, and far away. Very far away.

"No. I'll manage, don't worry. The kids are too young…"

"Hey, I'll be there in 24 hours if you need me. You know that, right?"

I nodded, then realised he couldn't see me.

"Yeah, I know. I'll phone if I need you. It's late now. Go to bed."

"Keep me updated on Uncle."

"I will. Give my love to all. Bye."

I hung up, then collapsed into the armchair, exhausted.

CHAPTER 60

I had to stoop to enter through the narrow grill-protected door to the bank. The queues were just as awful as I had predicted, and I was glad I had taken the day off to deal with banking matters. Waiting patiently in line, I could feel the man behind me move closer and I swung around to stare at him. He pretended to examine the ceiling, hands in his pocket.

"Can you keep your distance?" I said, loudly.

"What?" he looked at me, fake surprise all over his face.

"Keep your distance and keep your hands to yourself!" I hissed.

He stepped back.

"*Arey*, I didn't do anything, madam! You are just getting annoyed for no reason at all."

I turned my back on him but kept my elbows jutting out, just in case he tried any funny business again. What was wrong with the men in this country? Were they so sexually frustrated that any woman, young or old, was fair game? This was a bank, for goodness' sake! But then I thought back to how Bela had told me about being groped in a temple. No place was sacred to these creeps!

When it was my turn at the till, I was glad it was a woman I was dealing with. My relief was short-lived as I realised that she was going to make my life as difficult as possible.

"Madam, have you brought a copy of the power of attorney?" she asked, looking at me from over her half-moon glasses.

"Yes, here it is."

She examined the document for five minutes. Then she said, "And what is the purpose of the withdrawal?"

"It's for my father's hospital bills."

"You have broken his fixed deposit?"

"Yes, because we need the funds."

On and on she questioned me, but I kept my cool, knowing that if I let the slightest irritation show, she would deny me access to my father's funds. Petty power play. It happened everywhere, from banks to government offices to airports, taxi ranks, and even schools. No wonder Angad had emigrated.

After half an hour of questioning me and perusing all the documents, she finally agreed to let me have the money. My father's money that I needed for his hospitalisation. Yet, I'd been made to feel like a criminal.

I rang Amma.

"I'm on my way. How is Appa?"

"He woke up a while ago and had some soup. He's sleeping again."

"And you? Did you get any sleep?"

"A little. Are you bringing me a change of clothes?"

"Yes, Amma," I sighed, "I've packed an overnight case for you, but you must let me stay this time and you can go home tonight." Even as I said this, I knew she would never agree to it.

"What, Pari! How can you expect me to leave my husband like that?"

"Very well. I'll be there shortly."

Sometimes I wondered if I would ever meet a person who I could be as devoted to as Amma was to Appa, or someone who loved me as much as Appa loved Amma. Then I would push those thoughts away as useless junk. Who would want me?

·   ·   ·

In my twenties, I had been attracted to a man named Subhash who had moved into the flat across from us in Saket. He hadn't been conventionally handsome, but had a sweet smile and always offered to help with my grocery bags if we ended up shopping in the market at the same time on a Saturday morning.

We had even met up for a few lunches, where he had made gentle enquiries about my background and profession. We had shared similar tastes in music and movies, and watched 'A Beautiful Mind' in the cinema together, chatting about the film over cups of coffee. I had told him about Appa's strokes and how Amma cared for him. I'd spoken about my dream of being an economist, and how life had thwarted that. He had listened in sympathy, talking about how his own dreams of migrating to the US had not materialised.

Every day I had looked out of my window to see him standing there with his cup of coffee, waiting to acknowledge me with a wave. Every evening as I had returned from work, he had ambled over for a quick chat, talking about the news headlines and his wry observations of the people in the locality.

Then one day, suddenly and quite without warning, he had disappeared, only to resurface a month later with a shy young bride on his arm.

There had never been any promises made or broken. He may have only viewed me as a friendly acquaintance, a neighbour from across the street, but my heart had been crushed enough to steer clear of all eligible men ever since.

CHAPTER 61

"You know you could have asked for an advance on your salary, Pari." Margaret Ma'am handed me a cup and saucer before pouring the tea for me. She still had an old-fashioned tea set from the eighties, preferring to drink her tea from the same flower-patterned cups I remembered from my childhood. The rest of us drank ours from sturdy mugs that could be whacked down absently and still not break. But these delicate china cups gave me more comfort than those mugs had ever provided.

"I needed the funds urgently, Ma'am."

I fixed my gaze on the paisley design on the curtains, swallowing the lump in my throat along with my misgivings.

"Is this the last of his fixed deposits?"

"No. There is one more."

There was a flutter of panic in my stomach as I vocalised this. Appa's treatments cost money, much more than we had saved up. I tried not to think of what would happen once the savings ran out.

"What after that?" Margaret Ma'am, true to form, never shied away from the difficult questions.

"Sell the gold, I suppose." I took a sip of my tea, then glanced at her.

"Oh, my girl!" She looked pained.

"It's okay, Ma'am. What use is all that jewellery to me? I don't wear much anyway, and it's really quite heavy and old-fashioned for these times."

Excuses, excuses. It broke my heart to think of parting with my family's legacy. Jewellery that had been meant for Srinivas' bride, and for me when I became a bride. Then I had a brief flash of recollection from the past. *Paati* exhorting Amma to sell her earrings to get me my braces. Life had come full circle, very nearly.

Margaret Ma'am nodded, a sad expression on her face, as if she had read my thoughts. She had seen me through the worst. From Sri's death to everything that had followed, she had been there, either to hold my hand or to bolster me when I needed it. Quietly, she had given her support and her guidance, steering me towards teaching when everything else was falling apart. At my lowest ebb, she had reminded me that life was still worth living, if not for myself, then for the two people who had already lost so much.

It was no wonder that I had returned to my alma mater to teach. Not only was it my comfort zone, but she was my anchor. Greyer, older, still wearing her wire-rimmed glasses, she was the kindest person I had ever met.

"Do you think it's true?" I mused aloud.

"What?" she looked at me, confused by the sudden switch of topic.

"That more things are wrought by prayer than the world dreams of?"

"Oh." She turned to look at the framed picture on the wall behind her. "I suppose so. If your faith is strong, then you know that God above does listen to our prayers, but He grants us the ones that we need, not the ones that we want."

"Hmm."

I wondered which of all my prayers God had granted. I certainly hadn't needed all the pain He had granted so generously.

"How is your father now? It has been, what... a week?"

"Yes, they are discharging him tomorrow. He is a bit weak, but no worse than before he went in. The doctor has talked about hiring a nurse to care for him during the day, particularly as the dementia gets worse."

"And?"

"I think it might be a good idea. Amma is getting older too, and even though she won't admit it, she could do with the assistance."

"Let me know if I can help in any way, Pari. You don't have to be strong all the time, you know."

I set my cup and saucer down on the desk and stood up.

"Thank you, Ma'am."

How could two words sum up my depth of gratitude? Even if I thanked her every single day of my life, it wouldn't be enough. But she seemed to understand and gave me a small smile in return.

It was easy to forget that she was just as human as I was. What went through her mind when everyone came to her with their problems? Whom did she turn to? I often wondered how she managed on her own. She had never married either, and I wanted to ask her what life was like, in her sixties, all by herself. Was she lonely? Was she happy? Was she always this strong?

What would my life look like when I was her age?

Instead, I suppressed all my questions and smiled weakly before I let myself out of her office and shut the door silently behind me. It was time to get back to work.

CHAPTER 62

Appa was discharged as hoped, and as I wheeled him out of the hospital, I was happy to see a bit of colour in his cheeks. Amma walked a few paces behind us and I slowed down to allow her to catch up. For someone who had always lived in *saris*, she had finally succumbed to wearing a *salwar-kameez* in the hospital, unable to ignore the practicality of the outfit. But she still hated them, comfortable only when wrapped in six yards of silk.

We had nearly reached the car when she exclaimed, "Oh Pari, I left my flask in the room!"

Amma's flask was the one Appa had presented her with when they had been a young couple, and it meant a lot to her. I handed her the keys to the car and sprinted back to the room, hoping the flask was still there. Luckily, I'd worn jeans and not a *sari* as it was my day off from school.

Years ago, I'd been shopping for a card in Archie's Card Shoppe in South Ex, and a lady had come up to me claiming to be a designer. She'd asked me if I wanted to model for her new collection. I'd nearly laughed in her face, but she'd said something about my long legs walking the ramp, and now that strange episode popped up in my head, unaccountably. Anyway, the long legs, although never sporty in school, got me to the room double-quick. Even so, the nurse was already stripping the bed, but I spotted the flask on the bedside table.

"Oh phew! Thank goodness it's still here." I grabbed the flask, throwing her an apologetic smile. She smiled back and balled up the sheets before freezing on the spot. I froze too.

"Madhu?" My voice came out in a whisper.

She bundled the sheets under her arm and tried to leave the room, but I got to the door before her, blocking the exit.

"It *is* you, isn't it?" I looked at her tiny figure, dressed in a white, starched nurse's uniform. Her hair was knotted at the nape of her neck, her eyes as large and luminous as I remembered, her delicate features and wheatish complexion the same as always. It was her.

"Pari," she acknowledged flatly.

"How are you? Where did you go...?" I glanced at my watch. Appa and Amma were waiting outside. "I can't stay, but please, give me your number. I'd like us to catch up."

"I'd really rather not." She sounded angry and hostile.

"Why?"

"Our lives are on different paths now. I don't want to be reminded of my childhood or anything from that time."

She tried to get past me, but something within me wouldn't allow it.

"I understand, Madhu. I heard about what happened, but please, don't blame me. I had nothing to do with it. I really would like to meet you for lunch or something. Here," I scribbled my number hastily on a piece of paper, "Take this. I'll wait for your call. I must go now. My parents are waiting outside."

With that, I left with the flask in one hand, and my bag in the other, wondering if I would ever hear from her again.

After I had settled Appa and Amma in, I went for a walk to clear my head. It had been a shock to see Madhu after all these years, and I felt quite unsettled. So many memories had come rushing back, not all of them unpleasant. Why had I been so insistent about reconnecting with her? What did I hope to achieve by dredging up the past?

And Madhu did belong to the past.

I walked around the block, pausing momentarily in front of Subhash's flat. I could hear a child screaming inside and I moved on quickly. The past needed to be left where it belonged.

But when the news of what had happened to Madhu's father had filtered back to us, I had hoped that somehow, she would make it out of the mess in one piece. Over the years, thoughts of her had randomly accosted me. How had her loss affected her life? Where had she gone? What had happened to all her ambitions?

Running into her today felt like serendipity at work. I couldn't walk away without making an attempt at rapprochement at the very least. Her anger was understandable. I was angry too. But maybe fate had brought us together for a reason? Maybe we could help each other heal?

CHAPTER 63

Angad's money order arrived a fortnight after Appa's discharge. I rang him straight away.

"You shouldn't have!"

"I wanted to, Pari. If I can't help physically, at least let me help monetarily."

"Does she know?"

"No, and she doesn't need to, either. Let's keep this between us, okay?"

"I don't want you getting into trouble like the last time."

"I won't. I've covered my tracks well."

"She's smart though."

"I know," he sighed, "but you don't worry about it. Just focus on getting everything back on track."

"You really don't have to do this, Angad. I still have Appa's fixed deposits, you know."

"Pari, after everything your Appa and Amma did for me, this is the least I can do. Wouldn't Sri want me to?"

At the mention of Sri's name, my eyes filled with tears. I blinked them away rapidly, changing the topic alongside.

"Guess who I ran into the other day?"

"Who?"

"Madhu."

"Who?"

Then I remembered that Angad had barely known Madhu. He had only been in our school a few short months before Sri's death, and everything else that had followed.

"You remember the petite, skinny girl who always hung around Samira? She was the driver's daughter. A year junior to us?"

"Vaguely. Was it her dad who was killed...?"

"In the shootout, yes. Then Samira's family upped and left, and Madhu never came back to school, either."

"Hmm, it's ringing a bell. But that was a crazy time, wasn't it? So much was going on and honestly, it's all a bit of a blur now. Where did you meet her?"

"In the hospital where Appa was admitted. She's working as a nurse there."

"Wow! What are the chances?"

"I know. I've asked her to get in touch, but I'm not sure that she will. She seemed quite angry and bitter. Said that we were on different life paths."

"Aren't we all? Can you blame her, Pari? It's hardly like her life has turned out wonderful. Working as a nurse can't be all that..."

"Yeah, it's not. Not in India, anyway. I think she had wanted to be a doctor."

There was a pause, then Angad carried on.

"Why do you want to meet her, anyway?"

"Just. Old times and all that."

"Well, I wish you luck. Doesn't sound like she wants to revisit them. I don't either."

"You took a part of the old times with you to Sydney," I laughed, but it was a wry laugh, mocking nothing but the situation.

"Tell me about it. Wish I could've left them behind!"

"Shhh. Don't say it out aloud. Are you okay? How are the babies?"

"They are fine. Probably home from school now. Little one is so naughty! He reminds me of Sri, you know."

"And Ankita?"

"She's beautiful."

I could hear the pride in his voice. Paternal pride. Angad finally had the family he'd yearned for after losing his parents and then finding himself wading through our tragedy.

"And how is she?"

He understood immediately.

"Roma? The same. Sweet one minute, venomous the next. You know, Pari, I often think that she's the only one among us who hasn't been touched by misfortune or grief. Her life turned out exactly how she wanted it to. But nothing, and I really mean nothing, makes her happy! Not living in India, not living in Oz. Working, not working. Losing weight, gaining weight. I'm at my wits' end, Pari. I wish I knew what to do."

"Angad, you can only do what you can. You're a good husband and father. I know, I've seen it firsthand. She's so damn lucky and if she can't see that, then there's something wrong with her, not you."

"Pari?"

"Yes?"

"If you do decide to meet this Madhu, don't say anything about Roma to her, okay?"

"Okay, but why?"

"Roma has this thing about the past, about your friend Samira, and anyone who was associated with her..."

At my sharp intake of breath, he stopped for a beat.

"I'm sorry, Pari. I didn't want to bring back bad memories, but..."

"I get it, Angad, I do. I have to go now. Thank you for the money, and I'll speak to you soon?"

"Yeah. Take care, sis. Bye for now!"

After I had hung up, I stared outside the window for a long time.

Samira. The common factor between us.

Where was she? What was she doing? Did she think of us at all? Did she ever feel any regret, any guilt for everything that she had destroyed so wantonly? Or had she moved on without a backward glance, without turning once to view the devastation she had left in her wake?

Samira

CHAPTER 64

Nostalgia, a combination of homecoming and pain. I'd read that somewhere and had never forgotten it. My home, such as it was, had been lost to me a long time ago, but the pain was lodged permanently in my heart.

I pounded the pavement, inhaling and exhaling rhythmically. Running was the only thing that chased the monsters away. Mark had said to me once that I even ran in my sleep, my legs moving constantly as if I was escaping someone. He couldn't know that there was no escaping oneself.

Once I got to the flat, I stripped and got into the shower. The hot water sluiced my body, and I allowed my mind to calm down for those few moments. Then I heard the bathroom door open and sighed. Mark stepped into the shower with me, and my few moments of calm were banished once more.

Later, as I dried my hair, head upside-down, running the hairdryer over my tousled mane, I heard him say something in the background. I turned off the dryer.

"What?"

"I asked what time the filming is scheduled for?"

"Oh, not until the afternoon."

He stretched out on the bed, his T-shirt rising, revealing the slight belly that had formed in the last few years. Still, he was pretty fit for a fifty-year-old.

"Aren't you going in to work?" I asked him, running my fingers through the knots in my hair.

"Can't be arsed! Come back to bed," he grinned at me lasciviously in the mirror.

"No can do," I responded, giving him a quick smile. "Have to prep."

"Who are you interviewing today?"

"Some young singer about her new album."

"Anyone I've heard of?"

"Not unless you listen to rap."

"Good Heavens! Is that what you'll be listening to today? I'm getting out!"

Mark jumped out of bed and headed towards the wardrobe as I chuckled. He knew that part of my prep would mean blasting the music until I was in the frame of mind to interview the up and coming musical diva. Luckily, the rooms were sound-proofed to the outside world.

"Good call!" I cried out after him.

Once my hair was semi-dry, I put the heated rollers in and went to the kitchen to get my coffee and porridge. As I stirred the cream into my coffee, I stared out of the window at the garden outside. A small redbreast hopped from branch to branch, searching. I watched his progress with a smile.

"What are you looking at?" Mark came up behind me and nuzzled my neck.

"Nothing, really. You have a good day." I turned, the coffee mug between us.

He planted a quick peck on my forehead.

"The accountants are in today, so it'll be a busy one. I'll be home late. Are we still on for the weekend?"

"Yes. I promised him."

"Do we have to?"

"Come on, Mark! It's only a day."

"Fine, fine! Let's set out early, then. I want to get back in time for the 9 o'clock news."

"Sure."

I watched him shut the door behind him, then turned to watch the robin again. But it had flown away.

In the studio, Emily applied my makeup expertly, blending in the foundation, powdering my nose and forehead, and prepping my lids for the eyeshadow.

"Love the jade green on you, Sam!"

"Thanks Em."

"It'll pop on the screen."

She stuck the false lashes on my mascaraed ones with the lash glue she squeezed out of a tiny tube.

"You just have the most exotic colouring! I bet there's Italian in you somewhere."

I stayed silent as she applied the lipstick. No one here knew of my past, of where I'd come from and in what circumstances. By marrying Mark, I'd erased my last name and taken on his, disposing of the last clue to my history. But I lived in daily fear of being found out. Luckily, while I was well known, I was much too low-key of a celebrity for the tabloids to want to dig up dirt on me.

Once Emily had finished my makeup, I examined my face in the mirror. If I squinted at my image, I could see Mama in the mirror staring back. But if I looked at myself straight on, the woman in the mirror was a stranger.

"What's she wearing?" I asked Emily, glancing towards the changing room where the singer was ensconced.

"Something loud, low-cut and sparkly."

"Oh dear!"

"Yeah. She's one of those. You have your job cut out."

I closed my eyes briefly, took a deep breath and reminded myself internally that while it was a skill to coerce details out of a reluctant interviewee, it was equally a skill to steer the interview in the direction I wanted it to go. This one sounded loud and brash, and likely to try and take over. It would probably be the latter today.

Then I marched out towards the soundstage, looking every inch the glossy daytime television presenter.

CHAPTER 65

When Mark came in at 10 p.m. I was lying in my sweatpants on our teal-coloured chenille sofa, my face bare of makeup, a mug of chamomile tea in hand, feeling much more like myself. He poured himself a glass of wine and sat down heavily next to me.

"What are you watching?"

"Channel surfing. Nothing interesting is on."

"Fancy a wine?"

"Nope!" I took another sip of my tea.

"How was the little diva?"

"As expected. Full of herself."

He took the remote out of my hand and started flicking through the channels, too.

"Did it go well?" he asked, his eyes on the screen.

"It was okay. She said something about 'old people' not understanding her music!" I laughed.

He leaned back and looked at me.

"You can't be serious! She thinks *you're* old?"

"Bear in mind that she has only just turned nineteen. I must seem ancient to her." I grinned and grabbed the remote back from him. "How was work?"

"Busy. I'm knackered! Let's get to bed now. I need all the sleep I can get before facing your father tomorrow."

"Mark!" My objection was half-hearted, and he knew it. Facing Papa was a chore to endure these days. If I could, I would have wanted some liquid courage too, but I couldn't. Alcohol revolted me most times, but sometimes it called out to me in the most achingly seductive manner. A manner that frightened me. I couldn't go down the same road as Mama. I just couldn't.

"You coming?" he asked at the bedroom door, his silhouette in sharp relief against the background light.

"In a bit. Just need to unwind here."

Then I lay there, changing channels mindlessly with the sound on mute, wondering once again where it had all gone wrong.

At midnight, I wandered into our wood-panelled study and took out the large cardboard box that I kept in the bottom desk drawer. It had been a while since I'd visited it, and somehow tonight, exhausted as I was, it seemed appropriate. Mark had never once asked what was in the drawer, never once rifled through my things, and I respected him enormously for it. Our pasts were our own to do with as we wished.

I sat on the floor and opened the box, the pattern on it having faded with age. A musty, long-forgotten smell assailed my nostrils. Removing a layer of tissue, I took out the doll and looked at her face, her faded gingham dress, her dirty blonde curls, and grimaced. She hadn't aged well. I stroked her, recalling a moment in time when I had been truly happy, unaware of the devastation that lay ahead. I set my Pari doll on the floor and then rooted around under the little knick-knacks from fifteen years ago to find a small bundle of letters wrapped with a burgundy ribbon. With trembling fingers I unwrapped them, and read through them one by one, sentences running into each other, words blurring with the unshed tears that pooled in my eyes.

· · ·

... My darling Sam...

... With you, life seems as infinite as the Universe, a million possibilities of what may unfold...

... Meet me at the corner of the bookshop. I'll be there at two...

... You asked me what life means, and all I can tell you is that without you, it means nothing...

... Camus said, "If we believe in nothing, if nothing has any meaning and if we can affirm no values whatsoever, then everything is possible and nothing has any importance..."

... You are still so young and innocent. Sometimes I feel that I am soiling you with my thoughts...

... Pari said your mother was unwell. What can I do? Tell me how I can help. I want to be there for you...

... Why don't you answer the phone? What have I done? Why won't you meet me?

... I heard about Angad. If this was your way to wound me, you succeeded...

. . .

Nine letters that I had saved; nine letters that reminded me of what was, of what may have been, and what I had wilfully destroyed.

I set them down next to my doll and rocked back and forth, arms wrapped around my knees as I sobbed silently. Regret. What a powerful emotion it was! But ultimately it was a useless one. Nobody had found a way to turn back the clock, and even if they could, how many threads of lives, decisions, and emotions would need disentangling to undo a single tragedy?

Slowly, I placed everything back in the box and shut the lid. The past was done with me, even if I would never ever be done with it.

At 1 a.m. I crawled into bed next to my softly snoring husband.

CHAPTER 66

We were both in the car at 10 a.m, starting out a little later than we had wanted to. I had let Mark sleep in while I went for a run, then prepared us some eggs and coffee while he showered.

"Do we need the A to Z?" I asked, wrestling with the large book in the passenger seat.

"Only for the last bit. I remember most of the route there. M40, isn't it?"

I nodded, distractedly. Two coffees later, I still felt like a zombie.

"You look tired. Didn't get much sleep?"

"No, not really."

"It's like this every time, Sam. Why do you do it if it affects you in this manner?"

"He's my dad, Mark! I can't just abandon him."

"Seems to me he did a pretty good job of abandoning you..."

I stayed silent.

"Sorry. That was uncalled for." He reached for my hand and gave it a squeeze. "Will the wife be there too?"

"I guess so. They live in the same house." I squeezed his hand back, then returned it to the gearshift.

"Your mother's house," he commented.

"Actually, my grandparents' house."

"How the hell did he end up with it?"

"He didn't. It's mine, but I let him live there."

"With the new wife."

"Not exactly new. He's been married for eight years now."

"Sam?"

"Hmmm?"

"Nothing. I just..." He turned onto the motorway, focussing on the traffic, sensing that I didn't want to answer any more questions. Mark was good that way. Most days, he interpreted my moods correctly. Maybe that's why I had agreed to marry him.

I looked outside, letting the jazz he'd put on the radio wash over me.

Coventry held such sad memories that I could barely face returning there. Our hasty departure from India, Papa's hiding out, Granny's anger and disapproval, Mama's failing health, and my own anguish, were all tied to a house that I couldn't bear visiting, but couldn't bear to get rid of either.

Anya had scrubbed all memories of Mama clean from the house. Maybe she didn't want her husband, my Papa, living in the past too. But the house itself held all our secrets close to its chest, whispering them to me every time I visited.

Was it in those turbulent months that followed our flight that I had discovered that my idol of a father had clay feet? Was it then that I had realised that the mother I had hated had been equally betrayed? No amount of care I had given her reluctantly in the months preceding or willingly in the months after could heal the rift between us. Papa, through his deceit, his selfishness, and his inability to face up to his criminality, had killed every semblance of familial love that may have existed.

"What about Madhu?" I'd raged when more details had emerged. Details of her father's death, of Papa's culpability. Of how he had fled the scene, letting his loyal employee of several years bleed to death on the roadside. Of the tiny sum of money he had handed to Umesh Driver's family, promising them more, which he'd had no intention of sending. And Madhu? What had happened to that poor girl?

He had shrugged and looked away when I'd asked. It was Mama —pale, jaundiced, dying—who had called me to her bedside and whispered, "She'll survive, Samira. Madhu is... a fighter."

Abandonment and betrayal were my lifelong friends, nurtured by the false promises Papa had made to me all my life. Still, he was my father. The only family I had left. The only family that counted. Charming, cowardly, deceitful; my genetic blueprint. How much of him was in me?

I fell asleep for a while in the car, still exhausted from the previous night. In my dream, it was Sri driving while Mama croaked out instructions from the rear seat.

"It's too foggy, Nina, I can't see."

"If you had kissed me better, you silly boy, you would be able to see."

Then we were in a field, and Mama had been replaced by Madhu. She was looking directly at me, holding onto her chest as blood seeped out from between her fingers.

"You shot me, Samira*di*!" There was disbelief in her voice, and she turned to Sri to show him her wound, but he kept waving a book in her face saying, "To will is to stir up paradoxes."

I woke up with a start.

"You were muttering in your sleep," Mark informed me, a playful smile on his face.

"You should have woken me."

"And missed all the fun?"

"W... what did I say?"

"Just something about being shot." He grinned. "You've been reading too many thrillers."

"Yes, I suppose I have."

I leaned my head against the glass of the car window. Ghosts of my past travelled with me no matter where I went.

CHAPTER 67

Anya opened the door to us, beaming widely. I had often wondered how Papa had gone from a stunning woman like Mama to someone who looked like she'd escaped from a dairy farm in Poland. Her short cropped hair, large and squat frame, guttural accent and flowery dresses were a complete antithesis to Mama's exquisite taste and looks. But at least she wasn't a drinker. Her only tipple of choice was Baileys, and that too at Christmas when she dragged Papa to midnight mass at church, the only time he ever visited a place of worship.

"Aha! Come in, come in. You are looking so beautiful, Sam." She hugged me tight, and I allowed her, my eyes searching for Papa in the background.

Mark handed the flowers and wine to her while I went inside.

Papa was sitting in his rocking chair watching an old interview of mine on television.

"Hello, Papa." I bent down to give him a kiss on his cheek.

"Hello, my little star! Look, I'm watching you on screen." He smiled up at me before going into a paroxysm of coughing. "Anya, where are my cigarettes?"

"No cigarettes today. House has to smell fresh for our guests." Anya bustled about in the kitchen.

"Mark." Papa acknowledged him with barely a flicker, even as Mark held his hand out to be shaken. Papa had never gotten over the fact that Mark was only ten years his junior. Even Anya was younger than my husband.

"I have recorded all your interviews over the years." Papa turned to the shelf behind him, pointing to the rows of tapes he had. Ben Hur, Sholay, and Goodfellas jostled for space with Samira 1999, Samira 2000, Samira 2001.

"I know, Papa," I said, softly. He pointed them out to me every year.

"You are looking more and more like your mother now. Same cheekbones, same hair."

"I have your ears, Papa."

"Eh? What's that?" he cocked his head, and I couldn't be sure if he really hadn't heard me, or was fooling with me. Then he winked. The charm was still intact.

At lunch, Anya served us Kotlet Schabowy with boiled potatoes and warm beets. Typical Polish fare. It was tasty and Mark showed his appreciation by taking a second helping.

I watched as Papa could barely finish his first. My eyes met Anya's, and she inclined her head towards the kitchen.

"Let me help you clear up, Anya," I said, taking the hint. "Why don't you men move to the parlour? We'll bring the dessert out soon."

In the kitchen, her face crumpled.

"We have had all the tests, Sam. They haven't found anything, but he keeps losing weight."

"Don't worry. I'm sure it's nothing."

But I had seen the way his jacket hung off him, the gauntness in his face, the watch that kept slipping off his too-thin wrist, and couldn't help but worry myself.

She reached out and held my hands.

"If anything happens to him, where will I go? What will I do?"

Her gaze was penetrating, asking me the one question she could not verbalise.

"It's okay, Anya. You can carry on living here."

"Oh, you're a good girl, Sam! Such a good girl."

She pulled me into another hug, and underneath her musky perfume, I smelled her anxiety.

In the living room, Papa had turned the volume up.

I was sitting on the red couch interviewing a film star. This was one of my first interviews, and I could tell from the way I crossed and uncrossed my legs that I had been very nervous.

"What was he like?" Anya asked, a dreamy look on her face.

"Nice." I didn't want to mention how nasty he had been to the lighting director, or how his finger had stroked my arm after the interview, asking if I wanted a nightcap in his room.

"You are so lucky, Sam, meeting all these famous people," Anya breathed.

"My Samira is famous, too. Have you not seen her interview in Radio Times?" Papa nodded towards a pile of magazines in the corner.

"Yes, yes," Anya agreed with alacrity.

Mark stayed silent. Papa treated him like wallpaper most times.

"And you," Papa said suddenly, looking at him, "When do you plan to make me a grandfather?"

Mark blanched at the unexpected attack.

"Papa!" I hissed, embarrassed.

"It's been two years, Samira. High time you had babies."

On the way back home, I apologised for Papa and for the whole sorry situation. It had been an exhausting day, and I could tell from the way Mark's lips had settled into a thin line that he had not enjoyed himself.

"Can we not do this for another six months, at least?" Mark asked, wearily.

I nodded, shutting my eyes, and pushing all thoughts of Coventry to the back of my mind again.

CHAPTER 68

Leena was my only Indian friend in London, and we met up monthly at a cool underground pub in Covent Garden, which had exotic cocktails named after movie stars. Marilyn Monroe had nearly destroyed us the last time.

"Let's go easy tonight, hey?" Leena grinned at me, her heavy-lidded eyes sparkling with mischief.

"What do you suggest?"

"The Vivien Leigh?"

"Go on then."

We ordered our drinks at the bar and then took ourselves to a dimly lit corner farthest away from the speakers that thumped techno beats over the heads of the inebriated patrons.

"How's you?" Leena asked, taking a sip of the peach infused Prosecco cocktail.

"Been better."

"Work or family?"

"A bit of both. New boss doesn't like me much." I took a sip of mine. It was delicious. I had to be very careful or this could get messy.

"How come?" she asked, leaning in.

"Female, menopausal... you know..." I shrugged.

"God, they're such bitches at that age. It's like they know they're past it and can't bear it if someone younger and hotter comes along." She'd had her own trials in advertising, preferring her male bosses to her female ones.

"I don't know, Leena," I said, thoughtfully, "At first I thought it was going to be cool to be under someone like her. A famous international correspondent and all that. Now, I feel like every time she looks at me, she sees a bimbo who is content to do silly celebrity interviews. It's like she's dismissed me as a bit of fluff."

"Has she said that? Actually said that in so many words?"

"No, but I sense it."

"Maybe," she put her hand on my arm, "Maybe that's your own dissatisfaction talking? I mean, are you happy doing this afternoon show of yours? Don't you aspire to more?"

"All I aspire to is peace, a regularity and a rhythm to my life. This ticks all those boxes."

Leena looked at me carefully before saying, "Wine or another round of these?"

"You do realise that I only ever drink with you?"

"And I am honoured that you do! Let me get another round."

As she walked to the bar, I remembered the first time I'd met her in the loo of a famous nightclub. I'd been having a full-blown panic attack, and she'd steered me into a corner, talking quietly to me until I had calmed myself down.

"What about you?" I asked her when she returned. "What's latest in Leena-land?"

"The usual. Pressure to get married, boyfriend still being a dick, and work driving me crazy, but in a good way." She traced a line on the glass with her finger. "I'm thinking that maybe it is time."

"For what?"

"To head back home."

"To Manchester?"

"Yup. I'm tired of the treadmill, Sam. I'm thirty-five! Will is never going to commit, is he? Maybe Ma is right. It's time to settle down with a nice Gujarati boy."

"Isn't that giving up on all your dreams?"

"Dreams change, Sam. I'm exhausted, and sometimes when I look at what my parents have—the comfort, the security—I want a bit of that too." She gave me a rueful smile.

"But will you be happy with just comfort and security?"

"You are, aren't you? Nothing wrong with giving up life in the fast lane. We are all getting older."

I thought back to Papa's demand for grandchildren. We were getting older, and some nights I could hear my biological clock ticking so loudly, it was a wonder that Mark slept through it at all.

"Have you told Will?"

"I've threatened him often enough, but one day when I really do it, he will be in for a shock!"

Just then, a young man lurched up to us.

"Hey! It's you, innit? From the telly?"

I shook my head and got up quickly.

"Stay in touch, Leens! Whatever you decide to do, do it for you, and not because of Will or your parents, okay?"

"I will, Sam. You take care of yourself too and remember, you're not a bit of fluff. You are smart enough to take your boss on. Don't let her intimidate you!"

We gave each other a quick hug before parting ways.

That night, as I hopped into a black cab to head home, I thought about what she had said. People changed and their dreams changed too. I couldn't even recall what I had wanted to be as a young girl, but Hema Aunty's voice had always echoed in my mind, saying that I would make a good news reader. I wasn't too far off that estimation in my current position as an afternoon TV show presenter. Then why, after years of working to get to where I was, did I suddenly feel inadequate?

CHAPTER 69

On our third wedding anniversary, Mark took me out to our local Indian restaurant. The green tablecloths, the smiling waiters, and the smell of Indian cooking immediately transported me back to India. I stumbled a bit, and the waiter reached out and grabbed my elbow to steady me.

"Thank you," I muttered, embarrassed.

I let Mark do all the ordering. He had his favourites, and I really didn't mind what I ate. It was all delicious. I just wished I'd learned how to cook Indian food, but now I had neither the time nor the energy to devote to it.

When the *papadums* and chutney arrived, Mark asked, "Are you ashamed of being Indian?"

I recoiled, snatching my hand back from him.

"What do you mean?"

"Sam, you never once refer to your time in India. You pretend not to understand the waiters, even though I know you do. You don't cook Indian food at home, you never wear any Indian outfits or watch any Indian films, and your only Indian friend is someone who found you and not the other way round. What am I to conclude?"

"Shame," I choked out, "has nothing to do with it!"

"Then what is it? You know you can't hide behind Sam Shaw for the rest of your life. There is a Samira Sehgal in there too."

I dipped my head to hide my agitation. Why today, I wanted to scream! Why this unexpected attack? Instead, I composed myself and looked up.

"My heritage has nothing to do with my identity."

"That's where you're wrong, Sam," Mark interrupted. "It has everything to do with it."

He broke off a piece of the *papadum* and dipped it in the mango chutney.

"My grandfather was German. Did you know that?"

I shook my head. I had never really bothered to find out too much about Mark's family.

"He was also Jewish." He chewed on the *papadum*. "He didn't survive the Holocaust. But what really gets me is that I didn't learn about him until I was in my thirties. You know why? Because my mother wanted to obliterate the past by ignoring it, by burying it so deep that none of us would be touched by it. When I discovered the truth, I felt I had found a part of me that had always been missing. Our heritage *is* our identity, Sam. And until we come to terms with it, we cannot reconcile with ourselves."

"Why are you telling me all this today?"

"I've been thinking about what your father said when we visited him, about wanting to be a grandfather. I think I'd like us to have children."

"You already have children," I said flatly.

"Yes, grown-up ones," he responded softly, "and everything I did wrong there, I want to do right this time."

"So, you want children to right your wrongs?" I spat out, furious now. "And what does that have to do with my being Indian?"

"Sam," he looked sad suddenly, the groove between his eyebrows deeper, "I wasn't trying to attack you. It's just that if we did decide to have children, I would want them to be proud of their ancestry. German, Jewish, Indian—all of it!"

I took a deep breath. The food arrived just then. The waiters placed the *saag aloo, balti chicken, lamb Madras, naan, raita* and *biryani* on the table in front of us. So much food. Most of it would get packaged to take home for Mark to enjoy over the course of the week.

"I've never wanted children, Mark. You know that. I told you on our first date."

"Yes," he nodded, "I do know that. But if you ever change your mind, I want you to know that I'll be by your side every step of the way."

Later that night, I took out my box again. This time I looked at the old photos. Black and white ones from my childhood, polaroids from our holidays in England, class photos where I stood beaming next to an awkward-looking Pari and a grumpy-looking Roma.

There were several things in my past that I was ashamed of, but being Indian wasn't one of them. What Mark misconstrued as shame was my deep-seated desire to protect the only precious part of me that hadn't been exposed to this world. I was lucky that people took me to be English because of my name, my colouring and my accent. Assimilating had never been a problem for me. However, those memories of basking in the warmth and love of India were my only refuge, a place and time that I retreated to when nothing else in my life made sense. How could I allow that part to be tarnished by a divulgence that meant nothing to anybody except me?

CHAPTER 70

"Samira?" a voice called out from behind me. "Samira Sehgal?"

I turned slowly, my heart thudding with apprehension. Who had found me in the vegetable aisle of Waitrose, of all places?

A curvy young woman stood there in navy trousers and a tan coat, hands on a shopping trolley, peering at me as if she couldn't quite make up her mind. Something about her face seemed familiar, and I almost grasped the thought before it slipped away again.

"Yes?"

"Oh my goodness, I thought it was you! Hi!!"

"Hi?" I was confused. Who was this woman, and how did she know me?

A child came up behind her and tugged at her hand.

"Maa, let's go..."

She kneeled down to whisper something to him, and I looked around to see if I could make my escape.

"How are you?" she smiled at me when she stood up, waiting for a response.

"I... I'm sorry, I really can't place you!"

"Oh gosh! I'm sorry! I should have said. I'm Ria, Roma Bannerjee's younger sister."

That's when it clicked. Roma's sister, the cute one, the one who had hero-worshipped me, much to her elder sister's annoyance.

"Ria," I breathed, smiling back at her, "What are you doing here in Surrey? Do you live around here?"

"Actually, I'm visiting my sister-in-law. Husband's sister. I live in America, in New Jersey, and we have come here for the Christmas holidays."

"I see. Your son?" I nodded towards the little boy hiding behind her.

"Yes. I have a girl too, but she is at home with my husband. I mean, at my sister-in-law's place. It's only a five-minute walk away. Why don't you come and have a cup of tea with us? Do you live around here too?"

I took a step back. There was no way I would go to some stranger's home to excavate our past.

"Thanks, Ria. I'm in a bit of a rush right now, and no, I don't live in the area. I just stopped off to buy some milk."

"Samira *didi*, don't rush off. It's so nice to see you after all these years. Let us at least get a coffee here?"

She overrode all my objections with a tenacity that reminded me of Roma. I sat with my basket, her trolley, and her little boy in the little café while she bustled away to get us coffee.

"What's your name?" I asked him hesitantly. I'd had very few dealings with little people.

"Oroon," he mumbled, looking down at his lap.

"I'm Sam, Oroon."

He looked up at me.

"But that's a boy's name!"

"Uh…" Before I could say anymore, Ria was back, clutching two coffees and a slice of Victoria sponge cake for Oroon.

"There, that was quick! Now, tell me all about yourself."

I sipped on my coffee, not sure where to begin.

"Well, I live here now…"

"Yes, Bubu had told me you had moved to the UK. But imagine bumping into you this way!"

Fortunately for me, Ria proved to be one of those loquacious people who could do all the talking without pausing for a moment's breath. In the space of thirty minutes, I knew all about her life in New Jersey, her husband's new job, her daughter's teething and Oroon's bed-wetting.

"I took a break after Onima was born, but now I want to get back to work. What about you *didi*? What do you do?"

"I, uh, work in television."

"Really?" Her eyes went very wide. "As what?"

"Just, umm, as a presenter. Nothing fancy." I wanted this encounter to end. I wanted to get away from her, her incessant chatter, her probing, her rekindling of history.

"Bah, Bubu will be so jealous when she hears!" she exclaimed gleefully.

"How is Roma?" I didn't care, but I asked to be polite, hoping I could take my leave once she had answered.

"She is fine. Living in Australia now. For a while she did not speak to us at all."

"Oh?" I was interested in-spite of myself.

"You know she married that half-Muslim boy from school? Maa and Baba were so upset with her, they nearly cut her off."

"Who?"

"Who what?"

"Which boy?"

"Ohh, Angad. You remember Pari's cousin from Dubai?"

My hand shook as I placed the coffee cup down on the table.

"Ria, this has been lovely, but I really have to go now. Thank you for the coffee."

I dashed out of the store, leaving my basket behind, grasping at the scarf at my throat as she called out after me, "But... your milk..."

Outside, I got into the car and pushed the key into the ignition with trembling fingers. Then I sat there, teeth chattering, trying not to remember, but drowning; drowning under the flood of memories that engulfed me.

Roma

CHAPTER 71

I didn't consider myself a kleptomaniac. Not then, not before, not ever. I was a collector of things. Things that reminded me of people, places and times.

It wasn't like I got these sudden irrepressible urges to steal stuff. My theft, if it could be called that, was always a considered action. Forethought, planning and nerve worked in conjunction for me to acquire whatever I desired.

Over the years, my collection had grown, and I kept the items hidden behind my blouses and petticoats. Small things like pens or mix-tapes, I wasn't too bothered about concealing. It was the more valuable items, like bits of jewellery, or a silver idol that I'd filched from Angad's colleague's house, that stayed out of sight.

It wasn't like I couldn't afford to buy these things for myself, but over the years, I'd found that this was my little way of avenging myself against people who had irritated, ignored or belittled me.

I wish I could say I felt guilty, but the opposite was true. Each stolen item reminded me of why I had taken it, and while it gave me a lot of pleasure contemplating the pain I'd inflicted on my unsuspecting victim, it enraged me all over again, too. Which is why I felt justified in having done what I had.

Take Pari's Madonna tape. After I had introduced her to my music, shown her my Walkman, shared the novelty of owning an item like that, she had harangued her father into buying her one too. Had she shared that news with me first? Oh no! It was always Samira that she ran to. Served her right then that her favourite Madonna tape had gone missing!

There was an eclectic collection of goods from my time in school. Margaret Ma'am's glasses when she'd upbraided me for copying Pari's homework, Samira's T-shirt when she had snubbed me in front of Angad, Ashish's new pen that he'd boasted about incessantly, and even Madhu's clip which her Pitaji had bought for her birthday.

Funny that these were the ones I'd held on to. When we moved from Delhi to Sydney, I'd had to dispose of the rest covertly. Of course, the collection had grown once again in Australia, but the oldest items in there were the ones that held most of my spite within them.

Having replaced the items back in my wardrobe, I sat and painted my nails a pretty pink. Just the other day, one of the Ozzie mothers had said to me, "You have such beautiful hands, Mrs Bannerjee. Very artistic!"

It was the first compliment I'd had in a very long time, and I couldn't stop beaming all day. There were many things I hated about living in Sydney, but amongst the few things that I did like was the fact that no one asked me stupid questions like why I hadn't changed my name after marriage. Nor did anyone taunt me about my weight or ask me to go on a diet. For the most part, they left me alone, and that was fine by me. The occasional compliment, though, reminded me that I was still a woman who wanted to be admired. All I felt like these days was an unpaid housekeeper, a chauffeur, and a cook.

When had all my ambitions disappeared? Surely, I'd had some! I could have become a famous singer if I wanted to. Everyone had called me the nightingale of Kinara Public School. When had all that disappeared in my desire to become a wife? *His* wife!

"Come home no, Roma?" Maa would always say, every time I rang her. But where was home now? Calcutta, where Maa and Baba had settled in retirement, or Delhi, where I had spent nearly all my life? Sydney was not it. Despite all its conveniences—Angad's well-paid job, our beautiful home, the children's grammar school and the small circle of well-heeled Indian friends we had—there was always an undercurrent to our residency here. We were 'the others'; aliens in this land, trying to hold on to our Indianness in a different cultural landscape.

Still, it was nice to be noticed.

After I had let my nails dry, I ambled to the kitchen and rooted around in the fridge for last night's leftovers. Some of the Thai take-away was still sitting in the cartons, and I grabbed myself a fork and tucked into it without bothering to heat the Pad Thai.

The pressing question of the day was what to cook for dinner?

I opened the freezer and looked inside. There was some frozen pizza. That would do. The children loved pizza, and if Angad didn't like it, well, that was just too bad.

CHAPTER 72

I was sitting in the dark when he let himself in

"You're late," I said, noting with quiet satisfaction how he jumped.

He turned the lights on.

"Roma..." His appeasing face was on. The same one that I didn't trust one bit. *This* was the man I'd fought my parents to marry?

He came and sat next to me on the couch.

"I told you there was a client dinner tonight."

"No, you didn't."

"Roma, I did. Look, you must have forgotten, and I really should have called, but I thought you knew."

Gaslighting. That's what they called it. Telling me what I should and should not believe. Angad was so good at it.

"When did you tell me, huh? When?" I turned to face him, my voice calm but teetering on the edge of hysteria.

"Last week, Roma. I can't tell you which day exactly, but you were still in bed." He sounded apologetic. What was he apologising for?

"Tell me the truth, Angad. Who were you out with?"

"It was a client dinner!" Now he sounded annoyed.

"Was your client young, pretty, and female?" His face twisted as I said this, and a part of me wondered why I needled him this way. Another part wanted answers.

"Stop it, Roma. You can't punish me forever for one transgression."

"One that I know of."

"A drunken kiss at a Christmas party! Really, Roma? I was the one who told you."

"And I can NEVER TRUST YOU AGAIN!" I was screaming now, not bothered that the neighbours could hear me, or the children would wake up.

"Shhh!" he put his hand on my mouth. "Don't do this now, please. Let's go to bed. We'll talk tomorrow morning. Calmly."

I wrenched his hand away, but lowered my voice.

"It's always tomorrow, tomorrow, tomorrow with you! I want answers today!"

His shoulders slumped, and he looked older than his years. I didn't care.

"Okay. What do you want to know?"

For years, the one question that had been festering in me, the one question that had poisoned the very foundation of our relationship, bubbled up, and I spat it out at him with every bit of venom I could muster.

"Did you have an affair with Samira?"

He started, then gawped at me.

"With who?"

"Don't pretend! You know exactly who."

"Samira? Pari's friend from school?"

"Yes."

"I..." He stopped, as if assessing how to continue.

"Don't lie, Angad," I warned him, my voice low and menacing now. "Don't you fucking dare lie!"

He flinched, then swallowed.

"Yes."

His voice was so quiet that I had to strain to listen.

"Tell me more."

"There's nothing more to tell. It was short-lived. A month maximum. Then she broke up with me."

"Did you love her?"

"Love?" He laughed then, a short, sharp laugh. "What's that? Sure, I was attracted to her. She was beautiful and mysterious and seemed very sad. I wasn't in a good place myself and found myself drawn to her. Anyway, it was so long ago, Roma. Why are you dredging it all up now?"

"Because..." I stopped, not sure whether I could say it out loud. Whether saying it out loud would make my suspicion real, make it concrete somehow.

He waited, and I knew I had to say it. It had churned inside me for years. Every time he looked at me, every time we kissed or made love, I wondered. As he waited patiently for me to elaborate, I knew I had to say it. Now there was no walking away from it.

"Because I think you've always loved her, and you've never loved me." A tear trickled down my face as I finally pronounced the thing that had pulsated beneath our marriage all these years.

"That's ridiculous, Roma! Just listen to yourself. Samira was a stranger to me. Yes, we went out a few times, but it was never serious. And I married you! I've spent seven years married to you. Seven years of trying to make you happy! How can you even say that?"

And just like that, all my anger and fear evaporated. I grabbed his hand and started to kiss it.

"I'm sorry! I'm sorry, Angad! I don't know what came over me. I just... I'm so scared sometimes that you... Never mind. Please forgive me! I love you. I really, really love you."

He took me into his arms and kissed me, unbuttoning my top.

"No, not here," I whispered, pushing his hands away. "Come into the bedroom."

Later, much after we had made up in the only way we knew how, he turned his back on me and fell asleep. But I lay there thinking for a long time.

Had it all been my imagination? Or, underneath his lust, had the perfume of another woman still lingered on his skin?

CHAPTER 73

Subterfuge is an art. Much after Samira and Madhu had left school, much after Pari had gained a new circle of friends, I still did not give up on Angad. Every girl that he flirted with, I found a way to diminish or demonise. Every event that he went to, I turned up unannounced.

In those years, I finally got to grips with my eating habits, and slimmed down enough to be attractive by society's standards. I learned to flirt with boys, to wear outfits that called attention to my cleavage, to apply makeup to enhance my features, and to keep my hair long, loose and silky, swishing it with effect anytime an attractive man was around. Yet, my heart pined for Angad and Angad alone.

In time, he came to regard me as a close friend, confiding in me about his crushes, his ambitions and his pain of losing his parents so young. I provided him with a shoulder to cry on, a listening ear for all his troubles, waiting for just one opportunity to make the leap from friend to girlfriend.

Meanwhile, Maa and Baba became suspicious of our growing closeness, and banned me from seeing Angad, trying to steer me towards the nice Bengali boys in our community. In my single-minded determination to make Angad mine, I flouted all their rules, rebelled against all their strictures. Life at home was a living hell, but I always believed it would eventually lead to happiness.

Now, as I loaded the dishwasher, I wondered what happiness truly was.

Ankita came into the kitchen, rubbing the sleep out of her eyes.

"Maa, what's for breakfast?"

"Cornflakes. You sit, I'll bring it for you."

At seven, Ankita looked so much like Ria had at that age. The same curly hair, the same mischievous expression. Annoyance darted through me as I realised that I hadn't spoken to Ria in over a month. Why hadn't she called? Then I remembered she was visiting her in-laws in England.

"Has Jai woken up yet?"

"No, Maa." Ankita sucked on her thumb as she regarded me. "Why were you shouting at Baba last night?"

I halted at the sink, my mind whirring.

"Because Baba came home late. I was worried about him."

"But sometimes you come late to pick us up from school."

"Yes, that's true. I won't be late anymore, I promise. Now, eat up."

Timekeeping had never been my friend. In that, Samira and I had been similar, our mutual tardiness having been a source of annoyance for Pari and Madhu. These days my slowness came from a lassitude that filled my limbs, a heaviness that covered me like a blanket. I could not get out of bed in the mornings. Angad got the children ready for school, prepared their lunches, and drove them there. I would finally rise at around 10 a.m. then potter around the house in my nightie, not showering until it was nearly time to pick up the children. I had to change my ways somehow.

On Saturdays at around 4 p.m. I took the children to the park, where I met some of the local mothers. We would buy our coffees and sit together on the bench and chat.

Shalini, the gynaecologist, was there with Seo-Jun, the Korean chiropractor. They waved to me and I went over to join them, letting the children run off to play on the swings with the other kids.

"Roma, where's your coffee?" Shalini asked, holding up her paper cup.

"I forgot. I was in a rush." I took my water bottle out of my bag. "I'll drink this instead."

"Very healthy!" See-Jun nodded, approvingly.

I didn't want to tell them that lately I hadn't been able to stomach coffee.

"How's the Christmas shopping going?" I asked, sitting down next to them.

"Not well," Shalini admitted ruefully. "I just can't seem to spare the time, and Dan is completely useless. See-Jun was telling me there's a great sale over at the mall. Have you been yet?"

"No, not yet. We are still debating whether or not to head to India for Christmas."

"Why debating?" See-Jun asked.

"Angad's got a lot of work, and his new boss seems to be a real taskmaster. He may not get the time off."

"Why don't you go with the kids, then?"

I nodded and sipped on my water, letting their conversation carry on. I could go with the kids, but I didn't want to leave Angad behind on his own. Despite all his protestations, despite the ghost of his brief entanglement with Samira, despite our lovemaking, I still didn't trust my husband entirely. My leaving with the children for an entire month would leave the coast clear for him to do as he wished, with whomever he wished. There was no way I'd give him that opportunity.

CHAPTER 74

"Bubu, you'd never believe who I ran into in England!"

"Who?" I answered Ria on the phone, a bit distracted as I tried wrapping ribbons and bows around the last few presents. The children were finishing school today and I couldn't get the presents wrapped once they were home, so I was running against the clock. Typical Ria to call just then!

"Samira! You remember? That beautiful fair girl from your year. You were friendly with her, no?"

I froze for a moment, not sure if this was one of Ria's jokes.

"Bubu, are you there? The line is so indistinct!"

"Y... yes, I'm here." My voice came out strangled, hoarse.

"Did you hear what I said? I ran into your old friend, Samira."

"Yes," I composed myself, "I heard. Where did you meet her?"

"In a supermarket. I'd gone to pick up Onir's favourite cereal, and she was there. She's become some hotshot presenter on TV now."

"Oh, really?"

"But she was nice once she recognised me. She was asking about you."

"What did you say?"

"Just that you're in Australia with your husband."

"And her? What about her? Is she married?"

"Well, that's the strange thing. Before I could ask, she ran out saying she was busy or something. Left all her shopping behind too."

"Oh."

Ria prattled on about other things while my mind tried grasping the significance of the encounter. What did it mean? Why was Samira rearing her head in my life again? Had I invited her back in somehow by uttering her name?

"Bubu! Are you there?"

"Yes, I am. Sorry, I missed the last bit. What did you say?"

"I said it's a shame you're not going to Cal this year. Maa and Baba were looking forward to it."

"I know," I sighed. "Next year, perhaps."

"Let's all go at the same time. It will be so much fun! The children can all meet each other again. Feels weird to be living so far away from each other."

"Yes. Let's do that." My finger kept stroking the ribbon as I struggled to keep my thoughts from scattering.

"Bubu, have you found a job yet?"

"What?"

"We talked about it the last time, remember? Now that the children are in school, you said you'd look for a job."

"Oh that. Yes, I will, but in the new year. No point right now. Everything is winding down for the holidays."

"I can't believe how hot it is where you are. They are expecting a white Christmas here. I hope we get a bit of snow, but the in-laws say that's quite rare, and the snow hardly settles..."

Luckily, Ria had never needed encouragement when it came to talking, so I could carry on wrapping the presents, saying the occasional "hmmm" or "yes" for her to be content that I was listening. I often wondered if Ria and I weren't sisters would we even have been friends?

"Okay, Bubu, I'll call from Jersey next. Have a great Christmas and New Year, and don't forget to call Maa and Baba."

"I won't. And you too."

· · ·

When I had hung up, I inserted a CD into the player, and let Lata Mangeshkar's dulcet voice fill the room. I sang along with her, while finishing wrapping the presents. Music had always calmed me, and it worked its magic on me now as well.

The spectre of Samira had haunted me for fifteen years. Her sudden reappearance, even if it was via Ria, was jarring but not entirely unexpected. I had always known at some level that we had unfinished business.

I set aside the pile of presents and opened up my laptop. I had tried searching for Samira Sehgal many times before and never come up with any positive leads. Now, I typed 'Samira TV presenter' into the search engine and some other woman's images popped up in the results. Then I typed 'Sam TV presenter UK', and there she was!

I examined her face and figure. She was beautiful, there was no denying it. She went by Sam Shaw these days. Did that mean she was married? No results came up when I typed 'Sam Shaw husband'. I was curious, but was running out of time. I remembered my promise to Ankita about being on time at school, so I shut the laptop, vowing to myself to continue my investigation into Samira later.

Then I took the little pile of presents into the garage and hid them behind some old tarpaulin. The children wouldn't think to look there. I noticed a long thin blue box sticking out from under a plastic bag and pulled it out, curious. It was a Swarovski crystal bracelet, rhodium plated, delicate and pretty. How strange! Angad knew that I only wore pure gold jewellery. My skin reacted to all other metals. Alarm bells started ringing in my mind. Who had he bought it for, and why?

CHAPTER 75

On Christmas Eve, we went to Ashwin and Gita's house for a dinner party. Ashwin worked with Angad, and over time we had become friends with them, and through them the other Indians who worked in IT and lived around the area.

The suburb of Liberty Grove was lush, green, quiet, and a recent development. Ashwin and Gita's townhouse was what aspirational living was all about. It was rumoured that Gita had flown in a famous interior decorator to the Bollywood stars from Mumbai to have her home look like the interior of The Taj Mahal Hotel in Colaba. She never let slip whether or not this was true.

Prior to leaving, I fussed over the children, not sure if Chloe was up to the task of babysitting them all evening.

"Relax, Mrs B, they'll be fine. I've got all your numbers here, and if anything happens, I'll call you straight away."

Angad came out, fiddling with his cufflinks, and saw me reminding Chloe about the dinner again.

"Roma, leave the poor girl alone. It's not like she's never done this before." He laughed to take the sting out of his words.

I turned away, heading towards the TV room to give the children another kiss.

"Maa, you look so pretty," Ankita looked at me, momentarily distracted from the cartoons on the screen.

I had worn a pink *Patola sari*, a part of my wedding trousseau, perhaps to remind Angad of where his loyalties ought to lie, or perhaps to remind myself that he was still married to me. Once again, all my old insecurities had resurfaced. Was I not good enough for him? Is that why he was always out late? Is that why he had kissed that woman at the party? And was that all that he'd done, or was there more? Had he confessed to the lesser sin in the hope he could put me off the scent of his greater ones?

The thought of the strange bracelet still rankled. It had disappeared the next day when I'd gone looking for it, and even though I had looked for and felt every package that had appeared under the Christmas tree, I had not come across it again.

Angad came up behind me and slipped an arm around my waist.

"You look lovely tonight, Roma!"

I stiffened, then moved out of his grasp, placing a kiss on Ankita's head and then on Jai's, who stayed riveted to the screen.

In the car, on the way to the party, Angad asked, "Is everything alright? You're very quiet this evening."

I hadn't said a word to him, still fulminating internally from my raging thoughts.

"I have a slight headache."

"Why didn't you say?" He looked at me, fake concern in his eyes. "Have you taken anything for it?"

"No."

"Do you still want to go? I mean, we can head back and I'll just call and say you're not feeling well."

"And make me sound like the bitch?"

"Roma! That's not what I meant." He pursed his lips and went back to staring at the road.

Why didn't he want me to go to the party? Was there something or someone he didn't want me to see? Every sense was on high alert now. Angad was smart, much too smart to be caught with his hand in the cookie jar, but if I got him to ease up, maybe he'd let something slip. I suppressed my anger and turned to him, my voice placating.

"Sorry Angad. I've just been feeling a bit off all day. Listen, I will not drink tonight. Why don't I drive back, and that way you can enjoy yourself with your friends without worrying about alcohol limits and all that?"

"They're your friends too, Roma," he sounded hurt now. My God, he was good. A damn good actor, really.

"I meant *our* friends, of course!" I smiled at him, stroking his cheek, and felt him relax, visibly. Sometimes, if I tried hard enough, I could turn him to putty in my hands. The trouble was that these days I didn't feel like trying. Everything felt like too much of an effort. Marriage, motherhood, life.

"You do look lovely tonight," he said once again. "Pink is your colour."

I'd worn pink at our wedding too. I wondered if he remembered that. Such a blushing bride I had been, in a pink lehenga with delicate *zardosi* work on it. I should have worn a red *Banarasi sari* embellished with gold embroidery, with *alta* on my hands and feet, *mathapatti* and *mukut*, with red and white bangles on my wrists. Instead, I'd distanced myself from my family's traditions, my Bengali roots, to be the kind of bride Angad wanted. Modern, muted, doll-like. How much I had given up for him!

I looked at his profile as he drove, and once again reminded myself how much I'd wanted him back then, how hard I'd fought everyone to get him. All those years when Maa and Baba had refused to speak to me. Exhausted as I was from this sham of a marriage, I was damned if I'd let anyone steal him away from me now.

CHAPTER 76

The party was already in full swing when we arrived. Gita greeted us at the door wearing a long, black figure-skimming dress with a plunging back.

"Look at you, Roma! Love the *sari*. Wish I could wear more of my Indian stuff here."

I wondered what was stopping her.

"Thanks Gita, that's a very nice dress." I handed her the bottle of wine and, as Angad exchanged pleasantries with her, I made my way inside.

It was the usual suspects. Ashwin and his six buddies, plus their wives. With us, there were a total of sixteen adults. That wasn't counting Gita's parents, who were babysitting the children upstairs. It was a shame that Maa and Baba weren't interested in coming to Australia. Maybe if they did, Angad and I could have 'date nights' and 'soirees' too.

"Hi Roma!" one of the other wives called out to me and I went over to join the group. I was the only one in a *sari*. Everyone else was dressed in cocktail dresses or blinged-up jeans with sequin tops and velvet jackets. Why hadn't I been sent the memo?

"We were just talking about Amrita's new ring. Have you seen it?"

Amrita displayed a big, flashy diamond on her finger, and I made all the appropriate noises. With these women, the talk was always about jewellery, clothes, and parties. Aside from Gita and Shalini, the gynaecologist, no one else worked. I should have fitted right in, but didn't.

"Aren't you going to India this time?" Amrita asked me.

"No. You?"

"We're taking Mummy and Papa back after New Year's."

"Oh, are your parents here too?"

"Of course! They come every year for Christmas."

Once again, a familiar resentment welled up inside me. Everyone's parents but mine visited. When Angad and I had moved to Australia five years prior, I had made Maa promise they would come. All I'd had since then was excuse after excuse. "Your Baba is unwell." "We couldn't get the visa." "Such a long journey." "My passport has expired." I wondered sometimes if Ria was given the same reasons too. Why were my parents such sticks in the mud?

"... so we're wondering who will get to helm that office?"

"I'm hoping it's Bikram," Amrita said, lowering her voice. "I can't wait to go home."

"What are you talking about?" I asked, having tuned out the earlier bit of the conversation.

"The Mumbai office that's being opened. They haven't chosen the branch manager."

Mumbai. That name sounded and tasted unfamiliar. It had always been Bombay to my generation until the powers that be had renamed it. I wondered if Angad was in the running for the position, too.

"Dinner is served, ladies and gentlemen!"

The lavish spread was all Gita's handiwork, and it always amazed me that she managed to work, keep a beautiful home, entertain and cook such a variety of dishes, too. Then I remembered, she had plenty of help by way of her parents.

"This is *Nadan Kozhi Varuthathu*, a spicy chicken fry from Kerala."

"You made this, Gita?" one of the men asked.

"With a lot of help from my mother!"

I tucked into the food, enjoying the South Indian flavours. Malayali cuisine was quite different from Tamilian food, but something about the entire experience reminded me of all the years spent in Pari's house, eating the food Aunty had cooked for us. I looked over at Angad and saw that he was enjoying it equally. Did he feel short changed that I only ever made Bengali food and that too, only when I was in the mood to cook?

Years ago, he had confided in me that he missed eating meat. Pari's family were Brahmins and strict vegetarians, and loving and considerate as they had been towards a suddenly orphaned relative, it hadn't even occurred to them that familiar food would be something he would miss as acutely. His mother had converted his father to non-vegetarianism, even if she hadn't converted him to Islam. So, they were in the habit of eating lamb biryani, *mughlai* chicken and other such delicacies he didn't dare mention under Rajan Uncle's roof.

From then on, I'd cooked lovingly for him, smuggling dishes like *Mangsher Jhol, Kosha Mangsho, Shorshe Bata Ilish Maachh*—meat and fish curries that he consumed hurriedly, hiding behind the servants' quarters. Belching delightedly and thanking me with a grin. The way to a man's heart, Maa had once said. Had I ever unlocked his heart, or had I merely unlocked his inner glutton?

After dinner, the men retired to the balcony with their whiskies while the women sat around the coffee table with their liqueurs. I hadn't touched a drop all evening, choosing to drink sparkling water instead. I examined the tastefully decorated Christmas tree, looking at the various baubles that they had collected from their travels all over the world. From Palm Springs, California, to Cape Town, South Africa, even the tree was a display of their uber-couple credentials.

Suddenly, I felt the urge to heave, and hurried to the guest bathroom. Inside, I emptied the contents of my stomach into the toilet bowl, retching until only a trickle of bile emerged. I flushed and then sat on the toilet seat, shaking. What had I reacted to? Was it the chicken? Or was it something else?

As I stood up, I felt dizzy, and so sat down again. It took another five minutes before I felt I could stand. I looked at my face in the mirror. My skin looked leached of all colour, the pupils of my eyes unusually dilated. I splashed some water on my face and dried my hands on the towel. Perhaps it was time to head home.

Outside, I went towards the kitchen to get a glass of plain ice water, but stopped just short of entering when I heard my name being mentioned.

"She's such a grouch, Gita! Why do you even invite her?" Amrita's high-pitched voice was followed by Gita's low murmur.

"Hey! Don't blame me. Ashwin is really fond of Angad, and how can I call him without calling the wife?"

A third voice pitched in. Rita. Nita. Whatever her name was.

"And did you see what she was wearing? She looks like such an aunty*ji*! She thinks the *sari* will camouflage her blubber."

"Has she gotten fatter?"

"She looks it."

"How the heck has she held onto such a handsome guy?"

"My question is, how the heck did she get her claws into him in the first place?"

"Where is she, anyway?"

I backed away frantically, my face flushed, my heart knocking against my ribs.

Later, as I took her leave, Gita hugged me and said, "It was so lovely to see you, Roma. We must do this again soon."

I smiled and nodded, my eyes on the delicate Swarovski bracelet that glinted on her wrist. Her Bvlgari perfume sat in my bag, swiped shortly after I'd heard them bitching about me. I wondered when she'd miss it.

CHAPTER 77

I wanted to put the entire horrible episode behind me. Women like that were no friends. I was better off without them. As for Gita, the two-faced bitch! Did she not have enough, with a doting husband, parents that did everything for her, a high-flying career and a beautiful home that now she wanted my husband too?

Confrontation had never worked with Angad. He would either deny or stonewall. I had to be strategic in how I handled the situation; find another way to get rid of this latest threat without creating any fuss or drama. How stupid did Angad think I was? Did he really believe that I wouldn't find out? Yes, I had very little to go on. A bracelet that had mysteriously disappeared and reappeared on another woman's wrist. He'd say it was all my imagination. Never mind. Where confrontation hadn't worked, some subtle arm-twisting could yield better results.

As expected, on Christmas day I received a perfume, a silk scarf, a gold pendant, some fancy nail polish, and a CD of Rabindra Sangeet, but no Swarovski bracelet. I made no mention of it. As far as Angad was concerned, I was blissfully unaware of his latest fling. I played along, feigning surprise and gratitude, pretending I hadn't noticed his disappointment when he unwrapped his own present to reveal another boring tie.

After dinner, when the children sat watching a cartoon about cars, I asked him about the position in Mumbai.

"Amrita mentioned it at the party last night. Are you thinking of applying?"

He looked at me curiously, while tearing the wrapper off another chocolate. Where did he put it? He never seemed to gain an ounce of weight, whereas I just had to be in the vicinity of food and all the calories attached themselves to me like metal filings to a magnet.

"No, not really. It's a bit out of my grade and experience. Besides, I'm happy where I am."

I bet you are; I thought to myself.

"Don't you want to progress in your career, darling?"

I snuggled up to him, my hand moving up under his T-shirt, one eye on the children.

"Yeah, I do, but heading a branch would be way out of my zone of expertise."

"Your comfort zone, you mean?"

He bit into another chocolate, then shrugged.

"I suppose you could call it that."

"Are you scared of trying something new?"

"No, Roma. I'm scared of falling flat on my face trying something that I'm not ready for. I am the provider for this family. If I'm out of a job, who exactly is going to put food on the table?"

"I've never known you to be so cautious."

"And I've never known you to be so interested in my job. What's going on, Roma?"

That's when I started to sniffle.

"I miss home. I miss Maa and Baba. I thought that if we were in Mumbai, I could visit them more often. The children could get to know their grandparents better, too."

"I see." He sounded stiff and unyielding.

"Don't you miss India, Angad?"

There was such a long pause after my question that I wondered if he'd fallen asleep. I looked up to see him staring out into the garden with a distant look in his eyes. When he answered, his voice was soft and sad.

"India is home to you, Roma. My home was Dubai where I grew up with my parents. India reminds me of my loss, of tragedy and pain. While I will always remain connected to it through Rajan Uncle's family, I cannot truly say that I miss it."

I let the silence hang between us before pulling out my trump card.

"Angad?"

"Hmmm?"

"I don't want to have the baby here."

"What?" He sat up.

"Yes." I looked at him, my eyes filled with an unspoken supplication, gauging his reaction to the news, watching the excitement, fear and happiness flicker across his face. "I did the test last night. It was positive."

Happiness won out. He pulled me into a hug, whispering endearments in my ear. Family was everything to Angad, and the more members I added to it, the more secure my position would become.

"What are you doing, Baba?" Ankita came up to us, pouting, unhappy to be excluded.

"I'm hugging Maa and the little pea growing inside her," Angad said, laughing.

"You have a pea growing in you?" Jai asked, interested now.

I nodded, smiling through my tears.

"A little pea that will become a brother or sister to you both."

"Yuck!" Jai took a step back. "I don't want a pea as a brother."

"You silly!" Ankita smacked him lightly on the head. "It's going to come out as a baby."

They climbed up onto the sofa with us and as we sat there, hugging, chatting and planning, I knew it wouldn't be long before Angad applied for the position.

Madhu

CHAPTER 78

I always thought of life as divided into a 'Before' and an 'After'. In the 'Before' I knew where I was headed, where I belonged and what I wanted. In the 'After', I was lost.

Those few months after Pitaji's death took on a nightmarish hue in my mind. We fled the same night, taking bus after bus to reach the village. Lallan cried the entire journey, Mataji cried too. I was the only one who stayed resolutely silent. The fact of Pitaji's death had not sunk in, and somewhere within me, I believed that he was still alive; that it had all been some colossal mistake and that he would come for us in a few days, laughing at our panic, telling us how stupid we had been.

But no one came. Not in the next few days, weeks, or months.

Mataji took refuge with her sister and family. They spoke in whispers around us, and sometimes, when they forgot we were around, I'd hear *Mausi's* husband ask how long we were going to stay.

It's ironic how, even then, even after everything that had happened, I believed that Raj Uncle would not forsake us. He had given us money to tide us over the first few months. There would be more forthcoming, and at some point, they would return and call us back home.

When I'd had the temerity to say it out loud, *Mausi* had laughed in my face, saying to Mataji, "This girl needs a reality check, Sushila. Tell her no one is coming back."

I didn't believe her then, confident that we wouldn't be abandoned, that even though my life would not be what it had been before—surely, I would not rot in this backward hellhole forever?

Two months after Pitaji's disappearance, Mataji called me over to her.

"Madhu," she said, her face grim, "there is a *rishta* for you. You will be getting married in a month's time."

"What?! I'm sixteen Mataji! How can you marry me off? I need to complete my education."

"You can forget about that. I do not have the means to support you and your brother. This is the only way. He is not asking for much in dowry. He is a nice man, just recently widowed. Has two young children. I've told him you have experience with handling young ones and how well you handled Lallan when he was little." She massaged her temples before repeating, "He is a nice man."

"If he's so nice, why don't you marry him?" I cried, before running out of the hut into the field outside.

That was, perhaps, the moment that I finally realised that my life had changed irrevocably.

As a girl, I was a liability. As a partially educated girl, I was a liability with a voice and opinions, a fact that would not be tolerated. My brother, little as he was, had better prospects because he was a boy. Someday, he would grow up and support the family, bring in a wife and a dowry, and take care of my mother in her dotage. What could I offer her except amorphous dreams of what I could have achieved with my intelligence? Pitaji had seen a better future for me, Mataji had only seen marriage.

The night that I took Rs 5000 from the dwindling stash of money and made a run for it was the night I severed all ties with my family. I knew then that I could never return, that Mataji and Lallan were lost to me forever.

After all my years of living in the shadows, I had become a part of the shadows. No one noticed me; I blended effortlessly into the background. I could be a slim young boy, turbaned and quiet as I hitched a ride to the railway station. I could be a hunched old woman, covered in a blanket as I sat in a corner of the train compartment, heading towards New Delhi Railway Station. I remained watchful and cautious, frightened and reserved, but staunch in my conviction that this was the only way forward.

Mid-afternoon, when I arrived, I hired an auto rickshaw and went directly to our house in Gulmohar Park. I stood outside the locked gates for a long time, peering through the grills, wondering where the Gurkha was. It was the *press-wallah* who offered me a cup of tea and filled me in on what had happened after we'd left.

"Raj *sahib* and family left for England the same night. The police came the next morning and ransacked the entire house. They were looking for some papers, they said. Did you know that Raj *sahib* was a big smuggler?" Then he saw my wan face and nodded. "Of course, you know. I'm sorry, *bitiya*, I heard your father died in the shootout. Now, the police have seized everything. No one can enter the house. I doubt that the Sehgal family will return ever again."

I drained my cup, thanked him, and stood up.

"Where are you going? Where is your mother?"

"In the village." I answered only the latter question.

He looked at me, speculation in his eyes.

"You need a place to stay?" Suddenly, his concern had turned into something else. Something slimy and disgusting.

"No, I'll be okay."

I never returned to Gulmohar Park again.

CHAPTER 79

"Madhu," the nursing superintendent called me aside. "Bed 5 is not doing well. Dr Chhabra will give him his injection in half an hour. After that, you clean his bedpan and change him. At least let the man die in dignity, no?"

Dignity.

How loaded that word was, and how little of it I saw in my daily dealings with people. Disease and death stripped people of dignity. When your body betrayed you, its functions out of your control; when pain and suffering took over your senses—dignity was the furthest thing from your mind. In my twelve years as a staff nurse, watching people thrash and scream, submit to being handled by strangers, accept or fight their fate, I had seen dignity all but abandoned at the threshold of the hospital.

"Yes, Sister," I said to Amy Matthews, my superior and my friend.

She looked at me while picking up the next patient's clipboard.

"How long have you been on shift?"

"Fourteen hours."

"Then you should go home. You look tired."

"I will, after Dr Chhabra's rounds."

She nodded at me, no stranger to pulling double shifts herself.

. . .

Later, as I followed Dr Chhabra around, giving her updates on the patients in our ward, I once again noted to myself how young and pretty she was. Pink-cheeked and bright-eyed, she looked nothing like the rest of us tired and haggard lot.

"Madhu, did Amy fill you in on Bed 5?"

"Yes, Doctor. She said you were going to inject him?"

"You can do that. It's just morphine for the pain. He doesn't have long now."

"Yes, Doctor."

"Has the family come in yet?"

"They will be in the next hour or so."

"Do you want me to talk to them, or will you do it?"

"I can do it."

She smiled at me and patted the side of my arm.

"Thank you."

When she left, I noticed her *dupatta* was trailing on the floor. I nearly called out to her, but then stopped. Someone would tell her, no doubt.

Mentally, I chided myself for being petty. It wasn't Dr Chhabra's fault that she had been given the opportunities denied to me, that she was a doctor while I was a mere nurse. Our destinies were predetermined, this much I was sure of now. There was a time I would have scoffed at such beliefs, but now I submitted to fate.

As I cleaned out the bedpan of the patient in Bed 5, I glanced at his name on the chart. Mr Rohit Kapoor. Stage 4 Kaposi's Sarcoma with lymphoedema. His skin was stretched tight, lesions and sores on his legs where the delicate surface had burst and refused to heal despite localised treatment. Now, he was too far gone.

At first, Mr Kapoor had cried out in pain, and sometimes anger, when I changed his dressings or gave him a bed bath. But over time, his mind had started shutting down along with his body. Placid as a child, he submitted in silence to being heaved, changed, poked and prodded on a daily basis. He barely recognised his own family, and the occasional groan that escaped him was the only sign that he still felt something, even if he couldn't articulate it.

After I had freshened him up, I spoke to him quietly.

"You know this is not the end. You may be at the very end of the tunnel of this life, but the doorway that lies ahead of you leads to another future. There will be no pain there, no suffering either. Say your goodbyes to your loved ones today. You will meet them in another realm someday."

His eyes rolled in his sockets, mouth dribbling as he listened to me, uncomprehending, semi-conscious. Was anything I was saying penetrating through the miasma of pain? I hoped I was offering him some succour, however nebulous it was.

My own beliefs were a mishmash of Hinduism, Christianity, Buddhism, and Islam. I would not have considered myself particularly religious. I never went to any places of worship; I didn't even have any religious idols or symbols in my house. But I needed to believe in something. In an ocean of anguish, faith of any kind was my only mainstay.

Much after he had died, and I had spoken to his widow and two children, I went and wept in the bathroom. How many souls had I tended to in my nursing career? How many had passed away in my hands? And why did certain ones affect me so deeply?

Then I remembered suddenly. Mr Rohit Kapoor had borne an uncanny resemblance to Raj Uncle.

CHAPTER 80

I still can't remember how I found my way to Margaret Ma'am's house back then; how I'd even known where she lived. Maybe subliminally, I'd stored the details in my mind, foreseeing a time when they would come in handy.

As I'd waited outside the door of her apartment, my stomach had churned with anxiety. She was my last hope. What would I do if she didn't or couldn't help?

The guard to the apartment block had challenged me when I had asked to go to the apartment. My appearance was no better than a street sweeper, the old, patched up *salwar kameez* on my body having belonged to Mataji several years ago, the blanket something I had grabbed in a hurry from *Mausi's* pile in the corner, hair uncombed, face dirty. No wonder he had nearly shooed me off. It had taken every ounce of my courage for me to stand up to him, and tell him in perfect English how annoyed Margaret Ma'am would be with him if he didn't let me meet her. What was it about this language of our oppressors that it reduced everyone to a slave once again? Nearly fifty years since our nation had achieved independence from the British Raj, their language still seemed like it would enslave us forever.

I had no way of knowing what time it was except that it was still the afternoon. How long did I sit there, empty of thought and emotion, rudderless? I had acted on impulse, wanting to get away from a fate Mataji had designated for me, but now, the initial adrenalin having faded, I was passive as a fallen leaf that waited for the wind to take it where it wished.

When Margaret Ma'am found me on her doorstep, I was half-asleep, fatigued from my journey and the emotional trauma of the last few months.

"Madhu! Is that you, my child?"

She picked me up off the floor, holding me in a hug.

"Oh, you poor, poor thing! How long have you been waiting here? Come on in…"

She ushered me into her small flat, letting me sink into a chair while she prepared tea. The radio was set on some classical music channel, and as I listened to it, I once again sank into apathy.

"Here, have some tea. I've added two teaspoons of sugar to it, and here are some Marie biscuits. Now, tell me, how is it that you are here, and where is the rest of your family?"

The tea revived me enough to tell her the story slowly, haltingly. I watched the horror, fear, sadness and anger settle upon her features, then flee to make room for the next emotion, and I wondered why I didn't feel anything anymore.

"But you are sixteen! Why does your mother want you to get married so young?"

"This is what happens to the women in our village. My mother was married at fourteen. I am almost too old." A mirthless laugh escaped me.

"Oh, my girl! And now you have run away… but where were you intending to go?"

"I…" I stayed silent for a beat, then looked up at her. "I was hoping to get some news of Raj Uncle's family, hoping that I could join them wherever they are. Uncle wouldn't want me to abandon my studies. He is the one who insisted I join…"

I watched her face fall as I spoke, and I knew that whatever she would say next would wound me more than anything else had so far.

"My child, Mr Sehgal will never return to India. There are so many charges against him. Smuggling, trafficking, accessory to murder. I don't know quite how many criminal activities he and your father," she cleared her throat, "were involved in directly. But the crime syndicate they belonged to have thrown him under the bus. Our government is appealing to the UK government to have him extradited. If that happens, he will face a lifetime in prison. So, I'm sorry to say, there is no future with the Sehgal family."

A tear trickled down my face, and I wiped it away. I hadn't wept for my father; I hadn't wept at losing my home, and I wouldn't weep now. Not even when my future, that longed-for future, was being snatched away from me once again.

"Could I not return to school, Ma'am?" I whispered. "I cannot afford the fees, but I will cook and clean for you. I could be your maid. You do not have to pay me. You could use my wages as fees."

"Madhu, even if I wanted to, my hands are tied. The trustees would never allow it. The scandal hit the school as much as anyone who was associated with the Sehgals." She sat there in deep thought for a while.

"I could get you into a government school. Not here, but in Haryana. I have a friend who is a principal there. Anita Wadhwa. I'll contact her. It won't be a private education, but at least you will be able to sit your Board exams. You are a bright girl, Madhu. I know you will come out on top, no matter what."

CHAPTER 81

After my encounter with Pari, I retreated to the staff room, shaking with belated shock. How could life have thrown up a piece of the past in this way? What significance was there in this chance meeting?

Ever since my life had derailed fifteen years ago, I was always searching for patterns, for meanings in those patterns, as if to side-step any further calamities. Yet, time and again, life laughed in the face of my superstitions.

Amy walked into the room and looked at me as I stood with my hands wrapped around my body, trying to stop my trembling.

"What's happened, Madhu?!" her voice filled with concern, she moved towards me, but I backed away, still trembling. "You look like you've seen a ghost!"

A ghost from my past, I wanted to answer, but couldn't articulate anything for fear that everything, the ugliest of truths, would spill out of me.

"I think I'm coming down with something. I don't feel well." I managed to gasp out.

"Go home. Now!" Amy was suddenly my boss once again.

I capitulated, gathering up my belongings in a daze and rushing out, my stomach churning.

· · ·

At home, I unfurled the piece of paper I had shoved into my pocket hastily. Pari's phone number. I recalled her face, so filled with surprise, with pleasure even, to have seen me unexpectedly. There was no malice in her, there never had been. Then why was I filled with this powerful rage, this resentment towards everyone from my past? It wasn't their fault that my life had fallen apart. But none of them had suffered quite as much as I had. None of them had fallen quite as far as I had either. I had no way of knowing for sure, but was almost certain that their station in life was way better than mine.

The tea leaves boiled in the little pan on my gas stove as I stood there thinking. I added the milk and sugar and brought it to the boil again, making sure that the tea was the deep brown shade I preferred. After I had strained it into a small cup, I went and sat on a chair by the window with the little scrap of paper clutched in one hand.

I traced my finger on the numbers she had scribbled on the paper. I had calmed down enough now to see that what had happened was fate at work once again. The choice was mine now. Did I dare call her? Did I dare find out what had happened to everyone? Did I care? I folded the paper neatly and put it in my diary. If life had put Pari in my path, life would give me the answer on its own. I was in no hurry to make any decisions.

Later, as I cooked my *daal* in the pressure cooker, waiting for the last whistle, I remembered my years in the government school. Once again, I'd had to disguise my real self to become a part of an alien landscape. In this all-girls school, very few were truly interested in education. It was a perfunctory rite of passage before marriage or another perfunctory college education. But for me, it was better than nothing. I kept my head down and worked hard, speaking only in Hindi, and only if I was spoken to first.

Margaret Ma'am's friend, Mrs Wadhwa, had given me a small room in exchange for cooking the family meals. She was not as kind as Margaret Ma'am, but she wasn't unkind either. Early in the arrangement, she had spelled out my future for me.

"You can forget about medicine. You do not have the money for it, and regardless of the quota system, I cannot see how you will make the jump from a government school to medical school. At best, you can try nursing. That way, you will be in the field you desire, even if it is at a lower level."

Cleaning bedpans and dealing with daily abuse from patients and their families had been at a much, much lower level in the government hospital I'd landed my first job in. Not until many years later, not until I'd found myself in the private hospital I worked in now, did I ever think to question why the opportunity to become a doctor had been denied to me. Why hadn't I tried to argue against or oppose that which was thrust upon me? Had my only act of rebellion, fleeing from my family, taken every bit of courage out of me? Had my submission been my defeat?

And what of my erstwhile friends? Where had destiny taken them? Had they soared or been ground into the dust? A prickle of curiosity made me take the piece of paper out of my diary again. Maybe I would call Pari. If for nothing else than to find out whether life had played unfair with them, too.

CHAPTER 82

As the weeks had gone on, I had slowly lost the desire to call Pari. Yes, the curiosity was still there, but it ebbed and flowed like the tide. The truth was, I didn't want to know. Because then, I would have to face up to what I had become as well, how far I had fallen from the dreams I had nursed as a girl. How the only thing I nursed today were sickly people nearing the end of their lives.

When Sister Matthews called me into her office, Pari was as far from my thoughts as she had ever been.

"Madhu, sit down," she pointed to the chair in front of her. "All okay out there?" she jutted her chin out at the door.

"As okay as can be. Patient on Bed 3, Ward 2, keeps wandering off. We found her in the kitchen half an hour ago."

"What was she doing?"

"Peeling potatoes," I chuckled, "At least she's trying to help!"

"Alzheimer's?"

"Advanced. Doesn't even recognise the son anymore."

"What's she here for?"

"Had a fall. We are keeping her in for signs of concussion."

"Hmm." Amy played with the pen in her hand. "Are you still enjoying your work here?"

"Yes. It's civilised. No one has spat on me yet."

"I'm sorry. Your time at the government hospital wasn't..."

"It was an induction."

"Still, you are an excellent nurse. One of our best."

"What's this about, Amy?"

"Well," she said after a slight pause, "there's been a request. A family needs a day time nurse. The father has vascular dementia, and they are struggling to cope."

"Surely one of the junior nurses...?"

"Yes, but you see, they've asked for you. Specifically."

"Me?"

Then it dawned on me.

"Is it a Mr Rajan?"

Amy looked at me curiously.

"Yes, it is. Do you know him?"

"I used to know the daughter many years ago."

"Then you'll do it."

"No. Actually, no, I won't do it. You'll have to find someone else."

I stood up.

"Is that all? I have to get back to my rounds."

Amy looked at me, puzzled.

"You know you can talk to me, Madhu? About anything."

"I know. Thanks Amy."

While drawing blood from a patient in Ward 3, I wondered why I didn't talk to her. Amy had been a friend and confidante on many occasions. But I had never spoken to her about my past, about where I came from and where I had intended to go. All I'd ever told her about were my struggles at nursing school, my first job, and my daily irritations. It was as if the 'Before' Madhu was a completely separate entity from the 'After' Madhu.

The 'Before' Madhu had had friends, people she trusted, people she thought would be her pillars for the rest of her life. The 'Before' Madhu had been naïve enough to think she was wise to the ways of the world. The 'Before' Madhu had believed that parents always wanted the best for their children, that they would support their dreams at any cost.

The 'After' Madhu knew that trust, love, and loyalty were all conditional. When the going was good, everyone milled about you, pretending to be your friends and supporters. When it was bad, very few stood by your side.

Amy Matthews was an exceptional nurse and a decent enough friend, but I didn't want to test her beyond those parameters.

And now, when the two chapters of my life threatened to bleed into each other, I couldn't help but be afraid. In many ways, I had cut myself off from that 'Before' Madhu. That life and those dreams belonged to someone else. A girl who had ceased to exist after that fateful night.

Now, the past had come barging into the present, and refused to be ignored any longer. It was loud and demanding, insistent that I looked at it in the face. I would look at it, and I would tell it to go back to where it had come from. The fact that Pari had asked for me specifically meant that she would not let go unless I told her in no uncertain terms that I didn't want any kind of relationship with her. Whether that was as an employer and employee, or as friends.

The time had come to give her a call.

CHAPTER 83

I lived alone, out of choice. After I had paid my debt to Mrs Wadhwa, I had returned to Delhi. Having lived outside of the city for nearly six years, I found it a changed place. New flyovers had been constructed, erasing entire localities, malls had taken the place of local stores, and every household in affluent South Delhi boasted two cars and a satellite television.

An expensive city, the capital of India, a buzzing metropolis—New Delhi was still home to me. It would always be. But it also held so many memories of days gone by. Of good times and terrible times. Of days when the world had been my oyster, and days when it had shrunk to a pinprick.

My first visit had been to Margaret Ma'am. We had kept up an intermittent correspondence over the years and she welcomed me into her little flat, unchanged from the last time I had visited it, with the same warmth and concern she had displayed when I first turned up on her doorstep.

"Madhu, my girl, I am so glad to see you! Come in, come in."

Margaret Ma'am had looked older suddenly; her dark hair had taken on a salt and pepper colouring, and the lines around her eyes and mouth had deepened. She still wore the same wire-rimmed glasses, but now they had a thin silver chain that kept them on her neck at all times.

"Anita has kept me updated on how you have been doing, and I was happy to receive your letters, too. Are you well? Here, let me get some tea."

I perched on the chair, uncertain, worried that I had overstepped the mark once again by deciding to visit her.

"So," she returned from the kitchen carrying a tea set on a tray, "I have some Marie biscuits and fruit cake too. It was Christmas a few days ago, and I indulged myself. You will share some with me, won't you?"

She poured out the tea and waited for me to add milk and sugar before asking, "What brings you here, Madhu?"

"Ma'am, as you know, I was working in the government hospital in Haryana."

She nodded her head. I had told her this myself in a letter.

"I've just been offered a place at a private hospital in Jangpura, and I am moving to Delhi now."

"Do you need a place to stay?" her brow creased.

"No, actually, I have found a place quite near the hospital. They just need a reference letter, and I wondered..."

"Not a problem, dear child. Of course, I will write you one."

"Thank you. Also..." I stopped, unsure.

"Yes?" she nodded at me encouragingly.

"I brought you something." I handed her a brown paper package.

"What's this?" She took it from my hands and unwrapped it. A blue cotton *sari,* plain but for a thin gold border, fell out.

"It's for you, Ma'am. From my first salary. Just as a thank you for everything."

Her eyes filled with tears as she looked at me. Then she stood up and came towards me. Placing her hand on my head, she said, "I wish I could have done more, Madhu. If I'd had the means, I would have. But you have made me so proud. Thank you for this. I will cherish it."

I'd wondered then whether Mataji had received the Rs 2000 I had sent her as a money order, and whether she cherished that bit of my first pay cheque too.

I lived alone, out of choice, circumstance, and necessity. My one-and-a-half room and tiny kitchenette barely qualified as a flat, but it was the best I could do in the area with my salary. Perhaps a part of me had hoped back then that Mataji and Lallan would join me in Delhi, but when there was no response to my money order or letter, I realised my journey would always be a solitary one.

Yet, in a city like Delhi, a woman living alone was bound to attract suspicion and speculation. Manohar became my lover, protector, and sounding board. The owner of the local dry-cleaning company, he was a married man with teenage children. But he had enough clout in the area to ensure that I could live my life on my terms. Love wasn't a part of our arrangement, and that suited me fine.

I had no intention of tying myself to any man. Men, even loving men like my father, had done so much damage to me that I couldn't ever trust them again. Manohar knew nothing of my past, and when he probed, I deflected his questions with a finesse that I didn't know I possessed. I gave him my body in return for safety. Love wasn't a part of our arrangement, and it would never be.

CHAPTER 84

Pari sounded pleased to hear from me.

"I'm so glad you called Madhu. It's been over a month, and I had sort of given up on you."

"Can we meet?"

"I'd like to! How about lunch? Sagar Restaurant in Defence Colony? Just like old times." Her voice was warm, filled with nostalgia.

I flinched reflexively, recalling the many lunches we had consumed together, the four of us, gobbling down the *idlis*, *vadas* and *dosas* with the careless certitude of a healthy, youthful metabolism.

"Yes, that's fine. What time?"

When I had hung up, I wondered what Pari made of my deliberate coolness, and whether she would still try to breach my defences.

"It has to be you, Madhu," she said as she looked at me intently. Her *dosa* sat untouched on the plate in front of her. "Amma knows and trusts you, and she will leave Appa in your care happily. Any other nurse will have to earn that trust, and sometimes, I think there may not be enough time for that."

"What do you mean?" I bit into my *rava masala dosa*, unmoved. I had seen and heard worse sob stories, and my mind was already made up.

"Amma is older and much frailer now. I worry for her. She does every little thing for him, and it's exhausting. I try to help when I'm home, but the bulk of it has always been managed by her. The last fall that Appa had, she picked him up, but strained her shoulder in the process. Never said a word to me, not until after Appa had been discharged. Her body can't take it anymore. She needs help. We need help."

I closed my eyes momentarily, letting the flavours explode upon my tongue.

"Aunty's *dosas* were always so good," I said to Pari, remembering the occasional meals I'd accompanied Samira on. "These aren't a patch on hers."

"Yes," Pari smiled sadly, "Amma doesn't really make *dosas* any more. She doesn't have the time to prepare the *maav* the old-fashioned way and doesn't believe in using the mixie. We stick to rice at home."

"Hmm." I chewed silently, not giving my thoughts away. "And what about the caste issue?"

"What do you mean?"

"You are brahmins and I... am not. Having someone like me living under your roof, won't that bother Aunty?"

Pari bit her lip, then reached out and put her hand over mine.

"I have never cared about caste, you know that! I didn't tell Amma because, well, she was old-fashioned that way. But Madhu, she knows you and I think, today, even if I were to tell her, it wouldn't matter a jot. Times have changed, she has changed. People are people, and the caste they are born into doesn't determine their character or their destiny."

Something about the vehemence she said this with touched me, but I kept my expression impassive.

"Madhu, I really didn't mean to burden you with all this, but I thought perhaps you could see why I was insistent on having you." She finally broke off a piece of her *dosa* and dipped it in the *sambhar*. "If you don't want to do it, I understand. But I'd like you to recommend someone instead. Someone you trust."

We sat in silence as I tried to formulate an answer. Seeing Pari now, after all these years, had churned up all kinds of emotions in me. If I set aside my anger and resentment for a moment, underneath it lingered a longing to return to that time. A time when the only problem we faced was an unexpected test on a Monday morning.

"Are you in touch with any of the other... umm... girls?"

"From school?"

"Yes."

"Some from my batch. I mean, after you left. But mostly, I am in touch with the teachers."

She grinned at my startled expression.

"I am teaching in our old school. Economics. Can you believe it?"

I swallowed, slowly.

"Did Margaret Ma'am tell you about me?"

"Margaret Ma'am? No. Why?"

She looked confused, and I exhaled, relieved.

"Although, I have to say Madhu, that woman is an angel. She has been so supportive through everything. Lately, I've had to take a lot of leave for Appa, and she has been like a rock..."

As she spoke, I nodded in recognition. Yes, Margaret Ma'am had been my pillar too, and the fact that she hadn't betrayed my situation to anyone increased my respect for her a thousandfold.

"What would the salary be?" I surprised myself by asking the question.

She looked at me carefully before answering.

"You know we're not rich, Madhu, but I'd still pay you more than you're making at the hospital."

"Fine," I said, "I'll do it."

Maybe invoking Margaret Ma'am's name had worked as a charm, but there was a bigger pattern to these seemingly disconnected elements of our lives; a pattern that I could not discern at this present moment, but one that I could not ignore either.

This time, submitting to my fate didn't feel like failure, it felt like acceptance.

PART IV

Pari

CHAPTER 85

In a life filled with losses, the last one came as a relief.

I lost Appa in my forties. It was strange that despite his strokes, despite his dementia, he outlasted Amma for seven years. Amma, who was younger, more robust, and had no visible health issues, went to bed one night and simply didn't wake up the next morning. Maybe she died of exhaustion, but it was more likely that the heart that gave up on her had already been broken several years ago when Sri had died, and just refused to mend in the years that followed.

At any rate, Appa, befuddled and disorientated, would confuse me for Amma and Madhu for me, all the time. We went along with it, as it made him less upset if he believed that his family was still around him. Once or twice, he even asked where Sri was, and then, as if some distant memory had just resurfaced, he would clap his hand over his mouth and shake his head, his eyes filling with tears.

In the end, with his health failing dramatically in the last three months of his life, it became clear that caring for him was beyond Madhu's capabilities, and so we admitted him to the hospital. The last month was a struggle. His body started shutting down. He refused food, slipping in and out of consciousness, his breath becoming an ominous rattle in his chest. The coldness of his hands and feet and the blueness of his lips told us that his time was near. I prayed for his release daily, unable to watch my dear Appa suffering in this manner.

He died while holding my hand and calling out, "Hema!" I hoped that Appa, Amma and Sri were together now.

It would have been much harder to cope had Madhu not become the sister I never had. In the last eight years, our relationship had grown beyond that of an employer and employee. Not that I had ever considered her my employee. But she had been brittle and distant at first, eager to establish boundaries, refusing to speak of the past, and putting up so many walls that I wondered who she had become.

Yet, as a nurse, she was wonderful. As I had predicted, Amma was able to hand over the reins to Madhu, saying softly, wonderingly, "This slight girl has so much strength, so much compassion." As for Appa, his eyes would light up every time she teased him lightly, changing and medicating him without his noticing, and keeping up a constant stream of good-natured chatter whilst never allowing his dignity to slip.

In time, she opened up to me. We spoke haltingly of our childhood traumas, of our losses and how they had come to define us; of thwarted ambitions and shattered dreams. We were not that unlike Madhu and I. At the centre of our tragedies, one name remained unspoken: Samira Sehgal.

In the days that followed Appa's death and cremation, Angad and I had to stay home and pray for his departed soul. Madhu brought us food daily, as I wasn't allowed to cook at home. Friends, colleagues and relatives visited to condole with us, telling me many stories of Appa's youth, of his kindness and dedication to work. "A true gentleman," they said, and we nodded in agreement. Appa had never been less than a gentleman his entire life.

Angad, being his proxy son, had to take the ashes to Kashi, just like Amma's and Sri's had been taken. After one's death, an immersion of their ashes into the river Ganga was about setting their soul free of all its earthly bonds. But in the days prior, we were free to sit and mourn the passing of another loved one.

"Look at us, Pari," Angad had said into the fifth day of mourning, "just the two of us left here, while they are all having a party up there, somewhere!"

I chuckled alongside.

"Knowing Sri, there will be a bit of head-banging going on upstairs!"

"Aunty will be furious," Angad grinned.

"Telling him to turn the volume down..."

"But he won't be listening!"

"He never did."

We laughed through our tears.

"What are you both talking about?"

Madhu joined us, handing us a plate of *kadhi-chawal* each. She was a splendid cook, and I was deeply grateful that she had taken on the onus of feeding us at a time like this when we weren't allowed to light the stove in the house. The alternative would have been greasy restaurant food from the nearest *Udipi* place.

"Old times. Of Sri."

She sat with us, in silence at first, letting us reminisce, then slowly adding her own droll observations to the banter.

I looked at the two of them—Angad and Madhu—two people dearest to me in the whole wide world, and prayed that God would keep them safe and in His grace.

CHAPTER 86

"Have you heard?" Bela asked, looking up from the sheet she had been correcting. It was mid-April and exams were in full swing. The tension in the air was palpable. Students walked around looking stressed, the teachers even more so. We couldn't wait for school to break up for the holidays.

"Heard what?"

"The new principal is some man."

Margaret Ma'am had decided that 2011 was the year she was finally taking her bow. After having served as principal for thirty-seven years, hers were large boots to fill. A few of the teachers had half-heartedly applied for the position, but everyone knew the trustees were keen to bring in someone new and from the outside to the job.

"Well, I guess that could be good."

"Good? In what way?" Bela was annoyed. She had hoped it would be someone she knew in the position; someone who was as soft as Margaret Ma'am had been, someone who would turn a blind eye to her many absences and late entrances. Then again, I had benefited from Margaret Ma'am's leniency too, although I'd never abused it.

"I mean, it's a new chapter, isn't it? A new person, a man, might control the wayward kids a lot better." It felt like a betrayal saying this, but lately, with drugs, alcohol and social media infiltrating schools, Margaret Ma'am's softness had often been mistaken for weakness. A firmer hand was needed. Maybe this man could provide it.

"Bah! I saw him come in. He looks barely older than the Class 12 boys."

"He can't be that young, Bela."

"You'll see," she frowned, then went back to correcting the sheet.

I did see, and a lot sooner than I had expected. After the fifth period, I was called to Margaret Ma'am's office.

"Pari, come in," she smiled, indicating that I should take the seat across from the suited man who sat opposite her.

"This is our senior economics teacher, Pari Rajan. She used to be a student of mine too. If anyone knows this school better than me, it's her. And Pari, this is Gautam Upadhyay, who will take over from me next term."

He held out his hand to shake mine, while I folded mine into a *namaste*. It was true that he appeared barely thirty years old, although I conjectured that he was at least five years older than that. With his caramel skin, dark wavy hair and crooked smile, he looked more like a television actor than a principal-in-waiting of a large, well-established school. I realised I was staring and cleared my throat to say something, just as he spoke at the same time.

"Do you t...?"

"Will you sh...?"

We both stopped at the same time, and I flushed deeply. What was wrong with me?

Margaret Ma'am poured a cup of tea and handed it to me.

"I think Gautam would like you to show him around, Pari," she said, taking a sip out of her cup. "If you don't mind."

I shrugged to hide my embarrassment. "I don't, but I have a class in twenty minutes."

"I'll take over. It's just a filler class, anyway. Students will be self-studying. The exams are on," she said by way of explanation to him.

He nodded, his eyes still on me.

"When would you like to go?" I asked, flustered.

"Now is as good a time as any."

As I led him from Margaret Ma'am's office out into the hallway, he said, "What were you about to ask me?"

"Sorry?"

"When I interrupted you."

"Oh. I just wondered what subject you taught?"

"English. I teach English," he said, smiling at me. He was just a little shorter than me, and it seemed odd to be looking down at him as we spoke. I was seized by a sudden, unaccountable urge to kiss him, and I turned my head away before he could read my expression.

For the rest of the tour, I assumed a professional and detached air. Nothing that would reveal the chaos of feelings inside me. Mr Gautam Upadhyay wasn't the first man I had ever been attracted to, but he was going to be my boss. For all I knew, he could be married. No wedding ring, though. I cast him a sidelong glance. He was so well-groomed. From his navy pinstripe suit and red tie, the perfectly manicured nails to his gelled hair, he was just a little too perfectly put together. I'd heard about men like him. Men who took more pride in their appearance than even women did, although I had never met one before. Was he a metrosexual?

Then again, he could be something else entirely. He could be one of those men who preferred his own sex over the opposite one. I looked at his shoes that shone like mirrors and at the silver cufflinks glinting at his wrists. I breathed in the subtle, warm, woody fragrance he was encased in. He was perfect, impossibly perfect, and that set all my alarm bells ringing. The only Indian men I had seen who were that polished were never the ones interested in women.

He smiled at something I'd said, and my heart beat unevenly. Why were the good ones either taken or gay?

CHAPTER 87

Madhu dropped in every Friday. Now that Appa was not with us, I missed seeing her face daily, and had insisted that we set up a weekly routine. Some Fridays she would bring food, some Fridays I would cook Maggi noodles or order in some food. Tonight we had settled on our favourite Chinese food delivery restaurant again.

"Vegetable almonds?" I looked at her as I placed the order over the phone. I don't know why I did, because our order hadn't changed in all the weeks we'd been doing this, but it didn't hurt to ask.

She nodded and said, "Also, *Gobi* Manchurian, like the last time. That was tasty!"

She had already kicked her shoes off and tucked her feet under her. She looked like a little girl—prim, pretty and petite. Sometimes I felt like a lumbering giant next to her.

"Beer?" I offered, and she declined as usual. Madhu wasn't a big drinker, but could be partial to a nice bottle of wine.

Amma would have been appalled to find that I had developed a taste for alcohol, but beer hardly qualified, and one bottle at the end of a tough week was my little treat for myself. I had so few indulgences in my life, anyway.

"How was school?"

"Busy. The last exam was today, and you should have seen them running out of the classrooms afterwards. It was like they were being let out of prison!"

"Ah, to be young and carefree again." Madhu smiled.

"I tell you, though, youth is wasted on the young. They can't wait to grow up, and I want to tell them to slow down and savour these years. But will they listen?"

"Pari, I don't think we would have either, at their age." She shrugged, then looked at me. "And what about you? What are you going to do over the holidays?"

"Well, I thought of going to Mumbai to stay with Angad and family..."

Madhu's eyes widened. This was the first I'd spoken of it, and I carried on hurriedly.

"No, then I changed my mind. They are shifting to Delhi in a month's time anyway, so why bother them right now when they are in the midst of packing their lives up?"

"I didn't know they were shifting..." Madhu said, her eyebrows arching in surprise.

"Angad has been tasked with opening a branch here now. His company was very impressed with what he did in Mumbai, even though he didn't think he was capable of it. He's a lot smarter than he gives himself credit for."

"True," Madhu acknowledged, then paused before saying, "Well, that's nice. At least you'll have family close by again." She sipped on the *nimbu paani* I'd brought her. I wanted to say to her that just because I had family near didn't mean that I would abandon her or our friendship. She was far too precious for that. But before I could say anything, she asked, "Are you okay with Roma now?"

I frowned as I replied, "Never not been okay, Madhu. She's the one who blows hot and cold all the time."

"What was the last tiff about?"

"It wasn't a tiff exactly, but she spotted the Swarovski bracelet Angad had sent me for my birthday and asked me about it. I was so taken aback that I just blurted the truth out. After that, she didn't speak to me for months."

"Jealous?"

"Of what? Angad gives her everything, but it's still not enough."

"You know, I never really liked her when we were in school. There was just something shifty about her."

"Funny you say that. Samira used to say the same thing..." My voice trailed off. In all the years we had spent time with one another, we had always skirted the topic of Samira. Yet, today, her name had rolled off my tongue with a strange ease. Had I finally started to forgive her?

The doorbell rang just then, and I went to answer it, paying for the food and tipping the delivery boy.

As we ate and chatted, I marvelled at how some force had brought Madhu back into my life. I was immensely grateful for her and our bond, and couldn't help but say, "Madhu, never let any misunderstanding come between us, will you?"

"Why do you say that, Pari?"

"Dunno. I think back to all those years we spent together in school, when I was better friends with Samira and Roma, when I didn't really bother to get to know you properly, and I feel like kicking myself! Look at how those friendships turned out, and you, out of that whole group, have been the only one who has stuck it out with me."

"Not out of choice! You practically corralled me into working for you," she laughed, throwing a pea at me.

I laughed back, knowing that neither of us would have wanted it any differently. We were more than friends to each other now. We were family.

CHAPTER 88

"I wanted a house in Vasant Vihar, but this was all they could find for us," Roma sniffed.

"Defence Colony isn't too bad. Remember the library we used to visit? And Colonel Kababz, where you girls would get your *seekh kebabs* from? It's all just round the corner from you now."

"Hmm." Roma wasn't convinced, and for the umpteenth time I wondered how someone who had lived in a simple flat in an upper middle-class area like Saket had acquired such airs and graces. Had Angad's success at work really inflated her ego beyond proportion, or had she always been this way and I had never seen it?

"What about the children? Will you send them to our school?"

"What? Of course not! They will go to the American Embassy School. They've always had an international education, and I intend to keep it that way."

I sighed internally. There was no arguing with Roma. She always got her way, and although the children were very well-mannered, I felt no closeness to my nieces and nephew. On their part, they were as remote as strangers, displaying little warmth or affection towards me.

"How are Uncle and Aunty doing?" I asked, changing the topic.

"Maa and Baba are in America now, with Ria." Her answer was clipped, inviting no further inquiry. But I pushed on, regardless.

"On holiday?"

"Oh no. They shifted there a few years after I came back to India."

"Really? Well, that's nice for them. At least they are with one of you, no?"

"Yes, with their favourite daughter." Her nostrils flared as she said this.

"That's not true, Roma. I'm sure they love you both equally."

"Really? How would you know?" She stood up and glared down at me as if I had committed a crime of some sort. Then, just as suddenly, her mood changed. "What do you think of this colour on me? I bought it today from the Ritu Kumar boutique."

She held up a deep fuchsia kurta, and I had to admit the colour looked lovely on her.

Appeased, she twirled in front of the mirror. I couldn't help but notice how much more weight she had put on in the last decade. But she carried it well, and as long as it didn't bother her, who was I to say anything?

"You really should wear brighter colours, Pari. All these earthy tones are fine in some art movie but are really depressing in reality."

I smiled at her, letting it pass. Roma's little jibes had lost their potency over the years.

"So, how's school?"

It had taken her over an hour to ask me how I was doing. Then again, why did that surprise me? Roma's self-preoccupation was just another aspect of her personality I had to get myself used to all over again.

"Yes, it's fine. Margaret Ma'am's retired. A man has taken over her position."

When she raised her eyebrows speculatively, I could tell she wanted to know whether I was interested in this man, whether he was a prospect for little old spinster me. I don't know what made me say, "He's gay."

"He's what?"

"You know. He prefers men."

She grimaced. "I know what gay means! I'm just shocked that he got appointed, that's all. But I guess, these days, anything goes. Glad my kids will be going to a more conventional school." She dropped into the chair.

"There's nothing wrong with being gay, Roma." Her flippancy annoyed me.

"If you say so! I'm pretty certain I wouldn't want my children exposed to that sort of thing."

"That sort of thing? Same-sex sexual behaviour has been observed in the animal kingdom too, so who are we to pass judgement on what's normal and what's not?"

"What's going on?" Angad walked in just then.

"Pari is defending some homo at school."

"What?"

"Nothing," I muttered, "It's nothing."

Angad shot me a quick look before bending down to give Roma a kiss on her cheek.

"Where are the kids?"

She shrugged. "In their rooms, on their computers, talking to their friends."

Angad turned to me.

"Pari, you're staying for dinner, right?"

I glanced at Roma, who was filing her nails now.

"Umm..."

"I haven't cooked anything," she said, without looking up.

"It's okay. We'll order in," Angad said, throwing me an apologetic look. "It'll take a while to settle into the new house, anyway."

"And I hope we find a maid soon. You can't expect me to do everything, Angad."

I wondered what exactly she did do, and I felt desperately sorry for my cousin brother. I'd always known that Roma was a difficult wife, but never known the extent of the problem. Now that they lived in the same city as me, no doubt I'd discover how deep the rot ran.

CHAPTER 89

"I have to admit, you were right." Bela said, popping a grape into her mouth.

"About what?" I bit into my cucumber sandwich. We were sitting in our favourite corner in the cafeteria eating lunch.

"Mr Upadhyay."

"Right in what way?" I racked my brain, wondering if I'd let something slip. Aside from Roma, surely I'd kept my suspicions about his sexuality to myself?

"Things have improved with the discipline in the higher classes. There's just something about him that inspires awe."

"Must be those perfectly cut suits he wears," I grinned.

She grinned back, then offered me some grapes. I took a small bunch and set it to one side, indicating that I was still working on my sandwich.

"Someone said he studied at Doon school," she lowered her voice, "Very posh! I can believe it, with that cut-glass accent of his. Not married, either. Single, handsome and so very eligible. Lavanya has set her sights on him." She mimicked holding a rifle in her hands and taking aim.

Lavanya was the new dance teacher. Young and pretty, albeit not the smartest cookie. He would appeal to someone like her. He appealed to almost all women on the right side of sixty.

"Well, good luck to her," I shrugged dismissively. She was bound to find out that she was barking up the wrong tree soon enough.

"What about you, Pari?"

"What about me?" I looked up at her in surprise.

"Don't you want to settle down?"

I shut the lid of my tiffin box, then opened up a packet of biscuits to offer her one. Our teas were already forming a film of cream on them.

"Bela, I'm forty. Not exactly as eligible as Mr Upadhyay."

"Why not? You're tall, slim and attractive. Why are you selling yourself short?"

"I'm not, but you know, I made peace with being single quite some time ago."

"Look, your mum and dad are gone now. You have no other responsibilities. Maybe it is time to think about finding a life partner?"

"Are you suggesting I give Lavanya some competition in that department?" I chuckled inwardly at the thought.

"No, I didn't mean Mr Upadhyay. He's too young for you, but..."

"Ouch!" I made a big show of looking pained. "One minute you say I'm still young, and the next..."

"Hush now! I was going to suggest you meet my *bua*'s son. Recently divorced, but he's a really nice man. He's in his fifties, and a bit on the fatter side, but really, I think you could get along."

I listened politely, half-tuning her out. Nothing about this man she was describing appealed to me. A picture of Gautam Upadhyay floated into my mind and I dismissed it just as quickly. There was no point in even thinking about something as fruitless as that, and it was unfair to compare Bela's cousin to him, too. But this question of 'settling down' hounded me in one manner or another, as if I was incomplete on my own; a piece of a puzzle that could not be slotted anywhere.

Years ago, when I had asked Madhu why she didn't settle down with someone, she had shocked me with her brutal answer, "Pari, men are only good for two things—fixing broken things and fucking. I have someone who does both for me."

I had neither, and there were times I wondered what it would have been like to have someone in my life for companionship, love, a bit of sex even. Yet the thought of being forced into a relationship for the sake of it made my stomach turn.

"So, should I set up a meeting?"

"Uh, no. Thanks Bela, I just don't think I'm ready to settle down yet."

"Then when? You don't want to go back unpackaged, do you?"

I flushed a deep red then. Did everyone know I had never been with a man, or was this just Bela's way of prodding a reaction out of me?

"I need to go."

"Okay no, wait. Please. That was not a nice thing to say. I'm sorry. All I'm saying is, why don't you give Inder a chance?"

I sat down again. This entire conversation was wearisome, but I knew Bela wouldn't let it rest until I had met this man.

"Fine. I'll meet him, but no promises, okay? If I don't like him, I will not waste my time or his. Why did he get divorced, anyway?"

"You can ask him yourself, but I'm happy you've agreed. I've told him so much about you, Pari. He loved your name, by the way. Said it was so unusual. He asked me if you turned into a fairy in moonlight," she simpered, obviously finding his comment cute.

I didn't, so I retorted acerbically, "You should tell him I turn into a werewolf in moonlight. I actually howl at the full moon."

"Do you?" Mr Upadhyay stood behind me, a quizzical look on his face.

I stood up, muttered something unintelligible, and fled the scene. How much had he heard? And did he think I was completely bonkers?

CHAPTER 90

For some people, love happened all of a sudden. They fell into it, ready, willing, and able. For others, it crept up on them and wrapped itself like a boa constrictor around their heart, squeezing hard, and forcing them to acknowledge the truth of their state. And then, there were people like me. The idea of love—nebulous and hazy—seemed wonderful. Yet, if it were handed to me, I would drop it like a hot potato, not knowing what to do with it, whether it had come to me by accident, or whether it really belonged elsewhere like a letter posted in haste to an incorrect address.

Meeting Inder was every bit as disastrous as I had imagined it would be. Not that Bela had been disingenuous while describing him, but as a relative, she clearly viewed him through rose-tinted glasses. Although he wasn't physically unattractive, it was his personality that repelled me more than any obvious corporeal shortcomings. Pompous, entitled, secure in his masculine superiority, he took my smiles and silences as a sign that I was deeply impressed by him. Why wouldn't I be? As a single woman, I should have been ready to grab the hand of any man who extended it in my direction. Even if the only bit of interest he showed was in the strands of grey that had slowly started emerging in my hair.

"Don't you want to dye it?" he asked, belching loudly after the *paneer makhani* he had demolished.

"Sorry?" his question caught me by surprise. I had been wondering how soon I could make my excuses and leave.

"Your hair. Why don't you dye it? Makes you look older."

At that moment, my aversion solidified into dislike.

"I like it this way."

"There are many good hair dyes in the market. I use L'Oreal myself. My ex-wife introduced me to it. Gives a very natural tint to the hair."

That's when I figured that he truly believed he was helping. He couldn't understand why a woman, especially a woman in my situation, wouldn't want to hold on to her youth. Softening my tone somewhat, I asked, "Speaking of your ex-wife, why did you divorce?"

He took a gulp of his water, swished around in his mouth to catch the loose particles of food in his teeth, then swallowed. I could barely look at him.

"She said she'd outgrown our marriage and wanted to find herself." He looked sad as he said this, using the nail on his pinky finger to extract a bit of coriander stuck between his molars.

"Sorry?" I felt like a parrot, saying 'sorry' repeatedly. My stomach churned with disgust. How desperate did Bela think I was?

"Some Bollywood actress did it, and now it's become a fashion for married women to go looking for themselves outside of marriage."

"I've never heard of this."

"But you're not married, are you?" He rolled up the bit of coriander between his fingers and flicked it to the floor.

I nodded and flinched. He had a point. He was also a pig.

"She said she didn't love me anymore, that I wasn't the man she had married; that I was old, fat, and ugly. She wanted other things in life."

"Did you have any children?" I asked then, still trying to find something redeeming in the man.

"Two boys. They live with their mother. I see them every weekend."

"I see."

"I could take you to meet them." He seemed eager then, almost too eager.

All his pomposity had fallen away to reveal the desperation beneath. This was a sad and lonely man, with a sad and lonely life, and although I didn't doubt his version of the events, I knew his wife would probably have an entirely different take on the breakup. At any rate, my instincts told me to back away quickly. I had no wish to partake in this drama.

The following week, as I explained to Bela that Inder and I were really not compatible, my eyes followed a distant figure in a dark navy suit crossing the courtyard towards his office.

Bela's eyes followed my glance.

"I see," she said, softly.

"Pardon?"

"No, I really do see now. I wish you hadn't wasted Inder's time if your interest lay elsewhere."

I couldn't understand her pique.

"I can tell you though," she carried on, "there's absolutely no point in trying. Lavanya has given up on him. He's very polite but completely disinterested. She thinks he has a girlfriend tucked away somewhere."

With that final salvo delivered, she walked away from me. I had known Bela long enough to understand that her annoyance with me would be short-lived. When she came around, she would realise what a poor match I really was for someone like Inder, who needed a more conventional wife; someone who would overlook his shortcomings, simply happy to find a man who could provide for her.

What I couldn't understand was why my heart had fluttered the way it did when she had assumed that Gautam was the reason I had turned Inder down. Was he? And what shade of foolish was I to fall for a man like him?

CHAPTER 91

"Come in, Miss Rajan. Shut the door behind you, please." Gautam Upadhyay had been in the principal's position for forty-five days when he called me to his office for a meeting. He was behind his desk, in his usual uniform of a navy suit and red tie, looking as devastatingly handsome as the day I had first set eyes on him.

"Would you like a cup of tea?"

I muttered a quick yes, noting that Margaret Ma'am's lovely china had been replaced by rugged, grey-and-black mugs of strange shapes and angular arms.

"Do you like them?" he asked, noting my interest.

"They are unusual," I said, politely.

"An Assamese potter who specialises in making unconventional shapes."

"I see." I was still confused about the summons. We had only just had a staff meeting a few days ago, so what was this about?

"So," he said, smiling as though he had read my mind, "You're wondering what this is about."

He sat across from me at the same desk that Margaret Ma'am had sat at for all the years I had known her. In the past month and a half, he had already made subtle changes to the decor. The sign I had looked at for comfort and guidance, the one that said "More things are wrought by prayer than the world dreams of" had been replaced by a picture of two hairy dogs. The desk had been cleared of all the usual clutter, and a leather folder and granite pen holder were the only items on it. The paisley curtains had been replaced by black-and-white blinds. In short, the room had taken on the masculine and tasteful energy of its newest inhabitant.

"I've been talking to the trustees, and we've decided that Miss D'Souza never really got a proper send-off."

It was odd to hear Margaret Ma'am referred to by her last name.

"We had a staff party for her," I supplied, knowing that even at that moment, it hadn't felt enough.

"Right! Yes, of course you did. But there are staff and students from the past who never got to say a goodbye to her."

"What did you have in mind?" I was intrigued.

"A large farewell-cum-alumni-meeting at the end of September, where we could felicitate her for the number of years she served at the school."

I looked at his earnest face and wondered if he knew just what a colossal task that would be.

"Thirty-seven years' worth of students and teachers. How would we even track them all down?"

"There is a database here that has the details of everyone who stayed in touch with the school over the years, and the students that the school kept a track of. It's a start. We could also put the word out on social media."

I nodded, warming to the idea. If the trustees had agreed to the expense of it, I was more than happy to go along. Margaret Ma'am deserved far more recognition than the silver tea set and the silk *sari* we had presented her with at the party.

"What about Margaret Ma'am? Is she okay with it?"

"That's where I need your help, Pari. May I call you Pari?"

"Umm, yes. Sure."

My name sounded different when he said it. It sounded sweeter and more exotic. I wanted him to keep saying it, over and over. Then I pinched myself to disperse the dream and concentrate on what he was saying.

"We want it to be a surprise, so you'll have to bring her in on the day with some kind of excuse. Do you think you could manage that?"

"Yes, I suppose I could." I paused for a beat, then smiled at him warmly. "What a kind thing to do! Thank you."

His eyes crinkled at the corners as he smiled back.

"We come from a long line of educators. My mother was given such a wonderful send off from her school, and I just felt that anyone who has devoted so many years to a school should be recognised and celebrated. Don't you think?"

"Absolutely! Also, maybe, we can get a few students to make some videos about what Margaret Ma'am meant to them, what impact she had on their lives, etcetera."

"That's a great idea! Why don't you liaise with the Alumni Association on this? I'm so glad you're on board, Pari. It makes my job that much easier."

Just for a moment then, I thought I glimpsed something beyond the warmth. A flicker of attraction, an intensity with which his eyes probed mine to ask an unspoken question. Discomfited, I lowered my gaze. Later, I wondered if I had just made that moment up. Whether I had conflated fantasy with reality. And if on the slightest chance that I hadn't, what could it possibly mean?

Samira

CHAPTER 92

Life had led me down many strange alleyways, some blind, others not so, and I had learned over the course of the years that resistance was futile. So, I succumbed and allowed myself to go wherever life flowed, hoping that in time, my purpose and direction would be revealed to me.

Returning home from Syria, as I jotted notes on my laptop, I wondered what Christine would make of the story. She would change things for sure, adding enough of her trademark punchlines to keep the audience riveted, but allowing my empathy and compassion for my subjects to seep through. The mentor and mentee had amalgamated into an indomitable force. A force no-one, least of all I had foreseen.

For just a moment, I allowed myself to doze, then woke up with a start. My head was too filled with images of the violent clashes I'd witnessed between pro-and anti-Assadists. The Arab Spring of protest had arrived in Syria. It wasn't my first rodeo, but it still had the ability to chill me to my core. What power and ambition, religion and politics did to mankind was the stuff nightmares were made of. No wonder I slept so little these days.

Strangely, though, the more I found myself in these dangerous and life-threatening situations, the calmer I felt; as if I was sitting in the eye of the storm. Years of anxiety fell away like sloughed off dead skin. I couldn't remember the last time I'd had a panic attack.

At Heathrow, I waited in the queue at immigration. Sometimes, the immigration officers questioned me longer than others, trying to understand why I had travelled to these red-zone countries. That was, until someone put two and two together, recognising the dusty, weary traveller as the wandering reporter from television. I never begrudged them their questioning. I knew they were doing their jobs, just as I was doing mine.

Soon after our divorce, Mark had said to me that I seemed to have a "death wish". He had mocked my assertions of wanting a quiet life, saying that, in fact, the opposite was true. Christine had told me to ignore it. She'd told me that these were the dying gasps of a marriage that had self-combusted years ago. She herself remained happily divorced.

Christine. My boss, my inspiration. The one woman whose praise I craved like none other. Leena once phoned me out of the blue, asking what had changed; why I had given up my daytime show to do real time reporting in all these strife-torn, war ravaged regions of the world. All I could say was that it felt right. It felt truer than anything ever before. I didn't tell her that amid all that chaos and mayhem; I felt myself come alive again.

Now back at home, I turned on the lights and then put the kettle on. The milk had a rancid odour, so I poured it down the drain and made myself a black coffee. It was late, and I was too tired to edit, but I played the footage to myself once again.

Men shouting, fists raised, tempers running high, and a stampede in the distance; someone spitting before making a threatening gesture at us, lots of jostling where we lost focus for a bit. Then, a man screaming into the camera, flecks of spittle landing on the lens. I shut the laptop and sighed. This would take a lot of work, and I wasn't in the mood right now.

I ran the shower and stood under it, washing the grime of the last few weeks away.

Papa's last words on his deathbed came back to me unbidden. "I'm going to meet your Mama now," he had whispered unmindful of Anya, his wife of twelve years who stood next to me.

I had smiled through my tears, and said, "Say hi from me."

He had never felt the need to apologise to anyone. Displayed no guilt or remorse. It was as though he had done nothing wrong, never been culpable, never destroyed so many lives with his thoughtlessness and his selfishness. I supposed I wasn't that dissimilar to him. I hadn't even said sorry to Mark for the failure of our marriage.

Ewa, the cleaner, had put all my post in a neat little pile on the side table. I went through it, separating the bills from the junk mail, looking for something, anything that would show me I hadn't been forgotten entirely by the world. There was nothing there. Sam Shaw, the reporter, had plenty of fan mail. Samira Sehgal had no one who wrote to her.

I wondered how Mark and his new wife were doing. The last I'd heard, she was pregnant. Maybe I'd see them at Christmas. After all, ours was a very civilised set up. Ex-wife and current wife didn't just tolerate each other, we actually liked one another.

Perhaps the fact that I could still stay friends with my ex was symptomatic of what had been wrong in our marriage all along: I had never really loved Mark.

CHAPTER 93

"You need a holiday now," Christine said, brooking no argument.

"But..."

"No buts! You've been on the go for the last eight months. You'll burn out at this rate." She took me out to the smoking shelter and lit up her cigarette, offering me one out of habit. I shook my head as usual.

Christine's two-packs-a-day had given her a model's chic figure and the unmistakable gravelly voice most of the world recognised. Her perfume was an amalgamation of roses and tobacco. I often thought of her on those terms, too. You didn't see the softness unless you had made it past the steel.

"It's good footage. It's very, very good. But mark my words, it's going to get worse there, and I'll probably need you to go back again." She blew a smoke ring, squinting her eyes at the sun.

"I think so too. Assad is adamant that the insurgents are being funded by outside forces. The crackdown has been brutal, and there are deserters from his own army forming an opposition on the ground."

"Yes." she flicked some ash off the railing then looked at me, her gaze penetrating. "Aidan said that you barely slept there."

"I couldn't. What if we missed something important?"

"Sam, listen to me. I need you to take care of yourself, to conserve your strength for when you'll need it again. Okay?"

"I understand. But all I need is a couple of good nights' sleep in my own bed and I'll be right as rain."

"You may think that's all you need, but I'll tell you what I need. I need you to look good and feel good. Remember, it's your pretty face that got us all the ratings to begin with."

"Are you saying that's all I bring to the table?"

"Far from it, and you know that. I wouldn't have shamed you into leaving that stupid afternoon show otherwise. But let's face facts. No one wants to see an old warhorse like me on the screen, when a beautiful young woman..." she raised her hand to ward off my protests, "a beautiful, young, intelligent woman is risking her life to show them the truth."

She took a drag on her cigarette.

"Look at yourself in the mirror. You are gaunt and exhausted, and very far from what I need you to be. So, take that break! Go visit family or friends, or go on a solo holiday and make love to a stranger. Whatever it takes to put that bloom back in your cheeks."

I chewed on my lip. I didn't want a holiday. Where would I go? What friends? Which family?

"When will it be broadcast?" I asked, hoping I could find a way to stall her determined mission to pack me off on vacation.

"Friday, most likely. I'll do the voice-over, interspersed with your live footage. Usual format. Stick around till then, just in case I need to clarify anything."

"Sure."

I went back into the office and headed straight to the women's restroom. Fortunately, it was still quiet. I examined my reflection in the mirror. It was true that I had lost a bit of weight. The circles under my eyes were darker than usual, and my skin looked grey under the harsh lights in here, but I didn't look like a dog's dinner. Not yet, anyway.

"Hey Sam!" Cathy, the new accounts executive, walked in just then. "I heard you were back from Syria. How did it go?"

"Oh, you know..." I shrugged, "it wasn't pretty. How are you enjoying the job?"

"I'm loving it!" she beamed, before heading into a cubicle. I could have left then, but I lingered, still looking at my face in the mirror. There was no denying the contrast between my face and Cathy's. She was the picture of health with her pink cheeks, twinkly eyes and bouncy blonde hair. I, on the other hand, looked like death warmed up.

Cathy emerged from the toilet, smiled at me and, as she washed her hands, said, "Say, I have two tickets for an exhibition on Saturday. Fancy coming?"

My knee-jerk response would have been to say no, but I took a moment to consider my position. With no social life, very few friends, and my utter devotion to work, I had isolated myself completely. How could it hurt to venture out once again?

"What kind of exhibition?"

"Paintings. It's a small gallery in Shoreditch and I know the curator."

"That sounds nice. Yes, I'd love to come."

"Great! I'll email you the details. Maybe we can grab some dinner afterwards?"

"Why not?" It was impossible not to get swept up by her enthusiasm. I couldn't remember a time in my life when I had ever been filled with the sort of *joie de vivre* Cathy displayed. Maybe some people were destined never to derive joy from their lives. Maybe I was one of them.

CHAPTER 94

Years ago, I'd had a membership to the Victoria & Albert Museum. In those days, Mark and I would walk in to see the latest exhibition. From exotic jewels to beautifully imagined clothes to sculptures old and new, we had inhaled art in all its avatars. Then, as our marriage splintered and work became my passion, all such interests fell away. I let my membership lapse along with my marriage.

In coming to this exhibition, I felt like a dormant part of me was waking up. A part that had loved art; loved colour and creativity. And here I was, surrounded by it.

I stood in front of a large 20X29 canvas that was painted a deep, smoky grey except for a tiny red dot in the centre. If I focussed hard on the dot, the surrounding grey melted away, the red filling my vision with its energy and primal life force. Something about it fascinated me, and I stared at it for a long time, almost going into a trance.

"Clever, isn't it?" an attractive young Indian woman had come up beside me. She seemed to be admiring it as well.

"I suppose." Clever wouldn't have been the word I would have used. Strangely compelling was more apt.

"Its simplicity is deceptive. The more you look at it, the more it reveals itself to you."

"Is it yours?" I figured she was an artist from the lanyard that hung around her neck.

"Oh heavens, no! Mine are in that corner. This is Yuki's. He is our new Japanese artist."

I thought I detected a Delhi accent in her perfect intonation. Something made me say, "*Aap Dilli se hain*?"

She started and looked at me afresh. "I am from Delhi originally, although I haven't lived there in a long time. But I wouldn't have put you down as a Delhiite?"

I smiled at her and shrugged, not sure why after all these years, my Indian side had asserted itself in this unexpected manner.

"I lived in Delhi many, many years ago. I haven't been back in over twenty years."

She examined my face as I said this.

"Would you like to go back?"

"I... I'm not sure. There's no one to go back to."

"There doesn't need to be. You could just go visit Delhi. Maybe see how much it has changed in the interim?"

"There's a thought," I laughed to hide the sudden, piercing longing I'd felt as she'd said that. "I'm Sam Shaw." I held out my hand. She took it, her grasp warm and firm.

"I know. I've watched your programmes on the telly and I'm a fan. Not the stalker type," she amended hastily, with a sheepish smile. "I just admire what you do. It takes guts."

"Thank you." I didn't know what else to say, but she carried on smoothly, filling the silence.

"I'm Anu, one of the artists featured today."

I nodded in acknowledgement, suddenly curious about this woman who wasn't that much younger than me.

"Which ones are yours?"

I walked behind her, admiring her composure, her unfeigned self-assurance. How wonderful it would be to know one's place in the world with such equanimity.

"These are mine."

I looked at the riot of colours in front of me. Not every painting was to my taste, but I couldn't help but be drawn in by the vibrant paints, the use of multiple elements, and the abstract swirls.

"These are very... exciting!" I said, moving closer to the one I liked the most. "This one is a little different, though. Not as joyous as the others."

"Is that the one you like?"

"Yes, I suppose it is." I peered at it. "Why is it called 'Mama'?"

"I had made it in my mother's memory. She passed away a few years ago."

"It's beautiful, and... I'm sorry." Something made me reach out and touch her gently on her arm. "I lost my mother very young, but it never stops hurting, does it?"

"Especially if you had a complicated relationship with her." Her eyes seemed to probe mine, as if looking for validation. I looked away in confusion, not wanting her to read my thoughts.

"Anyway, Sam, there are so many other artists here. You should have a look around. Let Joan know if there's anything that interests you. She's the curator."

With a quick smile, she moved away to talk to another couple, leaving me rooted to the spot. Something about her had reminded me of Madhu. Perhaps it was her poise, her imperturbability, and her quiet dignity.

With a sudden pang, I realised that I did wish to return to Delhi, even if it was only to correct my wrongs. Was it too late, or was there still a way to reach out to those that had meant so much to me twenty-odd years ago?

CHAPTER 95

At dinner at an Italian Trattoria, Cathy asked me so many questions that I couldn't keep up.

"Whoa, whoa! What's this, the Spanish Inquisition?" I was mildly miffed, but kept my tone light.

"I'm sorry, Sam! This isn't relaxing for you at all, is it? It's just that you're such an enigma that all of us girls keep wondering what your life is really like."

"It's not as exciting as you think. Mostly it's exhausting, filled with jet lag, no sleep, and long stretches of tedium."

And lonely, I wanted to add, but didn't.

"You are such an inspiration, do you know? What a career..."

Cathy's hero-worship, lovely as it was, did little to satisfy my yearning for friendship; my yearning for those who had known me before I became Sam Shaw, those who understood me and weren't dazzled by the aura of celebrity.

After the dinner I jumped on the tube to head home. It wasn't late, but suddenly I couldn't rid myself of the thought that I had left it too long, that perhaps it *was* too late to make amends.

I looked at the people around me. It wasn't the usual scrum of commuters, students, and tourists. Today, it was mostly just tourists, and no one threw me curious glances wondering where they had seen me before. On my days off, I dressed down in jeans and wore glasses instead of contacts. This afternoon, however, I'd made an effort, pairing cream trousers with an inky blue satin blouse and pearls.

The dinner had been nice in the end, once Cathy had stopped gushing and asking too many questions. It felt good to talk to someone normal for a change. Not someone who was providing me a sound bite or would turn into a news story. Still, a part of me was relieved to leave as well. For all my people skills at heart, I was essentially a loner.

At home, I changed out of my clothes into my pyjamas, and picked up the book I'd been trying to read for the last two months. But somewhere along the way, I'd lost the thread of the plot, and couldn't be bothered to flip back to reacquaint myself with the characters. I set it down and picked up my laptop instead. Maybe I'd try to find a nice place to holiday in, a place where I could switch off and unwind, maybe even make love to that stranger.

There were five new emails, and I nearly ignored them but for my compulsive need to keep my inbox free of clutter. Three were spam that I consigned to junk, one was an article in Time Magazine, forwarded to me by Christine, but it was the last one that caught my attention.

~

Kinara Public School would like to invite all of its alumni and staff for a farewell lunch in honour of Miss Margaret D'Souza's retirement. Please RSVP latest by the 10th of September, 2011.

~

I sat staring at the email for a long time. It was almost too pat, too much of a coincidence; as if someone had eavesdropped on my thoughts and decided to present me with an opportunity that couldn't be ignored. I baulked at this happenstance. Life did not work like that. Or did it?

Shutting my laptop, I went to the kitchen and rooted around for that bottle of red I'd bought some months ago. Tonight I felt like a drink.

The first mouthful of the Cabernet Sauvignon felt dry. I closed my eyes and let the underlying supple, soft and plummy flavours burst upon my tongue. Uncharacteristically for me, I needed to pair some chocolate with it, and hoped there was still a Lindt bar leftover from Christmas somewhere in my little store room.

Chocolate and wine, the two indulgences that I rarely partook of, seemed symbolic tonight. As if life itself was exhorting me to take a different path. To let go of my inhibitions, to try something different.

In the years gone by, I had often thought of reaching out to Pari or to Madhu. I'd even made a Facebook profile in the hope that one of them would reach out to me. But I'd taken it down just as quickly. Fear, shame, regret, and an inability to explain my own actions or my father's criminality had superseded every decent instinct. Yet, the random panic attacks that came out of nowhere and disappeared just as suddenly, my holding on to the memorabilia from days gone by, and the guilt that gnawed at me constantly were all indicators that I had to, I *needed* to make peace with the past.

I grabbed my laptop and went onto the British Airways website. If I thought too long and hard about it, I'd change my mind. I booked a return ticket. Three weeks would be enough. Enough to explore the city that had once been mine, attend the lunch, and try to reconnect with old friends, if they'd have me.

Then I carefully worded a thank-you email to the sender, saying that yes, I would attend.

CHAPTER 96

I slept most of the way to Delhi, exhaustion ambushing me unexpectedly. The cabin crew were attentive, even a bit awe-struck as they recognised me from the programme that had aired just the previous week to record numbers. Fortunately, I was seated next to an older Indian lady who didn't have a clue who I was, and after smiling at me politely, didn't bother me for the rest of the flight. Little mercies.

At the airport, I found myself in the much shorter queue reserved for the First and Business Class passengers, and in less than ten minutes, I was in front of the poker-faced immigration officer.

"Samira Shaw?" he asked, looking at my passport.

"Yes," I kept my face impassive, but somewhere within me, an irrational fear erupted. What if they knew who my father was? What if they arrested me instead?

"Indian?" he studied my face.

"Half-Indian. My mother was English." I made myself sound as haughty and superior as I dared, hoping it would pay off. It did, as he stamped my passport and handed it back.

"Welcome to India."

· · ·

Alighting from the plane, the first thing that struck me was the smell. It was that warm, earthy, smoky odour that immediately assailed one's nostrils—a distinctive combination of cooking fires and diesel fuel, of car exhausts and *agarbattis*. A smell that I'd forgotten, but one that immediately reminded me I was home.

After collecting my luggage, I ignored the many taxi touts calling out "Madam, Madam...", and "Come, come... I will take you..." to look for the board that had my name on it. I had travelled to the most dangerous parts of the world, but my team had always accompanied me. Travelling to Delhi on my own was a different kind of adventure, one that I intended to accomplish safely. On the far right, I saw SHAW on a board held up by a short, portly man, and I headed straight for him.

"Sheraton?" I asked him, and he straightened up from his half-dozing posture.

"Madam Shah?" he mispronounced my name so charmingly that I smiled and allowed him to lead the way.

On the drive to the hotel, I marvelled at the quiet streets, remembering the noise and chaos from my childhood years. The city was sleeping at this time. Tomorrow, I'd be interested to see if it would awaken to the same frenetic pace that I remembered.

In the years that I had been away, I'd caught the occasional documentary or movie filmed here in Delhi. It always amazed me to see how much the population had swelled along with the chaotic traffic. Even back in the 80s, Delhi had been a city of contrasts; of broad boulevards and narrow lanes, green open spaces and confined housing blocks without a sprig of vegetation, five-star hotels and grimy guesthouses. Wealth and poverty had co-existed in relative harmony back then. Had that changed? How much had changed? I had no concrete plan of action, except for wanting to revisit this city of my childhood and youth, and look at it with fresh eyes.

In all my travels, I had never encountered a country like India, but maybe I was biassed. There was something about this place in that you could love it or hate it, but you could never, ever be indifferent to it.

"Madam Shah need driver?"

"Pardon?"

I was taken aback by this sudden interruption.

"For going here and there?"

I gathered that Ghanshyam, the driver, was offering his services.

"You will drive me around?"

"No, no Madam. My brother. You need?"

"Let me think about it."

It would be prudent to have a driver, but I wanted to experience the autos of my youth. Riding in these covered three-wheeled vehicles had been a joy I'd taken for granted as a teenager. You could be one with the rolling vistas, yet have a railing and a canvas roof that separated you from the traffic, the people, and the elements. But I didn't want to disappoint my sweet driver, either.

"Give me his number. I'll call him if I need him."

"Thank you, Madam. He very good driver. Most trusting."

At the hotel, the male receptionist was efficient and chatty.

"Are you here on work, Miss Shaw?"

"No," I smiled.

"Pleasure?"

"I hope so."

He took my passport to make a copy, and while I waited, I watched the few people who were still hanging around the lobby of the hotel at this late hour.

Years ago, when Mama had taken me to Vikram Hotel to have my hair trimmed, I'd thought it to be the height of luxury. The Maurya Sheraton far exceeded that initial experience. Hospitality in Asia wasn't just a byproduct of the tourism industry. It simmered beneath every interaction, every smile, every *namaste* one encountered. Yes, there were con men and cheats here too, crime was rife and the streets weren't safe for women after a certain hour, but by and large, India lived by the old Sanskrit adage of '*Atithi Devo Bhava*' which meant 'Guest is God'.

CHAPTER 97

"So, how's Motherland treating you?" Christine's voice sounded raspy on the phone. "I've got a ruddy cold." she explained.

"And I've got the Delhi belly," I groaned. Five days of exploring my city and I had finally been felled at the hands of a *golgappa-wallah*.

"A *what*?" Christine sounded confused.

"A street vendor serving these little puff balls filled with boiled potatoes, chickpeas, sweet and sour chutneys and flavoured water. I used to eat these little snacks all the time as a girl and nothing ever happened to me back then."

"Duh, child! You had the immunity back then. Well, I hope it was worth it." her sarcasm dripped down the line.

"I don't know." I was curled up in bed in a foetal position. "Can't keep anything down. It runs through me like water."

"Both ends?" she asked.

"Both ends," I answered.

"You poor sausage! You have to call a doctor."

"I know," I sighed. "Right now, I just want to sleep."

Ghanshyam's brother, Radheshyam, had proved to be an excellent driver and guide, taking me to long-forgotten corners of Delhi. From the Red Fort and Chandni Chowk to the streets of Janpath and my old haunts at M-Block, Greater Kailash, I had ventured far and wide

in search of my lost years. I had sampled all the foods of my childhood too, believing that my stomach could handle it; believing that it
was a lot stronger than my heart, which remained bruised after all
these years.

"Well, I just called to tell you that there's talk of us being nomi-
nated at the British Academy Television Awards," Christine snapped
me back from my reverie.

"What?" I sat up, felt dizzy, and fell back on my pillow again.

"Yes, my darling! Your coverage and the work you put into 'Syrian
Spring: Ground Up' is being universally lauded. I told you all those
years ago that you were wasting yourself on that stupid interview
show, and I have been proven right!"

"Yes, Mother." I groaned again as my stomach cramped.

"Right! I have to go, but as your boss and 'mother', I strongly
advise that you get checked out by a doctor. And get those pills, why
don't you? The ones that stop you up. Anti-diarrhoea, antiemetics?
Their chemists are brilliant! You'll find anything you need there."

"Hmm."

Much after Christine had hung up, and sleep was proving elusive, I
sat in bed looking at the photographs I'd clicked in the last few days.
It had been fascinating to see the city I had spent nearly sixteen years
in through a different lens: that of a tourist and an outsider.
Radheshyam had been delighted to discover that I could speak Hindi,
however haltingly, and had spoken to me in the lingo from that
moment on.

"Madam, you look foreigner but speak like Indian!" he'd exulted,
then said, "*Apne desh ki mitti, apne desh ki mitti hoti hai.*"

He was right. India still felt like home, and this fine desert dust
from Rajasthan that settled on my hair, my clothes, my skin was my
own *mitti*—the dust of my land.

I scrolled through the pictures, some that Radheshyam had taken
of me, some that I had clicked from the car hurriedly as we drove past
a landmark. There were also the ones that I had taken with great

intention, alighting from the car, framing the scene as I wanted, and taking the photo, which I knew would be good enough to display on a wall.

Then I stopped scrolling to scrutinise the one I'd taken of the tomb in Lodi Gardens. Once again, my heart constricted with all the memories. The cool darkness as we hid from the world exploring each other's minds and bodies, the feel of Sri's lips, the urgency of his lust, the awareness of being utterly engulfed by emotions alien and unfamiliar, the confusion that had followed, the truths that had felt like lies. In some ways, it seemed like a lifetime ago, in others, as if it had only been yesterday.

The school lunch was three days away, and I wanted to be well enough to face Pari and Madhu if they turned up. Only at that very moment did I consider the possibility that their lives might have taken them in directions far away from the alma mater. What if they didn't show? What if this entire trip was a wasted effort to build bridges with people who had long moved on?

Then, as another spasm made me drop the phone to the bed and draw my knees up to my chest, I was struck with the conviction that there was serendipity at work here. I was here for a reason, and they would be there too. Even if neither of them forgave me, I hoped they would at least give me a chance to explain. At the very least.

CHAPTER 98

It was a Sunday, and I had given Radheshyam the day off. Today was a good day to take a ride in an auto-rickshaw. The doorman at the Sheraton looked at me askance as I asked for a three-wheeler. He was used to calling for taxis for the patrons, and someone like me who didn't fit his idea of a local wanting an auto-rickshaw completely threw him. Still, to his credit, he didn't persuade me otherwise.

What did one wear to a school get-together? While packing, I'd thrown a few options into my suitcase, hoping the answer would come to me in the moment. But in India, none of them seemed appropriate. Instead, on one of my forays with Radheshyam, I'd stopped off at FabIndia and bought myself a turquoise cotton kurta with tiny gold *ambis* block-printed on it. This I'd paired with my white linen trousers and the little gold hoops Mama had left me. My sunglasses and a slick of lip gloss and I felt ready, if a bit shaky, on the inside. I kept reminding myself that even if no one I knew showed up, I'd still get to meet the lovely Margaret Ma'am, and maybe even a few other teachers who might remember me. I hoped they had forgotten the scandal my departure had created, and viewed me a bit more kindly with the passage of time.

Hopping into the three-wheeler, I covered my head with a scarf, remembering how the wind could play havoc with one's hair in this mode of transport. The driver was a taciturn young man, who spat out a stream of pan-stained spittle every ten minutes or so, and examined me in his rear-view mirror at every traffic light junction. I studiously ignored his scrutiny, choosing instead to focus on the few landmarks I still recognised on our way to the school.

As we passed the massive, glistening black sculpture of 'Gyarah Murti' near Willingdon Crescent on Sardar Patel Marg, I realised we were only ten minutes away from the school now. My fear had set up a drumbeat inside of me, and in order to distract myself, I focussed on the extraordinary sculpture of Gandhi leading an iconic retinue on his path-breaking Civil Disobedience Dandi March. As children, we had sometimes wandered here to examine the various figures depicted on the march, wondering who they were and how the sculptor had carved them so expertly to reflect a mood of hope, anticipation and optimism. Later, one of our history teachers had explained that aside from Gandhi, the other figures were merely representative of a nation of myriad people of multiple faiths and backgrounds.

"This sculpture contains a great truth. Anything worth achieving must be done in the spirit of collaboration. An individual can only take a movement so far; it is only as a collective that we will achieve long-lasting success. Our freedom movement is a prime example..."

"We are here." The auto-rickshaw driver stopped in front of the gates, and I returned to the present moment, with the same fear humming inside of me.

After paying him, I alighted from the auto-rickshaw, inviting curious glances from the other people who were entering the premises. Most had come in groups or pairs, and I, who looked so different from them, had come on my own. I could hear the whispers already. "Who is she?" "Did she study here?" "She looks foreign."

I took the scarf off my head and wrapped it around the handle of my handbag. Lifting my chin slightly, I started walking in, ignoring the looks, the casual curiosity. For eight years, I had studied in this school and, just like these people, I had every right to be here.

Just short of the entrance, there was a long table behind which sat people with badges. They were cross-checking our names against a chart. When it was my turn, a woman no older than twenty-five asked me what my name was.

"Sam Shaw. But you will have me registered as Samira Sehgal."

"Ah yes, here it is. And here's your name badge. Please wear it to allow other people to identify you."

"Thank you." I pinned the badge on.

As I moved through the crowds, looking for a familiar face, I was suddenly overcome with memories of the times I'd spent running in these fields, eating lunch under the fig trees, and buying *samosas* in the cafeteria. The times I'd spent fending off advances from senior boys, basking in the praise of my teachers, and all those occasions when I'd planned a future with my friends—a future in which we would all be in each other's lives, where we would attend each other's weddings and spend every birthday and festival together; where our children would be friends and our families so enmeshed that we couldn't tell one apart from the other.

Today, I stood here, a stranger amongst other strangers, wondering how life had butchered each one of those dreams.

Roma

CHAPTER 99

Sometimes I just wanted to walk out of my life and never return. To create an alternate existence in some place where no one knew me and where I could start from scratch again.

I was an unloved woman. My husband pretended but my children didn't even do that. It was obvious they preferred the *ayah* to me. They spent more time in her company, asking her to cook them their favourite foods, getting her to do their hair, iron their shirts, and play Ludo with them. They took advice from their father; they spoke to their friends into the early hours of the morning, lived their lives on social media, and when I entered their rooms, they schooled their faces into polite indifference. I was nothing but a figurehead to them. Someone who had birthed them but remained detached from their petty little lives and the dramas contained within them.

I suppose I was to blame in some ways.

In Australia I had tried too hard. I'd cooked, I'd cleaned, I'd chauffeured in my bid to be the perfect wife and mother. Then we had moved to India at my behest, and I'd been put on bedrest because of complications with my pregnancy. It was there that little by little I had given up control over my family. After Barsha's birth, the traumatic labour that had preceded it, and the long recovery afterwards, I had remained marginally involved in the running of my household, but my mind had preferred flitting into the lives of the soap operas that I devoured avidly. There were maids here to do all the grunt work. All I'd had to do was allocate the sums of money that Angad transferred into my account monthly.

Children grow up fast though, and those needy toddlers had transformed into distant and detached teenagers, save Barsha, who was ten and who I'd never really bonded with after the caesarean. Her bond was with her father, and she did little to conceal her indifference to me. Sometimes I thought it might have helped to send them all to boarding school, but then, whatever little value I had in the family would completely disappear alongside.

Right now, I was still a wife and a mother, even if it was in name only.

Everyone always talked about Angad in such glowing terms. About how wonderful a boss he was, what a great husband and father, such a warm and compassionate human being. They did not see what I saw. A man who cheated on his wife with impunity, telling one bare-faced lie after another. A man who acted as if his family meant everything to him, yet stayed out late night after night screwing anything in a skirt. This was the man, this was the family I wished to escape.

Ankita came into the room wearing impossibly short shorts and a tank top that left little to the imagination.

"Maa, I'm going out."

"No, you're not. Dress properly."

"What's wrong with what I'm wearing?"

"Everything! You look like a prostitute. Get changed now!"

"Everyone my age wears this kind of stuff!"

"I don't care. You won't step out of the house like this."

"You're horrible!" She stomped out of the room, slamming the door behind her.

These exchanges exhausted me. Everything exhausted me. Increasingly, the only thing that gave me pleasure was locking myself in the bedroom with the television on, as I worked my way through packets of *namkeen chivda* doused with tomato ketchup. Then I would fart into the bed, giggling to myself at the thought that Angad would climb into the same covers, clueless.

Over time, my phone calls to Ria had dwindled as well. She had accused me of being paranoid and jealous. I had accused her of stealing my parents away.

"They'd rather be with me than listen to you complain incessantly about a life that *you* chose!"

A life that I had chosen. A life in which I could have been anything, gone anywhere, and what had I chosen? To be a corpulent housewife, with no other interests than stuffing her face and living her life vicariously through fictional characters. Some life!

Pari had said to me on one of her infrequent visits that I could take up music again.

"You had," she'd corrected herself, "You *have* such a beautiful voice. Why not sing again? Take some lessons. It could be a lovely hobby."

I'd stolen her portable fan that day out of sheer annoyance.

Still, I'd pondered her words, wondering if I could make something of my life even now. I had no friends, my family had distanced itself from me, and there were days when I couldn't bear to look at myself in the mirror. Maybe I could take up singing again, just for the pure pleasure of it.

Then again, the very thought of going out into the world would debilitate me to the extent that only food could provide salvation.

CHAPTER 100

"Why do we have to go?" I looked at Angad adjusting his tie in front of the mirror and felt another prickle of anger.

"Because," he spoke to me slowly, as if I was retarded, "We are the alumni of the school. Besides, don't you think we owe it to Margaret Ma'am? You spent a lot longer at the school than I did, and you cannot deny that she was a wonderful principal."

I shrugged. I felt nothing towards her. Not gratitude, not obligation. Nothing.

"Roma," Angad turned from the mirror and looked at me directly. "I think you need to see a doctor."

"Why?" I asked truculently, already knowing the answer. He had been saying this for a while now.

"It's not normal, this shutting yourself off from the world. Maybe," he came and sat next to me, putting his hand on mine, "they could prescribe something? Something that would help with these moods of yours."

I snatched my hand away.

"Are you calling me mental? *Āmi jāni!*" I nodded furiously. I knew it! All he wanted was to certify me mad, so that he could snatch everything from me, stick me in a mental asylum and have his multiple affairs out in the open!

"Shhh, Roma. I'm saying nothing of the sort. Look, if I'm not well, if there's something wrong with me physically, don't I go to the doctor and get some medication? It's the same thing. Just have yourself checked out. If not for my sake, then for our children's sake."

I was so bored with this conversation, this repetitive drone of going to see a doctor. There was nothing wrong with me, and if he wanted me drugged up so that I would be oblivious to his activities, then he had another think coming.

Just to get him off my back, I nodded a yes, then stood up and headed towards the bathroom.

"And will you come with me on Sunday?" he called out after me.

"Where?" I asked, over my shoulder.

"To the school lunch."

"Oh," I stopped in my tracks, then said quietly, "Okay."

In the bathroom, I stripped down to my underwear and examined myself in the full-length mirror. I had never liked my body in all its softness, roundness, plumpness. But now, I actively hated it. The rolls of fat that started under my breasts, the drum-like belly that hung over to the top of my thighs concealing a long, horizontal caesarean scar, my chunky legs that were criss-crossed with stretch marks, my upper arms that dimpled with cellulite. I was ugly! I turned my face away.

I didn't want to go back to school and meet my old teachers and former classmates. I didn't want to see the pity in their eyes, or listen to their whispered comments—"What happened to her?" "God, she's so fat!" I didn't want to stand next to the elegant Pari, or the tiny matchbox princess, Madhu, and feel like a whale. And what if she showed up? What if my *bête noire* made an appearance?

I'd followed her career covertly through the last decade. From a glamorous television interviewer, she had evolved into a gritty, hard-hitting news reporter, travelling the world, covering live events as they happened. Over the years, she had only become more beautiful;

her features chiselling into something otherworldly, the planes and angles of her face lending themselves incredibly well to the camera.

It had always amazed me that Pari and Madhu never mentioned her. It was as if they had forgotten her existence. She who had harmed them far more than she had harmed me. But I was the one who refused to forget. I was the one who entered her name into the search engine of my iPad religiously, looking for every picture, every programme, every news article she had ever been featured in. And at the end of the day, before Angad returned home, I would diligently delete my browsing history.

Sam Shaw—beautiful, accomplished, fêted. Samira Sehgal hid behind this name and this persona.

How was it that people like her always landed on their feet? Like a cat with nine lives. After everything she had done, everything her father had done, there was never any payback or justice. If I ever met her, I'd scratch her eyes out and hand them back to her. Those honey coloured, almond-shaped eyes that seemed to carry a thousand secrets within them. Those eyes that had ensnared so many unsuspecting men. Those lips that lied as they smiled. That body. That sinuous, sexy body that she had been born with, that she had done nothing to deserve.

I turned the shower on and let the water run down my face, soaking my hair and drowning my thoughts out.

There was no way that hotshot Sam Shaw would show up for a piddly little school lunch. She had left her past behind a long time ago. I needed to do the same.

CHAPTER 101

There were so many cars parked haphazardly in the car park that Angad had to manoeuvre ours into a corner, parking at an awkward angle to allow me to exit.

"Are you okay?"

I nodded a yes, irritable to be beginning the day in this manner. Holding my *sari* by the pleats, I stepped out of the car and looked around me. I wasn't the only one in a *sari* thankfully, recalling the mortifying Christmas party in Sydney. Here, there were plenty of other women, younger and older, who took pride in wearing our national outfit. I'd chosen a deep cerise with a black border, striking enough to stand out against all the other colours. My hair, freshly shampooed and styled at the parlour, hung long and loose over my shoulders with the tiniest bit of curl at the ends. I had applied a Dior lipstick that matched my *sari* and my nails, and drenched myself in Miss Dior perfume. Today, I needed to look good. It was my armour against the past, a defence against the present.

After we had collected our badges, we walked towards the field at the back of the school building. This is where a large stage had been erected with a lectern and a microphone. A screen on which they planned to play a montage of films for Margaret Ma'am had been placed at the far end of the stage. Sofas and chairs were lined up in front of the stage, and on the periphery of the field, caterers were setting up tables to place the food on.

"They've done a fantastic job with the organisation of the event," Angad commented, looking around.

"What time is Pari coming?"

"She is picking Margaret Ma'am up along with Madhu. They should be here shortly."

"There's a lot of people here."

"I'd say at least eight hundred."

We looked around for familiar faces but spotted no one we recognised.

"Hey Roma, I think that's the new principal."

I looked in the direction Angad had pointed in. A very dapper man in a dark suit was talking to a chap fiddling with the microphone. He was handsome in a clean-cut Aamir Khan kind of way, but short. Way shorter than Angad.

"The homo principal," I commented, my voice flat with distaste.

"Homo? What makes you say that?"

"Pari told me."

Angad looked back at him with renewed interest. I observed Angad having already picked up on the many stares he'd attracted as we walked in. Still so handsome after all these years. Dressed in a pale blue shirt and dark wash denim jeans, he was effortlessly good looking. Such a shame that he was a serpent underneath that good-looking exterior.

"Angad?"

I turned to look at a dark, overweight man approaching Angad with what sounded like awe.

"Yes?" Angad was equally perplexed.

"Nitin Sharma. We were in commerce together."

"Oh, hey Nitin! Took me a minute there..." Angad was covering up for the fact that he still hadn't recognised him, turning to me, saying, "Remember Roma Bannerjee? My wife now."

Nitin turned towards me, trying to hide his surprise. "Hi Roma! You used to sing, right? I remember the assemblies..."

Just then, Angad's cellphone rang, and he held up his hand at us, indicating it was important. Who was ringing him on a Sunday, and why did he need to answer it? Then I remembered it could be the *ayah*. Maybe something to do with the children. I excused myself and rooted around for my phone in the bag, but no one had rung me.

Then Angad held out his hand to me, beaming.

"That was Pari. They're bringing Margaret Ma'am here now. Let's move to the front. I want to see her face."

We pushed our way through the throng towards the stage, and in a distance I spied the grey-haired, *sari*-clad woman flanked by Pari and Madhu. As she came closer to the stage and saw all the various pictures pinned on the boards, along with the messages from ex-staff members and students, she looked shocked and then, just for a moment, absolutely terrified. That's when Madhu whispered something in her ear, and slowly, the fear vanished, replaced by an unalloyed joy. Gratified, she accepted the bouquet of flowers from the Chairman of the Trustees to a thunderous applause. As the new principal held out his arm to take her up to the stage, I heard Angad say, "She's so happy! I'm glad we came. Aren't you, Roma?"

But I wasn't listening. My attention was on the willowy woman on the far right of the stage. Dressed in a turquoise top, her auburn hair caught the sunlight and glinted like copper. Her delicate wrists were devoid of any jewellery. Her hands clapped alongside the rest of the audience, and her lips curved in a radiant smile.

She was here. The woman who had haunted my every dream and nightmare was here. Samira Sehgal had, despite all indications to the contrary, turned up for the piddly school lunch.

CHAPTER 102

I wish I'd pretended an illness and gotten Angad to take me home then. I wish I had never gone to that wretched lunch. I wish I'd never set eyes on Samira Sehgal. But there she was, and I couldn't take my eyes off her.

She was slimmer in person, much slimmer, verging on being emaciated. What did they call it? Heroin chic? Maybe that's what kept her weight under control. Yet she shimmered with the kind of beauty that only the very fortunate were blessed with. When Samira's mother had been alive, everyone had said that Samira wasn't a patch on her as far as looks went. Today, she had far surpassed her mother. There was a strange delicacy to her, yet she also emanated a quiet strength. Where Aunty had been all style, Samira was all substance.

"Are you alright Roma? You look so pale!" Angad's voice penetrated my thoughts, jolting me back to the present moment. Luckily, he couldn't see past my sunglasses and did not look in her direction.

"I'm okay. Just felt a bit hot there for a second. Should we go and pay our respects? Then we can leave." I tried sounding nonchalant, as if nothing had bothered me, but my voice wavered towards the end.

"You want to go already? But we just got here. Let's catch up with a few friends first. I'm sure Nitin will know if anyone else from our batch is around."

I clutched my bag in a panic. There were so many people here. What were the chances that we'd actually come face to face with her? But inside me, a sinking sensation said that none of this was a coincidence. Something big was about to happen, something major was going to change.

"Shall we?"

I let Angad guide me towards the queue that had formed near the stage. Everyone wanted to meet Margaret Ma'am, and just for a moment I felt sorry for her. How tiring to trade pleasantries with so many people, most of whom she probably didn't even recall. Pari, Madhu, and the principal stood like sentries behind her, while the Chairman of the Trustees sat in a chair next to her. Someone had brought another microphone on the stage and placed it beside her. I guessed they wanted her to make a speech at some point. I hoped we'd get out of here before the full-blown nostalgia set in.

Eventually, it was our turn, and as I climbed onto the stage with Angad, I wondered what I could possibly say to a woman who had known me so briefly over twenty years ago.

I knelt and touched her feet as I'd seen the others do. It was a reflex, with no thought behind it, but she caught my hand in hers and held it tight while looking into my eyes.

"I hope you are well, Roma, my girl?"

Her skin felt dry and papery, and I blinked as her eyes bored into me. How could she possibly remember me? Had Pari been telling her tales?

I smiled weakly, muttered a thank-you and moved on. My eyes caught Pari's and in my indignation I thought, "Serves you right if I don't warn you about Samira's presence. I hope she catches you off-guard. I hope it comes as a bloody shock!"

She threw me an uncertain look as I walked off the stage. Maybe she had sensed my annoyance and was perturbed by it. Good! If she had been blabbing about me to Margaret Ma'am, I'd make sure to make her feel unwelcome the next time she "popped in" to see us.

I couldn't see Angad anywhere and as my eyes sought him out, I discovered him chatting to that Nitin fellow on the far left.

"Roma, Nitin was saying there's a few people from our batch here. Let's try to sit together. Where are you? Oh, yes. Come on, let's go there."

I allowed myself to be taken to a group that I had nothing in common with; that I barely remembered. As Angad chatted with and charmed them, I stayed stubbornly silent, refusing to mingle. The sudden desire to be back home and in my bed was so overpowering that I stood up.

"Excuse me, I need to find the ladies."

With that, I turned and left, winding my way through the various clusters of people. On the stage, Margaret Ma'am was still holding court. This could take forever! When would they show the film? When would the speeches happen? We didn't have all day to hang around here!

Then I spotted her. She was only four people behind the person speaking to Margaret Ma'am. Pari still hadn't seen her, but I could see the laser sharp focus with which Samira was looking at her. Something interesting was about to go down, and I'd be damned if I'd miss it.

CHAPTER 103

The moment that Pari locked eyes with Samira, I saw her freeze. It was at the same moment that Madhu turned from the principal and spotted Samira, too. If it hadn't been for Margaret Ma'am's composure, in the way she put her hand on Samira's head and spoke to her, things could have taken an ugly turn. Samira held her hand out at Pari, then at Madhu, but they stayed silent and unmoving. Her face fell as she moved off the stage. I stood back and watched as she walked towards the ladies' room. Then I followed her.

Inside, several women were chatting, reapplying their lipsticks and fixing the pleats on their *saris*, while Samira stood to a side, dabbing her eyes with a tissue. Even here, even amongst all these women, some of them quite attractive too, she seemed separate; a creature from another world. Incredibly beautiful and incredibly alone.

I moved closer to her, then stood right next to her, pretending to apply my lipstick. Her eyes swept over me and returned to her own image. She ran her fingers through her hair, took a deep breath, and then headed out. I remained fixed in my spot, shock reverberating through me. Samira had looked at me but not seen me. She had no idea who I was! She had completely forgotten me. This woman who I had been fixating on for the last two decades didn't even care that I existed!

Crushed, yet strangely relieved, I headed back towards Angad and the group. Maybe all of my worries had been for nothing. Maybe I could finally shake off the ghost of my past, of Samira, and move forward freely once again.

The speeches had started in earnest, and as I took my place next to Angad, I wondered what was going through Pari's mind. She had retreated to one side, but I could see her in a deep discussion with Madhu. Were they analysing their next move? Were they going to approach Samira or freeze her out? I hoped it was the latter. She didn't deserve any better. Besides, I didn't want Angad to see her. I didn't want any old feelings to resurface. Despite his multiple assurances that Samira had meant nothing to him, I didn't believe it. She had been like a siren, destroying anyone who was lured by her song. How could he claim he'd been immune to her charms, especially after their brief fling?

I tried looking for her in the congregation, but didn't see her. Could it be that she'd left? I sincerely hoped she had. She could go back to her perfect life in England and leave us be. We didn't need or want her back here.

Margaret Ma'am waved the bent microphone away, choosing instead to walk to the lectern. A sudden memory of morning lectures came to me unbidden. Back then, I'd barely concentrated on what she'd said, all my attention on a handsome boy who I'd wanted to make my own. Today, I figured, I could give her the consideration of actually listening. She was old, *so old*. Old people had earned the respect just by virtue of having lived long enough.

"How old do you think she is?" I whispered to Angad, but Nitin answered me, instead.

"Seventy-two. Not that old, really. She's still such a strong lady!" His voice was laced with admiration.

I nodded quickly, turning my attention back to her. She was

dressed in a blue cotton *sari* with a thin gold border, and the same wire-rimmed glasses she had always worn; her hair was completely white now, her voice surprisingly strong as she spoke,

"... and nothing has given me quite as much pleasure as to meet my old colleagues and students today. I am blessed that so many of you feel that I made a difference in your lives. When I was appointed the principal of this school, my only aim was that every student who passed out of here felt that they were a loved and valued member, and that they would take that same feeling out into the world and contribute to society in some small way. It makes me proud to see that so many of you have, far beyond my own imagining. As for this honour you have bestowed upon me today, all I can say is a deep, heartfelt thank you. A part of me will always live on in this school. With Mr Upadhyay taking the baton from me, I have no doubt that the school is in excellent hands, and will continue to flourish in the same way..."

Blah, blah, blah, I thought to myself, craving the comfort of my favourite television serial. When could we leave? But Angad was surrounded by his yesteryear cronies, and it looked as if we'd have to stay till the bitter end.

CHAPTER 104

A few days after the lunch, I invited Pari over, dying to know what Samira had said to her on the stage. I cooked first, hoping to soften her up.

"This is delicious, Roma! I'd forgotten how well you could cook."

I smiled and waved her compliments away.

"So, the lunch went really well?"

Pari was scooping up the last of the *shukto* and rice, and just for a second I wished she'd stop eating and focus on what I was saying.

"Hmm?"

"The lunch. It went well?"

"Oh yes. Margaret Ma'am was so surprised and happy. Madhu and I had to concoct a real whopper of a tale to get her to the school on Sunday. I'm surprised she didn't suspect something was afoot." She licked the spoon with relish before setting it down. "But you know, Gautam... uhh... Mr Upadhyay planned everything down to the tiniest detail. I mean, even the cake we had her cut had pictures of her time at school superimposed on rice paper... It was all so well thought out and sweet."

"Yes, yes. It was all wonderful. How about you? Did you enjoy the day?"

A shadow crossed her face as I asked her this, but she quickly replaced it with a smile.

"Of course! It was so good to see some of the ex-students and colleagues. Some of them were kids I'd taught too."

It was obvious she was unwilling to take the bait, so I switched tactics.

"I've got some *rosogollas* for dessert. Would you like some?" I knew Pari could not resist anything sweet.

"Yes, please!" she grinned at me. "Where's the *ayah*? How come you're doing all this cooking?"

"I'm not entirely useless, Pari! The *ayah* has a few days off. Some festival in her village."

"And the children?"

"In their rooms. Would you like me to call them?"

"No, it's okay. If they're busy, let it be." Pari had never bonded with the children either, more because I didn't want her to. Every time she came over, I instructed them to stay in their rooms.

I brought out the earthen pot in which I stored the *rosogollas*. I'd brought the pot from Cal, and always transferred the shop-bought *rosogollas* into it, knowing that the flavour would intensify in there.

"They are from Annapurna's in C.R. Park. Best *rosogollas* in Delhi, in my opinion, although not a match for Kolkata."

I served her two and then ladled two out for myself, along with the thin sugar syrup.

"Was that Samira I spotted on the stage?" I slipped in the question innocuously, watching Pari's hand freeze halfway to her mouth.

"W... what?"

"I thought I saw Samira talking to you. She looked older, of course, but not much different from school days."

Pari set the spoon down and looked outside the window. I could sense the internal struggle and waited patiently. This was not the time to push.

"Yes," she said slowly, "that was Samira. She said she wanted to talk."

"Talk? About what?"

"I don't know. Actually, I didn't really let her say any more. She reached out to Madhu too."

"And?"

"Well, neither of us was prepared, so we didn't... umm... respond well."

"What's there to talk about, anyway? She's been out of our lives for so many years. Now, she waltzes back in and wants to *talk*? The cheek of it!"

Pari looked up at me, her eyes filling with tears.

"Margaret Ma'am said it might be a good idea to meet her, to see what she has to say. It's an olive branch, she said. Why turn it down?"

"Why?" I was livid now at the interfering old bat. "Will the olive branch bring Sri back, or Madhu's father? What's the point of letting that horrid woman into our lives?"

"I don't know, Roma. There's a part of me that wants to know what she has to say. If only for my own peace of mind."

"And Madhu?"

"Madhu doesn't want to meet her. She is still angry, and very, very hurt."

"I don't think you should meet her either, Pari. Trust me, that woman only causes havoc wherever she goes. It's a bad idea. Let her go back to where she came from. Don't allow her to disrupt your life!"

She looked upset and, much against my wishes; I got up and hugged her. A little display of affection could swing this my way. She stiffened at first, then allowed herself to relax.

"Thank you, Roma. I just needed someone on the outside to point me in the right direction. You're right. After all these years, what good can any explanations do?"

I patted her back and kissed her on the cheek, suppressing a shudder. That had been close, way too close for comfort. Hopefully, Samira would get the message and go back home. We didn't need the likes of her in our lives anymore.

CHAPTER 105

"*M*emsahib?"

There was a knock on the door. I woke up from my snooze, disorientated.

"Wh... what? *Kya hua?*"

"*Memsahib*, should I put the food away in the fridge now? *Sahib* isn't back yet."

I peered at the bedside clock. It showed 11:15 p.m. This was late, even for Angad.

"*Haan*, put it all away," I dismissed her, then turned the volume down on the television. Where was he? Standing up, I brushed the biscuit crumbs off my top and onto the rug, then unplugged my phone from its charger. No messages. Normally I didn't bother calling, but he had never come home this late without informing me first.

His number rang and rang, then went into voicemail. I placed the phone to the side, then went out into the hallway, passing the *ayah* placing the food in the refrigerator. I opened the door to Ankita's room. Barsha was asleep on her bed, face down, one foot dangling off. Ankita was on her phone, as usual. She looked up, startled as I walked in, and tried to slip the phone under her pillow.

I shook my head and held out my hand. She handed the phone

over, a sulky look on her face. I pressed the home button and went straight to the directory. Then I dialled 'Baba' from her phone.

Two rings later, Angad answered.

"Akku, what's the matter? Why are you calling me at this hour?"

"This is Roma," I walked out of the room into the hallway once again. My voice was icy. "Where are you, and why didn't you pick up when I called five minutes ago?"

"Roma," he sighed into the phone, "Sorry! I was caught up. I was just going to call you back when the phone rang and I saw it was Ankita."

"So, where are you?"

"I'm just on my way home."

"I mean, where are you, *right now*?" my voice had taken on a hysterical edge.

"I'll explain when I get home." Then he hung up.

He walked in just past midnight, said a quick "hello" and went straight in to shower. When he emerged, I muted the television and glowered at him.

"So?"

He towelled his hair, then sat at the edge of the bed.

"I went to meet Pari and Madhu. They wanted to discuss something with me."

"You met Pari here the day before yesterday. What happened between then and now that required this urgent meeting?"

But I knew. I already knew before he even opened his mouth.

"You know that Samira Sehgal is in town?"

I nodded, not trusting myself to speak.

"She's been wanting to meet them and has made a few overtures. The last one came through Margaret Ma'am."

He plucked at the towel on his lap, his hair still damp from the shower, his face looking grim.

"They wanted to consult me as to what to do."

"What did you say?" My voice was just above a whisper.

"I said," he looked at me before looking away, "I said it would be a good idea."

"What?"

"Look Roma, this thing with Samira has hung over all of us in one way or another. Don't you think it's time we laid it to rest?"

"We?"

"Yes, we. All of us. You too."

"What have you suggested?"

"Well, actually, it was Margaret Ma'am's idea. She's asked everyone to come over to her place on Sunday. Pari, Madhu, you, me and Samira. That way, whatever needs to be said can be said, but it will remain civil. I think it's a good idea."

"I don't, and I don't want to go!"

"Roma, listen to me. Obviously, there's a reason she has reached out. It's only fair that we give her a chance to explain."

"You just want to see her again, don't you?"

"That's nonsense! I haven't thought of her in years. You are the one who can't seem to forget her."

"Don't lie to me, Angad!"

He stood up then and turned his back on me.

"The trouble with you, Roma, is that you can no longer differentiate between truth and lies. In fact, I wonder if you ever could."

He walked away then.

This was the harshest thing he had ever said to me, and after he'd shut the bedroom door behind him, I sat there in silence, staring at the muted screen of the television. I knew he'd spend the night on the sofa, as he had been doing lately.

I had to acknowledge to myself that even before Samira had re-entered our lives, our relationship had been on shaky ground. But now, now that we would sit across from her and listen to her speak, now that Angad would see how lovely she was in person, what being with someone like her could be like, would that finally sound the death knell for our marriage?

Madhu

CHAPTER 106

What was I afraid of? I hid behind anger and hurt, but really, it was fear that immobilised me. Fear that everything that I had built so painstakingly would come crashing down once again. Fear that my past would catch up to me and mock my assertions that I had moved on.

That moment, that first moment when I had looked up and stared into Samira's face, my heart had dropped like a stone. Everything around me had blurred, and it was as if I'd been transported into another time, another place, and the hand that had reached out to me placatingly was the hand of a monster. I had shrunk away from it, shaken and disbelieving, registering the hurt that crossed her face. On the outside, my body had carried on automaton-like, smiling, chatting, placing the flowers and gifts people brought Margaret Ma'am on the table behind me.

Why was she here? Pari and I, equally shocked, had spoken in undertones. What did she want?

"Can we talk?" she'd asked Pari, who had shaken her head reflexively.

Later, Pari had asked me if perhaps it would have been a good idea to say yes. I had vehemently disagreed. What was there to talk about? All those wasted years and loved ones lost to the callousness of the Sehgals? What good would it do to churn up the past in this way?

Yet, at night, as I lay tossing and turning in bed, I wondered how fair I was being in blaming Samira. She had been just as much a victim as I. A young girl whose life had been disrupted, just like mine.

Amy, my colleague and friend from my days as a staff nurse, had once told me it was at once a blessing and a curse to see both sides to a story. I had always known that life was shades of grey, and not black and white. Samira had been a friend and an older sister to me. Guileless in many ways, she had been swept up in the currents of our lives at a time when we had barely learned to row. Yet, there was no one else to pin the blame on. In my mind, even in Pari's mind, she became the monster that had ruined our lives.

Now she was here, and she wanted to talk. But why, after all this time? Surely, if she'd had an iota of affection for us, felt a smidgen of guilt, she would have reached out sooner? Why had it taken over twenty years for her to find us?

That's when I decided that the doorway that led to the past had to remain shut. Nothing she said or did could alter that which had already occurred. If she was here to assuage her own conscience, I wasn't willing to roll over and let her. Not even curiosity about where life had taken her would budge me from my position. Not even Pari's constant indecisiveness would change my mind.

I was done with the Sehgals, and that was that.

Then Margaret Ma'am called one day.

"Madhu, you need to see her. She has a week before she returns to England, and she's desperate to meet you both. What harm could there be in seeing her once?"

Margaret Ma'am was the only person in the world who had the

power to change my mind because to her, I owed everything I was and wanted to be.

Pari, Angad and I sat in a conference, talking through the ramifications.

"She just wants forgiveness," Angad said.

"But that won't bring Sri back. She broke his heart, Angad!" Pari cried out.

"It was sudden cardiac arrest, Pari. He was genetically predisposed to it. Our grandfather died young too, because of the same reason. Besides, his drug use..."

"And what about you?" I asked, quietly.

"Me?" Angad looked at me askance.

"I was there, Angad. I saw you with her. I let you into the house when you took her out the first time. You may have forgotten, but I haven't."

Pari looked between him and me, then turned to face him.

"You've never told me this! You dated Samira?"

"I did." He swallowed convulsively. "Only briefly, though. And I had no idea she had been involved with Sri. If I had known, I would never have... Pari, you have to believe me."

"I believe you," I interjected, making him turn his gaze away from Pari to me. "But why are you pushing us now to meet her? Surely, if anything, you know firsthand the damage she caused."

"Because, I think Margaret Ma'am is right. Sometimes the only way to exorcise our ghosts is to face them head-on."

Maybe that's what convinced me, or maybe it was the fact that Angad drove me home in utter silence, dropping me off outside my flat without saying a word. His silence spoke volumes, and I listened.

CHAPTER 107

Samira was already at Margaret Ma'am's when we arrived. Dressed in a lemon skirt and a white top, she looked thin and drawn. I had a sudden flashback to Nina*ji* during her last months in Delhi. How similar she was to her mother, how much more beautiful she had become.

We filed in one behind the other as Margaret Ma'am greeted us with hugs, leading us into her small living room, which suddenly felt very crowded. If Samira was startled to see Angad, she didn't show it. She had asked only to meet Pari and me, so she cast Roma a curious glance, but smiled politely at all of us.

Margaret Ma'am brought out her tea set with her favourite Marie biscuits and set them down on the coffee table. The silence was excruciating, none of us knowing how to break the ice. Margaret Ma'am obliged by getting Pari to pour out the tea and offer it to everyone, while she said, "Now, did you know that our Samira has become a very famous television reporter? She was just telling me about her time in Syria over the past few months."

Samira blushed and took a sip of her water, having declined the tea.

"So, children," Margaret Ma'am continued, "I've called you over because Samira was very keen to set the record straight. She called me several times over the past week in the hope that I would intervene and bring you to the table…"

"We are only here because of you, Ma'am," Pari said, tonelessly.

"Well, I am glad you are here." Margaret ma'am smiled at her, then at all of us. "Now, I know some of the things that happened. Samira here has filled me in on some of the others. But I don't want to interfere in any way, so I'm happy to go into my bedroom until you have finished talking."

"No, Ma'am. Please stay." Samira's voice was soft, but compelling.

Margaret Ma'am had half-risen, but she sat down again, looking around at us for approval.

"Very well, my child. I'll stay."

Suddenly, I noticed a picture hanging on the wall behind her. It was the one that used to hang in her office. The one that said, "More things are wrought by prayer than the world dreams of." I said a silent prayer in my mind.

"I…" Samira began, then stopped. She looked at Margaret Ma'am, who nodded her head encouragingly.

"I have wanted to do this for a long time, but wasn't sure how. There were things I needed to explain, but I didn't have the words for them. There's a lot I'm guilty of and there's some that I'm not. But I know, deep down, that I need to apologise. To you, and you, and you." She looked at Pari, at me, and at Angad. "I wronged you all in little and large ways. I wronged you by hiding things, by misleading you, by wilfully ignoring you, and most of all, by being confused and needy; desperate and ignorant. Please forgive me."

Her hair fell like a curtain about her face as she looked down at the floor.

"Why?" My voice came out in a whisper. "Why, after all this time?"

She looked up at me, her eyes large and luminous, tears pooling in them.

"I don't know, Madhu. It just felt right. I've never come back to India since that night, when we left in a hurry with just the clothes on our backs and a few precious belongings. I thought I never would.

Then, the invitation arrived in my email. I didn't even know that the school had my email address." She shrugged. "I guess it was time."

"And Sri? What about him? All these years that you have carried on, living, thriving, becoming this famous reporter, have you once thought of what you did to him?" Pari had two red spots on her cheeks and was breathing heavily.

"Every day, Pari," she looked at her, the tears spilling onto her cheeks. "Every single day. I have never loved another man the way I loved him."

"Then, why?" Pari was crying now, openly. Her anguish was plain to see.

"Because I was sixteen, Pari! I was young, I was confused. It was too intense, and I couldn't make sense of my feelings. Then Mama fell ill, and I was ill-equipped to deal with the emotional toll that took on me." She turned to me. "You were there Madhu. You saw."

I nodded my head.

"I did see. Then why Angad?"

"Because she knew I'd fallen for her. It was easy. She knew that I would talk to Sri about it, which I did. After that, he stopped bothering her. Isn't that true, Samira?" Angad looked at her, his face expressionless.

"Yes," she muttered, "it's true. What I did was wrong. Very wrong."

"Did you ever think what I went through when I read your love letters to him? Can you imagine the weight of the guilt I've lived under all these years?" he asked, his face twisting.

"I'm sorry Angad. I'm so, so sorry. None of it was planned. I didn't think any of it through. I was a young, stupid girl."

"Stupid and destructive," Roma spoke for the first time. I had almost forgotten she was there. She had been so quiet the entire time. "What do you want now? For all of us to say that you are forgiven, so you can shimmy back to your celebrity lifestyle with all your sins wiped clean?"

Samira looked at Roma, her mouth falling open.

"But Roma, I have nothing to apologise to you for. Why are you even here?"

"Angad is my husband!"

"He wasn't back then."

"You *knew* I liked him!"

"No," Samira said, her voice firm, "I did not know. Besides, you married him. So, why are you looking at me for an apology?"

"God, she's such a bitch! Let's go, Angad." Roma stood up, her large frame quivering with anger.

"Roma, please." Angad put his hand on her arm.

"Child…" Margaret Ma'am tried to speak, but Roma was already making her way out.

"Are you coming or not?"

Angad stood up, and with an apologetic look, followed her out.

Then it was just the four of us, and we sat in silence again.

"There is a lot of healing power in forgiveness," Margaret Ma'am said softly.

I looked up at Samira then. Her ashen face, her gaunt figure, her nails bitten down to the nub. I was overcome with pity, not just for her, but for all of us. For our inability to divorce our past from our present, for our vilification of a person who had suffered just as much as we had, for our anger and our resentment. For us as we sat here, in this present moment. If forgiveness was freedom, I wanted that freedom. If it was healing, we needed that healing.

"I forgive you Samira*di*. For everything."

I held my hands out to her and to Pari. They clasped fingers with me, hesitatingly at first, then firmly.

It was time to move on from the pain, the regrets, and the recriminations. It was time to let bygones be bygones. It was time to absolve ourselves.

Suddenly, I felt as if a huge boulder had been lifted off my chest, a weight that I had carried for nearly twenty years. Pari's hand was warm and Samira's was cool to the touch, but a strange electricity crackled between us, a reminder of the bond we had once shared. I looked up to see Margaret Ma'am smiling at us and knew then that I had done the right thing.

CHAPTER 108

I was back at the hospital, as a senior nurse now, overseeing a lot of what Amy used to do before she moved back to Kerala. A junior staff nurse knocked on the door to my office.

"Excuse me, Miss Kumar?"

"Yes?"

"There is a lady demanding to see you right now." The nurse, a new recruit, looked quite frightened.

"Is it a family member? Visiting hours aren't till later."

"No, sister, it's someone who asked for you."

"Okay, send her in."

Deluged as I was with work, I hoped whoever this was could be dispatched quickly.

A few minutes later, the nurse walked in with Roma behind her. Startled, I dropped my pen, then composed my face as I picked it up. I greeted her with a smile.

"What a surprise! How come?"

In fact, it was a shock. I hadn't been aware that Roma knew where I worked. Why was she here?

She glowered down at me and inwardly I quaked while putting on a brave face. I was well aware of her infamous rages and didn't want one erupting here, at my place of work.

"I needed to talk to someone! I can't talk to Angad, and I know Pari won't listen."

"Can this wait, Roma? I'm really busy today."

"No! I need to talk to you now." She stood in front of me, the window behind her, her large frame blocking the little bit of natural light that streamed in through the windowpanes.

"Okay," I sighed. "Would you like something to drink? Tea? Coffee?"

"Coca Cola." She looked at me as if challenging me to deny her.

"Sure. Mary, can you bring us a can of Coke and one *chai*, please?"

When the nurse had left, I asked Roma to take a seat and got up to shut the door to the office. That way, I hoped I could contain whatever was about to transpire.

"How can I help?"

"I need you to keep this between us."

"Okay," I nodded, curious now.

"Promise me."

"Roma, is that really necessary?"

"Promise!"

"Okay, I promise," I said, feeling like a five-year-old.

She put her hands on the desk between us, leaned forward, and said slowly, "I think Angad is having an affair."

I sat there in stunned silence.

"All this," she waved her hands in the air, "All this has been a big set-up." She put her hands back on the desk, her perfectly manicured nails painted the palest shade of pink. "This drama about Samira wanting forgiveness is all bullshit. They've been having an affair all along, and we've just been made fools of."

When I found my voice again, I stuttered out, "But why? What purpose would it serve?"

"Purpose? What do you mean, purpose? Angad has been having affairs all along. But this time..." She wagged her finger at me, looking mildly deranged, "This time, I'm telling you, she's got her claws into him well and proper."

"Are you saying that Samira forced this meeting so that she could carry on her affair with Angad? That makes no sense, Roma!"

"It makes perfect sense! She wants to get Pari on her side, then you, and that will leave me isolated."

"Roma, Samira doesn't even live here. She's only visiting. I think you've read way too much into this meeting."

"No, no," she leaned forward and put her finger on my lips, silencing me. "I think all of you are blind to the main plot. I'm the only one who knows what's really going on."

I slumped into my chair, not knowing how much more of this I could take.

"So, what's going on?"

"She wants him to divorce me, so that she can have him all to herself. She wants you and Pari to help her do this."

I goggled at her. Where was all this coming from?

The nurse knocked at the door and brought in our drinks. I handed Roma her Coca Cola, hoping she'd be distracted from her lunatic theories while I instructed the nurse to shut the door behind her again.

"Who have you spoken to about this, Roma?"

"No one else but you."

"Why me?"

I did wonder. Roma and I had never been close, and in the year since they had moved from Mumbai to Delhi, she had done little to re-establish contact.

"Well, it's obvious, isn't it?"

"What is?"

"You can't stand her either. You didn't want to make nice with her. Angad and Pari forced you to."

Then I remembered that she had left before she saw me forgive Samira. But what kind of convoluted thinking had brought her to my door? What did she want from me?

"I want you to spy on her. Call her over, get her to spill her secrets to you."

"Roma, honestly..."

"I *need* you to do this for me! Madhu, for old times' sake."

I nodded. She was getting overwrought and agreeing seemed the only way to calm her down.

"And what if there are no secrets to spill, Roma? What then?"

"We'll see." She stood up suddenly, her mood switching from mild elation back to a suppressed fury. "Call her, then call me."

After she had left, I put my head in my hands and shut my eyes. I could feel a headache forming behind my temples. A headache that would become a migraine, debilitating me for the rest of the afternoon.

What on earth was I meant to do now?

CHAPTER 109

On our Friday evening meeting, I vacillated between telling Pari everything, to wondering what good it would do. We hadn't even had a chance to discuss Samira properly.

"What do you want to eat?"

"I don't care. Anything, really."

"Pizza?"

"Why not? For a change!" I pulled a bottle of wine out of my bag. "I thought we could do with this today."

"Wine? Ooh, very fancy. Aren't you working tomorrow?"

"No, I've taken the weekend off. Perks of being a senior."

"Madhu...?"

"Hmm?" I wrestled with the wine opener while she fetched the glasses.

"Isn't Samira leaving in a few days?"

"I believe so."

"Do you think we should call her over? Meet her properly?"

"We could," I said, slowly, "I mean, the meeting at Margaret Ma'am's was very emotional, but we never really got to talk properly."

"That's exactly what I was thinking! It might be nice to catch up. Just the three of us." She looked scared. "I don't want Roma to know."

"Why?" I peeked at her.

"Well, you saw her reaction that day. But Angad called me last night, saying that she had become hysterical and accused him of having an affair with Samira!"

I stayed quiet.

"What? Aren't you surprised by this? Do you know something that I don't?"

"I didn't want to say, but she had come to the hospital yesterday, and was spouting all this mad stuff about Samira to me, too."

"Which is why I don't want her to know. I'd like just us to catch up with Samira. I don't think we can go back to being friends the way we used to be, but after all the effort she put in, how can we just let her go back without spending some time with her?"

"I agree. What did you have in mind?"

"How about dinner at Chungwa? She always loved that place."

Much after we had eaten our pizzas, saving a few slices for breakfast, we dimmed the lights and sat on the sofa, sipping our wine.

"Isn't life strange, Madhu?" Pari was staring into the distance. "For years, I blamed Samira for everything. Then, that day, when I saw her... the way she looked... She's still beautiful, but she looked broken. You know?"

"I do."

"I get the feeling she doesn't have anyone in her life."

"You could be right." I took a sip of my wine, then set the glass down before saying, "Pari?"

"Yes?"

"I don't think she's very well."

"What do you mean?"

"I've seen that look on patients before. She had this pallor, this sickly appearance, as if something is eating her up from the inside."

"Didn't Margaret Ma'am say she'd had food poisoning? That's why she was sticking to water."

"Yes, I know that's what she said. But my instinct is telling me that there's more to it, that she's not very well at all."

"Will you speak to her?"

"I'll try. But in what capacity? As a nurse, a former friend, their driver's daughter?" I laughed.

"Don't be silly, Madhu. No one has thought of that in years. I think you should tell her. Maybe she can get herself checked out while she's here? After all, we have some of the best doctors in the world, don't we?"

I picked up my glass and took another sip of my wine.

"Pari, you know the new principal?"

She sat up straighter immediately.

"Yes, what about him?"

"I think he has a bit of a thing for you."

"What?!"

"I mean it. He couldn't take his eyes off you the entire afternoon." I grinned at her, then winked. "Pari's got a boyfriend..." I sang the same silly song we used to in school. She threw a cushion at me, nearly hitting my wine glass. "Hey! This is expensive stuff."

"And you're drunk! I've told you, he's gay."

"What makes you think that, eh? What proof do you have?" I slurred the last bit, deliberately.

"I just know."

"Pari, you have a faulty gaydar! I've worked with gay men, and I can tell you, Mr what's-his-name Gautam yay-yay, is straight. Totally hetero!"

She sat in shocked silence, absorbing my words, then took a big gulp of her wine.

"You're mistaken! Definitely mistaken."

"And you, Pari Rajan, are afraid. Don't be. He seems nice," I chuckled.

"What about you, Miss Kumar? Anyone on the scene since you booted Mr Dry Cleaner out?"

I knocked back my wine, stood up, and started a mad dance.

"Pari's got a boyfriend, Pari's got a boyfriend..."

She got mad at me first, threw a few more cushions at me, and then later at night, after we'd brushed our teeth, and lay together on the bed, she said, "I think I'm falling in love with him, Madhu. What should I do?"

"Fall, Pari. Just fall. What's the worst that can happen?"

"He'll break my heart?"

"Our hearts have been broken before. They've mended too. Don't let fear stop you from letting something beautiful into your life."

After she had fallen asleep, and I could hear her soft snores beside me, I pondered my own words.

How long would I let fear dictate my life?

CHAPTER 110

For years I'd thought about it, dreamed of it, saved up for it, but something stopped me at the very last minute. Was I capable enough? Was I good enough? Was I too old? Would people laugh at me?

Then Samira had done the unthinkable. She'd walked back into our lives and begged forgiveness. How much courage it must have taken for her to travel thousands of miles to atone for her teenage mistakes! And I had been there. I had seen her struggle to cope with Ninaji's health, seen how often Raj Uncle abandoned the family without as much as a backward glance, seen the overwhelming amount of attention she had received from the opposite sex with no one to guide her or help her navigate that particularly sensitive time in her life. Yet, she had owned up to her mistakes with the sort of dignity that was rare to behold.

Her courage had emboldened me. So what if I was forty? It wasn't too late for me to become a doctor. I'd been in the field long enough to know that I would make a good one too.

I sat at home that Saturday afternoon, nursing a vicious hangover, as I filled in the application form for the MBBS course. I had to try, or I'd die wondering.

Pari had seen me off at the auto-rickshaw stand with a hug and a kiss on the cheek. She had to go to school for a meeting. I hoped she would bring those walls down enough to let Gautam through. She still thought of herself as an ugly, gawky girl with funny teeth, when in fact she was a tall, elegant, attractive woman with an enviable self-possession. I wished she could see herself through my eyes, and then she would know the sort of loyalty and love she could inspire in people, given half a chance.

She'd said to me once to never let any misunderstandings come between us. I didn't want to lose her either. She was the only family I had, and I wouldn't let anything upset our relationship. I never wanted to fall in her estimation.

I picked up the phone and rang The Maurya Sheraton.

"Could you put me through to Miss Samira Sehgal's room, please?"

"Just one moment." There was some rustling of paper in the background, then the operator returned. "Sorry, we don't have anyone by that name staying here."

"Oh, sorry!" I tried to remember the last name Samira had given us. "I think it's Shaw. Samira Shaw?"

"Oh yes. We have a Miss Shaw here. One moment. Connecting."

A few rings later, Samira answered. She sounded tired.

"Samira*di*, it's me—Madhu."

"Oh, hello Madhu. I'd given up on hearing from any of you again, and now, you're the second call I've received today."

"Did Pari call you already?"

"No. It was Angad. Actually, it was quite a strange call, and I'm not sure what to make of it."

"What did he say?"

"Just something about Roma being angry with me all these years. Madhu, I know we didn't really get along that well back then, but why is she still angry with me? I did nothing to her, as far as I can remember."

"Samira*di*, forget it. Roma is just highly strung, that's all."

"Yes, I got a sense that she was."

"What are you doing?" I tried to steer her away from Roma.

"Right now?"

"Yes."

"Well, I was just lying in bed, resting. I haven't been feeling too well lately."

"Samira*di*, if you like, I could organise a few tests for you at the hospital where I work. We'll get the results back within twenty-four hours."

"That's kind of you, Madhu, but I'm leaving on Monday. I'll get tested when I get back to the UK. I've probably picked up some kind of bug."

"Well, make sure that you do get tested..."

"Why does that sound so ominous?" She laughed at the other end of the line, and I didn't want to say, but couldn't help thinking that whatever she had, it was definitely worse than a bug.

"Just the cautious nurse in me talking! Samira*di*, before you go, Pari and I would like to take you out to dinner."

There was silence at the other end.

"Hello?" I said, wondering if the line had disconnected.

"That would be nice." Her voice sounded shaky. "I thought that I probably wouldn't see you again before leaving."

"We couldn't let you go back without having a proper catch-up." I tried to make light of it, but I knew that we nearly had.

"Where should I meet you?"

"How about Chungwa at GKII?"

"Oh my goodness, you remember?"

"How could we forget?"

"I can't believe it's still around!"

"Shall we say 6 p.m. on Sunday?"

"Sounds lovely. Oh, and Madhu?"

"Yes?"

"Thank you."

CHAPTER 111

I got to Chungwa just before 6 p.m. but Samira was already there, waiting at the table I had reserved. Dressed in a plain white T-shirt with an embroidered collar and pale blue jeans, she looked painfully thin, but she still attracted plenty of looks. She had always had an aura about her.

She got up as I approached and reached forward to hug me diffidently.

"You haven't changed, Madhu. You still look like a little girl."

"Bah! I'm forty Samira*di*, as you well know."

I handed her a little package.

"This is for you."

Surprised, she took it from my hands and said, "What's this? I haven't brought any presents."

"It's something very small."

"May I open it?"

"Yes, I'd like you to."

I observed her face as she unwrapped the package and took out the small, soft toy dog I'd bought her. She broke into a smile.

"Do you still collect soft toys, Samira*di*?"

"No," she responded softly, "not in years. I left all that behind in India."

"Well, maybe you could start again."

"Maybe."

"Are Nina*ji* and Raj Uncle still alive?"

"No, Madhu. They've passed on. And your mother and brother?"

"They don't stay in touch with me. It's a long story."

"Tell me. I want to know."

I stared at the menu cards the waiter had set down.

"Should we get some Talumein soup?"

"Vegetarian?"

"For Pari, but we could split a non-veg one."

"Okay," she smiled, "but let's order the rest of the food once she arrives."

After I had placed the order, she looked at me intently.

"What happened, Madhu?"

I shrugged.

"It was a long time ago, but Mataji was trying to get me married and I didn't want to, so I ran away from home."

She gasped, then her eyes filled with tears.

"You poor thing!"

I shook my head.

"Like I said, it was a long time ago. It doesn't matter anymore."

"But how could it not? They are your blood!" She brushed a tear off her face. "All this happened because we left, no?"

"Yes."

What else could I say? That one night had changed everything for me.

"Papa never spoke about that night, about what had transpired. But before Mama died, she filled me in on all she knew. Oh God, Madhu! All those years that I spent adoring my father only to discover that he was *khokhla* on the inside, a hollow man! How he betrayed all of us, but especially you."

I remained stoic, focussing on the tiny rosebud pattern at the neckline of her T-shirt.

"Are you married? Is there anyone in your life now?" she asked, concern lacing her words.

"There is... but..."

Her eyes searched my face.

"But?"

"I... I'm not sure... It feels right, but..." I had the sudden urge to tell her everything, and as she observed me closely and listened to me stumble over my words, a slow comprehension dawned in her eyes.

"I see." She lowered her voice. "I think I understand now. But I may have done something silly..."

She stopped just as Pari walked in, and I wondered what she had been about to say, and whether she would still say it. But as they hugged and wept, I knew that the moment had passed.

After Pari arrived and we had placed our orders, I took a back seat and watched them catch up in half-sentences, garbled explanations, laughter and tears. These two friends who had been separated by circumstances had never lost that deep-seated love for one another. They were grown women now, but as I listened to them giggle over memories, and cry over lost ones, they reminded me of the same girls I used to trail around school. I felt no jealousy, just sadness for all that wasted time.

"Then Mrs Nagpal's wig fell on the table..."

"And the boys kicked it around the room?"

"It was funny at that time... but how sad for her!"

"Mortifying!"

I joined in with a few anecdotes of mine, content to let them chat, satisfied that we had managed to have this time together. Perhaps we would never be the best of friends with Samira. Her life was in England now, and from the sounds of it, she loved her work. Just having this moment in time, though, felt special. After all those years of holding on to anger and animosity, it was liberating to let it go. Like Margaret Ma'am had said, there was a healing power in forgiveness.

"Samira, you need to put on some weight! You're too skinny." Pari was back to ribbing her good-naturedly.

"I know! I guess it's stress and bad eating habits." She cast a glance at me. "I've promised Madhu that I'll get a check-up when I'm home."

"Good! Here, look, your favourite American chopsuey has arrived."

The waiter placed the dish of crispy noodles, mixed vegetables, and chicken doused in a sweet Indo-Chinese sauce, topped with a fried egg in front of us.

Samira laughed. "In all my travels, I have never come across this dish in any Chinese restaurant in the world! This has to be an Indian invention."

She tucked into it with alacrity. "I used to tell my ex-husband about it. He thought it sounded disgusting."

Pari raised her eyebrows.

"I wouldn't know. I'm a vegetarian, remember? So, why did you get divorced?"

As Samira talked about her divorce, a sudden chill went through me. Pari noticed straight away.

"Are you okay Madhu? Have we been ignoring you?"

"No, I'm fine. Really. It must be the air-conditioning."

As they fussed over me, I couldn't shake off the sense of foreboding.

Then I looked up, and there she was. Roma, dressed to the nines, in a black-and-magenta *salwar kameez*, standing at the doorway, looking around. Her eyes met mine and there was the strangest look in them.

Triumph, anger, resolve.

She walked towards us with the sweetest smile plastered on her face, and I knew then that something awful was about to happen.

CHAPTER 112

When Pari saw her, she whispered to me, "What's she doing here?"

She looked absolutely petrified, as if she had been caught red-handed committing murder. I felt no better myself. How on earth had Roma found us? Who had told her we were meeting?

Samira stood up and welcomed Roma to the table.

"I'm so glad you could make it, Roma. Ladies, I know this has come as a surprise, but I'm the one who invited Roma here. I felt we'd gotten off on the wrong foot at Margaret Ma'am's and didn't want to leave India without making peace with Roma as well."

Roma sat down next to me, still smiling.

"Well, at least you thought of calling me Samira. These two would have kept it a secret forever."

"I, uhh, no Roma. I didn't think you'd want to come," Pari stuttered by way of explanation. I tried to catch her eye, but she was too busy tripping over her words. Instead, Samira looked at me and, with the tiniest tilt of her head, tried to reassure me.

"You've started eating already? I thought we were having dinner together."

"We started a little earlier, but we can order some more food. What would you like?" Samira asked, waving a waiter over.

"I don't really like Chinese," Roma huffed while scanning the menu, "but I guess I'll have the chowmein and fish in hot bean sauce."

When the waiter had left, I pushed the plate of spring rolls towards her.

"Try these, Roma. They are delicious."

She took one and bit into it, chewed, swallowed, then looked at Samira and said, "Well, why did you want me here? You have your two best friends from school already. Did you want to rub salt in my wounds?"

"No, not at all." Samira sighed. "Look, Roma, I know we haven't always gotten along, but I just wanted to apologise to you as well. You see, I really had no idea that you were interested in Angad back then. I was so wrapped up in my life, in my own issues, that I didn't think of who I was hurting or how much."

We stayed silent as Samira rearranged the fallen crumbs of pastry into a pattern on the table.

"That day at Margaret Ma'am's, you caught me by surprise. I wasn't expecting to see you there. I'd been preparing my apology to Pari and Madhu for so long that you were almost an interference. I reacted badly. Later, when I thought about it, I realised I had been dismissive of your feelings. I may not have hurt you deliberately, but I certainly did, inadvertently. And I apologise."

I felt Roma stiffen next to me and then relax the next minute.

"Well, I never thought I'd see the day when Miss High-and-Mighty Samira would apologise to me!"

She was practically gloating, but Samira remained impassive, letting Roma have her moment.

"We have to toast this reunion! What are you drinking, girls? Water? How boring! Waiter, bring us some vodka and diet cokes."

We looked at each other. None of us had wanted to drink, but Roma was almost euphoric and it felt wrong to break her strangely good mood.

"Roma, we have to work tomorrow," I interjected softly.

"So? Just one drink to celebrate our friend. Look at all this food. It will soak up the alcohol."

The evening felt strangely surreal after her arrival. Where conversation had flowed freely before, it was stilted now. Memories were confined to the ones Roma remembered. We had to laugh at her jokes, even if they were at our expense. She altered facts to suit her version of events and chugged back the drinks one after the other. After polishing off her chowmein, she ordered another plate, then turned up her nose at it once it arrived. She displayed a ghoulish fascination with Samira's divorce, asking her again and again who had left whom. When we tried to get a word in, she dismissed Pari and me as a pair of 'old maids', then launched into an unexpected diatribe against her *ayah* and how she had stolen her children from her.

At one point Pari said, "Roma, I think you've had enough alcohol for the evening. Please stop."

"Can you believe her?" she looked at Samira. "She thinks I'm going to turn into an alcoholic like your mother."

I winced, and Pari and I exchanged looks. Maybe it was time to call it an evening.

Samira remained composed throughout, as if nothing Roma said or did affected her. I thought I saw the tiniest flicker of pity in her eyes, but she veiled it quickly, keeping an expression of polite interest throughout Roma's ramblings.

At 10 p.m. I stood up.

"It's getting late, and I won't be able to get an auto. Let's make a move."

"Auto-shauto! I'll drive you home. Sit." Roma commanded, and I sat down, not wanting to make a scene.

"Actually, Roma, I think we need to get going. My driver Radheshyam is waiting outside. It's not fair to keep him so late on a Sunday evening." Samira called for the bill, but Pari had already settled it discreetly. We were going to split it between us later.

"You know what your problem is, S..Samira?" Roma slurred.

Samira smiled.

"I'm sure you'll tell me."

"You worry too much about the little people. That's his job! Let him wait."

Samira had already pulled out her phone to call him, but Roma snatched it out of her hand.

"I'll drop you! Tell him to go."

"Roma, you're in no state to drive. I was going to get him to drop all of us."

Roma slipped the phone into her bag and giggled.

"You're not going anywhere. Let's go for a drive. I know! Let's go get ice cream at India Gate. Remember? We used to go there as teenagers?"

There was a manic energy about Roma, and Pari mouthed to me, "say yes".

"Yes, okay. Samira*di*, let's go for a quick ice cream. Why don't you get your driver to follow us? Then, after the ice cream, we can head home. Is that alright by you, Roma?"

She was already on her way out, Samira's phone still in her bag.

Pari looked at me helplessly, then followed her out.

"Madhu, I don't think this is a good idea," Samira frowned, her eyes following them.

"I know, *didi*, but when she's in one of these moods, it's best to go along with it."

"Poor Angad." She looked at me searchingly as she said this, and I dropped my gaze and fumbled with my bag. Then we walked out of Chungwa together.

EPILOGUE

None of us escape life unscathed. Some of us carry our scars visibly, on the surfaces of our skins, as a conspicuous reminder of the chaos and frightening randomness of life. Others bury them deep where no one else can see them or fathom their existence. Yet, we know where they are and we worry at them constantly. Touching, smoothing, soothing the knotted cicatrix on our bodies, on our souls.

And the pain, like molten lava, throbs liquid-hot under the surface of those wounds. Those wounds that have scarred on the outside but still haven't healed completely on the inside. That pain can corrode you, if you let it.

I can't let it.

I won't let it.

I look at the long thin scar on my cheek in the mirror and think back to the night of the accident. We could have stopped it had we been brave enough to speak out or if we had read the signs correctly.

Roma had never forgiven Samira. That night, as she had pretended to toast her, all she had wanted from her was an admission of guilt. She had convinced herself that Angad was leaving her for Samira, and nothing would persuade her otherwise.

I still recall Samira climbing into the seat next to her, while Madhu and I sat at the back. I remember reaching for my seat belt, telling Madhu to do the same. Had Samira put her belt on? I can't remember.

A group of middle-aged women on a joyride with a reckless, drunk and dangerous driver at the wheel. Could we not have foreseen how it would end?

The doorbell rings just then, and I hurry to open the door. Madhu is standing there dressed in a peach *salwar kameez*, crutch under one arm. Her left leg had been fractured in multiple places. It is a miracle she can walk at all.

"What are we ordering today?" she asks with a wan smile.

"I thought I'd make Maggi noodles."

"Ah, a Pari special. Yes, let's do that."

I open the fridge to take out the vegetables I'd chopped up earlier and spot the bottle of beer I had bought nearly a year ago.

"Do you want a drink?"

"No." She speaks quietly, but I know what she means.

"Is it painful?" I ask, looking at her hobble over to the sofa.

She shrugs.

"I've felt worse. It is getting better."

Then suddenly, unaccountably, she bursts into tears. Madhu—who never cries, who has always been imperturbable in every instance, able to ride out every storm in her life with enviable equanimity—sits on my sofa sobbing piteously. I rush to her side.

"Madhu, no, no. Don't do this. It's over."

"But it's not. Not in my mind, Pari! I live with the guilt of it daily."

"Samira wouldn't want us to."

"If we hadn't agreed to go with Roma..."

"Yes, *we*. I was there too. Madhu, nothing we say or do can change what happened that evening."

"Is that you or Mr Yay-Yay speaking?" she smiles through her tears, using the back of her hand to wipe her face.

"Gautam has a way of putting everything in perspective."

"Like Margaret Ma'am."

Later, as I ladle the noodles into our bowls and hand it over to Madhu, I ask, "Have you been to see Margaret Ma'am?"

"She came to see me, and I told her everything."

"About you and Angad too?"

"Yes, and the baby."

"I'm so sorry."

When Angad told me about his and Madhu's relationship, I wasn't really surprised. At some subliminal level, I had always known. In the shy looks they had exchanged at first, in his insistence on dropping her home every time he joined us for dinner, in his growing disenchantment with Roma — there were clues that I had picked up on subconsciously. The fact that Madhu had miscarried their baby after the accident, a baby she hadn't even known she was carrying, upset me far more than the news of their affair. Another life snuffed out before it had even begun.

"What did she say?" I ask, wondering how Margaret Ma'am viewed us after the accident, after everything that had happened.

"Oh, you know... another one of her cryptic quotations. Let me see if I can remember it. Oh, yes! 'How shall a man escape from that which is written; how shall he flee from his destiny?' I think she said it was someone called Firdausi who had penned it."

"That's the amazing thing about her. She has never ever judged us. In our darkest moments, at our very worst, she has always believed we were capable of better." I say, laying my fork down, strangely overcome.

"Was Roma capable of better?"

"She wasn't well, Madhu. I really believe that. Look at all the stuff Angad unearthed afterwards. She'd been stealing for years. Probably lying too. And she'd suspected him of being unfaithful their entire married life. The irony was that when he finally cheated on her, she pinned her suspicions on the wrong person." I pluck at my hair. "We should have intervened. We should have got her some help. I wish I'd known the extent of the problem."

"No one did. Not even Angad, and he was married to her." Madhu looks thoughtful before asking, "Do you think she planned it?"

"No, definitely not. I don't think it was a suicide mission. She wasn't some kamikaze pilot out to destroy us all. I think she just lost control of herself and the car."

"I just remember all the screaming!"

"And the crash."

We stay silent, lost in our thoughts, remembering that horrific night. The voices, the police cars, the flashing lights of the ambulance, the car driver who had followed us from a distance crying out, "Samira madam, Samira madam!"

"Do you think they suffered?" I ask her. The question has plagued me for months.

"Roma died instantly, but Samira—"

"I heard her moaning when I regained consciousness."

"Poor Samira*di*!" A tear trickles down Madhu's cheek. "I used to think life had dealt me a poor hand, but when I think of her..."

"I know." It still hurt to think back to how I'd hated her for years, how little I'd understood her.

"But, you know, Pari, in a funny sort of way, I think she might have suffered more if she had lived."

"Why?"

"You know when she told us that Raj Uncle had died of stomach cancer?"

"Yes."

"I think she might have had something similar."

"What makes you think that?"

"It's just a hunch, but I've been around enough sick people to know that she wasn't well."

"Still Madhu. She could have gotten treated had she lived. We don't even know for sure..."

"No," she shakes her head, "we don't, and we never will."

· · ·

"Does the scar bother you?" she asks me later, after we have pushed our plates of half-eaten Maggi aside.

"Not really. I thought it would, but the outside matters so little to me these days. It's the inside that really counts, doesn't it?"

"So true."

Once again, we fall back into silence.

"How are the children doing?" I ask after a few minutes. I'd seen them at the beginning when they'd sat shell-shocked, still absorbing the news of their mother's demise. Things are still too raw for me to visit regularly, my relationship with them still too tenuous. Their healing has to happen with their father, with Angad.

"It will take a while. Gomti, the *ayah*, has been very good with them."

"And you? Are they accepting you?"

"It's too early for that, Pari. I don't even know if Angad and I have a future."

She sits across from me, a tiny figure, looking so forlorn that I reach over and put my hand on hers.

"Remember when you'd told me not to let fear stop me from letting something beautiful into my life? You too, Madhu. Don't forget it."

I wash up, then help Madhu change into her nightie. We lie together in bed, more sisters than friends, and say our prayers for those who are no longer with us.

Madhu falls asleep before me. As I lie there wide awake, I remember the first time I ever set eyes on Samira. How lovely she had seemed, how charmed her life had appeared. I think back to the innocence of those childhood days, when all that mattered was how I could get to be friends with the new girl. I fall asleep dreaming of that auburn-haired girl with the dimpled smile.

Somewhere, in a world beyond pain and guilt, beyond shame and sorrow, in a world where nothing ever dies, she is laughing as Sri whispers sweet nothings into her ear.

THE END

AFTERWORD

Word-of-mouth is crucial for any author to succeed and if you found this book interesting please do leave a review on your preferred retailer. Even if it's just a star rating or a sentence or two, it would make all the difference and would be very much appreciated!!

If you enjoyed this book, you can sign up to hear more about my new releases and any special offers!

Do visit www.poornimamanco.com to keep abreast of all my news.

ACKNOWLEDGMENTS

As always, my heartfelt gratitude to my wonderful editor, Charulatha, and my excellent advance reader team (ART) of Paul, An, Valerie, Mirielle, Maria, Hollene, and Sami. Also, to all the other reviewers who read the manuscript prior to it being published.

Writing has always been a cathartic exercise for me, and through this medium I have exorcised plenty of my own unresolved issues. However, above all else, I write for you, dear reader. In these characters, their lives and their journeys, I hope you find something you can relate to and learn from as well. These fictitious beings are always teaching me how to live, love, laugh, and forgive.

Editing services: charu.dpp@gmail.com

Book cover design: team@miblart.com

ABOUT THE AUTHOR

Author of five short story collections, one novella and two novels, Poornima has lived more than half her life outside of India, her birthplace. Still, you can take the girl out of India, but you cannot take India out of the girl. Nearly all her books and stories show the deep connection she retains to her motherland.

Poornima lives in the United Kingdom with her husband, two daughters and one very cute hamster named Atlas.

ALSO BY POORNIMA MANCO

Parvathy's Well & other stories

Damage & other stories

Holi Moly! & other stories

The Intimacy of Loss

Twelve - stories from around the world

Parvathy's Well & Other Stories: The India Collection

Eight - Fantastical Tales From Here, There & Everywhere

A Quiet Dissonance